THE GOOD VICAR

R.J. Whitfield

TSL Publications

First published as e-book in Great Britain in 2010
First published in print by TSL Publications (Lulu) in 2015
Reprint by TSL Publications Feb 2016

ISBN / 978-1-911070-03-0

The dream disturbed him. Something about it was too real, too vivid. There was something that spoke to him in words he did not want to hear. It was like no dream he had had before, none matched the intensity with which this one had come.

He lay awake staring into the dark, the warm duvet pulled up to his chin. A quarter past twelve. He sighed. The rhythmic inhale-exhale of his wife soothed his disturbed spirit somewhat, but it was not enough. Things had been stirred up and they could not be restored by man alone, or woman, he quickly added.

A car's lights briefly lit the room as it turned the corner and hummed off into the distance. This broke his mood and with a small sigh, he threw his legs out of the bed and fumble-shuffled for his slippers. His cotton pyjamas retained the warmth of the bed for a second before the cold night air began to take hold.

He paused at the bedroom door to grab his dressing gown and, while he tied the waist cord, he looked back at the bed. Marjory's head lay peacefully on the pillow, her greying hair catching the dull light, giving it a halo-like effect. Her mouth was slightly open and he could still hear her soft breathing. He held the image in his mind wondering how he should, or if he could, tell her about the dream. It was after all just a dream he told himself.

With another small sigh he turned and walked out the bedroom, his slippered feet hissing quietly over the thick carpet. The stairs creaked nosily as he felt his way down them and he cursed each one silently for the disturbance his weight caused as he moved from one to the next.

In the kitchen he snapped on the light and blinked as the brightness invaded his eyes. After a few seconds of adjustment he plodded over to the kettle, checked that there was sufficient water, then flicked the switch. As the water chugged to life he got himself a mug, grabbed a teabag from the canister marked 'Tea', dropped this into the mug and threw in a spoon of sugar.

'No, it cannot be,' he mumbled to himself as he got the milk out of the fridge. 'Not him, surely not him Lord.' The kettle clicked off as the steam bubbled out. It threw his attention across the kitchen and suddenly his thoughts moved inward. 'Not *me* Lord, surely…'

He left it hanging, too scared to continue. Tea. The hot water gurgled into the mug and he watched the inky brown stain spread outward from the bag. One second, two seconds, three seconds, then stab the bag with the spoon. Once, twice, then lift it out and wait for the dripping to stop before dropping it into the bin.

He didn't want to face the dream, didn't want it to be real, couldn't let it be real. Tea. The cold milk spread quickly, turning the orange-brown liquid a dark cream colour and he stirred, taking comfort from the ting-ting-ting of the spoon against the side of the cup. Two final taps of the spoon on the rim.

Tea. It was ready. He couldn't delay any more. The tea was ready. A smoky wisp of steam rose from the mug and he knew he must now face the dream.

Leaving the kitchen light on, he moved quietly down the passage and groped for the light switch in his study. The calmness of the room greeted him and the shelves of books that lined the wall immediately gave him comfort. He ran his fingers gently over the spines of one shelf, marvelling at the bumps and the knowledge hidden behind them.

The desk was a large, old oak one that had a green leather cover. It had been a present from his previous congregation when he had left nearly twenty years ago. They had been exceedingly generous he had thought back then.

He moved round the desk and eased himself into the armchair which sighed as it welcomed him into its softness. He loved his chair, it was so comfortable. He could think in it, it had that aura of calm about it.

And he needed to think now. He needed to think about the dream and decide what to do, or what not to do. He stretched over the desk and picked up the glasses case, snapped it open and took out his reading specs.

Then he took his Bible from the pile of books on his left. He stared for a moment at the faded cross on the cover where the embossed gold had worn away.

Is this necessary, he thought. Do I really need to check this or was it all just a dream? It had been far too intense to be just a dream, there had to be more to it, but, and this was a big but, these things never happened in this day and age, they only happened in biblical times.

The pause lengthened till his hand began to shake and he shuddered. He took a sip of tea, letting the hot, bittersweet liquid soothe him. Then he picked up the Bible and began paging through it.

Acts 9 v 10 – 12:

In Damascus there was a disciple named Ananias. The Lord spoke to him in a vision.

'Ananias.'

'Yes Lord,' he answered.

The Lord told him, 'Go to the house of Judas on Straight Street and ask for a man from Tarsus named Saul, for he is praying. In a vision he has seen a man named Ananias come and place his hands on him to restore his sight.'

He read the passage through twice, then stopped and removed his glasses. He pinched the bridge of his nose, closing his eyes tight while his mind churned over those words.

It had been just like that in the dream. *Andrew,* the voice had called. *Andrew, go and see him in Dartmoor, go and see Paul McCready. He is waiting for you, he is praying for you to come and restore him.*

'Andrew, are you okay?' Marjory's voice jolted him out of his thoughts and he looked up to see his wife standing, sleepy-eyed in the doorway.

'I…I…I'm fine,' he stammered, scrambling around in his mind for something to say. He dared not tell Marjory about the dream, not yet at any rate, not until he had had time to think about it himself.

'I…I just woke up with some inspiration for Sunday's sermon and thought I'd better jot down the ideas before I forgot them.' Lord forgive me for this small lie.

The sleepy eyes nodded and smiled. 'The Lord moves in strange ways; and at strange times,' they said. 'Don't be too long.'

The Sleepy Eyes turned and he listened to the plop, plop, plop of their feet down the passage, then the creak, creak, creak of the stairs. Some shuffling around followed by the sounds settling and then they faded.

He reached out an unthinking hand for his tea and staring after the sound of The Sleepy Eyes, gulped the drink down. Paul McCready. Surely not. Of all people, not Paul McCready.

---o0o---

'Did you get all your thoughts down dear?' Marjory's pale blue dressing gown asked as it swished past him in the kitchen where he sat at the small table.

'Hmmm?'

The Dressing Gown tugged the thin floral curtains open and the sunlight that had been building up behind them spilled into the room.

'Your sermon, did you get all your thoughts down?' The Dressing Gown was at the fridge. It would get out two eggs. It always got two eggs out.

'Oh. Yes. Well. Most of it.' Another lie, Lord forgive me again.

'That's good.' The Dressing Gown poured his orange juice. 'You'll be finished well in time for Sunday then?'

'Um. Well I hope so, still a lot of work to do to get it into a proper sermon. It was mostly ideas last night.'

'Oh.' The Dressing Gown sounded slightly let down as it placed the juice next to him, switched the kettle on and set about the crackle-pop business of frying eggs.

Andrew stared at the glass of juice. Should he tell her about the dream? Would she understand? The juice didn't answer.

The Dressing Gown meanwhile loaded a plate with the eggs and bacon, added a slice of hot toast then put it down in front of him. It turned and switched on the radio.

'...since fighting resumed in the Middle East,' the BBC voice informed them. 'Convicted child murderer Paul McCready has *claimed that he was left blind after a bright light flashed in his prison cell last night. The incident is said to have occurred at around 12:15. A spokesman for Her Majesty's Prison Services said that they are investigating the incident, but are treating McCready's claims with some scepticism. "This is not the first time he has made outrageous claims," the spokesman said. It is believed that an optician will be examining McCready later this morning. McCready is currently serving a life sentence for the murder of eight year old Chantelle Bridges, two years ago.'*

Egg and toast hung in mid-air pierced by a fork. The thick yellow yoke dripped a slow blob back onto the plate.

'Andrew? Andrew are you okay?' He looked up and saw Marjory in her pale blue dressing gown.

---oOo---

The air was fresh; it always was up here. He looked down at the town that lay set out below, his eye tracing the roads till he found first the church and then moved on to the vicarage. He had had to get out of there. The dream, the dressing gown, the BBC voice. They were all still there, filling up the house.

He needed to be away from the oppressive weight the dream seemed to bring to him in the house. He needed to think. He could not face Marjory at the moment. He had lied to her, once last night, once this morning before breakfast and then a third time as he left the house. *Just going to check on Peggy Deane, dear.* He would have to lie again when he got back. Lord forgive me.

He felt ashamed. It was unlike him to lie, even less so to Marjory. *If I had said I was going to check on Geoff Deane I wouldn't have been lying,* he thought with a faint grin. But the comfort of that faded as quickly as it had arrived and he turned to read the inscription on the bench on which he sat.

'In loving memory of Geoffrey Deane, 1927-1990. 'E loved this view.'

Andrew turned to face the voice. A short figure stood a few feet away, hands thrust deep into the pockets of its jacket, a sharp rat-like face peered out from beneath the furry hood.

'Di' jew know 'im Father? Geoff Deane. Di' jew know 'im?' The Rat Face moved to sit next to him.

Andrew slid sideways to place some distance between them. He never liked the youngsters with their hoods up, there was something sinister about them.

'Di' jew know 'im.' The Rat Face asked again and sniffed, pushing his hands further into his pockets.

'I...I sort of knew him.' Andrew's thoughts were wrenched away from the dream as Geoffrey Deane's dour features popped into his head.

'Wot wos 'e like?'

Andrew stared across at The Rat Face. Why did it want to know what long-dead Geoff was like?

The nose twitched and sniffed again in anticipation of an answer.

'Um...' Andrew hated this intrusion into his thoughts. He was supposed to be thinking about the dream and what to do about it. 'He was a good, kind man.' Why did The Rat Face want to know, besides he had never really known Geoff that well.

'Snot wot I 'erd.' The Rat Face was petulant. 'I 'erd he wos a pee-do.'

Andrew turned sharply. 'That's no way to speak of the dead. Geoffrey Deane was a good man. He was most certainly not a paedophile. How dare you accuse a man like that?'

The Rat Face laughed. 'Wot evah. But like I says iss wot I 'erd.'

Andrew glared at him, but the boy's blue eyes didn't falter, returning his stare with a look so intense that it seemed to be injecting evil into Andrew's soul, so much so that he nearly cried out in pain and turned his head back to the view, his hands shook as he felt his heart thrashing in his chest.

Andrew go to him in Dartmoor. Go and see Paul McCready. The dream pulled against The Rat Faced stare and he felt trapped between the two forces. He buried his face in his hands and his mind screamed out NO LORD! NOT ME!

He sat like this for a second, hoping, praying for an answer, but nothing came. A desperate sense of emptiness began to fill him and with a slow resignedness he looked up. The Rat Face was gone.

---o0o---

Peggy Deane's face was a wrinkled lump peering out the top of the duvet, her clouded eyes attached to reality by a mere thread.

'I've just been to Geoff's bench.' Andrew smiled. He felt safer here in the small bedroom surrounded by the clutter of age. In the background a carer beat out a clattered tune on the breakfast dishes.

The Clouded Eyes blinked a vague recognition of Geoff's name then sank back into their world. At least now he had not lied to Marjory, he was doing what he said he would do when he left the house this morning.

The problem he had now was that the words of The Rat kept coming back to him. *I 'erd 'e was a pee-do.*

He looked at The Clouded Eyes and wondered if he could ask them the question. *Was Geoff, you know? Well was he…did he…um…did he mess around with little boys?* The stumbled-over question remained unvoiced. There was no way he could bring himself to ask it, besides which, The Clouded Eyes would never comprehend even if he did ask.

He shifted in the chair and it creaked slightly. He had never known what to say to The Clouded Eyes at the best of times. It was always difficult to talk to someone who wasn't there. He glanced at The Wrinkled Lump again, then his eyes moved to the portrait next to the bed. A brighter, alive Peggy Deane smiled back at him while a slightly glum faced Geoff stared vacantly at the photographer.

He didn't look like a paedophile, but then what does a paedophile look like? The newspaper picture of Paul McCready jumped into his mind. To ward off this intrusion, he picked up the photo and studied it.

As he stared at the once alive couple he heard The Wrinkled Lump stir. She was stretching out a hand to him and he took it, shocked slightly at how cold it felt. A rasping intake of breath shook her and the weak hand pulled him closer with a sudden strength. He leaned in, sensing that she wanted to say something. The words came in a hoarse, quiet whisper.

'Go...see...him.'

He pulled back sharply and stared into Peggy Deane's clear brown eyes. They blinked at him, searching his face for a sign that he understood, then they clouded over again for the last time and her hand went limp in his.

---o0o---

Marjory sat on the comfortable floral sofa. She wore a bright yellow cardigan and a tweed skirt. A pretty floral tea cup was held delicately in her hand.

'I'm going to see him. That's what she said.'

'Oh, that is so sweet,' she smiled.

While walking back home, Andrew had convinced himself about Peggy's last words. She had been telling him that she was going to see Geoff again. She was in no way connected to the dream, telling him to go and see McCready. He had misheard the whisper.

'Yes, it was quite touching,' he sipped at his own tea. 'Geoff was a good man wasn't he?'

Marjory smiled again, 'Yes he was. They will be happy to be together again.'

Andrew nodded, then risked it. 'Did you ever hear any stories about him though?'

'What on earth do you mean Andrew?' She put the cup down and took a bite of a piece of shortbread, brushing the crumbs that formed on her lips into her mouth.

'Well it's just that I heard a rather disturbing claim today. Someone mentioned to me that they had heard that Geoff was some sort of paedophile.'

'Good Lord Andrew!' The shortbread paused just below lipsticked lips. 'That's just outrageous. Who told you such a thing?'

Andrew blushed. It was not exactly the most credible source. 'You know that young lad that hangs around outside the newsagent, always got his hood up, face like a rat?'

'Andrew, that's not a nice thing to say, but it does describe him well.' She gave a naughty schoolgirl giggle which she swallowed along with the last bit of shortbread.

'But why would he say such a thing, and why did he talk to you? He never talks to anyone.'

Andrew paused, contemplating his answer carefully. To hide his thoughts he picked up his own shortbread. 'Well...' he took a large bite; big enough to allow him time to think while he chewed. Marjory, God bless her, waited patiently for him as she always did.

He swallowed, then cleaned the inside of his mouth with his tongue, gaining a few more seconds thought time. Then he made his mind up.

'Well, actually I went up to Geoff's remembrance bench this morning before I went to see Peggy. I...I needed to think about something which I'll tell you about in a minute. Anyway while I was there The Rat, sorry that young lad arrived. He started asking me about Geoff and then just came out with his claim. I 'erd 'e was a pee-do.' Andrew attempted the boy's accent but it didn't come off well and he coughed nervously to cover his embarrassment.

'Well I've certainly never heard any claims like that about Geoff,' The Yellow Cardigan sipped its tea. 'Besides which young Alex, The Rat as you seem to like to call him, would only have been about one when Geoff died so he certainly can't be making this claim from personal experience can he? Whatever made you think there might be any truth in what he said?'

Andrew blushed. 'I don't know, it was just something in the way he said it, the conviction he had.' He stared into his half empty tea cup.

The Yellow Cardigan tutted and swallowed the last of its tea. Andrew stewed in his thoughts for a bit, still contemplating how to broach the dream with Marjory.

'Have you set a time for the funeral yet?' The Yellow Cardigan asked.

'Oh, I've suggested Friday at two to Pat. Doubt there will be a big crowd in. Can you arrange for the Women's Group to do tea?' Andrew wondered briefly if Pat could shed any light on the claims regarding Geoff, but it was not the subject you take up with someone when their mother has just died.

The Yellow Cardigan nodded while Andrew finished off his tea, then rose to clear away the dishes.

'Marjory, hang on a bit. I need to talk to you about something.' He looked up and watched his wife slowly lower herself demurely into her chair. She clasped her hands neatly on her lap and raised concerned eyes to meet his.

---o0o---

'Morning Father Andrew,' Eve laughed as he walked into the small Vestry Office of the church. Everything she said sounded like a laugh.

Andrew smiled a greeting at The Laugh. She was a plump and jolly woman.

'Morning Eve, how are you this morning?' He was in Good Vicar mode. Always show an interest in people. It's the sign of a good minister.

Eve had been the church secretary when they had arrived at the parish and she had served him well. In the early days he had found a strange attraction in the ever-cheerful demeanour of The Laugh. To his shame he had spent some of those first few months fantasising about him and Eve wondering round the Garden of Eden naked. Andrew and Eve. But she was not the usual voluptuous portrayal of Eve one saw in the classic paintings, she was larger and rounder and in his naughtier moments, he would forgo any fig leaf censorship.

But that was then. Nowadays, The Laugh irritated. No-one should be allowed to be that cheerful, not with all the problems of the world that constantly flowed across his desk. Every smile, every giggle, every moment of merriment grated, but he could do nothing but smile back. He was The Good Vicar after all. *For God's sake Eve, do you have to be so bloody cheerful all the time?* remained a pent up outburst.

'The man coming to do the quote for the organ overhaul rang to say he would be a bit late and Steve Smith said he couldn't come today to do the garden, but will definitely be in tomorrow. Also, Linda McLeod went into St Mary's last night. She will be operated on at one this afternoon, Roger asked if you could say a short prayer for her then. Cathy will be coming round at two on Friday to do the flowers for Sunday.' The Laugh rattled off the day's update.

'Friday? There may be a bit of a problem. Peggy Deane passed away this morning and it's likely the funeral will be then.'

'Oh, poor Peg,' The Laugh laughed. 'How's Pat doing?' Why must she laugh at someone dying?

'Pat is doing fine. It's been a long time and I think it was more a relief.'

'Well she'll be with Geoff now,' The Laugh smiled sweetly. Probably imagining the two elderly people running round in heaven hand in hand, he hid his grimace.

On a whim Andrew asked the question. 'Eve, have you ever heard of any funny business with Geoff. I mean was he ever in trouble or anything? I only ask because I heard something rather disturbing about him which I can't believe and I'd like to put it to rest.'

For the first time since he had known her, The Laugh's smile faded. It was only for a fraction of a second as her brow knitted.

'Geoff? Well before you came…no…those were just rumours.' The smile returned with a laugh. 'No it can't be that, Geoff was a lovely man, wouldn't harm a fly.'

Andrew nodded. So there was something to The Rat's claim.

---oOo---

Back at his desk, Andrew started to digest Marjory's reaction to the dream. He had had to dash out to a prayer meeting straight after morning tea and then had popped in to get the update from The Laugh in the office, but now he could think.

She had listened patiently as he explained the dream to her, telling her about the voice saying *go and see him in Dartmoor*. He had then explained that he was comparing that to the story of Ananias when she had popped her head round the door of his study last night.

She had smiled a sad, accepting smile when he apologised for lying about preparing his sermon. This annoyed him slightly, she was always so understanding.

She had sat upright in her chair, back straight, knees pressed demurely together and hands clasped neatly on her lap. Her greying head tilted slightly.

He had explained the similarity of his dream to that of Ananias years ago and then his shock at hearing about Paul McCready's flash of light. Had McCready really experienced a road to Damascus conversion and was God really calling him to go and see him, to go and cure his blindness?

He had tried not to sound too doubtful, it would not look good a man of the cloth questioning God's call. But these things never happened nowadays, besides which why him? He never knew Paul McCready and had never healed anyone, so why him?

'You'll need to contact Dartmoor I guess,' Marjory had said. He hated her blind faith, the way she just accepted that God had called him and he must obey. There was no question of McCready's blindness being a coincidence that happened to fit in with a weird, albeit intense dream. Why could he not have her simple accepting faith? Why could she not have his deep, well hidden cynicism?

And there was still Geoff to think about, The Rat's allegation and Eve's clouded look to analyse. Did Peggy really say *go and see him* or did he mishear? If anyone approached him with this problem his advice would be to go and pray about it. Find out what God wants of you. He closed his eyes and brought his hands together, interlocking the fingers rather than the classic hands together pose as he always felt embarrassed praying like that. Then he tried to pray, but all his mind could conjure up was the newspaper picture of Paul McCready below a headline that screamed GO AND SEE HIM!!

---oOo---

Andrew smiled at Pat. He had always liked her, she was an intelligent, caring woman, someone he could talk to.

'Thank you for coming Andrew.'

'How are you doing Pat?' He followed her through to the neat lounge and eased himself into Brian's chair.

'I'm fine.' It was a brave smile. 'Cup of tea?'

'A cup of coffee, if I may.' No more tea! He was beginning to feel tea'd out. Every cup since the dream seemed to have brought more anxiety.

Pat raised a surprised eyebrow then disappeared into the kitchen.

'You take your coffee the same way you have your tea?'

'Yes please.'

He listened to his coffee being made, letting the sounds of domesticity wash over his ruffled soul. He snuggled deeper into the comfortable chair and stared at his reflection on the grey television screen. This was where the heathen Brian usually sat.

He pictured Pat's husband loafing in his pyjamas on a Sunday morning, the newspapers spread out around him while his wife was bringing the collection plate up the aisle. Brian's road to hell was paved with the *Sunday Times*. He glanced round the room for any signs to back up this image but the lounge was tidy with everything neatly in its place.

The coffee announced itself with a slight rattle of the cup in its saucer. Pat placed the tray that also contained the obligatory biscuits onto the low table in the centre of the room. Andrew watched her movements, taking a little pleasure in being so close to this attractive woman. Pat had been a late surprise for Geoff and Peggy and was now a vivacious forty to her mother's seventy-five.

She looked up and caught the appreciative glance just before it scurried down behind the vicar's collar. She turned quickly, too quickly. Had she seen him? Was that a shy blush he saw? Her face held no clue when she turned back and handed him his coffee, following it up quickly with an offer of a custard cream.

'Where's Brian?' He needed to say something to break the moment.

'He had to go into work this morning. An important meeting that he's been trying to set up for ages. Said he would come home straight afterwards.'

Andrew nodded. It confirmed his belief that Pat's marriage was on autopilot. It needed someone or something to force it to land so that she could get off.

'Well I've set things in motion for Friday at two, is that okay?'

'That'll be fine.'

'We need to discuss hymns, who's going to say a few words and details like that.'

Pat nodded.

After the arrangements for the funeral had been finalised, Andrew stood to go. A few crumbs bounced off his lap and onto the carpet. He nonchalantly ignored them, hoping Pat had not noticed.

At the door he gave her a light peck on the cheek, then as an afterthought hugged her, enjoying the warm softness of her body against his.

'Call me if you need anything,' he said as he started down the short path to the gate. At the gate he paused to fiddle with the latch, then as he walked through he glanced up and found himself on the receiving end of a piercing stare from two rat-like eyes that glowed beneath a furry hood. The Rat grinned a knowing grin, then scurried off, leaving Andrew standing holding the gate ajar.

---o0o---

He stared at the phone. It sat cradled in its charger, grey and cold. He knew he should call the bishop and talk to him about the dream, get his advice. But he battled to think how he could open the conversation, let alone broach the subject.

He had already reached for the phone twice, then settled back into his chair, fearful of the voice that would be on the other end. It seemed sensible to talk to the bishop first before rushing off to Dartmoor, but…

The chair was comfortable and sitting back in it he could not reach the phone. He wanted to stay like that now, cocooned in his comfort. He knew it was dangerous to stay settled for too long, the inertia would become harder to overcome.

As a distraction from the task at hand he tried to summons Pat's face up in his mind, her wave of grey-tinged blonde hair, the gentle jaw, the ski-slope nose and the twinkle-brushed eyes nestled between the opposing arrows of crow's feet. It was a pleasant face, one that brought warmth to his troubled mind.

There was depth to her that Marjory lacked. Marjory, bless her, was sweet and totally loyal, but she lacked substance. She was somewhat two dimensional and as a parishioner had once joked with him, two dimensional only looks good on paper.

The sound of the front door drew him out of his thoughts and he glanced back at the phone. His hand stretched out again for it, then dropped back guiltily. What if Marjory caught him phoning the bishop? Would she be offended that he sought advice elsewhere? How stupid was that thought?

He listened to her dropping the keys on the table in the hall, then she began to clatter around in the kitchen. His thoughts wandered again. This time they visited The Rat. What had he been doing outside Pat's place? It was not one of his usual haunts, or at least Andrew could not recall ever seeing him there before. Then the thought struck – maybe The Rat was following him!

He looked up in shock just as Marjory appeared round the door, a mug of steaming tea in her hand.

'Bloody hell Marge, you startled me!'

'Andrew! Language!' She tutted and placed the mug down on the wooden coaster next to the phone. 'I thought you might like a cup of tea.' It was almost an apology and she began to withdraw from the room.

'No. Wait. I'm sorry love,' he gestured for her to come back. 'I'm just edgy about this dream business.' How he wished it was Pat he was talking to and not Marjory. Pat would know what to say.

Marjory hesitated at the door for a second then turned and, after a moment's contemplation, eased herself onto the arm of the chair opposite his desk and waited for him to talk. Her knees pressed together and bent slightly gave her body a neat zigzag shape. Her tight skirt had pushed up slightly and he could just make out the tops of her stockings. Years ago this would have excited him, but now he felt a little repulsed.

She noticed his glance and immediately stood to straighten the skirt, taking his look as a reprimand for showing too much, before sitting again, ensuring that she was decent. This annoyed him. Why was she so prudish?

'Thanks for the tea.' His trained voice was gentle and reassuring despite his annoyance. The zigzag nodded and waited. He didn't want to say any more, but having called her back he felt he should go on.

'I saw Pat. She's holding up well.' The zigzag shifted its bottom on the arm of the chair.

'Poor thing,' it said.

Andrew shook his head and the zigzag sighed.

'I suppose I should get on with things. I need to prepare for the funeral as well as Sunday.' He was dismissing her.

She stood to leave, then paused at the door again. 'I presume that you heard the news?'

'No, what news?'

'The optician couldn't find anything wrong with McCready's eyes. They say he's faking it, but he is still insisting that he's been blinded.'

---o0o---

In loving memory of Geoffrey Deane, 1927-1990. He loved this view.

Andrew fingered the plaque lightly. It was colder up here than it had been in the morning, but he felt better. The whole dream was just that, a dream. There was no hidden message or God calling him to go face that monster. It was all a coincidence, the optician proved it.

The weight of the day had lifted and he pulled his coat tighter round him as he traced the route from the vicarage to the house where Peggy Deane had died. His mind relaxed slightly as the reality of her passing sunk in. He no longer had to make a fool of himself going in there every so often, trying to make conversation with those lifeless eyes. He was free of that burden now.

He moved his gaze from Peggy's house to Pat's and again he pulled up the picture of her face that he kept stored in his mind, but this time he let his thoughts go further. He moved his inner gaze down her body, slowly stripping away the white blouse and black slacks that she had been wearing that morning. He let his gaze linger at the top of her stockings which were held in place by a suspender belt. This excited him. He moved her gently to the bed. Which bed? Hers or his? It didn't matter, the bed is not important, it's her and her body that matters. The underwear dissolved and he brought her naked body close, revelling in the warmth and smoothness of it.

'You shaggin' the pee-do's dorta?'

He jumped and stared at The Rat, acutely aware of the hardness that ached in his groin. He crossed his legs quickly to hide it and remonstrated with The Rat.

'No! No! What makes you think that?' He was shouting, a sure sign of his guilt. 'Why on earth would you suggest such a thing?' He forced his voice to calm down and with it his groin.

'I saw you there at 'er 'ouse. So you shagging 'er or wot?'

'No. I am not...' he paused a second before saying the word unfamiliar to his tongue, '...I'm not shagging her.' He was calm now and a hint of patronising crept into his voice, it was an 'explaining the facts of life to a child' tone.

'So why's it jew is always round 'er place when 'er ol' man's away?'

'I was there this morning because her mother had died.' Why did he have to defend himself to The Rat? 'There was certainly no shagging going on.' He tried to meet The Rat's stare, but it was too intense and he returned his gaze to the town.

'So the ol' lady's dead? Took 'er bloody time goin' din she? Djoo reckon she knew 'er ol' man was a pee-do?'

Andrew turned sharply and glared at The Rat. 'You have no evidence that he was a paedophile so I wish you would stop alluding to it. He was...' His voice melted under the stare and, '...he was...' he turned back to the town and drew strength from that. '...he was a good man.'

The Rat sniffed loudly next to him. He could almost see the busy nose wriggling in delight at his discomfort. How could someone so young have such a hold over him? This was not natural.

''e wos a pee-do oright!' The Rat was suddenly running off, shouting back loudly. ''e wos a pee-do, jus' like that McCready fellow!'

---oOo---

'Andrew.' It was that voice again. 'Andrew.' Soft, yet commanding. He wanted to wake up, to run away from the pain the sharp goodness of the voice brought. There were no visuals with the dream, just sounds like in the old days before TV.

'Yes.' He heard his voice plop into the thick treacle black of the dream. It was his voice but it was not under his control.

'Andrew, go and see him in prison. Go to him, he is waiting for you. Go and heal him.'

He scrambled madly in the dark, clawing his way up from the black depths of the dream, pushing the treacle down to cover the voice.

'Go to him, go see Paul McCready.'

He glanced down into the darkness below, a murky image of the tabloid picture waved in the pool of black and the voice began to grow softer, but no less urgent.

He turned and tripped upwards on the unsteady surface, pausing for breath on the gloomy plateau of semi-consciousness. The voice was now just a faint whisper, there was no longer a message, it was just sounds shaped as words.

He opened his eyes.

---o0o---

'Morning Andrew, to what do I owe this pleasure?' The Bishop's voice was warm with a hint of authoritarian.

One could hardly call it pleasure, Andrew thought as he went through the process of greeting and being polite. He had known the Bishop quite well back at uni and had kept in touch on and off. However, while Ian had quickly climbed up the ranks in the church (or the Stairway to Heaven as he liked to think of it), Andrew had been left behind to wallow in pastoral parishes.

'It's where your talent lies,' Ian had told him one day. 'You're just so good with people.'

If I'm so good with people, how come I haven't managed to manipulate a nice cushy Diocese for myself like you, Andrew had mused to himself. Maybe I'm only good with the wrong people. His bitterness surprised him. Long gone was the fervent passion of wanting to make a difference, wanting to spread the Good News that had burned so violently in him as a youngster.

He had had too many disappointments, too many unanswered prayers since signing up. Each set back threw further water on the fires of the Spirit until he was left with the merest glimmer of light in amongst the black coals of his soul.

But what could he do? A career change was out of the question, he was too far passed the point where it would have been feasible. So now he just plodded on, smiling when he needed to smile, comforting when he needed to comfort, chastising when he needed to chastise and preaching without conviction.

Then the bitterness had come. He began to resent the God that had called him into service, only to throw him into the mundane kitchen of life. The recruitment posters never say 'Your Country Needs You...To Peel Potatoes.' He felt swindled, like the youngster rushing off to sign up for king and country and spends the war defeating the enemy with the peeled spud.

With the resentment came the guilt. While he raged against his lot in life, there were always those sermons he had sat through, reminding him of a different kind of fire, one that consumed you in an agonising trap for eternity. There were days when he felt that he was surely destined for hell and that thought frightened him, but it only fuelled his anger at God for putting him in this position. 'My God, My God, why hast thou forsaken me?' He wanted to cry out. He wanted to curse God and die, but he did not have the guts to do so.

The pleasantries were over and he had to get to the reason for his call. He took a deep breath and plunged in, wondering to himself how the warm voice would react.

---oOo---

'Morning Father Andrew,' The Laugh bubbled. 'Are you okay? You don't look well,' she smiled.

'I'm fine thanks Eve. Just had a bad night, didn't sleep well.' He buried his face in the post he had picked up from the desk. The fury was sloshing around inside him in angry waves. He studied each envelope closely without seeing them. He didn't want to talk to Eve, he was in no mood for joviality.

'Roger McLeod rang. Linda is doing well. He said to thank you for your prayers and asked if you could be there when they get the test results next week.' The Laugh giggled.

'Hmmm?'

'Linda McLeod? Remember Father? She had surgery yesterday. You did prayer for her didn't you?'

'What? Oh yes of course I did.' Lord forgive me. 'When next week do they want me there?'

'Wednesday at three,' and a chuckle. The Laugh waited for Andrew to acknowledge this, but he continued to flick through the post.

'Father Andrew?' A concerned laugh that asked *how could you be lost in the post, they were all bills I've checked through them already?* He flicked over another envelope and seemed to study the address intently for a moment.

'Father Andrew?' A nervous giggle and a step in his direction. 'Are you okay? Can I make you some tea?'

'NO! No more bloody tea!' He threw the letters on the floor, watching them scuttle for safety from his anger. He turned and stormed out of the vestry, and despite his anger he managed to shoot an apologetic look at The Laugh. It was not her fault, but he was not in the mood to explain that, he merely needed to leave the door open for the full apology he would have to make later.

Outside the cold air quickly cooled his temper while he stood breathing heavily. One hand sought and found the rough stone wall of the church. It supported him physically but gave no spiritual comfort and this caused his anger to rise again. He needed to move on quickly. The Laugh would be coming to check on him any second and he could not face that. He moved swiftly onto the road and almost without a conscious thought, headed straight towards Pat's house, only half aware as he turned into her street of the rat-like eyes that followed him to her door.

---o0o---

'Andrew?'

'May I come in, Pat?'

She moved aside to allow him to pass and he walked straight through to the lounge and dropped into Brian's chair. Pat followed, the concerned look on her face mingled with puzzlement. She had never seen her vicar so agitated.

'Are you alright, Andrew?' He had heard that too often in the last couple of days. 'Can I get you some tea?' She stood at the door, seemingly too scared to cross the threshold, as if in crossing it she would somehow catch whatever it was that caused Andrew's distress.

He sighed and sank deeper into the chair.

'Yes please, Pat.'

Her name felt sweet on his tongue, a welcome relief from the bitterness in his mind. She disappeared into the kitchen.

Suddenly the comfortable chair was not comfortable anymore. It was Brian's chair, what the hell was he doing sitting in it. He stood and moved to the mantelpiece where he picked up a photograph. The image showed a younger and very vivacious Pat in her graduation gown, on her left was Peggy, all smiles and alive, on her right, the paedo.

He put it down quickly, in shock that his mind seemed to have embraced The Rat's accusation so. The chair was still uninviting and he was caught between standing around looking foolish and sitting feeling uncomfortable. He had just settled into the armchair when Pat arrived with the tea. There were rich tea this time. He preferred the custard creams, but he was too agitated to care.

Pat handed over the tea and biscuits and retreated to her chair opposite, sitting and waiting expectantly for the Vicar to explain his sudden appearance and mood.

What the hell am I doing here? He looked around the too familiar room, desperately trying to find words to start the conversation. The call to the Bishop flooded back to his mind and the humiliation and annoyance that it brought rose within him.

He took a deep breath then expelled it, hoping the unsettling feelings would go with.

'That's a lovely picture of your graduation,' he almost blurted this out in his desperation to start the conversation. Pat glanced nervously up at it.

'That was a long time ago,' she smiled.

He nodded, somewhat calmed by the smile and snuggled a little deeper into the chair that was now becoming more comfortable. He reached for his tea and it was only the rattle of the cup in its saucer that made him realise that he was shaking.

'Andrew.' The voice was soothing and concerned.

He looked up at the soft blue eyes. Her head was slightly tilted, her look a question mark and he melted. The story came tumbling out. Not the story of the dream, but about the call to the Bishop regarding *a certain problem*. How the Bishop had not seemed to believe him, almost laughed at him, saying, without saying, that Andrew was not high enough up in the church for God to even talk to him, let alone ask him to do something.

'Are you sure that's what he meant?' Pat could hardly believe it.

'Well, that's the impression I got.' He was calm enough now to sip at his tea and took a healthy bite on the rich tea, taking a reckless pleasure in letting some crumbs bounce down his stomach and accumulate on his lap.

'Well…' Pat drew out the word as she searched for the right ones. '…I suppose you must do what you think is right. If you believe God is calling you to do something then you should do it.'

Andrew nodded. It was exactly what Marjory had said, but somehow, coming from Pat, it made more sense. He dabbed at the crumbs on his lap and dropped them onto the saucer. 'Thanks, Pat. Sorry to have bothered you at such a difficult time.'

She smiled, feeling slightly awkward. 'More tea?'

'No. No thanks. I'd better go.' He stood and moved toward the door and she followed. In the small hallway he stopped and turned to her.

'I'm sorry to have bothered you.' He repeated.

Pat looked at him, the unasked question hung embarrassingly between them. *Why come to me, why not go to your wife?*

He saw the question in her eyes, in her look and fumbled for words to answer it, but she was in his arms and his lips were on hers before the words found his. Her minimal resistance was more surprise than repulsion driven. Then through the adrenaline fog came the voice. 'GO AND SEE HIM.'

He pulled back, staring into the startled blue pools that stared back.

'I'd better go.' He said and turned, the enormity of what he had just done sending shock waves through an already disturbed mind.

'Andrew.' She reached out a hand to bring him back, to stop him falling over the precipice. But his shame burned fiercely now and he couldn't face her. He moved quickly to the door and, pausing to throw a mumbled *I'm sorry* over his shoulder, left without looking back.

The door clicked closed and the gloom closed back round her. She stood for a moment, staring at the space Andrew had just vacated, the surprised look still etched on her face. Then slowly the expression drained away and a smile as light as the touch her fingers now gave her lips appeared.

THE GOOD VICAR

---oOo---

Back in his office, Andrew sat shaking. *What the hell are you doing?* He held his head in his hands while his mind screamed accusations at him. The kiss still burned on his lips and tingled in his conscience. He fought hard against admitting the thought that it had felt good and more scarily, it had not been rejected, if anything it had been welcomed. He sat still, forcing himself to breathe deeply and slowly till the intensity of the thought waned.

The phone rang, its metallic chirrup dragging the last pangs of guilt from him, replacing them with thoughts of hurt and anger as the call with the Bishop flooded back.

It was the funeral parlour wanting to talk about Peggy's funeral. He adjusted to Good Vicar mode, amazed at how easily it came to him.

'Yes Mr Greystone, two o'clock on Friday…No, I don' think it will be a big one…The Mother's Union are going to provide nibbles in the hall afterwards.'

He put the phone down and smiled. He was calm now, still impressed at his professionalism in dealing with the call, The Good Vicar to the rescue.

The Phone rang again.

'Good Morning, is that Father Andrew Compton?'

'Speaking.'

'This is Father Gregory Simms. I'm the prison pastor at Dartmoor. Do you have a moment?'

He recoiled from the phone, half throwing, half dropping it.

'Hello? Hello?' Father Gregory's tinny voice pleaded to be rescued from the fall and Andrew scrambled around madly for the phone and The Good Vicar.

'Hello. I'm terribly sorry, the phone slipped.' It was a distant cousin of The Good Vicar, but at least they were related.

'Is this a bad time?'

'No, No.' Yes it is a terrible time. 'Please go…' away '…on.'

Father Gregory hesitated for a second, almost as if he had heard the unspoken thoughts, but then continued, 'Well it's rather a strange matter. As I said I am the prison pastor at Dartmoor, and I've had a request from one of my parishioners. It regards the funeral of Mrs Peggy Deane who I believe was one of your flock?'

'Yes?' Andrew drew out the word knowing what was coming and furiously tried to work out how Paul McCready could know about Peggy Deane, let alone her death. Her body was just settling into the morgue.

'Well...' Andrew could feel the uncertainty in the voice on the phone and wanted to blurt out *it's about Paul McCready isn't it*. But he held his tongue, preferring to let the uncomfortable explanations be one-sided for the moment. Besides, his own confusion at the connection between Peggy and that monster was occupying most of his processing capacity.

'This parishioner of mine has asked if you could record the funeral service and send a copy up to him. There's no chance of his being granted permission to attend in person, he's not related to the deceased, just an old family friend he said. However...' Father Gregory paused, this was delicate.

Andrew waited, the slight feeling of power over the voice on the other end began to thrill him. He could put this man out of his misery, but he chose not to. Let him suffer like I have had to with these dreams.

'However, I'm afraid the parishioner in question is a rather notorious one and, well I guess it depends on the family's reaction. You should get their permission I guess.'

'Who is this parishioner?' A smile flittered over his lips, one that bordered on maniacal.

A large breath was taken in the small office of the Dartmoor Prison's Vicar.

'Paul McCready.' The name came on the exhale.

Andrew waited a suitable time before replying.

'I see,' then went silent again, imagining this Father Gregory squirming as he played with him.

The silence stretched long enough for the voice to snap.

'I'm sorry, I know it's an awkward one, but I'm rather duty bound here to at least make this call. If you don't want to talk to the family I'll understand.'

'Oh no. I'll talk to Peggy's daughter, that's not a problem.' It's never a problem talking to Pat, although…The kiss stung his lips again, but he refused to lose the upper hand in this conversation.

'I'm just rather curious as to how Mr McCready found out, I mean very few in my Parish know of Peggy's passing, her obituary hasn't even been printed yet. I wouldn't have thought news would travel that fast.'

The throat on the other end of the phone was cleared before an unsure voice said, 'I was rather hoping you wouldn't ask that, but since you have, here goes. He claims that…well he claims that God told him in a dream.'

---oOo---

The phone looked comfortable in its cradle. He didn't feel he could disturb it, not just yet. Maybe it would wake up by itself and start crying, then he could pick it up and comfort it. But for now…

Do phones dream? Do they eavesdrop on other conversations? Could they tap into the thousands, or millions even, of phone calls flying around the world? He imagined having the power to tap into all those private conversations. How much better could he know the hearts of men then?

He sighed. He was delaying another call. How could he talk to Pat after the way he had left her earlier, even more so, how could he ask her for permission to record the service because a convicted child murderer had been told by God that Peggy was dead and he wanted to hear what happened at the funeral? Why was he even interested in Peggy? Did he actually know her? He stepped back from the thought, unsure of the wobbly ground around it.

The ground around his trip to the prison was also suspect, but he decided to risk it. Why had he suggested that he should see McCready himself? He knew the answer, but how had it seemed to Father

Gregory? There had been, he was sure, a tone of doubt in his agreeing to the visit.

What would he say to McCready? What does one say to a man who used a cricket bat to smash the eight year old skull of an innocent, defenceless girl? They had never proved beyond reasonable doubt that any sexual misconduct occurred, but society and the press agreed between the lines that this had happened.

They also had not proven that McCready was responsible for a string of unsolved child murders and disappearances that had occurred over a period prior to his arrest. The fact that these stopped when he was incarcerated convicted him where the courts couldn't.

He looked back at the phone. It still lay snug and smug in its holder and for a split second he believed he could understand why McCready had used a cricket bat. He jumped back from the thought and the image of the shattered remains of the phone.

'This is completely different,' he told himself, his hands shaking. 'A telephone is an inanimate object. Smashing a phone is nothing like smashing a human skull.'

'I brought you some tea.' Marjory was at the door.

No more bloody tea! The cricket bat was in his hand again and swinging wildly. Bits of china mingled with bits of skull, red blood mingled with red tea.

'Thanks love, you always seem to know exactly when I need one.' The Good Vicar had slipped quietly into the room while he had been busy appeasing his base desires.

---oOo---

At the door he paused. Should he go to The Laugh and apologise for earlier, or should he head straight over to Pat's. He was not ready to face either just yet. He was also aware of the solitary typed sentence on his computer screen. This constituted the sum total of his sermon due for delivery on the rapidly approaching Sunday. He could just as easily return to staring at that sentence.

He fumbled around for the house keys that lay on the little table next to the front door. He could see them, but chose to ignore this as he was buying time to make up his mind. He did not want to get caught standing at the door trying to decide where to go so he invented this excuse. He cursed himself for not having resolved the issue before leaving the safety of his desk.

In loving memory of Geoffrey Deane. He couldn't go back up there, not now anyway. 'There wasn't time,' he mumbled out loud, trying to drown the thought that The Rat was waiting there for him to torment him.

Scooping up his keys and the image of Pat's soft warm lips, he opened the door. A well-dressed man stood on the doormat, his hand stretched out pointing at the doorbell. Andrew instinctively followed the finger while his mind processed the rest of the image.

'Brian?' He tripped over the name as images of a vengeful husband coming to retrieve a stolen kiss raced through his head.

'Andrew.' The man nodded formally. No 'Father' before his name, bloody heathen. Despite his thoughts The Good Vicar clung to his ground, hoping that the surprise on his face was perceived to be only because of finding an unexpected visitor on his doorstep.

'Well, that's a coincidence.' The Heathen smiled warmly. 'Were you just on your way out?'

'Yes…yes. I was heading up to the office.' Lord forgive me. 'But it was nothing too important. Come in.'

'Actually I'm here to see Marge.' He stood his ground while Andrew cursed his too familiar shortening of his wife's name.

'Marjory?'

'Yes. Pat asked me to come over. She wants me to sort out the snacks for Peggy's funeral. Is she in?'

Relief and annoyance flooded into Andrew as he was discarded in favour of something mundane.

'Yes, she's home. Marjory!' He shouted up the stairs, trying not to throw too much sarcasm into using her full name. 'Brian's here to sort out the nibbles for Peggy's funeral.'

Marjory appeared at the top of the stairs patting her greying hair into place, a warm smile playing on her lips. She was so good like that, the sympathy oozed naturally from her.

'Use my office.' He gestured grandly as The Heathen stepped politely inside, then added, 'If you don't need me I'll be off then.'

Brian nodded. 'Thanks, Andrew. I think we can manage from here.'

Leather on willow. He turned and started heading off towards the church, bringing his thoughts round to composing the grand apology that would be laughed off.

The small figure that jumped out from behind the bushes startled him.

''e's shaggin' yer misses you know.'

The nose twitched over the evil grin then it scurried off, leaving him caught between staring after his tormentor and staring back at his house.

---o0o—

'It's all rather complicated at the moment.' The Good Vicar was saying. Andrew sat back and watched him at work. The Bishop was right, The Good Vicar was good with people. Not the people who organised you a cushy Diocese of your own, but the people who made up the Diocese. He sipped on the tea that he didn't want.

She had already forgiven him, probably had done so as soon as he had stormed out. How can some people forgive so easily?

'I'm surprised you haven't lost your temper a long time ago,' she giggled. 'If I think of all the problems you deal with in this office, and those are only the ones I know about, well I think I would have gone crazy by now.'

What? You mean you're not already crazy with all that maniacal laughter that keeps pouring out of you. He smiled warmly, accepting the back-handed compliment and kept his thought unvoiced.

He had not given any details, just bandied about phrases. *A lot on my plate at the moment, things are getting to me a little bit* and *frustrated at not having all the answers.*

'I'm sure everything will turn out right. Remember, the Lord moves in mysterious ways. There must be a reason why all this is happening.' The Laugh's eyes sparkled kindly as she chuckled sweetly and, for just a fraction of a second, her plump motherliness charmed Andrew again and he wanted to rest his head on her inviting breasts, he wanted to lie naked with her in the warmness of fleshy sin, Andrew and Eve.

But the feeling passed as quickly as it had arrived and in need of a distraction he glanced at the neat stack of envelopes that stood on the corner of the desk. The Laugh had obviously cleaned up after his little tantrum and the letters looked accusingly back at him.

''e's shaggin' your misses you know. He allowed himself a smile at that. Having given it some thought he could now dismiss everything The Rat said. There was no way on earth that Marjory would be unfaithful to him, that went beyond the ridiculous.

He reached over to the pile of letters and began to open them methodically, flattening the folded bills into a neat pile. He glanced up and saw The Laugh smiling nervously at him. She was as skittish as her large frame would allow her to be.

'Don't worry Eve,' he smiled, 'I'm not going to throw them this time.' The Laugh let out a shriek and her whole body wobbled with the relief the humour brought. Andrew giggled slightly, more at The Laugh's reaction than at his comment. He took a mouthful of tea to suppress his humour, then opened another letter.

He unfolded what he expected was another bill and stared in horror at the crudely printed tabloid photo of Paul McCready. Underneath, in large print, the message read 'Look forward to seeing you.'

---oOo---

We all have our favourite meal – Sunday roast, fish and chips, chicken tikka masala...

The sentence stared at him from the screen. It was going to be a very short sermon unless he did something soon. And he still had to go and see Pat again to talk about...

The folded photo seemed to call out from his pocket.

We all have our favourite meal. The food was getting cold, the gravy congealing. Why wasn't there a sermon microwave where he could put in a cold sentence and a few seconds later take out a full blown sermon, piping hot and pulpit ready?

He was always putting something off. First he didn't want to do the sermon so that he could go see Pat, now he didn't want to see Pat so he could...what? He didn't want to do the sermon either. The five loaves and three fish, or was that the other way round, he could never remember without checking. It was an old story, one everybody knew. What new and exciting message could he bring to this stale meal?

Who had sent him the picture of McCready? He was putting that ponderance off as well, afraid of the answers it may throw up. Did Royal Mail do a collection from a big red letterbox in the sky?

We all have our favourite meal. He was suddenly hungry. Marjory must be out; she would normally have fixed lunch by now. Where could she be? He couldn't recall her saying that she was going out, but then in his present state of mind he could have missed her telling him. In one ear and out the other.

He walked to the door of his study and listened. The house was quiet. 'Marge?' he called hesitantly, recalling the familiar use of her name by Brian.

'Marge?' Louder this time.

Still nothing. He sighed and strode through to the kitchen and set about making a sandwich. *We all have our favourite meal.* Tuna sandwich was not his but it would have to do, bread and fish, it had been good enough for Jesus.

Where was Marjory?

He sliced the soft bread in half and sat at the breakfast table chewing pensively. He would go and see Pat as soon as he was finished. Brian would be around so he would not have to discuss the kiss, they could resolve that some other time. He felt the glow of a decision made and sat back smiling slightly.

---o0o---

'Brian not here?' he was surprised.

'No, I thought he was over at yours.' equally surprised.

This made it awkward. His hope of hiding behind The Heathen's presence to avoid discussing the kiss dissolved, and now it hung in its full, warm, puckered glory between them. There was no avoiding it.

'Look, about earlier Pat...' he cast a shy glance up at her and she blushed. 'I'm sorry. That should never have happened.' He glanced again and was shocked to see a fleeting look of disappointment flash across her face.

'Yes.' She was almost too pragmatic.

'Yes.' He agreed. 'I was distressed, a lot of things happening at the moment, distressing things. I should not have acted as I did.'

She nodded again.

'Come sit.' She gestured to Brian's chair and he sank uneasily into its familiar comfort.

'More calls to the Bishop?' She asked as soon as he had settled. At least she didn't want to discuss the kiss either.

'No, nothing like that.' He resisted the urge to giggle nervously. The earlier tantrum he had had about his little talk with the Bishop seemed distant and puerile now.

'There're a few things...look I don't want to bore you with all the details, but one of them affects you, other than my earlier indiscretion.' He added the last bit to what he felt was a decidedly naughtily raised eyebrow. He had not expected this. It had been a one-way affair to his mind until now.

'Well,' The Good Vicar slid into the armchair, 'I got a call from the vicar at Dartmoor. You know, the prison.'

'Dartmoor?' All naughtiness disappeared. 'Why would I have any connection to that place?' She shifted in her chair, intrigue and worry intertwined in her features.

'That's where I'm rather perplexed. You see, it seems that a certain prisoner, apparently a rather dangerous one, has requested that I record your mum's funeral service as he wants to hear it. There's no chance of him being allowed out to attend it, they said.'

Pat looked quizzical. 'Mum never knew anyone in Dartmoor. Who is it? What's his name?'

The Good Vicar sat forward in Brian's chair and took her hands in his. It was a comforting gesture, trying to protect her from the shock and relieve her obviously building distress, it was not Andrew the Stud Muffin making a pass.

'Pat,' he paused. This would not have been easy with any parishioner, but it being Pat made it a lot more difficult. 'It's a notorious criminal, I can't understand why he would be interested in Peggy's funeral at all.'

'Oh for goodness sake Andrew, just tell me who it is.'

Andrew was slapped by the fierceness of the demand. A mini struggle took place between The Good Vicar and The Stud Muffin as to who should answer before the voice calmly said. 'Pat, it's Paul McCready.'

'What! You mean the...'

'The paedophile, yes I'm afraid so.'

'Oh my God.' She cupped her hand over her mouth, her eyes expressing the horror. 'Oh my God Andrew. Is this some kind of a sick joke? What could that monster possibly want with mum? Andrew?' She was appealing to The Stud Muffin to comfort the distress away.

'Pat,' The Good Vicar answered, feeling like a cold-hearted bastard. He could let The Stud Muffin take over and exploit the vulnerability on offer, but he stood his ground. 'I'm sorry Pat. I know this is difficult, but I felt it was my duty to let you know.'

'You didn't agree to it?' The no-show of The Stud Muffin brought some venom into the remark.

'No, of course not,' he was indignant, but kept his tone calm. 'It's not my call, but...' he would have to tell her about the dream now, '...but there's more you should know before you make a decision.'

The Stud Muffin stood quietly and tiptoed out of the room, it had no part to play in the conversation to come.

---oOo---

'Where were you earlier love?' The Rat's accusation had no impact on the tone, there was no searching for clues in there; just a passing curiosity.

'Oh, um, Brian insisted on buying a few snacks for the funeral so we popped out to *Tesco*'s.' Marjory pattered her hair nervously. 'I see you made yourself some lunch.' She picked up the plate and cup that Andrew had left discarded on the table. The teacup rattled slightly in its saucer as she carried it across to the sink where she began rinsing the dishes off.

'Yes, tuna sarnie. Isn't it a bit early to be getting nibbles?' Again The Rat's accusation played no part.

'What? Oh, no. The stuff we bought should be fine, crisps and biscuits, nothing fresh. The Mother's Union will supply the fresh stuff – cakes and such like.'

'Okay.' A naughtily raised eyebrow suddenly appeared in his mind's eye. 'Oh, there's been a further development...'

The sentence was truncated by the shrill whistle of the doorbell. Marjory raised a well behaved eyebrow that asked *Who could that be?*

Andrew turned and walked slowly down the passage. Something was telling him that whatever was behind the ringing was not going to be welcome. A second impatient blast on the bell confirmed this.

'Alright I'm coming,' he called but didn't speed up his step.

'What the hell kind of a stunt you pulling!' The door was hardly open when The Heathen let rip. Andrew stepped back as the onslaught of wrath hit him. 'There is no way she's going with you and the service will NOT be recorded. Over my dead body. Peggy had no time for paedos, there's no way in hell she would have allowed her funeral to be heard by that…that…' he grabbed angrily for the word, '…that monster.' Having grasped it, he spat it out, disgusted that he couldn't find a more venomous word. 'You've got a bloody cheek coming round asking Pat to take part in your silly perverted games.' He stopped to take a breath and was about to continue when Marjory's voice cut him short.

'Brian? Andrew? What's going on?' She was at the door, almost pushing past her husband. Andrew looked sheepishly down at his feet while Brian struggled between continuing his tirade and behaving himself in front of Marjory. The frustration pulled his fingers tight into his palms.

Through gritted teeth, he hissed, 'Your husband,' icicles formed around the word, snapped off and fell to the ground narrowly missing Andrew's feet, 'sees fit to suggest to my grieving wife that not only does she allow the funeral of her mother to be recorded for the pleasure of a Dartmoor inmate, but he has the audacity to try and convince her that she should go along with him to visit this paedophile to see what a nice chap he's turned out to be. It's bloody…sorry Marge, it's completely outrageous.'

'Andrew?'

'I'm not having it. He's not taking Pat anywhere near that place and if I so much as smell a tape recorder within a mile of the church, there'll be hell to pay.'

'Andrew?' Her voice soft, but demanding.

'He's not bloody doing it. He…'

'Brian! Please?' Sharp then sweet.

Brian's anger was reduced to a glare which Andrew shrunk from as he scrambled around desperately for The Good Vicar.

'Brian, I'm really sorry to have upset you so.' Phew! He was there. 'I got a call from Dartmoor and, I must admit it shook me somewhat. I guess I just didn't think properly. Of course there's no question of taking Pat to see that man. It was silly of me to suggest it even. I'm really sorry I've upset Pat. Please tell her that.'

The anger writhed with furious irritation around The Heathen.

Gotcha! Andrew thought doing a mental victory dance. He could just hug The Good Vicar, but that wouldn't be good form. The quiet answer turns away wrath. One nil to the quiet answer.

'What about recording the service?' Growled.

'Out of the question too. I'm sorry Brian. I just thought it was Pat's call. Obviously she's more upset about it than she let on earlier. Please, please apologise for me.'

'Obviously *he's* more upset about it than Pat was earlier,' Andrew whispered to The Good Vicar, but was brushed aside.

'Well next time think before doing something stupid.' He turned and dragged his anger down the path. At the gate, the anger looked back and waved a threatening fist at Andrew while Brian fumbled with the latch.

Andrew watched him cross the road, then his stomach knotted as he saw a hooded young lad stroll up to Brian and start talking to him. Angry fingers were pointed back at him and Brian glared in his direction.

''e's shagging your missus you know,' Andrew could almost hear The Rat's whiney and unfounded accusation being made.

He turned and looked at Marjory who returned the glance for a second then walked away down the passage, her scornful look lingering in Andrew's mind.

---o0o---

In loving memory of Geoffrey Deane, 1927-1990. He loved this view.

He didn't really want to be there, but couldn't think where else to go. He was certain that The Rat would appear and he didn't want to face him, but felt a strange masochistic pull to have a confrontation. He watched the town below slip into late afternoon.

The sniff told him that The Rat was there, but he didn't move his gaze from the town. He could handle whatever The Rat said, but not the look.

'You can use this.' The Rat's voice was soft, almost kind and Andrew turned, half expecting someone else, such was the difference in tone.

The young lad, Alex, that was his name wasn't it, sat swinging his legs and holding out a small black machine just slightly larger than a penknife. His eyes were gentle, not the sharp stare of before, and he had pulled his hood back revealing an innocent young head.

'What?'

'You can use this. Issa dictaphone, you can then record the funeral. No one will know if you 'ide it in yer pocket.'

Andrew stared at the little machine then back at the boy.

'How...?'

''e told me when he left your place. Bloody angry 'e wos too. Whatcha say to make 'im so mad?'

'What did he say I said?'

''e said that you wanted to record the ol' lady's funeral for that paedo McCready. Issat right?'

Andrew thought for a second. There was no getting round The Rat. 'Yes, I got a request from the vicar at Dartmoor. He said that McCready wanted the service recorded.'

'Well you c'n use this.' The boy held out the little machine again.

'No, they made it quite clear that they didn't want the service recorded for that man.'

'Go on, they'll neva know. Besides, from wot I 'erd McCready's a new man. Reformed 'e is. Doan 'e deserve a chance?'

Andrew faltered. Maybe this was what the dream was all about. Give McCready a chance. Maybe he had been reformed in a *Road to Damascus* type conversion. Maybe God did need him to go and see McCready and see that he was a changed man. But...

'Take it.' It was almost seductive. 'I fink McCready needs someone to trust 'im and I doan fink that Mrs Deane's dorta is as against it as wot that Brian is.'

Andrew looked across at the young lad. The voice had been calm and mature. It was not the evil accusative voice that had tumbled from

The Rat earlier. The boy raised his eyes to meet Andrew's and he flinched, expecting that harsh, piercing look that he could not cope with, but it didn't come. The hazel eyes were gentle and brimming with childish innocence. They were…he caught his breath as the word came to mind, they were beautiful.

---o0o---

In the fading afternoon light he sat trembling at his desk. He felt dirty. The beautiful eyes kept appearing in their seductive way to him and he couldn't help himself thinking about how beautiful Alex had looked. With his hood down, he was no longer The Rat.

But while these thoughts raced around his brain, there was still The Good Vicar's voice berating him for his behaviour. What the hell was he doing? He was not a paedo but he was having lustful thoughts about this eleven year old boy. It scared him. He had managed to resist an overwhelming desire up at the bench, but had not stopped thinking about the boy since.

He tried to force images of himself and Pat passionately making love into his brain, but this seemed to have no effect. The images were rudely brushed aside by those hazel eyes.

'Dinner's ready.' Marjory's voice broke into his thoughts and he panicked. He had to compose himself before facing his wife. It was going to be hard enough dealing with the annoyance she seemed to show when Brian had stormed off without being seduced by the image of Alex on the park bench, so vulnerable and ripe for picking.

'In a minute,' he called back, then moved quickly to the little drinks cabinet, poured himself a measure of gin, downed it and braced himself to face Marjory.

---o0o---

He looked down at her head which lay on the pillow. Her rhythmic breathing had a calming effect on him. He still felt the chill of the reception he had had at dinner and the silence of the meal pervaded the house.

The bedside clock read 01:30 in bright red numbers and he rubbed his eyes. He was tired, but had been too scared to go to bed. Not only didn't he want to face Marjory's rising anger and the flashes of hazel eyes that were thankfully reducing, but the dream loomed large as well.

At least his sermon was done, even if it was a little half baked. There was enough there for the congregation to sink their teeth into.

He undressed quietly and slid into bed, his eyes were tired but he forced them to stay open for a bit before the effort of doing so outweighed the little strength that he had left to fight it with. He felt himself falling into the blackness of sleep.

---o0o---

He opened his eyes. Light was streaming in through the thin curtains. He lay in his warm, pre-conscious funk for a while before he slowly realised that the dream had not come and a smile spread across his face. He felt rested for the first time in a good while. Even the strange seductiveness of The Rat had disappeared. What had all that been about?

He looked over at the clock. 10:30. He sat up quickly, the fuzz of sleep falling away from him. Why had the alarm not gone off? Why had Marjory not woken him? She was not in bed with him, what was going on? He fumbled for his dressing gown and shoved his feet into his slippers before stumbling downstairs.

'Marge?' he called as he searched from room to room, but all the house threw back at him was silence. He was puzzled, but also aware of the need to move if he was going to make his appointment at Dartmoor in time. In the kitchen he flicked the kettle on, then ran upstairs to dress, carefully buttoning on his dog collar.

Back in the kitchen he made a quick cup of tea which scalded his throat as he gulped it down. He grabbed his car keys, then had a thought and moved quickly to his study, scooping up the phone from its cradle without walking round the desk. He dialled the number and waited.

'Pat? It's Andrew. Can you talk?...I just called to check if you still wanted to come to Dartmoor today, I know Brian...Yes, yes, I know, don't worry about that, I just wanted to check that it was your decision too...No, that's fine, I wanted to make sure. I got the impression that it was only Brian's view...No, that's perfectly okay. I know it was a shock yesterday and you've had more time to think, don't worry, I understand...Yes, I'm still going to go, I have to, I need to put my mind at rest about the dream...Oh, no I definitely won't be recording the service, don't worry about that. I've always maintained that it is your call.' He looked guiltily down at the little black machine that lay on the desk. '...No, that's fine. I understand perfectly, don't worry. Look I must dash. I'll come over when I get back, we still have to talk through some details for tomorrow. I must go...Okay, bye.'

He stared at the phone for a second, trying to shake off his disappointment, then headed out to the car. He wondered if the trip was really necessary given that he had not had the dream last night, but he had a nasty feeling that if he cancelled, then the dream would come back more forcefully. It was probable that the dream had not come because God knew he would be obeyed today. The thought comforted him, he actually felt like he was doing God's will, a feeling he had not had for ages.

He eased the car into a roundabout and as took his exit, he glanced at the occupants of the car that was slowing down to enter it. His car veered slightly as he focussed on Brian's car which came to a pause at the roundabout. In the passenger seat sat Marjory. They didn't see him.

---o0o---

He didn't look as sinister in the flesh as the tabloid photos made him appear. He had dark curly hair, his strong jaw and cheeks slightly darkened by a day in the shaving wilderness. But the most striking feature was the eyes. The photos had shown him with cold, hard, unrepentant eyes that stared out from the page, daring the world to take him on. Now as Andrew watched him move in opposite him, the grey-blue eyes seemed to stare lifelessly ahead, soft and contrite.

'Father Andrew, thank you for coming to see me.'

The voice was gentle and respectful. Andrew flinched slightly. He had been expecting something so much more vile and unclean that the calmness of the man almost seemed to offend.

McCready held out a hand, slightly off target and Andrew had to twist a little in order to shake it. He half expected some sort of electrical shock to come from the hand, but nothing except hard workman calluses rubbing against his soft vicar palms.

They sat down, McCready feeling around for the chair before carefully easing himself into it. Andrew studied the man's eyes trying to detect any hint in them that they could actually see. He wanted to wave his hand in front of McCready's face but The Good Vicar stopped him. Thank goodness he's here, Andrew thought, this is definitely his territory.

'Father Gregory would you mind if we talked alone?' McCready moved his head to where he thought the short, handsome priest stood, but again missed the target by about a foot. Father Gregory gave Andrew a questioning look and The Good Vicar nodded polite assent.

Once McCready was sure that the prison vicar had departed he turned back to Andrew. 'I guess this is all a bit strange to you Father,' he said.

The Good Vicar nodded, then remembering the lifeless eyes said, 'Yes. I'm not sure I understand why you want to have Peggy Deane's funeral recorded. The family don't know of any connection between you and her, and are very against me recording the service.'

'I see Father,' The Paedophile seemed disappointed.

The Good Vicar waited to see if he would go on, offer an explanation as to why he wanted to hear Pat's funeral, but the man remained silent, contemplating something. The silence stretched till Andrew couldn't take it anymore.

'Well?'

'The man was jolted from his thoughts and his unseeing eyes turned towards Andrew, this time they hit the mark and Andrew shrunk back slightly from the steel-cold stare.

'I am disappointed Father,' his voice said, 'I had hoped you would not have this problem.'

The Good Vicar nodded and said, 'I'm sorry to bring you this bad news, but you have to see it from our side, we know of no connection between you and the deceased. You have a notorious reputation, so unless we have more to go on then that, it's not too surprising that we are not prepared to grant your request. But that is why I am here,' he went on quickly. 'I wanted to find out what the connection is, perhaps then I can make a case to the family for them to allow the recording to take place. But as it stands…' He trailed off deliberately, this was a good ploy to get people to open up.

'I see Father,' the monster said again and fell silent. He was contemplating an answer so The Good Vicar waited. Eventually he reached a decision and looked up, hitting the target again, almost uncannily so. 'I'm afraid that I cannot tell you what the connection is at the moment Father, hopefully I will soon be able to, but the time is not right, not just yet Father.'

Andrew was not sure he liked the idea of *not just yet*, it implied that McCready expected to see more of him.

'Well I'm afraid I can't help you then.' The Good Vicar was so professional. He waited to see if this would coax more out of the man, while Andrew's curiosity willed him to give up his secret.

'That's the way it is, Father.' The voice understood.

'I'm sorry then, but I think I'm wasting my time here,' The Good Vicar moved to stand up.

'Father. Please.' The voice implored him to stay and he hesitated. 'If I may Father, I would like to ask that you trust me on this, I'm begging you, Father. It is important to me that I at least get to hear the funeral. I can assure you that there is a connection between us, but now is not the time to reveal it. Please believe me Father. It is very important to me. What harm can it do to record the service?'

There was something is his voice that made Andrew ease back into the chair. The Good Vicar was leaving, shaking his head in disgust.

Andrew waited a moment before saying, 'You say that now is not the time to reveal the relationship between you and Mrs Deane, when will the right time be? What is stopping you telling me now?'

'You will not understand, Father, no one will understand at the moment, certain things need to happen first before I can tell you, but for now, I'm asking you to trust me, Father. Will you trust me, Father?'

Andrew paused for a moment. 'Let me think about it.'

'The funeral is tomorrow, Father. Please!' There was now an urgency, almost a demand in the voice and the blind eyes that had dropped slightly glanced around desperately trying to make contact with Andrew's, but missed their mark this time.

'I have already told the family that I will not record the funeral unless they change their mind, but I think that that is unlikely. However,' he paused, enjoying the little bit of power he had over this notorious monster. McCready leaned forward in anticipation. 'as time is short, I will make a recording, but not hand it over to you until such time as I am satisfied that the connection you claim to have with Mrs Deane warrants me allowing you to hear it. That is the best I can do.' Lord forgive me.

McCready sat back, a half-smile played on his lips. 'Thank you, Father, thank you very much. You will not regret this, you have my word, Father.' The other half of the smile appeared.

Andrew moved to stand up, but the smile suddenly faded and McCready motioned for him to remain seated. 'Father, please, there is more.'

---o0o---

Andrew made a mental note to himself never to accept a post as a prison vicar, not if the tea he got was this vile stuff he obediently sat sipping on. Father Gregory sat opposite him in the small office.

'We prayed together for his sight to be restored,' Andrew explained, 'I'm sorry, but I do feel like I'm treading on your toes here.'

THE GOOD VICAR

'No, not at all, I've not been able to reach him, I'm just pleased that one of us seems to have some influence. I'm still not convinced about the blindness, what's your opinion?'

'I'm not sure. It appears genuine, and his sincerity during prayers, well I must say I've not often encountered the like in my time. But then one is always reminded of the character we're dealing with here. He could very well just be a very good conman. I must say I'm not totally convinced either.'

Father Gregory nodded his concurrence with Andrew's analysis.

'And this business of recording the funeral, what is all that about?'

'Inconclusive again. He would not offer up any real reason why he wanted the service recorded, despite me saying I had to have one before being prepared to do it.'

'So you're not going to record it then?' Father Gregory sounded a little disappointed.

Andrew recounted the story of the negotiation that had taken place, twisting the truth slightly.

'And the family, what are their views?'

'They're dead against it at the moment, but I'm sure I can convince them to allow the service to be recorded and only released if Mc-Cready offers a good enough reason is received.' He would not convince Brian, he knew that, and he seriously doubted that he would be able to fulfil McCready's other request, the one he said nothing about to Father Gregory. He had got the impression that achieving this request was one of the things that needed to happen before McCready would open up to him.

Father Gregory nodded. 'Good luck with that. I do feel that if we can grant him this request, we may just be able to reach him.'

The Good Vicar smiled. 'It must be difficult working with the men here, so many crimes that we seem unable to forgive, yet you need to see past that and look at the person behind the sin.'

Father Gregory smiled back, he had been asked this many times before, usually not so politely. 'It is hard sometimes. Take McCready for example. How does one even begin to forgive him for beating that poor girl to death, he seems to show no remorse, and refuses to admit to all those others that he is suspected of.'

'Do you think he did them?'

'I can't be sure, but from little things he has said, I wouldn't be surprised. I just can't help wondering about those poor parents still not knowing what has happened to their daughters. They need closure, yet still he holds back.'

'So how do you manage to even visit the man?' At least the biscuits were better than the tea.

'With difficulty,' Father Gregory replied. 'We always tend to look for the Satan in people, what I try and do is look for the Jesus.' He sat back with a satisfied, bordering on smug look on his face.

So is there any Jesus in McCready? Andrew almost asked, but thought better of it, opting to rather smile his agreement and saying, 'A good Christian way to view it.' He allowed his colleague a small moment of pride before continuing. 'Have you ever met with the girl's parents, you know, the one he was convicted for? The Bridges if I recall their name correctly?'

He watched the pride quickly fade and a semi-squirm take place. 'No, I…I don't think it would be appropriate for me to do so.'

'Has he ever asked you to talk to them on his behalf?' Andrew delighted in the shock now.

'No! He didn't ask you to, did he?'

'No,' Lord forgive me, 'I was just curious to know, given the other strange things he has done.'

Father Gregory relaxed slightly. 'I don't think I could face the parents, more so given my responsibility to the prisoners. How would you minister to those poor bereaved people? Who was it that had that horrible job? Father Bernhard something wasn't it? I remember seeing him on telly once, do you know him?'

'No, I remember the face. I think I may have seen him at some church conference before, but don't think I've ever spoken to him. Poor soul. That must be one of the worst things to have to do in our line of work. I just pray that I never have that task thrust on to me.' He tried hard to keep the dread he felt at having to face the Bridges, out of his voice.

---o0o---

In the car heading home, he shelved McCready's request that he go and persuade the Bridges to forgive him, an impossible task if ever there was one, and tried to focus his thoughts on the image of Marjory sitting in the passenger seat of Brian's car.

There must be some logical explanation, he thought, although The Rat's little voice *'e's shaggin' your missus,* kept ringing in the back of his mind.

Surely Marjory was not having an affair with Brian; that was unthinkable. She was dedicated to him, a good Christian wife. Those vows meant something to her, she wouldn't break them would she? Forsaking all others, those were the words.

He tried to remember back to his wedding day, to picture her in her white dress all shyness and smiles, but the only image he could call up now was the rather formal and demure portrait that stood on top of the television.

Where are we going to put that photo when one day we upgrade to these new-fangled flat screen tellies? There was no room on the mantelpiece with all the pictures of Jane and Sean there.

When last had they heard from Jane, she hardly ever rang these days? Then the thought struck him, how would he have coped if it had been Jane twenty odd years ago who had gone missing one day? The little pain caused by her not calling them these days would be amplified a thousand-fold. Image that anxiety and panic when she had not returned home when she was due.

Then the whole intrusion into your lives as the press try to help, brave faces in front of the cameras and bright lights, but tears and tensions behind the scenes.

And then the horrible news brought to you by the nice policeman who you have come to hate. He is just a decent fellow doing his job, but every time he appears you expect the worst. Day after day he torments you, arriving with his updates that end with the bottom line of 'still no news.' Till that one day he arrives, grim faced and you know there is news and it's not the news you want to hear.

'A body of a young girl has been found, we believe it is your daughter. We will need you to come and identify the body.' Poor man, he's just doing a difficult job, probably sitting there feeling thankful his own daughter or son is safely ensconced at school while he tells you that they *think* it is your daughter. Think? They *know*. They must know. Even if her head had been smashed in, they know.

How do you face going to see the body? Hoping against hope that it is not your daughter, selfishly wishing that it is some other poor couple that have to experience the dreadful pain of it being their loved one rather than you having to admit that which you have feared most.

Imagine that incredible, inconsolable pain that strikes you as you stare down at the battered, cold body lying in the morgue, that greying lump of flesh that had once been your lively, lovely daughter. All the tantrums and tears, all the disobediences disappear, she had been a perfect, lovely child.

The public thank yous would be difficult too. Thanks to the nice policeman who, despite wishing he could have done more, but knowing he did his utmost, had done a sterling job. You hate him even more now for not having saved your daughter's life, for being the bringer of the bad news. You want to scream at him, blame him but you know it is not his fault.

Then the evening after the harsh glare of the media spotlight fades away and you sit alone in the house, the silence of her absence screaming at you and the 'if onlys' hang heavily in the air between you. You want to accuse the other of neglect, of letting little Jane out to play on her own, but you know that you are just as guilty. You desperately need to pull close together to claw at the crumbs of comfort on offer, but you don't know how to move.

Imagine then the next visit of that policeman. They have a man in custody who they believe did this. How do you feel then? Kill the bastard! Even if the police have the wrong man, kill the bastard.

The court case would drag on forever and there would be all the defence arguments, trying to exonerate this man who is now a monster in your eyes and you want to scream out *LIAR!* every time he opens his evil mouth. You raped and killed my lovely daughter you bastard! But the legal system does not allow you this outburst.

Then finally you sit in court waiting for the verdict of the jury, hating them for taking so long to decide, it was bloody obvious that he did it. You glare at them, daring them to even try and consider the inconceivable notion that this monster is innocent, and then the relief that floods over you as the word *guilty* rings around the court. That bastard will pay for his actions. How you wish that the death penalty was still being used.

Out once more into the glare of the media's flashing lights. 'We are pleased with the verdict. Justice has been done. We can never get our Jane back, but she can rest in peace now.' We will never have peace in our lives again.

Then back home to the gloomy, silent house full of unspoken accusations and 'what ifs', full of the emptiness of the verdict. Guilty was not a strong enough word for what he did, there is no word for what he did. And the sentence is too meagre. Death would be too good for him. You want to rip his testicles off with a pair of rusty pliers and ram a red hot poker up his backside, then leave him to die a horrible painful death, begging for mercy. The house is full of this venom, there is no space for God, no space for forgiveness.

How do you being to talk to someone who has gone through all this and try and plant the seed of forgiveness in that hate-filled home? Why had he agreed to do this? Was he mad? Did he get too carried away thinking he was doing God's work?

Andrew turned into his street, knowing that The Good Vicar was going to have his work cut out for him. He looked up and saw Brian's car outside the house.

He pulled up a little way down the street and walked quietly up to the front door, his mind racing. This is foolish, there is no way Marjory would allow anything to happen. Why was he beginning to doubt?

The front door creaked slightly and he flinched, but moved quickly through and headed as quietly as he could up the passage. He paused at the door of the lounge trying to convince himself that there was no heavy breathing going on behind it, then he put his head round the door.

---oOo---

'Hello, Father Andrew. Are you okay?' The Laugh smiled.

Why the hell had he come here? There was no way he could think here, and he would never be able to discuss what he had just seen with The Laugh.

'I'm okay Eve, just a little tired.' The Good Vicar was on autopilot, the shock had even affected him. He sat down behind the desk and looked up at Eve who stood smiling opposite him. He glanced quickly down from her eyes to her cleavage that was partially on display before he politely looked away. He now knew why he was here, he wanted to bury his head into that motherly bosom and cry his pain away.

'Do you want some tea?' She smiled.

Is tea your answer to all life's problems? No I don't want tea, I want to be comforted by you. 'Yes please.' He watched her plump form move round the office preparing his drink.

She had been lying back on the sofa, her blouse unbuttoned, the sensible bra pulled to one side and Brian's hungry mouth was seeking out the small orange nipple that she was offering to him, while his free hand rode high up her skirt.

It now seemed strange how she had pushed him off her and fumbled madly to close her blouse. She knew he had seen her, why try and cover it up now, what good did that do? Did she really think that by suddenly appearing normal that he would believe it had never happened, that he had not seen anything?

Her voice was shrill and full of panic as she had tried to call him back, calling out his name in desperation.

Eve looked across at him and blushed slightly as she realised that he had been watching her every move. 'Father?' she asked with a nervous giggle.

Fuck it, he thought throwing away the sin-filled lounge.

'Eve, I desperately need a hug, I know this is rather unorthodox, but something horrible has just happened to me and I really need to be comforted. Would you mind?' He opened his arms hoping she would not reject him.

'Father?' A nervous giggle, then all the motherliness that was pent up in her large frame bubbled over. 'Of course.' She moved round the desk and drew him into her chest where he felt the relaxing balm of the warm contact immediately start to soothe him and he fought back the tears.

'Do you want to tell me about it?' Her voice echoed in the chest that lay beyond the muffling breasts.

He sighed heavily, he couldn't just come out with it. It would be all over the parish in a flash.

'I've just had a big shock,' he muttered into the wonderful smell of womanliness.

Eve pulled back slightly and looked down at him, searching his eyes, then said sadly, 'You found them together, didn't you?'

Andrew was shocked. Eve knew. How could she know?

'You poor man,' she smiled as she read the answer to her question in his face and then pulled him back into her breast.

Thoughts flew around his mind as he relied on the shock absorbers that his head lay on, to stop him screaming. He drew a big breath and swallowed hard, shouting for The Good Vicar to snap out of it.

Eventually he pulled his head back and felt the reluctance in Eve's hand to let him go.

'You knew about them?' The Good Vicar asked a slight tearfulness being kept at bay.

Eve nodded sadly and gave a nervous laugh.

'Does everyone know?'

'I didn't *know*, well no one knew for sure, but a lot of us have been suspecting for a while.'

'How long has this been going on?'

She shrugged sadly, 'A while now, we did hope it was not true, but he would always...'

'Please, Eve. No details at the moment. I can't face the details right now.' She nodded. 'Thanks,' he smiled without feeling. What did he do next? He couldn't face Marjory now, he needed to collect his thoughts before he even dared attempt that. That is of course if Marjory wanted to see him. The bench was out of the question, undoubtedly The Rat would be there. They knew, yet The Rat was the only one who'd had the decency to tell him, even if he hadn't believed it. That left Pat's.

'Does Pat know?' Suddenly he remembered that he was not alone in being cheated on. The adulterous kiss did not count in his scrambled mind.

Eve gave a stifled laugh. 'I don't think so, oh what a horrible time for it to come out, first her mother and now this. This is so horrible.' A small tear escaped from her eye and she turned away. 'I'm sorry Father,' she said.

Andrew was annoyed. She was supposed to be comforting him at the moment, not the other way round. He summonsed up The Good Vicar and with him some strength. 'We'll be okay I'm sure.'

The Laugh smiled through the tears, then laughed. 'Yes of course. Everything will turn out for the best.'

He wished he had her optimism. The return of The Good Vicar had sobered him up and he needed to be elsewhere, somewhere he could be alone.

He stood up. 'I'm going to go pray for a bit,' he answered The Laugh's questioning look. She nodded and smiled, her face saying how proud she was of her Vicar. Who could be so courageous in the face of such adversity?

---oOo---

The warm colours of the stained-glass window did little to dissipate the coldness he felt in the church. He walked slowly up the aisle and moved quietly into the side chapel. He shuffled into the pew, dropped a kneeler onto the floor and then eased himself onto his knees, expelling a large breath as he did so.

His hand automatically made the sign of the cross over his troubled breast and he raised his eyes to the light that came in through the window. It was not a picture he particularly liked, the figure of Jesus was too otherworldly as it stretched out a hand to touch and heal a far too well dressed beggar. *Your sins are forgiven.* He imagined those words coming out in a speech bubble from Jesus' mouth in cartoon fashion. Then it struck him that that was what was wrong with the window, it looked too much like a cartoon.

Your sins are forgiven. He remembered the text where Jesus got into trouble for speaking those words. How dare he play God and forgive sins.

Dare he, little old Father Andrew Compton, dare he consider playing God and forgive Marjory her sin? It hurt too much right now for him to even consider this.

Or was it just the shock that hurt? He had been so convinced that she would never stray. His thoughts about Pat and to a degree about Eve suggested to him that perhaps there was no love left in the marriage, so why should he feel so betrayed? Marjory was just doing what he desperately wanted to do himself. Maybe it was the shaking of his belief that the love would never end.

He pulled himself up onto the pew. He was not praying, so why bother kneeling? Should he pray? He didn't feel like praying. Despite all that was going on in his life, he did not feel he could turn to God for comfort or advice.

What was he going to do now? He could not face going home, could not face Marjory just yet. God, his life was a mess. It had been okay a few days ago before the dream came. Well maybe not completely okay, directionless and rather empty, but now it was cluttered with unpleasantness.

He heard the door of the church rattle and ducked down in the pew.

'Father Andrew?' The Laugh's voice echoed in the empty building. He lay still, wondering why he was hiding. The Laugh's breath was a little laboured as she shuffled unsurely up the centre aisle. 'Father Andrew?' She stopped and Andrew held his breath.

'He must have gone home,' he heard her whisper to herself. 'Poor man, I hope everything will be okay.' She turned and he listened to her soft steps pad to the main entrance. The big doors clunked closed and he heard the key turn in the lock. Instinctively his hand went to his pocket to check if he had a key, then suddenly he smiled. He knew where he was going to spend the night.

---o0o---

This was not a good idea. What time was it? He longed for the morning. The kneelers did not make as comfortable a mattress as he had hoped, and his robes were not keeping him overly warm.

He pushed himself slowly onto his feet. His hip hurt from where he had been lying on his side. He moved stiffly around a step or two before a loud bang echoed in the silent church and the pain shot up his leg from his toe. 'Fuu...' he swallowed the rest of the word just in time. It would not do to swear in a church. He lowered himself into a pew and massaged his toes while wondering if mentally swearing in a church counted.

He rubbed his face with his hands and looked around in the dark. It felt menacing. Churches are supposed to be welcoming he thought and closed his eyes.

---o0o---

His neck hurt. Sleeping while sitting in a pew was also not good. He rolled his shoulders to ease the stiffness, but felt too tired to move. He sighed heavily and stretched himself out on the pew without opening his eyes. He fumbled for a kneeler to rest his head on.

---o0o---

The pew was hard, and in the fuzziness of his mind he thought he heard Marjory's voice calling him. He pushed himself up and listened.

The creak of the pew cracked loudly in the silence that hissed back at him once he had settled himself into the sitting position. He strained to hear above the noise of the silence, but there was nothing. He rubbed his chin, feeling the roughness of the stubble that was growing there. What time was it? Will morning ever come? He now regretted having hidden when Eve came to check on him. Let's try that kneeler mattress again, he thought and lowered himself onto the makeshift bed, pulling his robes around him for warmth.

---o0o---

It was Brian's face, but he knew it was McCready. He watched as the evil figure stared at him over the head of another, smaller one that knelt on the floor in front of him. Brian/McCready looked at him, his steel-greys full of menace and slowly the prone figure began to light up and he could see her features. It was Jane and she was looking at him smiling. He struggled to move and cry out but couldn't. Brian/McCready lifted a cricket bat and laughed, the vile sound echoing in his brain. The bat was lifted, ready to strike. He looked at Jane, no fear was showing on her face, it was like she was welcoming the blow to come. The bat began to descend with force, but in slow motion. He wanted to move, to prevent the blow, but he felt that his hands were tied.

The robes had caught up around him and restricted his movement. After an initial panic, he forced himself to calm down and slowly manoeuvred his trapped body free of the tangle. He was shaking.

---o0o---

What was that sound? He opened his eyes, more awake than the previous times. He had only dozed this time. He longed for his duvet and the warmth of Marjory's body in the bed beside him. He listened again and yes, there was definitely a noise, feet were scrunching on the loose gravel outside the door.

A sudden panic took hold as he sensed that what was outside was evil in nature. He crossed himself quickly. 'Lord protect me from whatever is at the door.' His mind screamed the quick prayer.

A loud clunk made him jump as the latch on the big doors was tried. The door rattled, gently at first, then a little more violently. His heart thrashed in his chest and he clung to the pew, paralysed with fear. 'Lord! Lord!' was all the prayer he could summons up.

The footsteps moved away from the door and round the side of the church and the menace seemed to fade with them. His heart slowed and courage returned. Quietly he moved down the centre aisle to the main door and drew his eye to the old-fashioned keyhole. In the dull glow outside he could just make out the bushes a little way off.

The footsteps were returning and with them the feeling of dread, but he held his ground. Suddenly a small figure moved into view. It had its hands pushed deep into its pockets and a hood up over its head. It paused on the path that led up to the door of the church and sniffed before moving towards Andrew.

He pulled back from the keyhole as The Rat tried the door again, this time with some force. At last he gave up and Andrew felt himself relax as the crunchy footsteps faded.

He wanted to light a candle, bring some brightness in to dispel the darkness that was full of fear and foreboding, but he didn't dare light one now. He moved silently over to the pulpit and climbed up to the little fortress there and sat on the ground, his knees pulled up and, resting his head against the wall, felt his heartbeat return to normal.

---oOo---

Geoffrey Deane sat in the front pew, his trousers round his ankles and The Rat was busy…'

He turned off the dream in disgust and pulled himself up out of the sleep. The cold hardness of the pulpit floor seeped through the seat of his trousers. He got slowly to his feet and peered out into the dark body of the church. Nothing stirred. How long would this night last?

---o0o---

'Father Andrew.' He felt someone gently shaking him. 'Father Andrew.' The light burned orange against his closed eyelids. 'Father Andrew!' The shaking and voice were becoming a little anxious.

He dragged his eyes open slowly, the bright light hurting and he blinked quickly, his gaze slowly focusing on the concerned face of Eve. She let out a snort that was half laugh, half relieved shriek.

'Father Andrew.' Can't she say anything else? He pushed himself up slowly. 'Careful!' Eve warned as he nearly fell off the side of the altar. He shook his head and slowly swung his legs over the side, then, with Eve clutching at the air around him in touchless support, he slid down to the floor.

'You didn't spend the night in here did you?'

His mouth tasted sour, a dull pain thudded just behind his eyes and a wave of nausea shuddered through his body. He managed a nod and rubbed his eyes gently.

'But? But I checked before locking up. I didn't see you. I'm so sorry.' She looked about to cry.

'Oh, it's not your fault, Eve, I heard you but was busy with my prayers. I thought I had my keys with me so didn't answer. I thought I could let myself out. I was in the side chapel.' Even The Good Vicar could tell a little white lie if he needed to.

'I'm so sorry,' she repeated, 'if I had known you were here…'

'Please don't worry, Eve. It was my fault, I really thought I had my keys on me but I didn't.' Lord forgive me, Andrew shot a bleary-eyed prayer off quickly. 'I really should have checked.'

'We do need to update these locks,' she laughed. 'You shouldn't be able to lock someone inside the church.'

'Yes, you're right.'

He felt horrible. His body ached and all the problems of the last few days were piling back on top of him, crushing his spirit.

'Marjory called the office a minute ago. She was in quite a state, worried sick about you. Shall I go call her?'

'No! No.' Sharp, then gentle. 'What did she say? What did you tell her?'

'She just said that you had not come home last night. I didn't know where you were. I was as concerned as she was. You must go to her. You two need to talk.'

He nodded. 'I suppose I must. Did she say where she was?'

'Yes, she said that she was going to wait at home for a bit to see if you came. I told her I would call if I heard anything. Are you sure you are alright? Do you want some tea or something? Another hug?' The last offer came shyly.

He looked up at her and smiled kindly. She loved playing mum. A moment of sadness passed over him as he realised that she had never married, never had a chance to be the mother she now seemed to be aching to be.

'Thanks Eve, but maybe just a cup of tea, no wait make that coffee, have we got any?'

'I'll raid the Mother's Union cupboard,' she giggled, refusing to show her disappointment at the declined hug. 'Where do you want it, here or in the office?'

'In the office, thanks Eve. I'll be there in a minute, I'd better tidy up here first.'

She started to say that it wouldn't be necessary, that she would do it, then catching Andrew's look, thought better of it and with a small laugh headed off to find the coffee.

He stared around the church. It held none of the menace it had had during the night, looked inviting even. His gaze settled on the altar and a picture of him curled up in the foetal position, a sacrifice waiting to happen, jumped up in his mind. This was not a pleasant image and he threw it aside, choosing to busy himself sorting out the strewn kneelers, finding solace in action.

At the door of the church, he paused as The Rat's strange and sinister prowling came back to him. Had that been real or a dream? It had felt real in the darkness of the night, but now in the light of day it all seemed too surreal to be true. Despite this he moved quickly across the small path, not wanting to linger where he felt spiritually unsafe.

He sipped his coffee under The Laugh's watchful eye, smiling reassuringly back at her, wishing his drink wasn't so bloody hot. He wanted to gulp it down and be out of there. At last he stood.

'Where are you going to go to?'

'Home,' he replied, 'I need to sort myself out for Peggy's funeral this afternoon.'

'Good heavens, I'd clean forgotten about that what with all the excitement this morning.' She gave a laugh that was too loud. 'Are you sure you're okay to go there? I mean if you want to use my place, you're welcome.'

He hesitated a second, almost tempted to take her up on the offer. 'Thanks Eve, but no. It probably wouldn't look good if anyone saw me coming out of your place, besides, I need to change.'

The Laugh gave a muted shriek as the implications of The Good Vicar's statement hit home. He chuckled gently, enjoying the humour and then felt his mood go as the prospect of facing Marjory hit him.

---o0o---

He slid the key into the front door, the stealth of yesterday's entrance burning hot in his mind. He stood inside the hall for a second listening, almost conjuring up the sounds of arousal that had led to his horrible discovery, but there were none.

There was, however, movement in the kitchen and, after a moment's contemplation he walked quietly towards it. The Pale Blue Dressing Gown stood at the sink, its back to him. As he watched, it lifted the phone to its ear and he shrunk back slightly into the shadows of the passage.

'Brian…yes it is…I don't know, he never came home last night…' the voice sounded cracked and raw, '…what am I going to do? I'm so worried…of course Brian, but this is not easy…Brian, Brian, please don't be like that…of course I do Brian but…Brian, this is not helping, look I need to speak to him before we do anything.' Suddenly there was more strength in the voice. '…Brian, have you said anything to Pat yet?…of course no, not now that would be horrid, but all I'm trying to say is that your time will come…thanks Brian, look I must go. I need to find out what's happened to him…thank you…you too…bye.'

The Pale Blue Dressing Gown stood for a few seconds longer staring out of the window then replaced the phone and turned as Andrew took a step forward.

'Andrew!' Her eyes were bloodshot from what? Lack of sleep? Crying? Both? He wanted to reach out to her and drag her into his chest, hold her tight and tell her everything was going to be okay. He wanted to call her Margie like he had when they had first started dating, but he stood his ground.

She took a step towards him then stopped, realising that he didn't want her close. She lowered her eyes, accepting the punishment.

'Marge.' He managed a formal greeting. He may as well be saying hello to a less well known member of the congregation after church.

She lifted her eyes, grasping at the acknowledgement. 'Andrew, where were you? I was so worried. Andrew I…'

He silenced her with a gesture of his hand. 'Not now Marge.' He turned and moved upstairs, ignoring the pleading cries of his name.

'Andrew! Andrew! Please?'

Let her suffer.

He reached the bathroom and closed and locked the door behind him. The nausea that had grabbed him again bubbled over and he dry-retched into the toilet bowl. He then sat back on the floor breathing heavily. There was a timid tap at the door.

'Andrew are you okay? Andrew?' He decided to ignore her for the moment, yes it was childish, but he was not up to talking just yet.

However, sitting on the bathroom floor sulking was not very dignified. He pulled himself to his feet just as Marjory rattled at the door gently.

'Andrew?'

He removed his shirt and stared at his reflection in the mirror, grabbing the sides of the basin to steady himself.

'Andrew?'

'Not now Marge,' he growled, then let The Good Vicar add in a slightly less rough tone, 'I'm not ready to talk just yet. I need some time and space. We can talk this evening, I promise.'

'This evening,' it was tearful.

'Yes. I promise.' He listened as she moved slowly away from the door, then sighed and returned his attention to the Father Andrew in the mirror. It was not a pretty sight. He watched as his reflection turned the tap on and began to apply lather to the green-grey face. The dark rings under the sunken eyes looked sinister as they stared back at him.

Tonight, what the hell was he going to say tonight?

---o0o---

The Pale Blue Dressing Gown had completed most of the breakfast routine by the time he walked into the kitchen. He was not hungry but didn't have the energy to excuse himself. He did feel better though for having showered. This was going to be awkward. He switched on the radio, leaving the volume soft enough to hear, but not too loud as to be obvious.

The Dressing Gown placed his breakfast down in front of him and he grunted a thanks then started eating without looking up. The Dressing Gown stood for a second, then moved over to the kettle. He dipped a chunk of bacon into the egg yolk and began to eat without tasting. He stared at his plate as he chewed. This is pathetic, he told himself.

'Are the Mother's Union ready for this afternoon?'

'Oh yes, Cynthia has done her usual chocolate sponge and Shelia is doing a batch of her famous choc chips, your favourite.' She grabbed at the lifeline gratefully.

He glanced up at her and smiled gently, he did like Shelia's biscuits. Hopefully he would get to the plate before they were all gone.

'I'll make sure she puts a few aside for you,' reading her husband's thoughts she smiled sweetly back.

'I still need to sort out what I am going to say this afternoon. There has been so much going on that I haven't had a chance.' He was not accusing her, but she lowered her eyes.

'Where did you go last night?' She asked meekly, scared that he would reject her again.

'I ended up sleeping in the church. Eve found me curled up on the altar using a kneeler as a pillow.' The distance from that incident allowed him to chuckle at the image and Marjory joined in.

'I'm sorry Andrew,' she said as the laughter faded, 'You could...'

'Not now,' he interrupted gently. 'Let's just...' in the murmur of the radio noise he caught the name McCready and he motioned for Marjory to be quiet, cocking his head toward the BBC voice.

'...*McCready who claimed to have lost his sight after a blinding light flashed in his prison cell has said that the miracle occurred soon after a visiting priest prayed with him for the restoration of his sight. Father Gregory Simms, the Vicar of Dartmoor Prison confirmed that Mr McCready had had a visit from an outside priest, but would not divulge any further details. A prison spokesperson said that they remained sceptical about Mr McCready's claims. Mr McCready is busy serving a life sentence for...* '

'I was there, that was me that visited him.' He stared across at Marjory and she looked back at him a little confused.

'I must call Father Gregory, will you excuse me.' The whole episode with Brian and Marjory was momentarily forgotten as he moved quickly through to his study where he fumbled around for the number then grabbed the phone and dialled.

---o0o---

Pat deserves better he thought as he straightened the papers he had just printed. At least I won't have to wing it; that would be worse. He looked at his watch. It was a quarter to one. Should he have lunch before he went? He didn't feel hungry, the joy he had experienced earlier while talking to Father Gregory had not worn off. God had answered a prayer!

It didn't matter that the recipient of His grace didn't deserve it, it wasn't McCready's miracle, this one belonged to him. He was suddenly convinced in his mind that the blindness had been real and that he, Father 'Ananias' Compton, had been called to cure it. This was two fingers reverently stuck up at Bishop Ian.

He stapled the pages together, ready to deliver in an hour or so. Then, as he placed his address on the desk next to the Book of Common Prayer, he noticed the little black machine and clicked his tongue; he had not managed to speak to Pat about that. He picked it up and examined it, noting the record, stop and play functions. Surely she would understand even if Brian didn't. Anyway Brian owed him one, he had only stolen a kiss from Brian's wife but Brian, the greedy heathen bastard had stolen his whole wife. He felt the hollow emptiness eat at his stomach as the thoughts returned and he pictured his wife and her lover, caught like fumbling teenagers pawing away at their curiosity.

It shocked him as he recalled the passionate embrace, that Marjory, his Margie, was still interested in sex. He could not remember when last they had been passionately intimate, certainly a good while before they had last been dispassionately intimate and that was long enough ago to be a distant memory in itself.

If he could just re-kindle that passion…

He sighed as the words *you too* came back to him. They could only have been in response to *I love you.* Had he really lost her love as well as her passion? Could he ever win them back? Did he want to win them back?

He sighed again and slipped the little back machine into his pocket. It would be too late for lunch now. He hurriedly gathered together all he needed for the funeral.

Marge had already left to sort out the Mother's Union so he moved quickly to the front door and opened it. A bright light flashed in his face and blinded him.

---oOo---

He moved slowly up the stairs to the pulpit and surveyed the small congregation from his tower. He didn't like what he saw. The coffin, dark brown and shiny stood at the front of the church, the flowers on it neat and unobtrusive, that was okay. As was Pat in the front row, stony faced in her black, and if it were a happier occasion he would have said striking, dress. A number of old folk, mostly women, were dotted around the church; old friends perhaps, or just members of the Mother's Union giving moral support while they waited to serve tea afterwards. They were okay too, expected even.

But it was the others he didn't like. The Heathen sat next to Pat, clasping her hand in his adulterous one in a gesture of comfort. His business suit, neat and tidy, made him look like one of the undertakers, downcast eyes refusing to meet his.

'The guilty bastard,' Andrew thought.

Marjory sat a few rows back on the other side of the church, a respectable distance from her lover. Her eyes did not leave her husband, perhaps fearing that the slightest glance in The Heathen's direction would be misconstrued.

Eve sat in the same pew, but at the other end, a sad, silly smile on her face.

At the back a small hooded figure lurked, almost hidden behind the pews. What was The Rat doing here? The sense of foreboding he had had the previous night tickled in his stomach.

Just in front of The Rat was Father Gregory. He would have had no issue with his fellow priest being there had it not been for the two rather scruffy looking characters who sat in the pew opposite. The one had taken the photo as he had stepped out the door while the other had immediately bombarded him with questions.

'Tom Watson from *The Express*, is it true that you were the priest who cured McCready's blindness? How do you know him? Do you think it's right to help a paedo? Was he really blind? Did you heal him?'

How the hell had they found out it was him? He had stumbled down the street, blinking away the blindness the flash had created, another miracle, while blurting out 'No comment,' to his tormentors. He wished he could have said more, denied it, but all that he could summons up in those few seconds was *no comment*, in other words *guilty as charged*.

He focussed on Pat. This was her mother's funeral after all. She deserved the best. Then as he began talking he started to wonder if Marge suspected him of any involvement with her lover's wife, so moved his gaze to Marge. She sat upright in the pew staring straight ahead now, his words washing right over her. He lost his confidence, stumbled over a sentence and forced himself to look round the church generally, flitting his attention from one person to the next. As his confidence returned he felt the little black machine weighing heavily in his pocket and for a fleeting second imagined that he could see McCready sitting in the church, but this faded as quickly as it had arrived.

The Good Vicar had settled down and was delivering a pretty good talk, despite the lack of preparation. He was just relaxing into this when two men came quietly into the back of the church. One carried a large camera and he recognised the other as a BBC news reporter. They slipped into a pew and looked around. Their gaze settled on Father Gregory and the reporter whispered something to his cameraman who nodded. Andrew felt a cold fever grip him and he held tightly to the lectern to keep from crumbling.

---o0o---

'Gentlemen, please. Have a little respect. This is a funeral it has nothing to do with why you are here. Please let the family have some privacy.' Father Gregory was trying to shepherd the growing group of reporters away from the church hall. 'Please, please let this family grieve in peace.'

'Why were you at the funeral Father Gregory?'

'Was Father Andrew the one who healed McCready's blindness?'

'Is there a relationship between the deceased and McCready?'

'Who is the deceased?'

Andrew listened in terror to the questions that he knew that he was going to be hounded with shortly.

'Gentlemen, please, if you will just let this funeral finish and I will arrange for a proper press conference in the church hall in an hour and a half, but please leave the family alone, this is very unfair on them. Please gentlemen, I don't want to see any of you near the church for the next hour and a half otherwise we will not answer any questions at all, is that clear?'

The noise slowly dissipated and Father Gregory came back into the church.

'I'm so sorry Andrew, one of the warders must have spilt the beans, got your name and details from the visitors' register. It was the only thing I could do to get them to go away, I hope you don't mind me arranging the press conference. If only I hadn't come down, this is going to make things a lot trickier. We must get our stories straight so that we sing from the same hymn sheet.'

Andrew nodded his tired agreement.

'Let's meet in an hour's time,' Father Gregory continued. 'Hopefully the funeral party will have moved off by then. You must go and tend to your flock. I'll stand guard so to speak. It would be nice if one of those vultures did show their face, then I could call off the press conference, but I suspect they'll obey me, they're hungry for a story.'

Andrew nodded again. He felt desperately tired now and stood alone in the church for a moment rubbing his eyes. At length he moved slowly over towards the church hall. The tea was in full swing with a respectable murmur bubbling round the hall. He looked round quickly, but could not see The Rat, thank goodness. He was not sure though if that was entirely a good thing. If he was here, he could keep an eye on him. This was preferable to having him wondering around with all those journalists on the loose, he could blurt out anything.

He saw Pat talking to one of the older women whom, he remembered, had been a good friend of Peggy's in happier times. The Heathen was standing next to them looking like a spare part.

'Pat, Audrey.' He joined the group. 'Pat, I'm so sorry about all those people. We have managed to get rid of them for the moment, they won't bother you again. I'm terribly sorry about all this, it was really awful of them to descend on your mother's funeral like that. Very unprofessional.'

Audrey sniffed and headed off while, out of the corner of his eye, Andrew watched The Heathen bristle. One word, go on, one word and I'll let your wife in on our little secret, funeral or not.

The Heathen seemed to read his thoughts and glanced down at his shoes for a moment before shuffling off. He watched him go, checking that he wasn't going to talk to Marge, and smiled inwardly as he saw Eve intercept him, her consoling laugh could just be heard over Pat's reply. Good old Eve, he owed her one.

'Andrew what is going on? Did you really heal McCready? What did you say about him wanting to record the funeral?'

'I've said nothing yet. I'm going to talk to Father Gregory, the priest you saw at the funeral. He is the vicar at Dartmoor. We're going to plan what to say.'

'But Andrew, what are you going to tell them about him wanting the service recorded, I don't want mum's funeral turned into a media circus.'

'I don't know yet, but for the moment, make sure that you and Brian say nothing. I think it will be better for everyone concerned that if the question does come up we lie.'

---oOo---

'Yes, I did pray with Mr McCready yesterday for his sight to be restored.'

'Do you believe his claims?'

'The optician that examined him could find nothing wrong, so I am still sceptical about his claims.'

'So you don't believe him?'

'That is not what I said.'

'Why did you pray for him if you didn't believe him?'

'It is for God to judge this, not me. If he was lying about his blindness, then he will have to answer to God for that.'

'Why was Father Gregory at the funeral service this afternoon, is there a connection between the deceased and Mr McCready?'

'Father Gregory came here to discuss the restoration of Mr Mc-Cready's sight. When he arrived, he realised that I had the funeral to perform and so he sat in on it while he waited to speak to me. There is no connection between Mr McCready and the person whose funeral it was today.' Lord forgive me.

'I have heard that McCready requested that this funeral service be recorded so that he could listen to it, is that true?'

That damn Rat! Andrew had had a nasty feeling that this would come up and was prepared for it.

'Am I right in saying that your source on that is an eleven year old boy?'

The man who had asked the question blanched as his fellow journalists giggled childishly at him.

'I am not at liberty to disclose my sources,' he muttered.

Gotcha you bastard! 'I'm afraid we have a young lad wondering round town who has a vivid imagination, he suggested to me once that I record the funeral service *for other people to hear* as he put it. He seems to delight in making wild suggestions. I suppose he also told you that I was having an affair with the daughter of the woman whose funeral it was?'

The man's face was crimson with rage and embarrassment, it admitted all that Andrew had accused him of and the questions dried up soon afterwards.

'You handled that well,' Father Gregory came up to him after ushering the last of the mob out of the hall. That bit about the young lad, stroke of genius it was.'

And about the only bit that was true, Andrew smiled wryly to himself. He was completely drained and feeling sullied by what had just transpired.

'I don't like this, I keep feeling that we will get caught out somehow. The church doesn't exactly have a high standing amongst the heathen out there. If we're caught out it just gives our enemies more ammunition,' he said.

'Don't worry, I'm sure this will all blow over soon.' Father Gregory offered a comforting smile.

Andrew wasn't comforted, but nodded a thanks.

'We must still discuss this McCready issue, but I need to get back to the prison. I have a meeting with the Governor. Call me tomorrow.'

Andrew watched his colleague leave the hall and then sat down heavily, burying his face in his hands. He had a nasty feeling about all this.

'Got out of that one.'

He hated that little voice. He waited for the sniff and only after it came did he look up. The Rat had his face covered by the hood for which Andrew was grateful, he could not handle another episode of the temptation he had had before, not now.

'You wos lucky. Maybe next time you won't be so lucky.' The hooded figure scurried out of the hall leaving Andrew staring after it.

---oOo---

'Andrew, thanks for coming, please come through.'

He wondered if he should sit in Brian's chair as usual but wasn't sure if The Heathen was around.

'Please sit,' Pat indicated his usual chair from which he deduced the answer to his thoughts. Where was Brian then? *'e's shaggin' your wife.*

'Brian not around?' Hell I hope she doesn't take that as a come on.

'No, he went off to settle up with the funeral people, then he said he had another important meeting that he couldn't miss. I'm so sorry about his outburst yesterday. He was shocked by this whole McCready thing. We both were. I tried to stop him rushing off to your place, but you know what he's like. He's not a bad person really, just a bit hot headed at times.'

Hot headed? Hot blooded more like.

Andrew nodded. The Heathen had obviously not said anything to his wife about being caught canoodling in the Vicar's house, and he wondered if it was his place to say something now.

'He certainly was hot under the collar yesterday.' Andrew nearly grinned at his oblique reference to the scene he had witnessed in the lounge, but swallowed the smile quickly. 'Good thing Marge was there, Brian calmed down quick enough when she came out to see what all the fuss was about.'

Pat smiled sweetly, she knew nothing.

'Oh, I haven't offered you tea. Would you like some?'

'Yes please.' He actually did feel like a cup for once. And custard creams, not those rich tea, they're a bit dry, he hoped.

'Why don't you come through to the bedroom, we can talk while we make love.'

The Good Vicar quickly interjected into Andrew's mind 'kitchen not bedroom, make tea not love' and he sadly acquiesced. Pat was looking quite striking in the black dress now that the funeral was over.

The kitchen was airy and bright, which lightened his mood and, so it seemed, Pat's as well. She moved fluidly around the room, putting the kettle on, getting the milk, sugar and teabags.

'Can you grab some biscuits, they're in the top cupboard there,' she pointed.

Great, definitely the custard creams then.

He opened the cupboard and cursed silently, Brian The Bastard must have eaten them all, rich tea then I guess.

'Why don't we sit here,' he suggested, 'it's brighter than the lounge.' It was a bit of a gamble, he hoped she would not feel restricted by convention, and the kitchen was more relaxing.

'Why not,' she smiled and gestured for him to sit at the little table.

The cups remained formal despite the dress down meeting place.

'Andrew, the other thing I wanted to talk about…' she took a quick sip of tea, '…was about this McCready fellow.'

He tensed up. Was she going to question him about recording the service? Maybe The Rat had blabbed again.

'Yes?' He drew out the word.

'Well...oh do help yourself to a biscuit, don't you just love rich teas?'

He lied.

'Anyway, there is something I think you should know about him.'

Andrew's hand hovered over the biscuits while the knot tightened in his stomach. What was coming now?

'I don't quite know how to describe it, but when he was arrested mum acted very strangely.' She was unaware of Andrew's discomfort. 'You know she was still *compos mentis* back then, but when they caught him it was as if she felt sorry for the man. Little things she would say, nothing obvious. If you remember, the whole nation was baying for his blood, but mum...it was like she forgave him before he was even found guilty. I have been thinking about that ever since you first mentioned him to us. Maybe I was a little harsh in not allowing you to record the service. I think Brian got to me on that one.' She stopped to take a bite of her boring biscuit, brushing the crumbs onto the floor without thinking. 'I mean what harm could it have done. I'm sorry I said no to you on the phone.'

She looked across at him now, the little black machine burning clear in his mind. 'That's okay, there's nothing we can do about it now.' Lord forgive me.

'I can't help feeling that mum would actually have wanted it. I think I've let her down. I'm going to miss her so much, even if there wasn't much of her in the last days...' A tear rolled down her cheek, the first one he had seen since Peggy's passing.
 He wanted to reach out and gently brush it away, his hand lingering on her soft skin. He felt the pull of her wanting it too. His arm twitched as he prepared to launch his comfort missile when he heard the front door close.

'Pat?' The Heathen's voice pierced the moment.

'In the kitchen dear.' The back of her hand did the job that he had so wanted to do.

Brian strode into the kitchen and stopped, his expression going from disinterested to shock in point one of a second. Andrew reacted quickly, standing up and putting himself between Pat and Brian. He gave Brian the slightest shake of the head before moving aside, watching the relief drain into his adversary's face while wondering why he hadn't let the bastard suffer.

'I think her mum's death is finally hitting home,' he said softly and with some feeling. 'I'd better go, I think she needs some loving and you're best suited for that.' He enjoyed the sharp look he got, then turned to Pat to say goodbye.

'Thanks for the tea. If you need anything else, just shout...' he had to swallow hard as the look he got from her seemed to scream *don't leave me with him, he is an adulterer, he cannot give me the comfort I know you can.*

'Thanks Andrew,' her voice was ragged. The Good Vicar could be a complete bastard when he had to, he thought as he let himself out the front door.

---oOo---

How could he win her back if he could not get rid of the image of her offering her body up to Brian's searching lips? How could he rid himself of the anger and betrayal he felt if that scene kept coming back every time he looked at her? How could he forgive her and try to win her back when he longed to be with Pat?

Dinner had been eaten in silence, although she had fussed over him a bit and had even cooked his favourite meal – shepherd's pie, the way only she could cook it. He had grinned inwardly at the connection between dinner and his sermon, but could not decide if this was just an offering to try and lessen her guilt, or if there was any attempt on Margie's behalf to win him back.

He had had seconds, not out of any sense of accepting the possible apology, but because it tasted so good. He had tried not to show too much response to Marge's sweet smile when he had asked for more, he didn't want to give the wrong impression.

Now they sat in the lounge, him in his usual chair that did not feel as comfortable as The Heathen's, and Marjory on the adultery sofa.

She was in her usual pose, hands resting demurely on her lap, knees pressed together. He wondered where to begin. The Good Vicar would probably know, but this was one time when it was not appropriate for him to be there, this was between Andrew and Margie. The Good Vicar would have a conflict of interests if he tried to play marriage councillor.

He took a breath to speak, but Marjory beat him to it, patting her greying hair into place as she began. 'Andrew, I'm so sorry you had to find out like you did. I never meant for you to get hurt, but things just developed between me and Brian. I didn't set out to have an affair.'

'Margie,' he was on the back foot already.

She smiled sadly at the use of her courting day's name, but went on, 'I couldn't help myself. I was feeling so lonely at home. Sometimes I felt as if you were looking right through me. You are always so caught up in the problems of others, giving so much of yourself to your congregation that by the time you got home, there was nothing left for me. I kept telling myself that it was okay, that you were doing God's work and I must support you in it. But when Brian started showing an interest in me, well, it was if I was young again. I felt wanted and special. Andrew, I don't think I can go on playing second fiddle to your work.'

He stared at her, anger growing at being made to feel that he was the one to blame here.

'Has Brian told Pat?' The question was out before he had even thought about it.

'Andrew!' Her composure left her. 'There you go again, thinking of others, can't you just for once think about us?'

What us! He wanted to scream at her. You're so prudish and cold to me and then go running off to screw The Heathen, there is no 'us', your passion is elsewhere now.

'I can't help it Margie, it's who I am. But we can work at it, please, let's at least try and work something out.' He was grovelling, why should he be? She should be the one begging for forgiveness, not him.

She patted her hair again, this time nervously.

'I'm going to stay with Jane for a bit, I think it will be better if we were apart for a while.'

'Jane?'

'Your daughter remember, or have you forgotten her as well?'

'Marge!'

'I'm sorry that wasn't fair.' She looked away from him now and he thought he caught the hint of a tear in her eye and he softened a bit.

'I've made up the bed in the spare room. I'll sleep there tonight. Jane's coming to pick me up tomorrow morning.'

Bitch!

---oOo---

Why had he insisted on sleeping in the spare room? She was the transgressor here, she should have been left to suffer. The bed was too small and the mattress too uncomfortable, no wonder Jane never came to stay.

He wanted to go and climb into bed with her and be wanted there, but he could not bring himself to look past her infidelity. He hated himself for these confused feelings. How can you love and detest someone in the same feeling?

He turned over, listening to the bed creak under his shifting weight, but his thoughts were the same on his left side as they were on his right. He rolled onto his back and stared at the ceiling, that dark cloud that loomed over him, heavy with despair. He searched for a silver lining but found none. This was no good.

He closed his eyes and regulated his breathing into a relaxing and slow rhythmic beat, trying to black out all thoughts. He felt the sleep slowly fold in around him and fell into its soft embrace.

She was lying back on the sofa, her striking black dress was pulled off the shoulders. The sensible bra was pulled to one side, revealing Eve's large breasts. A dark figure hovered over her, its hungry mouth seeking the offered nipple.

A small figure in a pale blue dressing gown stood nearby, egging then on. It sniffed and shoved its hands deep into the pockets of the gown.

He turned and looked at Pat. She sat naked beside him, her eyes transfixed on the couple on the sofa. From what he could tell, she was aroused by what she was seeing. He pulled her to him, frantically searching for her lips, desperate for the passion they would bring.

It melted and he felt the hardness of his erection fighting with his pyjama trousers. His breathing was ragged. Slowly he calmed his body down before he opened his eyes. He swung his legs out of bed and fumbled for his dressing gown.

In the kitchen he flicked the light on and blinked away the pain its brightness brought. He could ill afford another sleepless night, but this was preferable to those dreams. Tea. That was the only option now. Coffee would definitely keep him awake. Did they have any hot chocolate? He opened the cupboard. There was an unopened packet of custard creams next to the tin he was looking for. His hand hovered momentarily over it, then in a decision-making grab, took up the tin and quickly closed the door.

While the kettle began its uphill battle, he sat trying hard to think how he could clear his mind of all that was happening so that he could just sleep in peace. Everything was bouncing in his mind, not giving him any space for himself.

The kettle snapped off and the bubbling faded to a wisp of steam. With an effort he got up and poured his drink. The gurgling in the cup stopped and was replaced by a low whimper.

He started. The whimper came again, quiet, pathetic and pleading. It was coming from outside the back door. Cautiously he opened the door and stared in shock at Alex who stood on the step shivering. He was completely naked.

---oOo---

'He was here, really Marge, he was.'

Marjory looked at her husband with a mixture of concern and annoyance. She pulled her pale blue dressing gown tighter round her and let her look ask the question.

'I don't know where he's gone, but he was on the doorstep, stark naked and shivering. He was there. I brought him inside, put him in that chair and ran to get a blanket to put round him. He was still shivering so I gave him some tea. Look, there's his cup.' He pointed to the empty tea cup on the table next to his hot chocolate one.

'Did he say anything? Did he tell you why he was running around naked?'

'No, he just sat there shivering. I kept asking him where his clothes were, but he wouldn't answer.'

He just looked at me with those beautiful eyes of his, and kept throwing the blanket aside so that I could see his soft white skin. I wanted so badly to touch him, but I am not a paedophile. I know I am not. The Good Vicar kept telling me that and I kept covering the boy up again, but he wanted me to see him, he wanted me to be seduced by his youthful beauty.

He could not tell Marjory all this so he said, 'That is when I came to call you. I thought he might talk to you.'

Marjory surveyed the scene, still unsure of what had really happened in the kitchen.

'The blanket has gone.' Andrew added sheepishly, trying now to convince himself that it had really happened. Given his dreams lately, it was just possible that he drank the tea and the hot chocolate himself and his battered mind had filled in all the sordid details. He sat down heavily and stared at the cups. A craving for custard creams rose suddenly, but he did not have the energy to move. In the back of his mind he realised that his actions were admitting to Marge that he had dreamt it all. But it had felt so real.

What was that look she was giving him?

'Maybe you should go to bed. You can talk to his parents tomorrow, see if they know anything. For now though, I must get some sleep. Jane is coming early.'

So that was it, she thought it was a hoax her had made up to guilt her into staying. Pretend you're losing it so she feels she can't desert you right now. The look said *you're pathetic*. He watched the pale blue dressing gown disappear out the room and sighed. Then on a whim he ran his tongue round his mouth. Hot Chocolate. That proved nothing, he could still have drunk the tea followed by the hot chocolate.

The custard creams called out for him again and he got the packet from the cupboard, it was one of those large double packs.

He sat down again and helped himself to a biscuit. The strange attraction to the naked young boy suddenly started drifting back into his mind and he felt a stirring in his groin. He panicked and ran from the kitchen to his study where his screaming mental mantra of *I am not a paedophile* slowly calmed down to a whisper, then a wisp of a whisper and was gone, leaving him badly shaken.

---oOo---

'Dad, you look like shit.'

Thanks and so do you. 'Hello Jane come in.'

He hated the nose ring, and why did she need so many earrings all the way up the one side of her left ear, why not the right one also, give your head a bit of balance.

'How's things?' A spider had tattooed its web up the back of her neck, almost climbing into her dirty unbrushed hair. And Marge is going to stay with this?

'Okay.'

'How's Harry?'

'Fine.'

Has he got a job yet? Andrew opted instead to ask the second question that came to mind, 'And Arkayic?'

'She's in the car if you want to go and see her.'

'I think I will.'

He had managed not to laugh at the reply he got when he had asked why they had chosen that strange name for his granddaughter, although 'strange' was omitted from the question.

'Well we didn't want an old-fashioned name,' Harry the layabout had said.

'Mum's upstairs,' he said as he moved to the front door, silently cursing his daughter for the look she gave him, like he was the guilty one chasing her mum out of the house.

He was half tempted to grab a glass of water from the kitchen and give Arkayic a quick baptism while Jane wasn't there, but that would not be right. Maybe, with a bit of luck, Arkayic would grow up to accept the faith that her mother had so firmly rejected.

Arkayic gurgled happily when he lifted her from the car seat. At least they hadn't given her dreadlocks or a tattoo yet. She still looked like a normal kid.

'Hello Arkayic. Hello Arkayic. Who is it? It's grandpa. Say grandpa.' The innocence and happiness of the little child was a strong antidote for his current predicament. He bounced her gently and she clapped her tiny hands, delighted with the attention.

'And who is this Father Andrew?'

'Ah Audrey, good morning. This beautiful little one is my granddaughter Arkayic. Say hello to Auntie Audrey, Arkayic.' He stooped to allow the old woman a better look.

'Hello Arkayic.' She tickled the little tummy 'Blblblb.' Andrew braced himself, preparing to catch the false teeth should they fly out while she did her baby talk routine.

'Is this Jane's little one?'

Andrew nodded relieved that normal talk had been resumed. Who else's could it be? He only had two kids to produce grandchildren, Jane and Sean, and Sean was gay.

'How is little Jane. We don't see her anymore?'

And I don't particularly want you seeing her now either. I couldn't stand your self-righteous judging of me by how my kids have turned out thank you very much, so bog off will you before she comes out.

'She's fine, she's in with Marjory at the minute.'

Audrey's looked confirmed that she had heard about the recent 'little incident' in the lounge, probably from Eve the blabbermouth. At least she seemed to be siding with him on this one. Maybe, the sight of Jane and Marge together would transfer the blame of not bringing the kids up properly onto his better half.

'They should be out soon if you want to say hello.' Arkayic hic-coughed and he burped her.

'I'd love to, but I really must get going.'

'She couldn't face your grandmother with the knowledge she has now could she.' He said as he watched the old lady disappear down the road. Arkayic thought this was hilarious.

He could almost hear the tearing sound as he placed her back in the car seat. Marge was already in the passenger seat, not having even looked at him as she had walked out. Jane slammed the boot on the suitcase.

'Make sure she's properly strapped in,' she called and climbed in behind the wheel. He watched as the car sped off down the road dragging his guts behind it. There had not even been a good bye from either woman.

A cheerful whistling behind him made him turn around. The Rat was rapidly approaching, hood up and hands thrust deep into his pockets.

'Mornin' vikka, sleep well last night?'

---oOo---

He would phone Brian and demand that he tell Pat if he hadn't already done so. It was the least The Heathen could do. He would threaten to tell her himself, give him an ultimatum. He could already picture himself in that comfortable chair, explaining things to her and being there to comfort her as the shock took hold.

He looked down at the empty packet that once contained a double row of custard creams. Did he really devour the whole lot last night as he sat in his study fighting off sleep and thoughts? The crumbs under his chair convinced him of that, and the fact that he was not hungry despite Marjory not having bothered to make him breakfast before she ran away.

Her words from last night came back to his tired mind now. *You can talk to his parents tomorrow.* Who were The Rat's parents? What sort of parents let their child wonder about the neighbour-hood so freely late at night? He forced himself to think of the strange behaviour of The Rat outside the church, too scared to bring himself to bring up the image of the naked child in the kitchen. Who were his parents? It was not a large town, but he had no idea who The Rat belonged to. He would have to ask Eve.

He leaned forward and picked up the phone.

'Hello Pat, is Brian there?'

'Oh Andrew, you poor thing. He told me everything last night. How are you doing?' Were the tears in her voice for him or ones of self pity?

'I'm holding up okay,' Lord forgive me, 'How you doing?'

'Not so well. I...I...' The tears took over.

'Do you want me to come over?' Please say yes.

'Gnff.'

'Pat. Come on Pat, you need to be strong.'

A loud sniff echoed down the phone. 'I'm sorry Andrew, I'm just so upset at the moment. Yes, please come round if you can.'

'Give me half an hour,' he said remembering that he apparently looked like shit.

As he looked in the bathroom mirror he thought that Jane had been rather kind in her analysis of his appearance.

---o0o---

Apart from it being in Pat's house and the fact that it was really comfy, the other thing Andrew liked about The Heathen's chair was that it was unsullied by any thoughts of The Rat.

'He's gone to work. I don't know what to do. I can't stand the thought of seeing him tonight, but I have nowhere to go.' This brought on a fresh bout of tears as she was reminded that her parents were now both dead.

You could move in with me.

'You should stay here, send him packing. Tell him to go stay with his brother for a bit. You've got your friends here, we'll look after you.' That was more subtle.

She smiled sweetly at him. 'Who's looking after you?' she asked, wiping a tear off her cheek.

'I have a funny feeling that I'm going to be mothered to death by a few of the old folk in the congregation.'

She spluttered a laugh through the tears. 'I can guess at who those might be.' It was good to see her smile again.

He laughed gently with her and then the laughter gurgled away and a serious look took hold of her features.

'Kiss me Andrew,' she said.

---oOo---

Brilliant timing Eve, The Good Vicar congratulated while Andrew cursed. He had been this close to her lips, this close to the passion he desperately craved. But no, bloody Eve had to come ringing on the bell to check that everything was alright.

She giggled as she sat between them, tea in one hand and a custard cream in the other.

'No. Thanks,' Andrew felt repulsed by the biscuits.

'Sorry, that's all I've got. We finished the rich tea yesterday.' What he wouldn't give for a rich tea now.

'I remember when my mother died,' The Laugh was giggling again, 'I was twenty-five at the time, or was I twenty-six? I don't remember exactly now. Twenty or twenty-six. Anyway…' Andrew tiptoed away from the conversation, leaving The Good Vicar to nod politely where required. Once she got going there was no stopping her.

He began to think about the Bridges. How could he get hold of them? And even more of a problem would be getting them to agree to see him, especially if the press splashed his face all over the place, he would be the last person they would want to see. Okay, maybe the second last person.

Perhaps Father Gregory could help. He seemed a decent fellow, and quite organised. Maybe he could help set up a meeting. But that was the easy part. How could he even begin to ask this bereaved couple to consider forgiving McCready?

He was extremely curious to know what the connection was between Peggy and the paedo. He glanced up at Pat. 'I think my sister took it a lot harder than I did, but of course she was a lot younger than me. What would she have been...' He drifted back out.

Could he and Marge patch things up? It would be best for his career if they did, but right now he felt he could give all that up for the completion of the interrupted kiss. He felt the stolen kiss he had had with Pat on his lips again, it tasted so good. He watched as Pat began to strip for him, slowly undressing herself. This was good.

'Andrew. Andrew.' Pat's voice broke the spell and he opened his eyes, looked around and tried to update his brain on what was happening.

'I'm sorry, I must have drifted off. I didn't sleep much last night.' The tiredness nausea was swirling in his mind as two pairs of eyes looked sympathetically on.

'You poor thing,' The Laugh chuckled. He glanced momentarily at her chest, then away quickly as he remembered that Pat was there.

'I...I think I'd better go and see if I can get some rest. I'm sorry Pat.' He hauled himself up out of the chair, fighting against his spinning head. He felt exhausted and realised with horror that his legs were melting underneath him. He sank slowly to the floor.

---oOo---

Black. Grey. Dark blue. Light Blue. Orange. Brightness. He opened his eyes slowly. The room smelt slightly of Pat and he clawed through the fog in his brain to remember what had happened. Slowly the fog lifted. He gazed down the length of his body, expecting to find something missing, but it was all there, except his shoes. The bed was soft and welcoming. How had they managed to get him here?

He felt relaxed, his troubles, although still sloshing around in his mind, did not feel as menacing. He slowly moved his feet off the side of the bed and pushed himself up. He waited for a moment while the whirlwind that erupted in his head calmed to a slight breeze, then steadied himself, ready to push to stand when the door opened.

'Oh, Father Andrew! You're okay! You gave us a huge fright.' She was next to him in a second and his head was buried in the softness of her chest before he could answer or move. 'We were so worried,' the echoing voice said.

He moved his head slightly to get some air and saw Pat standing at the door, a look of relief and amusement on her face. Slowly he extracted himself from his padded cell.

'How are you feeling Andrew?' Pat's voice was calm and soothing.

'I'm okay, I think. What happened?'

Eve launched into a detailed account of his collapse to which he half listened, nodding when he thought it was appropriate. He kept an eye on Pat, looking for a signal, something to say that the interrupted kiss was still on the agenda, but nothing came.

'We're waiting for Dr Phillips to come,' he caught a sentence out of The Laugh's barrage.

'No, I'm fine really,' he interrupted, 'I don't need to see the doc. Just exhaustion, I haven't been sleeping well.'

'But you must see Dr Phillips. You've been out like a light for four hours.'

'I'm fine now, really. I just haven't slept properly for two nights now and it all rather caught up with me. Pat?' He wanted her on his side. 'Please let Dr Phillips know that his services are no longer required.'

Pat paused for a moment, then nodded.

'Okay.' She slipped quietly out of the room and Andrew looked at Eve and smiled. She laughed back, unsure of herself.

'Where are my shoes?' Apparently this was an hilarious question but it did produce his footwear and he busied himself putting them on, taking his time doing the laces. He felt The Laugh's questioning eyes on him the whole time.

'Father Andrew?' she giggled as he re-tied his left shoe for the second time. He could hear Pat's muffled voice on the telephone in the next room.

'Hmm?'

'Father Andrew, who is Alex? You kept mumbling his name.'

---oOo---

The house was quiet. Too quiet. Why had he insisted on coming back here? Well to get away from The Laugh for one, and the imminent arrival of The Heathen if he really needed another reason. He looked at his watch. It was 4:30. What could he do? The sermon was done, it was too early for there to be anything decent on telly. He wasn't hungry yet, but he knew he must do something to occupy his mind.

He could phone Father Gregory, but that would drag him back into all the stress that had brought about his collapse. A picture of Sean bubbled up in his mind. When last had he spoken to his son? He recalled the harsh words when they had last parted. He shouldn't have been surprised when Sean came out, he had already half suspected it, but the timing had been bad and he had not handled it well. Since then, there had only been a few stilted calls aimed at reconciliation, but always falling wide of the mark.

The trial (was it a trial?) separation with Marge at least gave him a reason to call and just maybe it could muster up some sympathy from his son to allow them to talk a little.

The phone rang before he had settled on making the call.

'Hello?'

'What the hell's going on then?' The Bishop's voice was angry. 'Have you really been running around healing blind paedophiles?'

How did he find out? 'Um...'

'It's all over the front pages. *McCready blindness cured by village priest.* I like the word village, a nice touch. *Father Andrew restores McCready's sight,* and then my personal favourite *Church Aids Paedo.* The pictures of you are enough to frighten people away let alone the headlines. I wonder if you could take a few moments out of your busy healing schedule to explain to your superiors exactly what is going on?'

'All I did was what God asked me to do.' The statement was air conditioned.

'Are you referring to that silly little dream you had?'

'God told me to go and see him and I did. I prayed for him and that was it.'

'I thought we had discussed all this when you called last time. I don't recall telling you to run off and heal people.'

Andrew was getting angry, but he let The Good Vicar keep control of his words. 'All I did was pray for him, God was the one who healed him.'

'Don't give me that, can't you see what's happening here? Andrew, that monster has been playing you for the fool you are. He was never blind, this is all an elaborate hoax thought up by a twisted mind for some or other twisted purpose. McCready does not need more attention, he's had enough already. Hopefully all this nonsense will blow over quickly. It's not fair on the victims' families. In the meantime, I don't want to hear of you having anything to do with that man. Is that clear?'

'But...'

'No Andrew, nothing to do with him, do I make myself clear?'

'Yes.' It was no use arguing.

'Good. Look, you've got to be careful with those sort of things Andrew, they can blow up in your face without warning.'

Don't patronise me you bastard.

'Yes Ian, I'm sorry Ian.' God he hated that soppy little subservient idiot who sat in his study. He replaced the phone in its cradle and stared at it for a long time. Eventually he moved with some determination to pick it up again.

---o0o---

The pub was rather dingy and he stood for a moment in the doorway letting his eyes adjust. Sean was standing at the far end of the bar, a half-drunk pint in front of him. He looked up as Andrew made his way over.

'Dad.' Neutral.

'Hi son, thanks for coming out to see me.'

Sean nodded, still non-committal. I don't blame him really, Andrew thought.

'Want another?' Andrew indicated to Sean's glass.

'Thanks.'

Andrew leaned forward on the bar to get the barman's attention, but he was busy serving another customer.

'How's Gary?'

'Fine.'

God this was hard work. 'He still working at that Insurance place?'

'Yes.'

The barman was free now, thank goodness.

'Pint of lager and what do you want, another half, or a pint?'

'Pint please.' Hooray a two word sentence.

'Make that two pints please.'

They stood in silence watching the man draw their beers. Sean made some inroads into his half-pint. The barman came back with the drinks, put them down and took the money Andrew offered him. He paused for a moment, staring at Andrew.

'You not that priest who healed that paedo are you?'

'What? You mean that McCready fellow? No, I'm not a priest, I'm a plumber, funny though, my missus said just this morning that I looked like that paedo.' Lord forgive me.

'Funny that.' The barman moved off and returned with the change, the suspicious look still on his face. They watched him as he moved down to the other end of the bar and started talking to some patrons who looked like regulars. A few glances were shot their way.

'Come let's find somewhere to sit, somewhere a little more private.'

They found a cubicle in a darkened corner and shuffled into it.

'What was all that plumber stuff about dad? It was you, wasn't it?' Sean was suddenly more alive now, but about the wrong stuff. 'Did you really heal him?'

Andrew shrugged. 'I don't know. He claimed to be blind, I went to see him about something else, he asked me to pray for the return of his sight, I did and now he claims to be able to see. I don't know if he really was blind or if it was a hoax.' The Bishop had stolen his miracle from him. 'Anyway I wouldn't say that too loudly in here, I don't think it'd go down too well.'

Sean nodded, but his eyes were bright with excitement.

'But I didn't call you down here to talk about that,' although I wish I had, his mind added as the glow faded from Sean's eyes. 'There're a couple of things I want to talk to you about. Firstly,' he took a swig of beer, 'I need to talk to you about mum.'

'You guys split up?

Andrew glanced up, shocked.

'Jane told me. She rang last night after mum rang her. So what's the deal there?'

Andrew sighed, 'I don't know what the deal is. I walked in on your mum in a compromising situation with another man. I've been having a rough time with some other things in my life, so I've probably not handled the situation too well, and she's decided to go and stay with Jane for a bit.'

'So you going to patch things up or what?'

'I don't know. I think that depends a lot on your mum. If she's dead keen on this other chap over me, then there's not much I can do.'

Sean leaned forward. 'What, just like that, you not even going to try and win her back.'

Andrew shrugged. 'I'm not sure I want her back.' Sean looked shocked. 'It's not that...well it's all a bit too fresh at the moment. I am still angry that she was not faithful to me. I don't know if I can forgive her for that, and, if the truth be told, I've become rather keen on another woman. Please don't tell your mother this. The problem is that it makes me rather a hypocrite if I hold a grudge against your mum for her infidelity.' He could sense more strange looks being directed his way from patrons in the bar. 'It's all rather confusing at the moment. I don't know what I want. I need to work through it all, but I just wanted you to know what was happening.' He had never been so open with his son before.

Sean nodded slowly. 'I think I understand. I won't say anything to ma, you two need to work it out between you.'

Andrew gave a half laugh. 'That's what your mum used to say about you and me.' His smile faded. 'That was the other thing I wanted to talk to you about.'

'Excuse me, sir,' the barman was standing next to the table and Andrew knew what was coming next. 'I'm afraid that I'm going to have to ask you to leave. You are that priest aren't you? And we don't want your sort, you people who help paedophiles, we don't want you here. You should be helping the victims, not the criminals.'

'Hang on a minute,' Sean was on his feet.

'Sean, it's okay,' his voice was calm while inside tears of joy were flowing that his son would stand up for him. He took a long gulp of beer and stood up.

'Come on, let's go.' He walked out, ignoring the looks he got and hoped his son was following him. At his car, he felt his legs begin to go and he grabbed the bonnet for support.

'Dad!' Sean was there and helping him.

'I'm fine son. Look I'm sorry I dragged you into this. I think I might have bitten off more than I can chew with this McCready business. You probably won't be able to show your face in this pub again. I'm sorry.'

'That's okay, I never really liked the place.' They both laughed and Andrew felt his strength return.

'Look Sean, I was just going to say that I'm sorry about the way I took it when you told me that you were moving in with Gary. It was a bad time and I said things that I regret. I don't want us to spend the rest of our lives with you hating me.'

'Dad I…'

'No, don't say anything now. I just want you to know that I am truly sorry for what I said and that I want you to forgive me.' He waved away any response, 'I've been thinking a lot about forgiveness lately and am beginning to realise that it's far easier to preach about it than practise it. What I want is that you go away and think about forgiving me, I mean really forgiving me.' A few of the patrons were at the door of the bar looking at them, this did not bode well.

'Promise me that,' he said quickly. 'Promise me that you will go away and think about forgiving me.'

Sean could not see the men as he had his back to them, but Andrew pushed the urgency into his voice.

'I will dad, I promise, but…'

'No son, we must go now, I think we may be in trouble if we don't.'

---oOo---

By the time he was back in the town (not a village), he had stopped shaking and was actually feeling quite good. He hadn't really thought about what he would say to Sean, it had just come out in the heat of the pressure, but now, as he thought about it, it made some sense of his life.

How many times had he stood in the pulpit and preached about forgiveness without really knowing what it meant, what sacrifice of emotions had to take place for true forgiveness to occur. He still didn't fully understand the concept, but he had a much better idea now.

For him to forgive Marge would not be a huge thing. At the moment he was not so hurt by her actions to make any forgiveness he may be able to muster of such magnitude to be a huge sacrifice on his part. To forgive her would be like cleaning a speck of dust off an otherwise blemish free surface.

Had Pat not been in the picture, and had they not drifted apart like they had, and if Marge's accusations of him not noticing her were unfounded, then yes, the forgiveness that would be required would be of a far greater magnitude and much more difficult to give.

He had not quite worked out yet what level of sacrifice Marge would have to make to forgive him his sin of neglect.

Sean would require more effort. It had been good that he had agreed to meet, it showed willing. And the way he reacted this evening was a good sign that he was well on the way. It had just taken a gesture on his behalf.

But the Bridges…The crime against them was so huge, unforgivable many would say. For them to forgive McCready would be just about the greatest forgiveness a human being can give. He was now determined to work on the Bridges. This was God's calling.

He turned into his street and saw the small crowd of journalists outside his house.

---oOo--

'Andrew?'

'Hi. Um. Would you mind if I slept here tonight? There is a herd of journalists outside my house and I can't face them tonight.'

'Did you really heal that man?'

'I don't know. I prayed for him and he says he is now healed. God knows if he was genuine or not. It is not for me to judge. I will tell you all about it, but tonight I can't face that crowd, I need time to think. I'd really appreciate it if you could put me up for the night.'

'I'll make up a bed in the spare room.'

'Thanks Eve.'

---oOo---

He watched The Yellow Dressing Gown move round the kitchen. Those large breasts did not hold any attraction this morning. He felt relaxed.

'How do you want your eggs, Father?' she smiled a happy morning after a night of new passion smile.

My godfathers Eve, all I did was sleep in your spare room. Nothing happened remember, unless you were dreaming…oh my god! He smiled back in what he hoped was an excessively platonic way. 'Boiled if that's not too much trouble. You really don't need to.'

'Oh it's no problem, besides, it's not often one has the Vicar to breakfast.' Was she flirting? Please God no. He remembered how The Laugh had interrupted him kissing Pat and images of a jealous rivalry flared up in his mind. Marge's bed was hardly cold and suddenly it seemed that two women were vying for the position.

'Toast?' The Laugh was over anxious.

'One slice please. I suppose I will have to go home soon, I need to change and pick up my sermon. I hope those vultures have left by now.'

I don't, The Laugh's look said, but she nodded her head.

'Tea or coffee?' She adjusted her gown inexpertly, giving him a better view of her cleavage.

'Coffee please.' He was not sure what disturbed him more, The Laugh's awkward attempt at seduction, or the greenshoots of an erection he was feeling. She seemed to sense his arousal and adjusted the gown again, her breasts practically hanging out, and giggled girlishly.

How could he stop her without hurting her feelings? Where was The Good Vicar?

'Is that the time?' He knew that he had to be cruel to be kind. She straightened herself up quickly, an embarrassed laugh falling from her lips.

'Oh yes, I'd better get a move on if you're going to get to church on time.'

---o0o---

Nearly all the regulars were there, quite a lot of the irregulars sat dotted around, and the rest of the nearly packed church was made up of the journalists. So far nothing had happened, but as he climbed up the stairs to the pulpit to deliver his sermon, he felt a shift in the atmosphere. There was an expectation, an excitement, a tension. He did not like it.

He got into position, crossed himself and began. 'Everyone has their favourite food, fish and chips, roast beef, chicken tikka masala. Mine is shepherd's pie...'

'Father Andrew.' So this was how it was going to be. Roger McLeod stood in his regular pew, about halfway back on the left. Linda was not with him. That was strange. Then he remembered the operation.

'Yes Roger?' Remain calm. They were all looking at the interrupter expectantly.

'Before you continue with your sermon, I thought you might like to enlighten the congregation about the newspaper reports you have been featuring in recently.'

'You mean the issue with Mr McCready I presume?' Of course he means the issue with McCready unless I missed the report about Village Vicar scores winner for Man. United.

'Yes. I think the congregation deserves an explanation as to your behaviour in this matter.'

Andrew didn't like the tone of the words 'your behaviour'. It implied wrongdoing and he was damned if he would admit to wrongdoing in this matter.

'My behaviour is quite simple Roger, I went to see Mr McCready, he asked me to pray for him so that his sight may be restored and I did. That is what happened.'

'I see, but why did you go and visit him?'

'He requested that I go and see him.'

'Does he know you?'

'I have not had any contact with the man before. He may have known of me as I know of him.'

'So why did he call for you in particular?'

'I don't know. He wouldn't say. Now perhaps I can go on with my sermon?'

'Just one more thing, Father.'

'Yes?'

'Do you think that it is right to minister to people like this McCready fellow?'

'Roger, our Lord ministered to the outcasts in his society. We have a duty to minister to whoever needs our help.' He sensed what was coming next, but that did not make it more bearable when it came.

'I'm afraid, Father, that I do not feel I can trust a man who helps out paedophiles with preaching the word of God to me, or with administering the Eucharist for me. Your hands have been dirtied by what you have done and I for one do not want to have anything to do with you. I don't know about the rest of you.' The last comment was directed at the congregation in general. He then excused me his way to the end of the pew and started walking down the aisle.

After a few seconds of looking round at each other some more of the congregation began to move, first the irregulars, then the regulars. Andrew waited patiently till the movements had stopped, then surveyed the crowd.

The journalists were still there, although some cameramen had left to get pictures of the *crowds deserting the paedo vicar*, they would probably return soon. A few faces that he vaguely recognised were still there, then there were those that he knew well and was grateful to see still sitting in their normal places. Eve was smiling nervously; Audrey looked shocked while Pat seemed concerned as did the others who had stayed.

'Father Andrew?' Another voice came out of the congregation.

'Yes?' He looked round to see who had spoken.

'I was wondering if you could clarify something regarding Mr McCready.' It was one of the journalists.

'Sir, this is a house of God,' he tried not to be too patronising, 'I will not answer any questions regarding that issue during the normal service time. I still have some of my congregation left and I intend to minister to them. If you wish to sit through my sermon, you are more than welcome, as are you welcome to join us in the Eucharist afterwards. You will not get anything else from me today.'

The Laugh looked like she was about to get up and applaud. 'Please don't,' his silent plea went out. Slowly the journalists moved out of the church. Once they had gone, Andrew looked round at the few people who remained and smiled.

'Now where was I?'

'Shepherd's pie!' Eve blurted out a little too enthusiastically.

'Ah yes, shepherd's pie. Thanks Eve.'

---oOo---

His chair was comfortable but he felt unbearably tired sitting in it. Maintaining his composure in the pulpit while watching those hypocrites desert him when he needed their support had drained him.

There were so many things to think about; *Go and see him; In loving memory; 'e's shaggin' your missus; Look forward to seeing you; Who is Alex? Church Aids Paedo; the yellow dressing gown; Kiss me Andrew.*

The sweetness of the last one appealed, but he decided to deal with the yellow dressing gown first and keep the kiss for deserts. Why had he let his mind take hold so drastically this morning? Yes, The Laugh had been friendly at breakfast, friendly with a hint of flirt, but there was no way she would have been so graphic. So why had he fantasised about her revealing her breasts to him? Freud would have an explanation he was sure and possibly he wouldn't be too far off the mark. In his beaten state, surely he was craving some sort of motherly comfort and Eve seemed to be best able to offer it.

Not having kids of her own meant that all those pent up instincts were still pure and piled up in that ample bosom. Maybe it was the closeness and, since the hug he had received from her, availability of it all that had excited him.

Still, he needed to control himself, or rather his thoughts, better. It had taken a few minutes before he felt safe to stand up without pointing at Eve's breasts. He made a silent promise to himself to be better behaved and threatened his mind with a few hours of counselling from The Good Vicar should anything like this happen again.

Who is Alex? He had managed to brush that one aside when Eve asked, saying that he (making a point of saying he) was someone with a problem that he had been trying to help. He would possibly have to ask Eve about The Rat and his parents but he didn't want to think about that now, he wanted something sweeter.

Kiss me Andrew. They had been three little words dropped like pearls into the muck of his mind, cleansing and soothing. He would take her up on her offer; that was a certainty. The urge to call her and pick up where they left off was great but the timing wasn't right. It needed a trigger of sort and, as he thought more about it, he realised that this needed to come from her.

He sighed as he filed that in the out-tray, knowing, hoping that it would come back into the in-tray marked urgent.

He skipped over the other items in his in-tray and went with some reluctance to the in-deeper tray. Ian's words still rang in his ears and, he conceded, the Bishop had a point. The walk-out in church this morning, although not totally unexpected, was a sharp reminder of Ian's concerns and he needed to sort out for himself who he needed to obey, the church or God. But before he could decide on this, he needed to work out if it was actually God or his warped mind that was in battle with the church at the moment. It was not a debate that he relished.

Saved by the bell. Who could that be? He hoped it wasn't the press, he had finally got rid of them by late afternoon by being particularly evasive.

'Hi, have you had dinner? I've rustled up a little shepherd's pie if you want some.'

That was quick he thought looking at his in-tray.

---oOo---

He looked down at her and smiled. He couldn't recall feeling this good for a long time. There was a euphoric glow that warmed his soul. She was more beautiful in the flesh than he had fantasised.

She returned the smile, slightly shyly as his eyes sucked hungrily on her naked body.

'Andrew?'

'Hmm?' It was dreamy.

She pulled herself up on her elbow slightly and he marvelled at the changing shape of her breasts.

'Should we feel guilty?' Her smile faded a little.

He thought for a second, clinging to his euphoric glow, not wanting it to fade, but feeling it slipping from his grasp. He lightly touched her cheek with the back of his hand.

'Pat,' he caressed her name out of his mouth, 'let's not talk about that just yet. Right now I don't think I've ever been happier in my life, I want this moment to last as long as possible.' He kissed her gently and watched the smile move to her eyes as her lips were busy.

His free hand sought the warmth of her smooth skin and he marvelled that at his age he was ready to go again so soon. He pulled her close to his body and blocked out the banging of The Good Vicar on the door of the little room in his mind that he had locked him up in.

---oOo---

'Are you shagging the pee-do's daughta?' The time for guilt had come and The Rat's accusation came to mind as he lay, eyes open, in the dark.

The warm glow along with the warm impression she had left on the sheets had cooled and now an almost icy guilt stabbed at his guts. Why? Why? Why? He slammed a fist into the pillow where only a few nights previously, Marjory's head had looked quite saintly as he had struggled with the dream.

He hated this guilt. Why should something that felt so good and positive in his life feel so utterly wrong in the cold analysis The Good Vicar was giving?

The passion had erupted from the dining room table. The shepherd's pie, which he now had to admit secretly to himself wasn't quite as good as Margie's, had been mostly finished and the small talk of the evening had dissolved as their eyes met over red wine glasses raised to kiss hungry lips.

The dinner was abandoned in a groping, snatching, clawing frenzy. They were half-naked by the time they were kiss-fumbling up the stairs, and completely naked by the time they fell lustfully into bed.

His own urgency astounding him only marginally less than Pat's frantic tugging of him into hers. Andrew the Stud Muffin had shaken off all staleness and was freshly baked and crumbling into bed.

'I'd better go.' Those words so full of sense had felt like the most ridiculous suggestion ever, but fires were dying down and he could hear The Good Vicar picking the lock of his little prison.

He had watched her dress and then had hastily thrown some clothes on to see her to the door. Returning to his bed he lay back and picked at the scraps of warm glow left. Eventually, with a huge sigh that seemed to reiterate to him the emptiness of the house, he turned onto his side and, praying quickly for a peaceful night, slid slowly down the black slope of sleep.

He hit the bottom with a loud crash that sent him straight back up at breakneck speed. Sitting up quickly he brushed aside the heaviness of sleep and listened. The crash had been real! Quickly he grabbed his gown and shoved his feet into the waiting slippers.

In the front room he surveyed the broken glass and felt the cool air coming through the jagged window frame. The dull streetlight teased his eyes as he tried to look past the ghosts they threw up to see if anything real moved. And then came the sniff.

---oOo---

'I don't think he did this, but he must have seen who did. You know the lad I'm talking about? Looks like a rat, I believe his name is Alex.'

The one policeman cast a quick glance over at his partner, then returned his serious face to Andrew and gave a half shrug, half nod.

'You say you recognised his...' he consulted his notebook, a disbelieving look on his face, '...his sniff?'

It sounded silly coming from another mouth. He had heard the words coming from his own mouth in a flow of pure sense, but now, somehow, this policeman had reduced his testimony to a ridiculous comment. He nodded miserably.

'You didn't actually see him then?'

'No.' Okay no need to rub it in. I get the point.

'And you say you've spoken to him a few times before.'

'Yes.'

'But you don't think he did this. Why not?'

A hunch, don't you bastards work on hunches all the time? 'I'm not sure. He's never been aggressive or anything like that with me. I don't think it's in his nature.' He's far more devious, throwing a brick through my window is not his style you wanker.

'Any ideas who might have done it then? Anyone got it in for you, Father?'

About eighty per cent of my congregation you arse. Don't you pigs follow the news?

'No, no idea.'

---oOo---

In loving memory of Geoffrey Deane. The early morning air was cold. He pulled his coat tighter and drew a slug of determination from his mental hip flask. He had been sitting here for about half an hour without so much as a sniff of The Rat.

A few cars glided noiselessly round the streets below and, he thought, he could just make out the boarded up window of the vicarage. He began to wonder if it would be The Rat or Alex that came, or neither. He sincerely hoped it would be The Rat. Where the hell was he?

He took the mental hip flask out again; it felt nearly empty. Slowly he lifted it to his lips and was just about to down the dregs when the sniff came. See constable, I can recognise that sniff anywhere.

'Who did it?' He jumped straight in, not looking up to see which of the young lads had arrived, not letting him get in first.

'Wot?'

'Who did it, who threw that brick through my front window?' It was angry and growled.

'Doan know wot jew talkin' about guv. Did somewun frow a brick frew your winda?'

Andrew turned his head sharply and glared at The Rat. 'You were there, you saw who it was, tell me who it was.' The sentence slowed like a train chugging to a halt, each word louder than the previous one.

'Not me guv, I weren't nowhere near your place last night.'

Where the hell were you then? Andrew discarded that sentence and opted rather to lunge at The Rat, grabbing at his jacket, pulling the hooded head close to his face. 'Tell me!' he hissed, sending shivers down The Good Vicar's spine at the anger and evil that seemed to encase the words.

'Orite, orite, lemmigo.' The Rat wiggled. 'I'll tell ya, jus' lemmigo.'

Andrew felt the anger cooling in him and he slowly released his grip on the coat. The Rat wiggled free, took a step back, straightened his coat and then gave a little laugh. ''ad you goin' there for a bit din I?'

A small growl escaped from Andrew.

'Orite, orite. Lemmie jus' sid down 'kay?'

Andrew nodded and The Rat eased himself into a slouch on the bench, thrusting his hands into his pockets. He sniffed then said, 'It wos that geezer wot stood up in the church.'

'What? Roger?' That was impossible. Roger was a respectable man. He might not agree with what Andrew was doing about McCready, but there was no way he would stoop to such low tactics. He was a lawyer for goodness sakes.

'I dunno 'is name, but if you say 'e'e Roger, then that's 'im.'

Andrew leaned forward and rubbed his face with both hands. 'Thank you,' he mumbled.

''s orite.' The voice had changed and instinctively Andrew knew that the hood had been drawn back. He dared not look, but hazel eyes were flashing in his mind and his head turned almost involuntarily.

'Wot jew gonna do?' It was not eyes that held his gaze now, it was the soft young lips, gently rose coloured and inviting as they worked their way around the words. He wanted to kiss them, lose himself in their innocent lure. He leaned forward slowly as in a dream.

---oOo---

The Good Vicar was having a right go at him, hammering away about how he needed to have more self-control. This was obviously an attack by evil forces on him, leading him into temptation. He must pray harder, especially the bit about lead us not into temptation.

His head was pounding and he fumbled for the aspirin in the bathroom cabinet. His shirt drenched with feverish sweat. Using a trembling hand he filled a glass with water and threw the pills into his mouth, quickly washed them down, then raced to the bed where he collapsed, breathing heavily; his eyes closed against the spinning of the room.

Slowly, as the bed accepted him into its comforting embrace, he felt the nausea of his migraine subside and was relieved to be left with only the splitting headache. The light coming through the window hurt, but the fear of returning fever held him to the bed.

What, he asked himself, would have happened if that old man with his dog hadn't come walking past just then? What perverted acts would he have committed? The loss of control he had experienced disturbed him deeply as he could not put it down to natural causes. There had to be some force working its magic on him, he was not a paedophile under normal circumstances, so he had to conclude that Alex's effect on him was unnatural.

And Roger? The accusation was as absurd as 'e's shaggin' your wife. The Rat had not lied then, in fact, other than teasing him about not being around last night, The Rat had never lied to him. But Roger?

Thinking hurt and he forced himself to relax his temples, easing the pain a little. The phone rang and he winced, then rolled slowly over to grab the sharp intrusion before it did further damage.

'Yes?' he groaned.

'Andrew? Are you okay?'

'I'm fine,' his voice said, despite the protestations from his body.

'But I heard on the news that they had thrown a brick though the window. Is that right?'

'Yes,' he kept the voice calm.

'Did it break anything other than the window, I mean, it didn't hit the display cabinet did it?'

'No, just the window,' but scared the living daylights out of me thanks for asking.

'Do you know who did it?'

Roger Bloody McLeod. 'No.'

'Well I don't like this. I'm coming home.'

He grabbed frantically for the image of him and Pat in bed together as it floated away from his grasp.

'Okay Marge.'

---oOo---

'Sir! Sir! You can't go in there, please.'

'Andrew?'

He shot a quick 'you see he is not with a client, how dare you lie to a vicar' look at the secretary and she faded away after a brief nod from Roger.

'Look Andrew, what I said in church yesterday stands. I, and many others, do not wish to be associated with you if you pursue this line of helping paedophiles. This is not the sort of behaviour we tolerate from a vicar. I will be attending St John's in future. Barging in here like this is not polite either, so would you mind leaving before I call the police.'

Roger's attack took a small measure of wind from his sails but, the aspirin had worked wonders and he was up for a fight.

'Maybe we should call the police, Roger. They may be interested in your whereabouts last night when a brick came flying through my front window.'

The surprise lasted a fraction of a second, but it was enough to convict the lawyer.

'I…I don't know what you're talking about.'

'Oh I think you do Roger, in fact I have an eye witness placing you at the scene.' The lawyer was shaken, but too many hours in the courtroom helped him overcome this quickly.

'I was at home with Linda, she will vouch for me.'

Andrew stared long and hard at the lawyer before saying, 'Don't ever do anything like that again.' He felt The Good Vicar shudder at the evilness of his voice and took a perverse pleasure in that. Roger too seemed disturbed by the tone but before he could answer, Andrew turned and walked out feeling great.

---o0o---

He was not sure he wanted to be there to welcome Marge back. Jane would most certainly give him the 'it's your fault' look while survey-ing the damage, and possibly pass a sarcastic comment about his not having cleaned up the broken glass. He longed for the comfort of Pat's presence, but The Good Vicar had been working overtime on the guilt gland since that demonic, yes that was the word for it, demonic outburst in Roger's office. He shivered now as the growl came back to him. What was happening to him? The Good Vicar usually had such a grip on his behaviour that he would never have made threats in such a voice.

But the vice-like grip on his life by The Good Vicar seemed to be being slowly pried apart by other forces, evil forces, and there were only two he could think of at the moment that may be guilty, Mc-Cready and The Rat.

Despite this analysis, he still felt the attractive lure of the two. He wanted to understand McCready, fathom out the connection between him and Peggy. He wished to delve into that dark mind and dig up that treasured nugget that would answer the question that was on the country's collective lips – Why?

Then there was The Rat/Alex. Sweet and sour. The dark menace with the hood, and that sweet angelic, beautiful boy. He knew he wasn't a paedophile, he hoped he wasn't a paedophile, but his encounters with Alex were making him doubt this. But surely his experience was different to normal paedophiles. He was not the one doing the seducing, he was the seducee.

He needed to move before Marge got home so he pushed himself out of his chair and headed out the front door. He paused for a second at the gate and glanced around. There was no sign of The Rat, but a man sitting in a car nearby lowered the newspaper he was reading. Andrew moved off quickly, listening to the sound of the car door being opened and shut, then steps clunking dully on the pavement as the man followed him.

---oOo---

Dear Lord God, please damn the press to hell. He desperately wanted to pray that prayer as he sat in the side chapel. He had hoped to go and see Pat, but having that pesky journalist tail him meant that he would have to be more subtle. What did they want from him anyway?

He looked around the quiet church, the man had thankfully not followed him in here, but the emptiness of the place did nothing to bring solace, rather it threw up little bubbles of memory of the night he had spent here. One thought would surface, pop and fade, only to be replaced by the next one. This powerful mix was going to his head. Why could he find no shelter in God's house?

He rose unsteadily and panic-fumbled his way out the church and into the vestry where he felt slightly calmer. He wanted to call Pat and have her come round. It was The Laugh's afternoon off so it was unlikely that anyone would come to the office. But as The Good Vicar rightly pointed out, you can't carry on an extra-marital affair on hallowed ground unless you want to apply for the role of spit roast star in the afterlife. His whole being screamed its protest at The Good Vicar.

There was nothing to do in the vestry and he knew he would have to go home soon and face Marge. How would she treat him? With pity for being attacked? With indifference, her concern being more about the damaged property and the endangered display cabinet? Or would she be angry at him for getting himself into such a position?

---oOo---

Anger it was. He had offered The Good Vicar good odds on it being indifference, but he was suddenly relieved that The Good Vicar wasn't a gambling man.

'You brought this on yourself, running off to see that monster like that. What did you think would happen? Did you think that no-one would notice? Look how close that brick came to smashing my mother's china tea-pot.'

What had happened to the demure Marge that had suggested that he blindly follow what he thought was a call from God. All that was suddenly gone in the flick of a brick. She looked almost ugly now, pacing around the glass-splattered carpet, her greying hair seemed greyer and unpatted. Maybe she had let herself go since The Heathen wasn't around to look good for.

Maybe it was The Bloody Heathen's doing this. Her attitude was now decidedly un-Christian like. Perhaps all the ungodliness of Brian was rubbing off on Marge and she would soon be spending Sunday mornings in bed getting her hands dirtied by the ink of the Sunday papers while suckling The Heathen at her saggy little breasts.

'Why haven't you cleaned away the glass?' Jane was in on cue, her snaky dreadlocks writhed angrily on her head. He ignored her, he just had to reach the sigh and then he knew he would be okay. That womanly sigh that says I'm done moaning, it obviously no use dealing with men, I will have to sort it out myself.

'Who did this?' Marge was demanding.

He shrugged his sigh inducing shrug and gave his sigh inducing mournful glance round the room. He could sense that he was nearly there.

Marge and Jane sighed almost simultaneously. Two for the price of one, bargain!

'I'll get the dustpan,' Jane said, casting a look at Andrew and pushing past him.

Marge's strength seemed to leave the room with her and she sank onto the sofa, burying her face in her hands. He stared down at her for a second, feeling a strange anger arise in him. She had deserted him when he needed her to be there, she had seen his growing madness as a desperate, childish attempt to try and keep her. She had drawn strength from her daughter when she was there, and now that Jane was out the room, now that there was no one else to look to, all options depleted, only now was she turning to him.

The Good Vicar was nowhere to be found so he moved quietly out of the door and headed to his study.

---oOo---

'Oh hello Andrew, you alright? I read about the attack and have been meaning to call you.'

'Just a brick through the window, no other damage.'

'Well that's a relief, reading the papers one could have believed that it was a full on air raid.'

'Just missed my wife's china teapot that she inherited from her mum, would have been World War Three had it been on target.' Both men chuckled.

'I'm glad you're okay. I guess you're calling to tell me that you want nothing more to do with McCready?'

'On the contrary, I'm more determined than ever to get to the bottom of all this business with the funeral and everything else.'

'I'm impressed, but Andrew, you mustn't do anything foolish. That brick could just be a warning.'

'Thanks, but I don't think the person who threw that brick will be doing it again.'

'You know who threw it?'

Andrew felt a twinge of smugness creep in, 'Yes. I did a bit of detective work and confronted the perpetrator this morning, he's not a dangerous man, in fact he would usually be regarded as an upstanding citizen so one threat to expose him as a hooligan should make him think twice about any brick throwing urges he may have.'

'Well, well, well, you're a braver man than I am.' Andrew was beginning to like Father Gregory.

He gave a dismissive snort before saying, 'Well given that you work with the genuine criminals, I'd say that you're the braver of the two of us.'

The dismissive snort was played back to him and he let it bounce out of the court.

'Anyway, I think we must meet up to discuss how we take this issue forward with McCready. Problem is I have a tail at the moment, think he's from *News of The World* or one of the red tops. I think I can shake him though. Can you meet me tomorrow at ten?'

'Can do, did you really record the service?'

'Yes.' He picked up the little black machine and caressed it gently.

'And the family, have you spoken to them yet?'

'No, not about this, but I think I can convince them.' After all I have a special relationship with her now.

He was glad that he kept that thought as a thought. Marge stood in the door way, an envelope in her hand. She slipped into his study, threw it onto his desk and with a faint flick of her head, mock-stormed out.

---o0o---

Dear Father Andrew

I was sorry to hear about the attack on the vicarage last night. Please find enclosed a donation of £200 which I hope will cover the cost of repairing the window. Please let me know if there is anything else I can do to help at this trying time.

Yours in Christ
Roger McLeod

Hypocrite!

---oOo---

They had cleaned up the front room nicely, so well that it squeezed a drop of guilt out of him. But that quickly evaporated as the sofa, soon to be his bed, taunted him. Marge was, he presumed, already tucked up between the adulterous sheets of last night, hopefully not smelling the scent of Pat's naked body that he had, until now, been hoping would linger for a while.

Jane would probably be tossing and turning in the uncomfortable spare bed. He took a small delight at this thought and accepted The Good Vicar's rap on his knuckles with the grace of an unrepentant school boy.

It was not just the prospect of trying to sleep on the sofa that he dreaded, it was the possible dreams that would come that scared him more. So he dallied between the heavy tiredness that beset him and the sofa of potential nightmares.

Eventually he resigned himself to the inevitable and slowly began to unbutton his shirt. His tired-glazed eyes watched double sized fingers fumble awkwardly with the buttons, while his mind allowed in a small ration of the sound of tapping on the front door. His fingers shrank slowly to their usual size as the mind allowed a bigger dose of sound in.

A tightness formed in his stomach and he quickly re-buttoned his shirt. There was definitely someone out there. He stumbled slowly into the hall, visions of an angry congregation bearing torches and pitchforks sparred with his sense of duty to answer the knocking.

'Who is it?'

'It's me dad.'

'Sean!' All his senses lit up and he pulled the door open.

'Are you okay? I only just heard the news, thought you might have gone to bed already.'

'Sean, come in.' He desperately wanted to hug his son, but his arms hung bound to his side by a lifetime of tradition.

'Mum and Jane are upstairs, they're probably already asleep, so keep your voice down.' He said as he led his son through to the kitchen.

'Mum's here?'

'Yes, she came running back as soon as the story broke. You want a drink?'

'Tea please.'

It felt good to have him here and he smiled quietly as he set about boiling the kettle and preparing the mugs.

'It's not as bad as the press made it out. Just a brick through the window last night.'

'Do you know who did it?'

Yes and the bastard has already sent a cheque to pay for the repairs.

'No, I spoke to the police last night, but you know what they're like. I don't think we'll get anywhere on that.' Lord forgive me.

Note to self, get more custard creams.

He took out a packet of rich tea.

'Has this got anything to do with that paedophile?' Sean was sitting at the small table idly fondling the salt cellar.

'I...I guess so. Most of the congregation walked out of the service yesterday morning and some looked quite angry. Could be one of them although I'd like to think not. Darn we're out of milk.'

'That's okay, I'll have it black.'

I was thinking more about my own cup, but I suppose I'll be a martyr like you.

'You sure?'

Sean nodded and turned his attention to the pepper cellar.

'As I was saying, it could be one of them, but then again, it could be anyone from round here, there are some rough youths that hang about the place.'

He put the tea down in front of Sean and offered him a biscuit.

'You not got anything nicer? Bourbons or custard creams? Mum always kept a good stock.'

'Nope, that's all that's left. I must confess to finishing up the custard creams last night and I haven't had a chance to get more.'

'Dad, you're slacking. No milk, no proper biscuits and mum's only been gone a day. What are we going to do with you?' The sparkle in his eye told Andrew that his son was just teasing and he smiled warmly as he eased himself into the other chair.

Sean's smile faded and he returned his attention to the salt cellar.

'Dad, I've been thinking a lot about what you said about forgiving you.'

---oOo---

It felt strange having his whole family under one roof, so close and yet so fractured. How had he let it happen? The split with Marge, the disdain, bordering on hatred he received from Jane and the huge rent in the father-son relationship. At least the latter was thankfully being bridged.

He watched Sean as he stripped down to his boxers and felt the melancholy drag him down. It was surely just yesterday that he had cuddled that tiny child in the hospital. It was a clichéd thought he knew, but sometimes there's a good reason why things become clichés.

Sean stepped out of his jeans and Andrew sneaked a long look at his body while his son folded his clothes up neatly. There were no feelings in there to explain his strange attraction to Alex. He was not aroused by the male nudity on display. He had become concerned that perhaps there were latent, suppressed homosexual urges that were suddenly coming to the fore in his behaviour towards Alex, but nothing came as he watched Sean. Then again, Sean was his own flesh and blood and that could explain the lack of interest he had. He sighed inwardly at the lack of answers.

'Dad, you're staring.'

'Sorry son, miles way.' Oops.

Sean climbed under the blanket on the other sofa and Andrew began undressing himself again. He was even more reluctant to sleep now despite the almost sickening tiredness that weighed heavily on him.

They had talked for a long time. Really talked. Sean had forgiven him, not just an *oh I forgive you* laughing it off as a minor incident. This was a well thought out, calculated forgiveness that analysed the transgression, analysed the transgressor, took a long hard look at oneself and the role one played in causing the issue, then purged all anger, purging all bitterness and purging all resentment that related to the issue. Then finally accepting the transgressor as you had done before the offence occurred.

Sean had managed this and, given the things Andrew had said at the time, it would not have been easy for his son to forgive so lightly. But still Sean's forgiveness would be far easier to give than it will be for the Bridges.

There had been his apology and the request for forgiveness to start with, but McCready was something else. You don't smash someone's head in then calmly say, *Oh I'm so sorry, please forgive me.* No one believes you. Andrew was not totally convinced of the repentance of McCready, but The Good Vicar did seem more sure of it.

Then there had to be a willingness to forgive on the side of the one transgressed against. Sean was more than willing, something he should have seen ages ago. Marge had hinted at it to his selectively deaf ears on a few occasions. 'Call him, talk to him, say you're sorry.' But he had been too scared of the rejection. Sean had been willing, but would the Bridges be?

McCready wanted real forgiveness, not just words. Was he asking the impossible? Could one fake forgiveness? Could he train the Bridges to fake forgiveness? He thought back to what McCready had said to him and wondered if he meant what he had hinted at, or if this was all just more evil tricks.

'Forgive them, for they know not what they do.'

At the foot of the cross Marge and The Heathen were twisted together in an unsightly embrace, their bodies intertwined as hungry faces seemed to simultaneously suck the other's being into itself. It was like one person, one body of concentrated passion.

'Forgive them, for they know not what they do.' The voice came again from the cross and he struggled to lift his life-weary eyes to peer into the gloom that enshrouded him. The voice sounded familiar. Slowly the face of the crucified came into focus and he scrambled backwards, clumsily trying to run from the blasphemous image.

McCready spoke again from the cross, a crown of snakes writhing in his dark curly hair, 'Forgive them.'

He tried to shield his eyes from McCready's face. Everything seemed wrong. Then he heard Marge's voice, small and frightened.

'Help!' The word plopped into the sticky bog of his dream and he wrenched his terrified eyes from the blasphemous McCready Christ. The Heathen, eyes aglow, was swallowing her whole, sucking her into him. Her legs flayed frantically as her body disappeared slowly into his hungry mouth.

'Andrew.' It was Pat. She stood near him, reaching out to him and he felt himself tearing in two as he tried to rescue Marge and find solace in Pat's warm embrace.

He took a step back, hoping to step out of the dream, but fell over a small figure that sniffed as he did so. There was no surface to catch him and he hurtled downwards into a black void that slowly faded till he opened his eyes.

In that strange suspended world between sleeping and waking, he heard the sniff again, so real and yet so surreal. He jumped up quietly from the sofa and padded to the front door, opening it quickly. The night greeted him with phantoms, bits of darkness thrown up and twisted in an invisible wind, movements that shuddered, shimmied and disappeared. But he could not hear, nor see anything that would convince the jury of his mind. He turned slowly back inside and wished he had bought some custard creams.

---oOo---

The house yawned and stretched around him as the dim light of a cloudy day apologised for calling time on the night. He listened to the toilet flush and floorboards creak of the family waking, this fractious family of his.

Sean would be the last one up, he always was. Andrew shifted in his chair, he felt numb and sore from sitting in that usually comfortable chair in his study, but now each movement he made seemed to bring aftershocks of that blasphemous vision. He had sat rooted to his seat most of the night, hoping, praying that his fragile soul would not be held responsible for conjuring up the McCready Christ.

There was nothing Christ-like in that man. Maybe he had repented, but unlike Christ, he bore the stain of terrible sin, Christ was spotless. He was confronted again by the F-word – forgiveness. To forgive McCready, properly forgive him, would be to give him that Christ-like innocence, not just a case of no longer noticing the sin stain, but a complete washing away of the mark, better than any washing powder could ever claim to do.

But how Lord? How can we mere mortals come close to giving that kind of forgiveness? Even if he could bring himself to offer mortal strength forgiveness to Marge, that nipple hungry mouth stain would always remain, he would never be able to purge it completely from his mind. Far easier to preach it than practise it.

Someone was coming down the stairs and the gloomy day flicked absent-mindedly at the remaining dust of the night. He forced himself to move and winced at the flash of the McCready Christ's face, but it was a more opaque vision which heartened him. Like pins and needles, he now knew that moving around would rid himself of the pain.

He turned his mind back to his family. Breakfast was going to be interesting.

---o0o---

The Pale Blue Dressing Gown was there, almost as if it had never left.

'Morning.' He tried to be as pleasant as he could. Marge turned and gave him an almost friendly smile. Perhaps she had actually realised that he had not brought the attack on himself, that it was the small mindedness of others that was at fault.

'Sean's here,' he announced, trying to keep the pride out of his voice.

'What? When?' Her brow wrinkled.

'He came tapping at the door late last night. Slept on the other sofa.'

'You mean he spent the night in the same room as you? I'm not saying I don't believe you,' she added quickly, 'but last time I looked you two were hardly talking.'

Andrew's smugness dissolved quickly as The Good Vicar gave him a small slap on the back of his head.

'We've sort of patched things up.'

'Andrew! That's great.' Her pleasure was genuine. 'But what brought that on?'

You leaving me you bitch. He got another slap for his thoughts.

'I'm not totally sure, but when you…well when you left, I needed someone to talk to, you know, someone outside the congregation, so I rang him. We had a long chat.'

She smiled warmly again. Was it for him, or for Sean the smile? He suspected the latter.

'We'll need four eggs then.'

Great, she was going to make breakfast.

'Oh dear, there are only three left.'

And no custard creams. I'll have to do a shop soon, unless she decides to stay.

'Don't worry, I'll just have toast, there is enough bread isn't there?' He decided to play the martyr.

She checked, nodded and then continued getting breakfast ready. She could have offered to forgo her own egg. He kept the bitterness out of his face.

'You'd better wake Sean, breakfast will be ready soon.'

'Sean's here?' Jane looked like shit, but then that was normal. A pang of pain passed through Andrew as he realised that his only ally in the house at the moment would soon be the centre of attention of the others.

'Morning all.' Sean answered Jane's question by swaggering into the kitchen. He ran his hand through his hair, his eyes bemused-brushed.

'Sean!' His mother made the first kiss claim on him, followed quickly by his sister.

Andrew stood a spare-part distance off, watching. As Sean hugged his sister, he raised his eyes to meet Andrew's.

'Morning son,' he smiled back at the warm look he got and Sean nodded a greeting. 'Sleep well?'

'Yeah, great thanks dad. The sofa is surprisingly comfortable. You alright? You haven't got a cold have you?'

'No. What makes you think that?'

'I thought I heard you sniffing a lot last night. Must've been dreaming.'

---o0o---

At least they did the dishes, he thought as he opened the fridge for the milk for his morning custard cream-less tea.

'Bugger! I must do the shopping,' he told the fridge, then moved back to scoop up his black tea.

The eggs had been scrambled for breakfast to try and get enough for four out of three. The movement after breakfast had been scrambled as Sean had had to dash off to get to work and Marge, now happy that the damage to the Vicarage was not serious, had felt a need to get back to being separated as soon as possible. Jane was worried about leaving Arkayic with Harry for so long, and rightly so, he thought.

The phone rang and as he went to answer it, he realised that he had not spoken to Pat at all yesterday. That must look bad, but he had an excuse. She could have called me. Why didn't she? She must have heard the news.

'Hello?'

'Andrew?'

'Pat. Hi…I…'

'I…' They faltered together.

'Sorry, no you go first…'

'No, you go…' This was silly, like teenagers in love.

'I was just going to apologise for not calling yesterday. You heard about the brick, I'm sure?'

'Yes. I was sorry to hear about that. Who would do such a thing?'

'I don't know.' Lord forgive me. 'The police are looking into it.'

'I was going to call you but Brian came back to pick up some things. We had a terrible row and just as he left Eve arrived and spent the whole afternoon, you know how she can talk. Left me quite exhausted and I went to bed early.'

'Sorry to hear that. Actually I'm surprised that Eve didn't come over or call here,' the thought suddenly struck him.

'Didn't she? She said she was going over to you straight after leaving here. That's odd.'

'That is odd. It's not like Eve. I'd better go and check up on her.'

'Good idea.'

'Pat.'

'Yes?' It was expectant and he hated having to say what he had to say.

'I think it's best if we do not see each other alone for a bit.' He could feel the disappointment pouring out the phone. 'It's just that the press are trailing me and I think it's better we're not seen together too much. It'll lead to nasty questions and conjectures.' He paused to control his own feelings before trying to placate Pat's. 'I really desperately want to see you again, but we do need to be careful at the moment. I don't want to drag you into this McCready mess any more than is necessary.' It was The Stud Muffin talking, but it was The Good Vicar's calming, reassuring voice. Andrew marvelled at the combination, and the effect it had.

'I understand. I don't like it, but you're probably right. Call me though, just hearing your voice will help.' A small sob caught in her throat.

'I will, but now I must go and find out what happened to Eve.' A horrible sense of foreboding came over him as he put the phone down.

---oOo---

The office was eerie without The Laugh. The white walls were colder and blander without the warmth she usually brought. He stayed only long enough to shuffle the papers on the desk, then headed out to her house.

The doorbell sounded hollow in the vacuous rooms that lay beyond the obstinate front door. He rang three times, then turned his concerned chiselled face to the reporter who had tailed him.

'Anything the matter Vicar?' He had an unpleasant leer as though he was enjoying the distress being suffered by the paedo-loving priest.

Andrew landed a fist twice the size of his own on this intrusion's nose while The Good Vicar ignored the fantasies and replied, 'No,' and added in a stage whisper to Andrew who was enjoying watching the journalist lying flat on his back, clutching a bloodied nose, 'We must not panic yet.'

'No one at home. Will that make the front page?' Andrew took over control of the vocal chords for a second and took a little delight in the look he got from both the journalist and The Good Vicar. 'I'm now going to return to the Vicarnage, you can use that one if you like – Vicarnage.' He pushed his way politely passed the slightly bewildered man and strode off down the road, listening for the footsteps that he expected to follow him, but heard nothing.

---o0o---

'Eve!'

'Hello Father Andrew, I was just over at your place.' She giggled and looked a little lost in the middle of the pavement.

The desire to hug her was strong, but he held back.

'I was just over at yours,' he wanted to laugh at the almost comic scene but needed to express his worries before he could allow any mirth. 'I was concerned. Pat rang this morning. She said that you were going to come over after seeing her and…well I must admit I panicked a bit there.'

'Oh Father Andrew, I'm so sorry. I didn't think that you and Pat would talk so soon. I was going to come over but,' she paused to let out a small giggle for no apparent reason, then went on, 'I bumped into Mr Williams, you know Clive. Well he invited me for a cup of tea at Le Café, even promised to pay for some scones and cream. You know how persuasive and charming Clive can be, and, with all our chatting, Pat had forgotten to make tea for us, not her fault really, poor thing, I mean what with her mum dying and then all that business…' She suddenly realised where that was heading and veered back to her story. '…anyway, I was so thirsty and I didn't think we'd be too long so before I knew it,' a chuckle, 'I was sitting there, chatting away to Clive. He's such a charmer,' pause for a faint blush, 'and, well, when I eventually looked at my watch it was far too late to come over to see you. I'm so sorry. I really did mean to come over especially because of the bricks and all, but Clive can talk.'

So can you when you get going. Do you ever stop to draw breath?

'Anyway, one of the things Clive said was that he saw you up on The Ridge with a little boy the other day, you know what,' she dropped her voice to a conspiratorial level, glanced around quickly, gave a stifled laugh for good measure then almost whispered, 'he said that it looked like you were about to kiss the little boy, on the lips like.'

She straightened as a cold fear gripped at Andrew.

'I told him not to be silly of course,' she gave a less stifled guffaw. 'He's getting old, must've been seeing things told him. Maybe it's all this horrible news about that paedophile that's gone to his head. But I told him off and told him not to go round spreading indecent gossip like that otherwise he would have me to deal with.' She smiled a *didn't I do well* smile to which Andrew managed to warm up a *thank you* smile response from his cold sweat body.

'Thanks Eve. Come let's go back to the Vicarage and discuss a few things.' He felt the time was right to broach the subject of The Rat with her.

---oOo---

Bugger! He had forgotten to get milk. And there were only a couple of rich teas left. He really had to do the shopping.

'I'm out of milk, will black do?'

Eve sat on the edge of the sofa, her large frame supporting her slowly turning head as she surveyed the damage. She swung her head back to the door at the sound of his voice and giggled.

'Oh I much prefer mine white. That's a shame.' Then suddenly a light lit up in her eyes, 'Let me pop down to Jim and get some, it'll give you a chance to let Pat know I'm okay.' She wobbled to her feet.

Of course, Pat. Andrew cast an annoyed eye at The Good Vicar. It was his job to think of these things.

'Oh that's very kind Eve. Marge has only been gone a day or so and look at the state of things already.' He shook his head sadly and enjoyed the warm glow of motherliness that Eve exuded. 'Would you mind perhaps getting some biscuits as well, we're pretty much out of them and you never know when they might be needed.'

'Sure. Any particular type?'

Custard creams. 'No not fussed. Just not rich tea, we've got a few of those left. Thanks Eve, you're a lifesaver.'

He ushered her and the desire to talk about The Rat out the door and, hoping only she, the milk and the biscuits returned, headed to the phone.

Pat's voice soothed from the first hello and he was irritated by the intrusion of The Laugh's return, but still put the phone down with a warm feeling induced by his agreeing to see her that evening. It should be safe now, there had been no sign of the journalist since this morning.

He took the packet from The Laugh and cursed silently as he saw the box of jammy dodgers through the opaque plastic. Not jammy bloody dodgers. How could he as a priest talk seriously to a parishioner about a spiritual problem while offering them a jammy bloody dodger. Besides, there was something nasty about them. As a child he had always associated the red jammy ring with the stigmata of Christ. How could you eat a biscuit that looked like nail holes through the hand? And full cream milk, why not semi-skimmed like normal people, no wonder she was the size she was. He accepted the slap on the back of his head from The Good Vicar.

'Thanks Eve. Don't know what I'd do without you.'

She blushed, giggled and arranged her plump form on the sofa in one rippling move.

His tiredness gnawed at him as he made the tea and by the time he eased himself onto the chair opposite The Laugh, he was feeling quite exhausted, a mild headache was starting to throb behind his eyes.

Should he talk about The Rat? He had no desire to do so now, but having invited The Laugh in, he needed to say something.

'Clive was half right in what he saw,' he watched The Laugh lean forward slightly as he began. 'I was up on The Ridge with a young lad, but I wasn't about to kiss him as Clive contends. Maybe he saw me leaning closer to hear what the boy was saying.' Lord forgive me. 'You remember I mentioned Alex a little while back?'

The Laugh nodded and gave a small chuckle as she took a breath to launch into an extended monologue of the circumstances in which Andrew had mentioned The Rat, but seeing the danger, he made a pre-emptive strike.

'Well the young lad I was talking to was Alex. Do you know him? Hangs around the shops a lot, always on his own, a hoodie, looks a bit like a rat.'

Eve shrieked at the description. 'That's naughty Father, but I think I know the boy you're talking about.'

'Do you know anything about the boy though? I mean like where does he live? Who his parents are? That sort of thing. He won't tell me anything and I can't help him unless he tells me those things.'

A dark look passed briefly over The Laugh's face, reminding Andrew of the look she had given when questioned about Geoffrey Deane's possible shady past.

'You know what, that's strange. Now that you mention it, I haven't a clue about any of that and I think I know most of the people in town.' Her usually jolly face creased at the brow and a look bordering on horror flashed across her features.

'Goodness Father, you don't think he's homeless? I can't believe we could have had a homeless child living in town all these years; that would be criminal of us to let such a thing happen.'

Andrew felt the knot tightening in his stomach. *All these years.* What could that mean?

'How long has he been around?' His throat was dry and he gripped the armrest of his chair watching the horror he was feeling being reflected back at him.

'Oh my god Andrew!' She was a half pace behind him in his thoughts. 'Oh my god Andrew! He's been in town for over twenty years and…'

'…he's never grown older.' Andrew heard his voice finish the sentence.

Eve gave a very nervous laugh.

---oOo---

How could no one have noticed? Even he had been blinded to the fact that The Rat was still as young as he had been ten years ago when they had first moved there. He had always been aware of The Rat being around, but it was like he was part of the town's furniture. Some things changed and some things stayed the same and, so it seemed, the whole town had got used to this. He was that lamp that sat in the corner of the room and was never used, never noticed, but would give the room an odd appearance if it was suddenly removed.

He had threatened The Laugh with hellfire and damnation should she utter a word of their discovery, The Good Vicar caught between disapproving his using emotional blackmail and a rather satisfied glow at the re-ignited passion with which he delivered his micro-sermon.

He opened a tin of baked beans and spooned some into his mouth, his mind oblivious of his body's actions. Despite his warning, he did not think that Eve would keep her mouth shut and it worried him. He needed to get to the bottom of this mystery and do so quickly. The uneasy feeling that McCready was somehow involved would not leave him. Should he broach the subject with Father Gregory? His mindset had been geared towards discussing the Bridges. But now...

He shovelled a heaped spoon of beans into his mouth and jerked forward to let some rogue sauce drip into the sink instead of down his shirt. He wiped the excess from his chin and an expletive from his lips with a piece of kitchen towel, then took a final careful mouthful of beans before placing the half-empty tin down on the counter with a rattle of the spoon.

He needed to move if he was to be on time to meet with Father Gregory. He glanced round the kitchen quickly and his eyes fell on the packet of jammy dodgers. He grabbed one from the packet and raised it to his lips then paused. Slowly he lowered his right hand from his mouth and placed the biscuit onto his left palm. He watched it melt into his hand, leaving a red stigmata wound.

He stared for a long time then, refocusing his eyes, picked up the biscuit and shoved it into his mouth, chewing quickly as he went in search of his car keys.

---o0o---

'Andrew, I was just beginning to wonder. Were you getting rid of your tail?' It was good to see the smiling face of Father Gregory.

'Managed to get rid of him yesterday thankfully, but I have a funny feeling that they'll be back.' He slid into the chair opposite his colleague and smiled.

'Coffee?'

Andrew glanced round the little tea room. Other than his companion and himself, there were two elderly women who sat at the window shaking over a cream tea and reminiscing for the sake of talking. A young, attractive girl sat in a corner reading a book while absent-mindedly rocking a small child in its buggy. The child flapped at the air and occasionally tugged a rattle into its mouth. It was all decidedly normal and it soothed him.

'Please. Maybe a slice of cake as well. What do they do here?'

Father Gregory motioned for the waitress to come over. She was a young mouse of a girl with a ferret face. Her tight white t-shirt exaggerated her bee-sting breasts while the tight fitting black trousers were dusted with just enough flour to have that slightly soiled look, but not enough to be obviously dirty. She kept her spectacled eyes glued to the small pad as she wrote out the order in a meticulous hand. 1 x coffee, 1 x Earl Grey tea, 2 x chocolate fudge cake. Without lifting her eyes, she slowly read the order back to them and at last glanced up, her face flushed from the exertion of having social contact.

Father Gregory smiled warmly and nodded a thank-you while Andrew relaxed further, there was very little here to indicate trouble about his paedo-healing escapades.

'How you holding up?' Gregory had a good vicar too, Andrew noticed.

'I'm...' he wanted to say fine, but he couldn't, he couldn't lie to a vicar could he? '...not so good.' He shook his head.

Gregory leaned in closer, using a pose that The Good Vicar himself often adopted. It opened up the body, ready to receive, inviting a person to spill all their problems out, leaving them feeling that it would be impolite to turn the offer down.

Andrew hesitated, should he fall for the trap or should he keep it all to himself? He opted for a middle road.

'I'm sure all my troubles stem from McCready. There is something strange, sinister almost about him. I mean over and above the evilness of his deeds. I don't know if we can trust him, especially...' Andrew remembered just in time that he had denied it when Gregory had wanted to know if McCready asked him to go see the Bridges.

'I'd better back this story up a little, small confession I need to make.'

Gregory nodded his eyes in forgiving acceptance as Andrew explained his little white lie. The Good Vicar went on to explain his theory that McCready may just divulge details of the other murders, the ones he was suspected of, it he could receive the Bridges' forgiveness.

He paused as the waitress returned and placed their order on the table, mumbling what each item was, in case they couldn't work it out from their appearance.

'I don't blame you,' Father Gregory forked a chunk of cake into his mouth.' I would have been a bit bewildered by it all myself, not sure who to trust and all that.' He smiled an *I'm glad you trust me now* smile. 'So what do you want to do?'

'I'd like to try and meet with the Bridges. Do you have any contacts I could use? It'll be delicate and I think I'll need a go-between.'

'Gregory Go-Between at your service.' He almost saluted then sheepishly backed off. 'Er…that's if you'd like my help of course.' His voice faded.

Andrew gave his best *put 'em at their ease* smile and lowered his eyes. 'That's very kind. Are you sure? It may not be too safe, you haven't forgotten the brick incident have you?'

'No, of course not, but I really have begun to feel that we're doing God's work here and with His help, we're bound to succeed.'

Andrew handed over control of his facial features to The Good Vicar while he wondered if he could ever really believe that. He wished he had Gregory's faith.

'Let me do a bit of detective work and I'll give you a call later in the week. Okay?'

Yes and synchronise our watches shouldn't we?

'Good, thanks.'

'You going to eat your cake?'

'What? Oh…Yes. Got too caught up in everything.'

He picked up his cup of coffee and breathed in its rich aroma before taking a large sip. The magnitude of his task was suddenly hitting home. He had gone through the theory in his mind, but now as he faced the reality, it became a daunting task, dark and insurmountable.

He turned his thoughts to Pat and their impending meeting, sweetening his mind while the cake took on that task with his taste buds.

---oOo---

The chair welcomed him and he eased back into it, closing his eyes. The tiredness pressed heavily on him and he ushered the impending nap into his mind. He felt the tension slipping from his body and he drew a deep breath, held it for a few seconds then exhaled slowly.

He steered his thoughts towards Sean, the happy re-uniting with his son. He ran through the conversation they had had last night. How good it felt to feel forgiven. That millstone that weighed so heavily round his neck had been cut loose and he revelled in the weightlessness he now felt.

Slowly his mind moved on. The recent events had such a stranglehold on him that he could not enjoy his forgiveness for long. He began to feel guilty that he had been forgiven but had so far done very little to obtain that joy for McCready. Did he owe it to him? How could he owe McCready anything?

The tabloid face wavered in front of him, those steel-grey eyes seemed to implore him to do something. Perhaps, he wondered, perhaps this was a deal God was doing with him, he got his forgiveness from Sean in return for which he had to procure a forgiveness for McCready. It hardly seemed fair given the relative sizes of the transgressions. But God had dragged him into this mess hadn't he? Or was it just his mind playing cruel tricks?

He turned to The Good Vicar for help, but The Good Vicar was already asleep.

---oOo---

The sniff came from the thick pungent darkness. He peered into it, trying to make out The Rat in the swirling patterns, but the blackness held on to its secrets.

'Where are you?' he screamed. The sound shuddered to a standstill.

The sniff came again, louder and closer. He sensed an evilness growing out of the dark and shivered. He wanted to turn round, to run away from the terror, but his feet sank further into the dream and he felt it closing in around him. He was struggling to breathe and began to thrash about.

A third sniff came clearly to him and the closeness of the dark began to melt. He could see the silhouette some way off. The figure was dark but surrounded by a faint glow. He stared hard at it, trying to make out its features. It did not look like The Rat. Slowly it began to glide towards him, floating over the black surface of the dream. It was growing quickly, too big to be a boy. And the sniff. It was growing louder. It was The Rat's sniff, but this was not The Rat.

Slowly, as it drew closer, details began to fade into the outline and Andrew stared, icy pins shooting through his veins as a pair of steel-greys stared back at him and sniffed. A long way off a bell rang.

---oOo---

'Andrew! My goodness are you okay? You look terrible.'

He half gestured, half pulled her into the hall and quickly shut the door before grabbing her in his arms and drowning himself in soft lips, hungrily breathing in the warm, womanly smells and soaking himself in the balm of her embrace.

She breathed in heavily through her nose, her eyes wide open with shock and delight. A slight groan rumbled in her throat.

He felt the sanity seep slowly back into him and eventually disengaged his lips but still held her close. He stared into her questioning eyes and murmured, 'I'm so much better for seeing you.' He was too tired to cringe at the corniness of his comment. 'Fell asleep at my desk and had an awful nightmare. No, I'd rather not, not just yet.' He answered her quizzical look. 'Come,' he gestured for her to go into the front room. The boarded up window made the room seem dark and close, like the dream. He snapped the light on, dispelling the eeriness and flooding the room with a cosiness, made warmer by Pat's presence.

She smiled kindly as he eased himself in next to her on the sofa, her soft hands guiding his face to hers, enfolding his lips in hers.

The stain of Marge's adultery, still so fresh on that chair, was nowhere near his thoughts. And later as he feasted on the sight of her beautiful, naked body next to him on the bed, he fought hard against what he knew he needed to talk about, but he had to come clean.

He started the conversation with a light caress, running the back of his fingers gently over the slopes of her side.

'Pat.' His voice sounded detached, something like The Good Vicar's, but it was not The Good Vicar talking. Maybe he *was* The Good Vicar now, watching from a distance, approving this confession while Andrew was out there doing the talking, laying himself bare before his lover.

Her eyes met his and smiled. *Tell me, tell me everything, unburden yourself, I'm here for you,* they said. So unlike Marge. She had been there physically, but he could not remember the times when she had actually listened to him.

'I have a confession to make.' It felt strange saying that. I have a confession to make. People usually confessed to their ministers not the other way round.

'You remember you were saying that you regretted not allowing your mum's funeral to be recorded?'

Pat pulled herself up slightly in the bed, her one hand fumbling for the duvet which she pulled over herself. This kind of confession did not require her to be naked.

Andrew considered covering himself as well, but resisted, preferring to get on with the task at hand.

'Yes?' She settled under the bedclothes, but he could sense the discomfort she was feeling. Maybe he should have chosen a better time, but he had started…

'Well I did. Tape it that is. But…' he quickly went on before she could intervene, '…I have not let anyone hear it yet, no-one, especially not McCready.'

He wished he was clothed, but covering himself now would indicate shame at what he had done and he was not ashamed of recording the service. He felt his nakedness acutely as she raised her eyes to his, and in the split second before she began to talk he tried to gauge her reaction. He read confusion, he read relief, he read betrayal and he read anger.

'Why Andrew? We asked you not to and you still went ahead. Why?'

He fought back the growing urge to cover himself and, borrowing the calm, reassuring voice from The Good Vicar, began to explain.

'I thought that it may be important at some point. I can't really explain why, but there is something about McCready that made me feel that perhaps recording the service would prove to be invaluable in getting to the root of what he's about. Gut feel I guess you could say, but one thing's for certain, I will never release the recording to anyone without your express permission. I promise you that.'

He watched the anger and betrayal fade as he spoke, now all he had to deal with was the confusion and, because he didn't have the answers, he knew he had to quell it by appealing to the relief.

'I'm sorry I was deceitful, but with everything happening with Brian I thought it was best at the time to go ahead and then sort it all out later when things calmed down and we could all think rationally. You remember a little while back you told me how your mum reacted to McCready's arrest and you said then that you perhaps regretted that we didn't record it. Well I think that was when we started to think rationally about it all.'

The anger and betrayal were completely gone now and the confusion had subsided to a slight lingering puzzlement.

'I'm not too sure how I should feel,' she said and pulled the duvet up slightly higher, 'but I think you may be right. There was certainly something about McCready that made mum react the way she did, but just what it was, I don't know. He's obviously not said anything to you?'

'I only met him that one time. He insisted that there was a connection, but he would not say at all. He wants me to talk to the Bridges, you know, the parents of the girl he killed. He wants me to convince them that he is truly sorry for that crime and is looking for their forgiveness.'

'No! You are kidding aren't you? I mean how cruel would it be to confront those poor people with that. No-one could forgive such a crime.'

'Sometimes forgiveness is the best way of recovering from such an event.' The Good Vicar did not feel comfortable speaking from a naked body, but knew he had to have his say here. 'Harbouring hatred and bitterness does not help heal the wound. Of course it's not easy, of course very few people are able to do this effectively but I have to at least try. I suspect that McCready may just divulge details of his other crimes if I can persuade the Bridges to forgive him. I know it's a type of emotional blackmail, but I have to do it for those other parents who don't know. They need the closure. Maybe I can just persuade the Bridges to feign forgiveness, that might work, but I really do feel that I have to try. I think that God is calling me to do this.' Either God or my own morbid curiosity.

'I think I understand,' she said and lowered her eyes while she thought it through. Eventually she looked up at him again and smiled, then said, 'Just out of curiosity, how did you manage to record the service. Brian checked the sound system before and did a sweep of the church. He didn't find anything.'

He was glad of the slight change of subject and grinned. 'A digital dictaphone. Tiny little thing stuck in my pocket. The sound quality is remarkable, you can hear everything. Amazing what modern technology can do nowadays. Come,' he said climbing off the bed, 'I'll show you.' He desperately needed an excuse to get dressed.

In his study he snapped on the light and swaggered over to his desk. 'Have a seat,' he called back as he moved behind his desk and sank into his chair. He felt comfortable again. Pat eased herself into the chair opposite and he pulled the drawer open.

'Andrew, what's wrong?' Pat responded quickly to the alarm on his face.

'It's gone!'

'What?'

'The dictaphone, It's gone. Someone's taken it!'

---oOo---

It had to have been The Rat. Who else? They were the only two who knew about it. But how? He tried to recall if he had seen the machine since the strange naked appearance of Alex that evening. Even if he had not been taken then, the unnaturalness of The Rat's existence might make it possible for him to walk through walls. He shuddered at that thought. He didn't believe in ghosts and didn't want to start, but...

It was too late to go up to The Ridge, but he was definitely going up there first thing in the morning.

Pat had eventually left after he had given numerous assurances that he would retrieve the machine. He paced the carpet in the study, willing the dawn to come, fighting off the tiredness that pushed down on him and the dread that welled up in him.

He could not sleep. Sleep brought dreams and dreams damaged him. He could feel his body call out for rest, the tense muscles screamed to be relaxed, his racing mind yelled at him to stop. But he could not. He was trance-like as he paced. If he stopped he would die. He had to keep moving. Where was Patmarge? She would look after him, she would protect him.

At least he was awake.

Maybe tea...or coffee...yes toffee. Where was Patmarge?

And a custard dodger. His legs felt weak, creaking under his weight. Maybe he should shave, he needed to look good for Alex. Alex's skin was so soft and smooth it would not do to have a prickly, scratchy face when he kissed Alex.

Why had the ceiling become the wall?

'Patmarge!' he yelled but forgot to use his vocal chords. He felt the blackness coming like a blanket to cover him, take him away and he screamed to make it go away, but it kept coming and slowly he gave himself up to it, feeling the tension in his body float away as he gave himself up to his fate.

He sniffed, then shuddered.

---oOo---

The floor dug into his hipbone and the bright light shattered against his eyelids. He groaned and forced his eyes open, blinking furiously to ease the pain. His temples throbbed in time to the booming bass of the headache and he wondered why he had been licking the carpet all night.

He rolled onto his back to alleviate the weight on his hip and waited patiently for his brain to update him on why he was lying on his study floor. I need to start work on my sermon was the first thought that came through.

He pushed himself up and then dragged his body into the chair, sinking into its softness where he stayed motionless for a while to let the beats per minute in his head reduce to an acceptable level.

In the kitchen he ran his hand though his hair, feeling the slight greasiness of it, then put the kettle on. He found his painkillers and set about assassinating the drummer in his skull. He had left the packet of jammy dodgers open on the counter and was onto the third one before he realised how stale they tasted. He washed what remained in his mouth down with the scalding tea, cursing first the heat of it, then the bitterness of the milk that had also been left out overnight.

The sauce of the baked beans had congealed and blackened round the rim of the tin, but the beans themselves looked, and thankfully tasted, okay. The sweetness of the second (milkless) cup of tea slowly brought him round to feeling half normal again and he cuddled the mug in his hands.

The fog was slowly freeing his mind up to go over the events of the previous night. A slight annoyance took hold as he realised he was experiencing a morning after the night before without having had the pleasure of the night before. And why did the name Patmarge keep coming to him?

He put that question aside as the missing black machine took on the starring role. He cursed out loud and braced himself for the reproval of The Good Vicar, already wincing at the pain the clip round the ear would add to his still throbbing head, but it didn't come. He looked round the kitchen, half expecting to see a physical manifestation of what he sometimes thought of as his altar ego. There was nothing there. This was odd. He tottered between panic and glee, then with a slight glint in the eye he addressed the kitchen with a loud experimental expletive.

Nothing. A twisted grin took over his mouth and he let a few more four lettered words fly, rising to his feet as his body seemed to gain strength from each one. Soon he was dancing around the room, his arms flailing in wild abandonment while the dam of pent up abuse waterfalled from his lips.

At last he leaned on the counter, gasping for breath, his head bowed. Then slowly his body began to shudder as the giggle grew to a full blown laugh and he raised his eyes to look out the window at the new world that lay outside and stared straight into the eyes of The Grinning Rat.

---oOo---

It was Eve at the front door and she ushered in The Good Vicar along with her big frame and a nervous giggle. 'I'm sorry, Father for coming round so early, but I couldn't sleep. I kept thinking about that young lad all night and I…'

She swallowed a nervous laugh that was about to bubble over as the state of her vicar hit home.

'Andrew?' He struggled to work out if it was an exclamation mark or a question mark that followed her outburst. A quesclamation mark. He wanted to grin evilly back at her, show her his new found freedom. But he had lost that as soon as The Rat had scurried away and he had answered the doorbell.

'Sorry Eve, you've caught me at a rather bad time. I…I think I collapsed on my office floor last night. Exhaustion. I haven't had a chance to tidy myself up. I must look a sight.'

Andrew, are you sure you're alright?'

No. 'I'm fine Eve. Funnily, falling asleep on my office floor like that has done me the world of good, I actually had a good night's sleep for the first time in a while.'

'And a most of the morning sleep too.' Eve added.

'What time is it?'

'Twelve-thirty.'

Andrew stared. Had he been asleep for that long? He was beginning to feel the benefit of it now that the grogginess of waking was fading.

'I really must clean myself up. Will you excuse me for a few minutes?'

'I'll make some tea.'

'Thanks. Oh, the milk's off. I forgot to put it into the fridge yesterday after you left.' He followed her through to the kitchen where she was already tsk tsking.

'Okay,' she laughed as she took in the scene in the kitchen. 'It's obvious that you can't look after yourself on your own. You go up and wash and I'll look after things here. Give me the front door keys too so I can go get a few things from the shop.'

He tumbled into the warm motherliness of Eve's suggestions and handed over the keys before heading upstairs. The shower refreshed him further and as he shaved, he watched himself carefully in the mirror, wondering at how glad he was that The Good Vicar had not abandoned him, and puzzling at how glad he had been when The Good Vicar had abandoned him.

The smell of frying bacon and eggs further warmed his mood as he walked downstairs. He half expected The Pale Blue Dressing Gown to be in the kitchen and that everything would be back to its pre-dream state, so much so that seeing Eve's smiling face as she placed a large plate down on the table just as he reached the door came as a slight shock.

'There you go Andrew,' she laughed, 'come and eat up.'

She manoeuvred herself into the chair opposite, a mug of tea in front of herself and watched as he sat down.

'Eat up.' She gestured with her head. With a smile he began to pick at his breakfast, but as the flavours mingled in his mouth, his hunger woke up and he tucked into the hearty meal, relishing the food and the care with which it had been prepared.

The Laugh watched him, ensuring that he was going to eat it all before she began to relax.

'Oh, I saw that young lad Alex outside the shop. I tried to talk to him, but he just ran away. We really must do something Andrew, we can't just leave him on the streets.'

---o0o---

'So you sendin' your fat bitch after me now?'

He held his temper, not looking in the direction the sniff and the voice came from.

'Nope,' dismissive. 'She did it of her own accord.'

'So you *do* fink of 'er as a fat bitch?'

Damn you, you bastard!

'Nope. There is only one person I know who has tried to speak to you recently, so it must be her you're talking about.' He turned now and stared straight into The Rat's eyes.

'You have something of mine.' He could feel the youngster try using the stare, the one that he could not look at, but Andrew did not flinch. 'Give it to me!'

'Snot yours. Remember I gave it you.' There seemed to be a slight panic in The Rat's voice.

Good, thought Andrew, he no longer has that power over me. 'So you do know what I'm talking about then. Give it to me.' He held out his hand for it, not taking his eyes off The Rat's.

The Rat shuddered slightly and seemed unsure of himself.

'I doan got it, whateva it is, I doan got nuffink of yours.'

Andrew flapped his hand at The Rat, his look demanding the machine.

'Orite.' The Rat lowered his eyes. 'Orite I jus' wannid to hear the funeral again meself.'

Should he believe that? He watched the young boy dig into his pocket and produce the machine. It felt good having it back in his hand, like it belonged there. He could almost feel The Good Vicar's voice delivering that half-baked eulogy.

---oOo---

'Well done Andrew, where was it?' Pat's relief was tangible when he produced the machine.

'Long story, but I'll give you the highlights.'

He filled Pat in on The Rat's involvement to date but didn't mention the fact that he appeared to have eternal youth.

'Are you sure he hasn't recorded over it or anything like that?' Pat asked once she had the full story.

'Goodness, I hadn't thought of that,' a panic knot tightened. He picked up the machine and rewound it slightly then pushed play.

'Go in peace,' he heard The Good Vicar addressing the congregation and felt the knot loosen.

'In the name of Christ, amen,' a few ragged voices replied, followed by the noises of some shuffling.

'Well that seems to be okay,' he breathed out his relief and leaned forward to turn the machine off when it suddenly sniffed at him and he pulled back as though burnt by it.

Then The Rat's tinny voice came out of the machine, ''e wants your gran'dorta. McCready says 'e wants your gran'dorta Arkayic.'

---oOo---

'Calm down dad, she's fine, she's with mum now. What is the matter?'

How could McCready get to Arkayic? He was safely tucked away in jail, there was no way he could do anything. And what about The Rat? Could he possibly have meant that he himself was after Arkayic? Unlikely. How could he get down to London anyway?

'You can ask mum, I'll call her.'

'Wait!' Andrew called to the abandoned phone.

'Andrew? What's going on? Why are you scaring Jane like that?' He knew the tone and hated it.

'I've just received a message threatening Arkayic and I needed to check that she was okay.'

'Who? Who's threatening Arkayic?'

He paused.

'Who, Andrew?' The impatience was growing.

'McCready.' He lowered his eyes and felt Pat's hand on his shoulder.

'McCready?' Another quesclamation mark. 'How Andrew? How would a man who is locked up in a high security jail do any harm to Arkayic?'

'I don't know. I just got a message saying that McCready wants Arkayic.'

'And who gave you this message?'

He glanced up at Pat, trying to get an extra supply of strength.

'That young lad, The Rat.'

'What? Alex? You are joking aren't you Andrew? How can you take anything that little hooligan says seriously? Can't you see...' Andrew heard a penny drop, but could tell it was the wrong currency. 'Oh I get it. You've got to stop this Andrew. Making up these far-fetched stories to try and make me come back will not work. This is ridiculous. You've got to stop it. And it's unfair on Jane, scaring her like that. Grow up will you.'

'Marge...'

'No Andrew, enough's enough. I don't want you calling here again making up stories. It won't work. I won't have it.'

'But…'

'No buts Andrew. Enough of this. Please don't call again.'

'But Marge, Pat heard…' he told the click on the other end of the line.

He sank back in the chair while Pat massaged his shoulders.

'What did she say?'

'She didn't believe me.'

'Oh Andrew, I'm so sorry, but Arkayic is alright isn't she?'

He nodded. 'She thought I was just trying to get attention.'

Pat gave a sad smile and he sighed.

'Okay, let's think logically about this.' He sat up a bit. 'We got into such a panic when we heard the message, but how can McCready get to Arkayic? Either he would have to break out of prison, or get someone else to do it. Now from what I remember from the press reports around the time he was caught was that they said he was a loner, so that's unlikely.'

Pat nodded. 'I recall that about him too. So why did that young lad, The Rat,' she seemed embarrassed by calling him that name, 'Why did he make such a suggestion?'

'He is rather prone to outrageous suggestions, but the scary thing is that he's never been wrong.'

---o0o---

He put the cup down on its coaster then settled into his chair, watching the computer screen as it booted up. He stretched across to grab the custard cream off the saucer. It felt good to have done some shopping, it brought a degree of normality to his life. It was amazing how much of the emptiness of the house could be filled with a few groceries.

The computer whirred and clicked under the desk and he let his thoughts wonder about Marge. He still had a nagging worry about the safety of Arkayic, but having logicked things out with Pat earlier, he felt that she was surely safe for the moment.

He had not really had the luxury of thinking about his future with Marge, if there was to be one at all. She was certainly not interested in getting back together at the moment and this, so it seemed, was without The Heathen being around. He hadn't heard mention of Brian from Marge and it would be unlikely that he could be with her at Jane's. Maybe he was staying nearby them in London. He made a mental note to ask Pat, gently of course, if she had heard from Brian.

The thought that The Heathen had just been an excuse, a manifestation of a greater issue, began to gnaw at his brain. He remembered Marge's accusations that he was always so caught up in the affairs of his congregation, leaving him with nothing in the emotional tank for the family. Had Marge's little fling been purely about getting an attention fix? She could have done better than The Heathen though. There were plenty of more suitable men in town, you only had to listen to Pat talking about Brian to realise what sort of an uncaring bastard he was. Never paid any attention to her needs…

His thoughts trailed off as he realised where they were leading. Was he, was The Stud Muffin, merely a distraction, a reaction, a search for some attention for Pat?

He sat back and cursed that thought with all its 'tions'. Even if it was true, why could he not be left to enjoy the moment? He knew where the thought came from and wanted to scream at The Good Vicar. Get out! Leave me alone! Let me live my life! But he knew now that The Good Vicar was such an integral part of him that they could never be separated. That little spell where he thought that he was free of that part of his conscience, exhilarating as it was, could never be permanent. The Good Vicar was attached with a spiritual superglue which there was no solvent strong enough to dissolve.

A picture of a tranquil beach, white sands, blue sky and turquoise sea flashed up on the screen and his attention shifted. A few clicks later and he was staring at a blank page. He rifled through some papers on his desk and found his list of readings for the year. He needed to start his sermon, life went on despite his personal turmoil, he still had some remnants of a congregation to serve.

The readings for Sunday included Matthew 18:21-35. Without picking up his Bible, he knew it was the parable of the servant who was forgiven his large debts by his master but failed to forgive a fellow servant who owed him a small amount. He stared at the reference for a long time.

---oOo---

'Just a follow up visit sir, may we come in?'

He was surprised, but ushered the two policemen into his lounge. The man who was going to replace the broken window was due in tomorrow he reminded himself as The Good Vicar offered the coppers some tea.

'Don't give them the custard creams, there're some stale jammy dodgers to get rid of,' he told The Good Vicar and got a clip over the back of his head which he took a strange delight in. Once in the kitchen he beat The Good Vicar to control of the hands and the jammy dodgers were on the plate and heading back to the lounge before anyone could say 'stigmata'.

'I'll bring the tea through in a second,' he said, leaving the two men to help themselves. He regretted not being there to see their faces as they realised how stale the biscuits were, but having played his practical joke, he wanted to think, to prepare himself for whatever the cops were going to say. There was something out of place here, unless Roger had run out and confessed to his brick throwing crime or, less likely though, The Rat had been a good citizen and reported what he had seen.

He quickly shovelled a custard cream into his mouth as he made the tea, ignoring the looks The Good Vicar gave him.

He poured, distributing the cups to the two uniformed men in an officious manner.

'Do have another biscuit,' he offered the plate.

'I'm fine thanks.'

The other one declined with a hand gesture.

He thought of pushing the issue slightly, doing a motherly Eve thing, *go on, there's plenty more,* but was afraid he would not keep a straight face so put the plate down.

The older of the two men sipped his tea, then began. 'Well sir, it's about that young lad that you think witnessed the incident, the one you say you recognised by his...' Oh yes, you do your very clever I don't believe you pause, '...his sniff.'

'Yes?'

'Well, we have not been able to locate him, he's not been hanging around his usual haunts and we were wondering if you perhaps knew where he lived?'

The two men leaned forward, just slightly, watching him closely.

Bloody Eve, she had gone and blabbed. He shot a warning glance over to The Good Vicar to say that this would probably not be the best time to be completely honest and open and was slightly surprised when he got an agreeing nod in return. Be sparing with the truth, but don't lie.

'No, I'm afraid I have no idea. I can ask around if you like. Eve, my secretary has lived here all her life, she knows just about everyone in town. Maybe she can tell us.' The Good Vicar winced at the way the truth was being stretched and brutalised, but said nothing.

'No, that won't be necessary. I'm sure he'll turn up somewhere.' It was Andrew's turn to watch closely and he knew for sure then that Eve had grassed. For a second he wished that God would bring down all the punishments he had threatened her with, but suspected that He was on Eve's side on this one.

'How long have you known this lad Father?' the older looking of the two men asked, trying, but failing to keep the suggestion that this must have come from Eve, out of his voice. It was an attempt to be offhanded, but the tone held too much interest.

'I can't say really. It's only been in the past few weeks that he's actually spoken to me. I guess he's just reaching that age where they're confident enough to be cocky. I think I may have seen him around once or twice before that, but you know how the kids all seem to dress the same, well I've never really distinguished him from the pack.'

The older policeman shot a *should we believe him* glance over at his colleague who replied with an *I guess so, he's a priest after all* look.

Andrew watched the interchange and then fired a *fooled them, didn't I do well* look at The Good Vicar who glared back at him.

'Have another biscuit,' he held out the plate, 'go on, you may as well finish them.' He grinned inwardly as the men squirmed out their declinations. He showed them to the door, then started to head back to his study. Even The Good Vicar was annoyed with Eve. This would just bring more unwanted attention to the whole miserable case. He could picture the headlines; *Homeless Boy Not Ageing, Youngster Stays Young,* and from the tabloids; *Ratboy Finds Secret Of Eternal Youth,* or even *Eternal Youth Rattles Town.*

He stopped in the hall for a minute wondering what to do about all this. Could the police really have believed Eve's story? Had it actually been Eve who had gone to them, or was it someone else to whom Eve had let slip that had called the cops? And what exactly had they been told?

The phone rang, its tone as always was completely neutral. It never said 'good news coming' or 'bad news coming'. It just demanded. 'Answer me! Answer me!' As with a child crying 'feed me! Feed me!' you just had to respond to the call and then deal with the shit later.

Father Gregory's voice was very welcome.

'I've pulled some strings, called in a few favours and managed to get you some time with the Bridges. Tomorrow evening if you can do it?'

'That's great,' Andrew said while wondering if it really was. 'Well done.'

---o0o---

The bed looked too big. It was meant for two and, as he undressed, he wouldn't have minded who was to lie next to him, Pat? Marge? Eve? Hell, he would even take Audrey tonight despite her being old enough to be his mum. He just wanted someone to be there, a womanly presence to soothe his passage into sleep.

He stood naked, folding his clothes away, then turned back to the bed. Two lifeless eyes peered at him over the bedclothes. Instinctively his hands covered his nudity but other than this, he did not recoil from the vision.

Peggy had never threatened when she was alive and now, in death, he did not even have that uncomfortable feeling that he had when he spoke to those lifeless eyes.

He waited for her to talk, somehow knowing that she had a message for him.

Without the slightest flicker of life from the corpse-spirit on the bed, her voice came. It was strong in tone, but ethereal and distant in volume.

'Go back to see him. Talk to him. He does not understand.'

'Understand what?' Now he did feel a little foolish talking to the ghost in his bed.

'He is going about things the wrong way. Tell him that. Tell him Peggy says that this is not the way.'

This was not making sense and the ghostly Peggy seemed to register frustration without any of its features changing.

'Tell him Peggy says this is not the way and tell him that she says that she is sorry.' The voice was suddenly urgent and Andrew realised that she beginning to fade.

'Tell him,' she urged, 'tell him, or Arkayic will die.'

---oOo---

The phone stared sullenly back at him, daring him almost. The urge to ring Jane and check on Arkayic thundered in his breast, but he dared not. He glanced at the clock. It had been at least ten minutes since he last looked at it, but it only registered two of the ten. He gritted his teeth and sighed. Should he make another cup of tea? That would help pass another five minutes, but he couldn't face a third cup.

He didn't feel like having any breakfast. Not yet, not until he had made this call. He stood up, paced round his desk and made toward the door where he stopped and listened to the silence of the house. It seemed to whisper, *tell him, tell him, tell him.*

He nodded without knowing he had done so, then turned back into the study. The clock had ticked on another two minutes.

He had tried to figure out if last night had been a dream after he had gone to bed, or a vision as he was getting ready for bed, but each time he had tried to focus his mind on the question, his head had filled up with the sound of laughter, Peggy's laughter.

He tried a different approach now. Was what he experienced last night a message from God, a message from Peggy, a message from…you know, the one from the really hot basement, or was it all just his fatigued and deranged brain making it up?

There was no laughter at these thoughts, but no answer forthcoming either.

'What is not the way? Why is Peggy sorry?' He tested out another approach, his verbalised thoughts pushing the quiet aside. The silence answered by returning in a crashing wave, covering over the question and burying it in its eerie surf.

The clock. Four more minutes. Maybe he gets in early. His hand reached for the phone then fell back again. He must wait. He could not say why he had to, but something told him that he could not call before nine. It was irrational but it also made perfect sense. Three minutes.

He drummed his fingers lightly on the desk and stared at the clock. Two minutes. He drummed some more. One minute.

Suddenly a fear took hold of him. What if… he started to think. What if…

The clock ticked over to nine and he grabbed at the phone, telling The Good Vicar that he needed to be in on this conversation.

---o0o---

'It's risky.'

'I know, but I must do it.'

There was a long contemplation-filled silence before the voice came back. 'I'm not sure the powers that be will allow it.'

'It is really important.'

There was another long pause before, 'Okay. I'll see what I can do, but I'm not making any promises.'

---o0o---

'Harry?' What an unpleasant surprise. 'It's Andrew, Jane's dad.'

The Layabout grunted what Andrew took to be a grunt of vague recognition but wasn't sure if it was recognising him or Jane.

'Is Jane there?'

'No.'

'Marge?'

'No. They've gone out.' Hooray, more than a syllable.

'Is Arkayic with them?'

'Nah, left me to look after her didn't they?'

It could be worse I suppose.

'She okay?'

'She's fine, sleeping at the moment. Shall I tell Jane you called?'

'Um…No. Don't worry. I'll call back later.'

A grunt.

He hung up and stared into the mid-distance for a moment. He could not shake his unease over the safety of his granddaughter.

---o0o---

'Morning, Father Andrew.' A decidedly nervous laugh followed. And so she should be nervous, he thought. He wondered if he should get The Good Vicar to handle this, or could he trust Andrew to do it?

'Morning Eve,' The Good Vicar stepped in, almost as though he sensed that this was his territory. Eve, despite her transgressions, was one of the few allies he had left.

'Cup of tea?' The voice bowed and scraped while the frame from which it came stood a few paces further away than normal, wringing its hands.

'Please.' Andrew prevented The Good Vicar from following this up with a smile, the result was a sort of kind grimace. 'And a biscuit if we've got, unless they're rich tea.'

'I'll check. I think there may be some jammy dodgers; your favourite.' She giggled.

My favourite? Since when? He tried to think when he had ever given any indication that he like the stigmata biscuits.

'Thanks.' The Good Vicar said while Andrew picked up the pile of post on the desk.

Eve snorted a frightened laugh and scurried away from the potential postal eruption.

'You should have the quote for the organ overhaul in there, the man promised to send it out this week,' she laughed as she returned with the tea.

'Yes, it's quite a bit more than I expected. We're going to struggle to raise the money.'

'We've always managed in the past,' Eve tittered kindly.

'Yes, but that was before I chased half the congregation away,' mostly the rich ones, Andrew added to The Good Vicar's comment. His sentiments sounded as empty as he expected the church to be on Sunday. What had he done? Should he be spending time on one probably condemned soul at the expense of those ones who had, until last Sunday, regularly attended his church? But then again, it had been God who had called him to minister to McCready, hadn't it?

'We'll find a way,' The Laugh interrupted his thoughts and he knew that he had to move on to the issue of her not keeping their little secret.

'The police came by last night.' He watched her closely for a reaction, but there was just the nervous giggle, then a slightly furrowed brow.

'What did they want?'

'They said they were following up on the brick through the vicarage window.' Still nothing more than the usual skittishness.

'Do they have a lead?'

'No, but they did ask about that young lad Alex, The Rat.'

'Why would they be asking about him? Do they think that he threw that brick?'

Andrew was puzzled. He had been convinced that Eve had been shooting off her mouth about their theory on The Rat, but she was showing no sign now that she may be guilty of having done so. Normally she was easy to read, but the word guilt was not what was coming up at the moment.

'No, I don't think he threw the brick, but I told the police that I think he saw who did.'

'Oh, so maybe that's why they were asking.' Then suddenly the thought struck her and she half hiccoughed, half laughed, 'You don't think that they…' Her eyes widened.

'Maybe, I'm not sure. They may have asked a few questions around town and reached a similar answer to what we did. They did seem edgy about it all. You haven't told anyone have you?'

She fired off a shriek of laughter, but suddenly swallowed it. 'No Father, of course not.' She seemed almost hurt by the question and he needed to act fast.

'Oh, I wasn't accusing you,' The Good Vicar glared at Andrew, annoyed that he had been forced into telling a white lie. 'I was really asking the question given that you wouldn't tell anyone, why do they seem suspicious? I trust you Eve. I'm sorry I didn't mean to sound accusing, it came out all wrong.'

Eve laughed a slightly forced laugh and wobbled an acceptance of the apology.

Andrew's sense of relief was minimal. He could trust Eve more than he thought, as long as he threatened her with the fires of hell, but the worrying thing was that the police seemed to be nosing around about The Rat's strange existence. They may take him into council care if they thought he was homeless. This would be a catastrophe. The Rat was a vital piece of the McCready puzzle that he could ill afford to lose.

---o0o---

Oh good, that should be Father Gregory. He dropped his keys on the hall table and dashed through to his office and grabbed the phone.

'Hello,' he heard the cheerful, hopeful tone in his voice.

'Andrew.'

'Marge?' His stomach knotted, there seemed to be a touch of hysteria in her voice.

---o0o---

'Andrew? It's your bishop speaking.'

'Ian, how are you?'

'Fine. I was just calling to see how you're doing. No more strange dreams or healings of paedophiles or anything like that?'

'Oh no, not at all,' he gave a fake chuckle.

'Good, good. That's what I like to hear. Now Andrew listen to me. I want you to make it public that you regret the whole debacle. We can't have people deserting the Church. You need to win your congregation back. You made a mistake and you need to correct it, do you understand me? I don't care how you do it, but you need to restore the damage you have done.'

'Yes Ian. I'll do my best.' He listened to the detached voice that meekly betrayed his boiling anger.

---o0o---

'Gregory?' He had not had time to think between the two previous calls, but hopefully this third one would bring good news.

'It's arranged. I had to pull a few strings and call in one or two favours, but you should be safe. The Governor has agreed, but it took some convincing. Hopefully this yields some dividends.'

'Thanks Gregory. When can we do it?'

'How soon can you get here?'

'Give me an hour.'

---o0o---

Marge's anger at him calling again and the bishop's patronising demands stayed in his study as he quickly readied himself. He was just at the front door when the phone rang again.

'Bloody hell!' he cursed and hurried back to answer it.

'Yes?' he demanded angrily of the receiver.

'Oh, sorry Andrew, have I called at a bad time?'

'No, no,' his emotions back-pedalled quickly. 'Sorry I was just on my way out.'

'I'm sorry. It can wait, I can call back later.'

'No, it's okay. I'm not in that much of a rush, what is it Pat?'

'I was just wondering if you'd like to come over for tea later? I've been thinking about this McCready business and was wanting to discuss some things with you, but it's not urgent.'

He paused for a second then said, 'Actually I was just on my way out to see him. Do you want to come with?'

---o0o---

They had kissed, a warm lover's kiss, but there was no time for more, The Stud Muffin must wait. The car hummed along the motorway and he felt strangely content. The woman beside him was beautiful and he was in love again, enjoying the discoveries one makes as one moves from friendship to intimate: the two freckles on her belly, the subtle scent of her shampoo and the way she drew her legs up on the couch and wriggled her toes, an action that their pre-lover meetings had been too formal to admit.

She seemed contented too as he shot a glance over at her. Her posture was relaxed, her alert eyes caressed the passing countryside and her lips betraying the merest hint of the full blown smile that lay beneath.

Suddenly he wanted to keep driving and never stop, forget McCready, forget The Rat, forget Marge, forget Eve, forget the lot of them. Just him and Pat forging a new life, a happy life somewhere.

But he knew that he could not. The dream would chase him wherever he went. He had to see this one through.

'Andrew.' He loved the way her voice caressed his name. 'Andrew, I want you to play Mr McCready the recording of mum's funeral. I've given it a lot of thought and, well I think it's what she would have wanted. The more I think about it, the more I believe that she seemed to feel that she owed him something. I can't quite put my finger on what exactly it is that makes me think that, maybe it's just a mother and daughter sixth sense thing. I really don't know, but will you do that Andrew. Will you let him hear the recording?'

He paused before answering. Granting Pat her request was tempting, doing something to please your lover always seemed like a good idea. It helped store up points for when you needed something, but, as The Good Vicar reminded him, he needed to think of the bigger picture.

'I will, I promise, but not just yet. Certain things need to happen before I can let him hear the recording.' He shuddered as he played the words back to himself. They echoed McCready's words during his first visit.

'What things?' He couldn't hear any disappointment in her voice and was relieved.

'The funny thing is I'm not sure. McCready must divulge the link between him and your mother for one, but he said he wouldn't do so till certain things had happened, but I don't know what they are. The recording is the only card we've got to play with and we have to be very careful as to when we finally use it. We can't play it too soon.'

Pat nodded and gently rested her hand on his thigh.

'Okay my love. I'll leave it up to your judgement.' She turned slightly in her seat and smiled.

His leg tingled where she touched him and her words tingled in his ears. He waited for The Good Vicar's rebuke, but it didn't come, instead he found The Good Vicar nodding back sagely. The issue at hand was bigger than infidelity.

---oOo---

Father Gregory paced the floor nervously.

'You trust this guard not to say anything?' Andrew was being infected by his colleague's mood.

'He's one of the few I trust implicitly. A good Christian fellow and not bigoted at all. He's the only one I've seen who treats McCready with any decency. The rest hate his guts and it shows. McCready's sort are the lowest of the low here.'

'And the Governor?'

'Oh, he'll not say anything. He's going out on a limb here so hopefully we get a result. What's taking them so long?' He checked his watch. 'It's not too far to get to the Bridges', but I don't want you to have to keep them waiting.'

Andrew suddenly found himself wondering how Pat would cope with waiting in the car, both here and at the Bridges'. He could not ask her to join him, especially not at the later appointment. He hadn't thought that through when he had invited her to join him. Maybe she could go shopping for a bit while he met with the Bridges.

He opened his mouth to try and calm Father Gregory down when a knock came at the door.

Gregory jumped across the room and wrenched the door open. McCready was ushered in by a young, serious looking guard. He looked straight across at Andrew, locking him in with his steel-grey eyes, eyes that were now full of life.

'Good afternoon, Father.' The words strolled out of his mouth and a grin tugged at his lips.

Andrew stood and nodded his greeting, then flinched slightly as an aftershock of the McCready Christ dream flashed briefly in his mind.

'Paul, please sit.' Father Gregory was like a nervous teenager entertaining his first date.

The convict moved into the offered chair and half slouched in it.

'May we speak alone?' he turned to face Father Gregory for the first time since entering the room.

'Afraid not. This visit is pretty hush-hush. You're here under the pretence of visiting me so if I'm not here, people will get suspicious.'

'I'm quite okay with Father Gregory hearing what is said.' The Good Vicar thought that this would help.

McCready contemplated this for a few seconds then nodded his head. 'So be it, Father.' He addressed Andrew. 'Firstly I want to thank you for restoring my sight, Father.'

'It was not me that cured you, it was God.' The Good Vicar said before Andrew had a chance to comment.

'But you were the one who prayed for me, Father. No one else would believe me, Father.'

'Who says I believed you?' Andrew chipped in before The Good Vicar could answer.

McCready raised a mildly surprised eyebrow. 'You didn't believe me, Father?'

'I don't know what to believe about you, all my dealings with you have been…er, peculiar to say the least. However, it's not important what I believe about you, but it's what God knows that matters.' The Good Vicar had grabbed the microphone back in a comic battle for the limelight.

McCready eyed Andrew suspiciously for a moment, then flung his head back and laughed. It was a surprisingly pleasant sound, not the evil, maniacal laugh Andrew had expected.

'I'm sorry Father, you're quite right. I must say I was sceptical about the whole thing myself. Not about me being blind, I can assure that I was, Father. But I was sceptical about whether you would come that first time.' He smiled a warm genuine smile that echoed back off Andrew although he felt a little uncomfortable returning it.

'So Father, are you going to let me hear Peggy Deane's funeral service?'

'Are you going to explain the connection between you and her?'

'I told you Father, things must happen before I can divulge that.' His eyes took on a hard glint like he was daring Andrew to defy him.

'And I told you that until you told me the connection I would not let you hear it. That was the deal.' He sensed Father Gregory lean forward and knew a comment regarding catch 22 was about to be launched from that direction.

He felt The Good Vicar give a quick glance over at Father Gregory, warning him to keep silent. A warm glow flowed through Andrew as Father Gregory sat back. The Good Vicar was trusting him with these negotiations.

McCready's glare lasted a moment, then slowly faded to a smile which Andrew could not help thinking was insincere.

'A bit of an impasse, Father. But don't be concerned, Father, the things I talk of will happen, I can assure you of that, Father.'

Andrew nodded, then remained silent for a few seconds till he heard Father Gregory's chair creak as his colleague shifted his weight uneasily. McCready had not taken his eyes off Andrew's.

'Before I came here the first time,' he measured the distance between each word, 'I had a dream. In the dream a voice told me to come and see you.'

Father Gregory and The Good Vicar looked up, surprised. McCready nodded as though agreeing with something he already knew.

'I have had another dream and that is why I am here.' He paused, waiting for The Good Vicar to stop him, but no rebuke came so he went on. 'I dreamt of Peggy Deane. In the dream she told me to tell you two things.'

McCready's eyes registered his surprise and he leaned forward slightly.

'I think we need to be very careful here,' Andrew continued, 'I am not sure that any of us know what we are dealing with. This may all be strange coincidences, dreams brought about by stress. We must be careful not to read too much into it.'

'What did she say?' McCready had shifted forward in his seat and his voice was tinged with a begging tone.

Andrew waited a second before answering, once again enjoying the power he held over the monster sitting in front of him. Then he drew in his breath and began.

'The first thing she said to me in the dream, and I must add that it was a dream and may well mean nothing, but the first thing she said to me was that you are going about things the wrong way.' He stopped to let it sink in, watching The Paedo, watching his steel-greys all the time, hoping for a sign or something.

McCready sat back, a look that was a crossbreed of bemusement and puzzlement was etched on his face for a second, then left, leaving a stony ponderance imprint. He nodded slowly, then said, 'And the second thing?'

Andrew could detect that something in his voice had changed. It was very subtle, but it seemed the assuredness had dropped a fraction. He shot a quick glance over at Father Gregory to see how he was reacting to this. He was studying The Paedo intently, seeming to be trying to read how McCready was taking this, although there was also a hint of puzzlement in his look too. The Good Vicar was also eying the prisoner closely.

'She also said to tell you that she was sorry.'

The steel-greys hadn't left Andrew's eyes in terms of the direction they looked in, but which had appeared to have lost a bit of focus, now jolted into full concentrated focus for a moment before hurriedly hiding the shock that had suddenly appeared and then guiltily slunk off to the side.

A thought brushed lightly through Andrew's mind that there was a welling up in those steel-greys, but it floated off before he could lay any grasp on it.

There was a long silence. Father Gregory was now staring at Andrew, his mouth slightly open. Andrew stared at McCready, feeling almost detached from the emotions he appeared to have stirred up in the man. McCready stared blankly at the floor near Andrew's feet.

He waited, knowing it was not up to him to make the next move and in the silence Andrew heard his heart beating loudly in his ears, then the whispered voice of The Good Vicar came. *Hold your nerve, hold your nerve.* Out of the corner of his eye he caught a slight movement from Father Gregory and with a minimal shake of his head he shot a warning glance over at him. Father Gregory shrunk silently back in his chair.

Almost a full minute passed before McCready finally stirred. He did not raise his eyes, but pushed himself up slightly in his chair and said in a hoarse whisper, 'If you follow the canal north from behind your church for about a mile and a half, you will get to a lock. A hundred yards up from the lock on the left hand side, there is a storm drain that is no longer used. In there you will find the remains of Shirley Creswell.'

---o0o---

'Have you heard from Brian?' For some reason Andrew didn't want to talk about his visit to McCready. He should have been feeling elated, vindicated even that his persistence had paid a dividend. The Creswells could now have closure over their daughter. Of course they would prefer to have found her alive, but at least now they knew. They could bury her and put an end to the torturous wondering.

He heard Pat answering his question, but it was a mumbled murmur against the angry roar of his thoughts. McCready was toying with them. Despite all the contemplative looks and emotional confessions, Andrew could not shake the feeling that it was all part of an elaborate act, that he was stringing them along, tossing them this little carrot to spur them on to something else, but what? The Good Vicar concurred with Andrew's sentiments.

Father Gregory had been ecstatic. McCready had asked to return to his cell soon after revealing the whereabouts of Shirley Creswell's body. He had not said anything further, just sat staring at the ground.

Once he had been escorted off by the same serious guard, Gregory was on his feet and pacing the room again.

'That was brilliant Andrew. Stroke of genius playing him like that with the dream of Peggy Deane. I mean it's quite obvious, looking with hindsight, that he has some attachment to Peggy, but you...' he stopped pacing and looked across at Andrew, a huge grin on his face, '...you had the foresight to realise that this was a way to get to him. Brilliant! How on earth did you think up the dream story? I am in awe...' His voice trailed off while the smile stuck around for a few moments feeling foolish before slinking away too.

'What is it Andrew?'

He looked up from his thoughts and smiled weakly.

'Just a bit overawed I guess. I didn't think it would have had such an effect.'

'Andrew? Andrew?' Pat was calling him back to the present.

'Hmm? Oh Sorry Pat, you were saying?'

She eyed him for a moment, her brow slightly crossed.

'I was asking what happened with McCready.' He heard a note of exasperation and winced. It was just like Marge when he hadn't been listening to her. 'Did you hear anything I said about Brian?'

He shook his head, then cast a quick glance over at her, smiling sadly.

'I'm sorry Pat. Yes, I was miles away. Something very strange happened with McCready and I was trying to get my head round it.'

'Oh, I'm sorry. You should have said.' He could hear that she was just like Marge used to be when they had first married. He hated these kind of thoughts. They were the kind of thoughts he expected to come from a pious looking Good Vicar, but these weren't coming from that quarter.

'No, I'm sorry. I really need to learn to pay attention to those close to me. I get too caught up in things sometimes.'

'That's okay Andrew. What happened with McCready then?'

'Tell her everything,' The Good Vicar whispered in his ear. 'She deserves to know the truth.'

So he told her, but not the truth as he knew it, but rather the truth as Father Gregory had seen it. How could he tell her that he had had a vision involving her dead mother?

She listened without interrupting and only when he stopped did she say anything.

'I don't quite know how to feel. I am happy that he has confessed to Shirley Creswell's murder but I don't feel comfortable with you using mum's death like that. Are you sure *you're* going about things the right way?'

He wished now that he had told his version of the truth, but it was too late. To deflect he said, 'Well, we can't jump the gun on this, we still need to see if his story checks out.'

'Humph.' She saw through his feeble attempt at changing the subject and he felt that the love he thought they had was ebbing away almost as quickly as it seemed to have welled up. Maybe it was just a rebound thing, for both of them. He wished he had paid attention to her answer about Brian now. He could have perhaps judged if there was any feelings left there. And he wanted to slap that smug look off The Good Vicar's face.

'I'm sorry Pat. I wasn't using your mother's death against Mc-Cready, I did have that dream. I don't know what it all meant, but I thought that maybe I would get an answer if I told McCready about it. It obviously touched a nerve, but I'm still none the wiser as to what the connection is.' He shifted the car down a gear to take a sharp bend, then glanced across at Pat after he straightened again.

Her mouth was slightly opened and she was staring at him but she could not take his gaze and looked away as soon as their eyes met, her lower jaw snapping closed. He could feel the wedge being driven between them and wanted to cry out for it to stop, the thought of driving off somewhere, anywhere away from all this, surged in him again.

'Pat?'

'I…I don't know what to say Andrew. I am pleased that you seem to have made progress with Mr McCready, don't get me wrong, but I just wish that mum wasn't involved, real or dreamt. She's hardly been gone and already there seems to be things trying to sully the memory of her. I…I don't want that to happen to her, not like with…'

Dad! She was going to say 'dad' wasn't she? Andrew ached to coax the word out of her but The Good Vicar had been half a step ahead of him and grabbed the vocal chords.

'Pat, don't let that happen. You have your memories of your mother, good memories. She was a good woman, nothing can change that. You must remember the positive things about her.'

'But how?' She almost wailed and it sounded so strange coming from her, she always seemed so calm and rational. 'It seems that she is linked to that monster. How can she be good and connected to that murderous man?'

Andrew fumbled for a reply and was relieved when The Good Vicar answered.

'It seems that your mum was able to see past the sin of the man and see the man himself. Love the sinner, not the sin we as Christians preach. It is not an easy thing to do, even more difficult when dealing with the evil that McCready did. I know. I struggle to see him as anything but an evil man. But your mother, she was a special person. I can see that now, she practised what we preach. I wish I could be more like she was. She was a true Christian, a good Christian woman.'

The Good Vicar eased back slightly now as he felt his words having an effect. He was caught between continuing to comfort Pat and risk reversing those hinted at feelings that she was beginning to cool in her relationship with Andrew, or continue to comfort her and in effect condone this adulterous relationship.

Andrew saw his chance and jumped in. 'Can you see her in that light, my love? Can you see that any connection she could have with McCready would have to be good. That is what she was like.'

Pat gave a teary smile and a half sob. She nodded, then sniffed.

'You're right Andrew.' She wiped the tear away and mumbled a thanks. After a few seconds she put her hand on his thigh again and stroked it gently. He shot a glance across to her and their eyes met. She smiled an *on the road to recovery* smile.

They pulled into the street where the Bridges' lived and Andrew thought for a second about putting off this visit. He was afraid of what it would bring to light and didn't want to face that. Also, he didn't want to leave Pat now when she needed him.

But duty called and Father Gregory's voice saying he had had to pull a few strings to get this meeting set up rang in his ear.

'We're here,' he said pulling up to the curb. 'I'll have to go in alone, you understand?'

Her head nodded 'yes' as her eyes screamed 'no'.

'Do you want to go into town, there's that nice little coffee shop that should still be open. I could meet you there?'

He watched her walk up the road and wrestled with The Good Vicar who was busy preventing his legs from following her. At last he turned and faced the Bridges' front door. It was a non-descript door that didn't want to be noticed. It seemed to scream out that nothing of interest happens behind it so clear off, there's nothing to see. He took a tentative step down the path.

---o0o---

Although he had never set foot in the house before, Chantelle's absence seemed to scream out at him from the moment David Bridges opened the door.

The scream came from the haunted, drawn features of the slight man in the doorway. It yelled in the silent darkness of the hall behind him, it trilled in the musty smell of the close lounge he was ushered into and echoed in the empty womb of the mousy, nervous woman who sat wringing her hands in the rather old fashioned, floral covered sofa.

But worse than the screams were the accusing look that he got from the gaunt face of David Bridges. For just a second he thought he heard The Good Vicar say, *why didn't I follow Pat to the coffee shop,* but when he looked over at him, The Good Vicar had a determined, set look on his face.

Kirsten Bridges would have been a pretty woman had it not been for the mad glint in her eyes that took over her features. It was a deep-shock madness and she seemed to cower in the corner of the sofa on which she sat.

'Kirsty, this is the priest I told you about.' The Accusing Eye's voice was soft and had a tearful tinge to it which surprised Andrew. He did not look like the tearful type. He was hard and tough, a nude woman stretched lazily down his upper arm from the sleeve of his football shirt and his square jaw sported a dark fuzz of metal filings stuck to a magnet.

Kirsty fluttered frightened eyes at Andrew and tried to move deeper into the sofa.

'I'm sorry, but she's been like this pretty much since she saw...' David lowered his voice slightly but it was still loud enough for all to hear, '...you know, the body.'

Andrew was shocked. He had not been expecting this. He didn't know quite what to say.

'Please sit.' David offered him a seat which he gratefully took, noting that the tearful note had left the voice. He eased himself into the slightly uncomfortable chair and pushed The Good Vicar forward.

'I want to start by saying that I am truly sorry for your loss. I cannot begin to imagine what it must be like for you.' He was addressing The Frightened Eyes but sensed that his words were bouncing off a protective shield her madness had created around her. He would need something special to get past the shield.

He glanced across at David who nodded and shrugged simultaneously.

'I don't know if you are aware that I have visited the man who caused you this hurt.' He was caught between addressing The Frightened Eyes or The Accusing Eyes so he spoke to the naked woman on The Accusing Eye's bicep. David had been unnervingly civil so far and Andrew hoped it would stay that way.

'And I feel that I owe you an explanation. I can't imagine that what has happened in this case would meet with your approval at the moment.'

He paused and met the accusing eyes, waiting for the accusing words. David shifted uneasily, but did not falter in his gaze.

He wants to be angry, but is scared of the priest's collar, Andrew whispered in The Good Vicar's ear. *I knew that* came back in a look.

It would be nice if we were offered some tea, and a biscuit, I could do with a custard cream, he thought, but left it a thought to allow The Good Vicar to continue.

'Are you a religious man Mr Bridges?' That took The Accusing Eyes by surprise.

'Not really,' the reply was defensive.

'And Mrs Bridges?' he asked the naked woman, then shot a glance over at The Frightened Eyes. They shrunk back from him.

'She was, before all this happened.' There was anger in the voice and, Andrew noted with a bit of worry, confidence. 'Went to church regularly till her God...' Andrew looked straight into the accusing eyes, daring them, '...until her God let her down.' It was almost mumbled.

Andrew wanted to cry out and say, 'That same God has let me down,' but he had the upper hand now and couldn't flinch if he wanted to hold on to it.

'I'm sorry to hear that,' he managed to get a drop of judgement into The Good Vicar's heartfelt reply. 'It may be a little difficult for you to understand my actions, but I will try and explain them anyway. I did not go to see him on my own volition, I felt that God had asked me to go.'

'Yeah, that same God you don't really believe in,' Andrew piped up and was given a withering look from The Good Vicar.

'I had a dream saying that I should go and see McCready and...'

As he said the paedophile's name Kirsty Bridges moaned loudly and he cast a glance over at her. There was a split second of pain the uttering of that name caused before she sank back down into her madness. He looked quickly at The Accusing Eyes, fearful that he would lose the hold he seemed to have over the man.

'...well in the dream I was told that he needed my help. I realise that this sounds rather crazy in this day and age, but I do believe that it was God calling me to this task.' Andrew stared at The Good Vicar. He did not believe that it was God's calling, but The Good Vicar didn't lie, he was prohibited from lying. Did a part of the whole, a part of the human being called Andrew Compton, a part of him that he referred to as The Good Vicar, did this slice of his personality really believe that?

'That is why I went to see him,' The Good Vicar went on, oblivious of Andrew's thoughts. 'I did not go lightly into it, I spent a lot of time thinking it over and making sure in my own mind that this was God's call.'

'Speak for yourself,' Andrew let the thought float by unspoken.

'I hope you can understand what I am saying?'

The Accusing Eyes betrayed little but seemed to give a slight nod as if to say 'go on, I'll make up my mind when you're finished'.

As The Good Vicar drew in a breath to continue, Andrew was sure that he saw the naked woman wink at him.

'You probably heard on the news about his blindness?'

The Accusing Eyes nodded and the nude woman winked again. Andrew wanted to wink back, but restrained himself. It was really The Stud Muffin's job to wink at naked girls, but he was not here, he stayed in the bedroom.

'Well I cannot say with one hundred per cent confidence that he was actually blind, but he did give the appearance of being blinded. Amongst other things he asked me to pray for his sight to be restored. Again you must understand that it is my duty as a priest to pray for the sick. It was a tough call for me to make. I was not convinced that he was blind and I did not want to offer a prayer based on a lie, but I also could not deny the request if it was genuine.

'I decided to leave it to God. I prayed out loud for his sight to be restored, while silently I prayed that God would judge the man accordingly if he was lying.'

'He was lying.'

Andrew's eyes came a close second to The Accusing Eyes in meeting the mad ones and caught them just in time to see the madness come crashing back down on the sliver of sanity that had briefly sparked there. Out of the corner of his eye, Andrew thought he saw the naked woman cover her breasts, almost as if she was ashamed of her nudity as Eve had been in the Garden of Eden when God came calling.

'Kirsty?' David Bridges was at her side, grabbing her hand, a pleading look on his face. He had not seen the madness fall back into place.

'Kirsty?' he pleaded but she shrank back from him.

Suddenly The Accusing Eyes were on Andrew, but they were slightly damp and softer.

'Pray for her Father. Pray for her like you did for that monster. She deserves it more than he ever did. Pray for her.'

The Good Vicar was wrong footed by this sudden plea, but after his initial shock he nodded slowly.

Andrew tried to scream at The Good Vicar. 'No! McCready was faking it, Mad Eyes is not. How will it look if you supposedly cured the paedo but can't cure his victim? Not a good advert for the Church.'

But The Good Vicar brushed him aside as he made the horizontal bar of the cross in the air, then took the hand of The Mad Eyes.

---oOo---

The Good Vicar was pensive in the car on the way home, wondering if he had done the right thing. It had seemed right at the time, but now...?

Pat seemed deep in thought too, but he did not have too much time to concentrate on her and what was worrying her, so the journey passed in silence.

He was nowhere closer to working out if he had done the right thing by the time he turned into his road after dropping Pat off. He had not arranged to see her again and she had not invited him in.

As he drew near the Vicarage, he noticed a figure pacing on the pavement in front of the house. It quickly crystallised into Sean.

'Dad, Arkayic is missing!' He had not even opened the car door or window, in fact, he was not even certain that Sean's lips had moved, but he heard the message clearly in his head.

---oOo---

'Calm down Marge,'

Because you're gabbling and I can't understand a word you're saying you silly woman.

'I need you to be calm, please, talk slowly. When did it happen?'

Slower still would be nice.

'I see, and what do the police say?'

Didn't I warn you? Didn't I tell you that she was under threat?

'Of course I'm upset Marge, I just need to understand what's happened.'

But no, you wouldn't listen. You thought I was just trying desperately to get you back. Don't you understand that this is far bigger and more complex than either you or I could begin to comprehend?

'I need some time to think. How's Jane doing?'

Yes, I realise not fine, but under the circumstances, how's she doing? Is that layabout being of any use?

'Is Harry with her?'

Well at least I was physically around and not down the pub every time we had a crisis.

'Okay, you go look after her. I will see. I think Sean will come down.'

But somehow I feel that I need to stay here. The answers to all this will be here, not in London.

---oOo---

'But she needs you dad. You have to go.'

This was going to be tricky. How do you explain that you've got a feeling that you should not go down to London to comfort your wife and daughter when they need you more than at any time previously? You weren't even sure that the feeling you had was coming from a good or evil source.

'I can't Sean. I know that what's happened to Arkayic is somehow connected to what is happening here and that I have to stay here to save her. Can you go? Mum needs someone there for her I realise that,' and I don't want her running back to that heathen. 'Can you go as my deputy? Please son. I can't explain why, but...'

The phone interrupted his sentence.

'Andrew?'

'Gregory?'

'You'd better get down to the storm drain. The police have found something. I think you need to be here.'

'What Gregory? This is not a good time.'

'Get here as quick as you can. Look, I've got to go.'

---oOo---

He had seen these scenes on TV before, the white forensic tent, the men and women in their white spacesuits and the yellow 'do not cross' police tape, and for a while as he hurried up the dimly lit canal path toward the bright generator fed lights, he felt distanced from the scene, like he was just seeing it on TV. But as he drew nearer, he felt the scene begin to close in around him, sucking him into its surreal breast. He felt its hot, excited breath on his face and smelt its foul, acrid smell of wrongdoing.

Father Gregory was talking to a man who Andrew guessed was a detective. He moved toward them, but was stopped by a uniformed officer.

'Sorry sir, this is a crime scene, you can't...oh it's you Reverend.'

Andrew stared at the man, his features slowly focussed in the gloom. Oh great, he thought, it's the sniff police.

'Good evening sergeant, I need to speak to the vicar over there. He called me here.'

The sergeant eyed Andrew for a second then indicated with a jerk of the head for him to follow. As he turned, he gave an exaggerated sniff and, Andrew thought, his shoulders shook a little with laughter at his own childish joke.

He was still a few steps away from Father Gregory and the detective when the prison vicar glanced up and saw him.

'Andrew, come over,' he looked grim.

The Good Vicar did not reprimand him for the smug look he gave the sergeant before moving over to Gregory.

'Andrew, this is Detective Smith. Detective, Father Andrew Compton, the one I was telling you about.'

He shook hands with the policeman, trying to quell the anxiety and curiosity that mixed in his belly.

'It was as he said,' Father Gregory interrupted the handshake. 'We found some human remains which seem to match the description of Shirley Creswell in terms of size and the clothes. The Forensic guys are going to take them away to confirm DNA and all that.'

Andrew was not surprised. He had felt that McCready was not lying, but The Good Vicar needed to be on show now.

'Those poor parents, have they been informed yet?'

'No, the police want to make sure before notifying them, but there's more Andrew.'

'More children's remains?'

'No, a live child, a baby.'

Andrew felt the loud thud of his heart.

'Arkayic?' He whispered.

---o0o---

He was not concerned about her health as he sat in the waiting room at the hospital. She was fine, he could tell from the way she had gurgled, smiled and clapped her hands when they had brought her to him.

There was a mild streak of impatience running through him as he flicked over the page of an ancient *Hello*! magazine, his gaze not taking in anything of the pictures or text. He knew she was okay, but the authorities had to convince themselves as well as making sure that the child was his granddaughter.

Sean should be heading back with Jane and Marge by now. Andrew allowed himself a small smile as he imagined his son's face on arriving at Jane's place only to be told that Arkayic was safe and he needed to turn round and head back. He could picture the two women being already packed and almost bustling out the door before Sean had had a chance to draw breath.

Two things puzzled Andrew as he sat in the waiting room. Firstly, the physical. How had McCready physically managed to abduct Arkayic and bring her all the way up from London when he was locked away in prison? It had to be him behind this. He must have an accomplice. But who could that be?

The second puzzling thing was the mental side of it. What was McCready trying to say or prove by doing this? Was this a show of power, a warning to play by his rules? Andrew shuddered at this thought and then watched as The Good Vicar offered up a quick prayer that good would triumph over evil in this battle. Father Gregory interrupted his thoughts by announcing coffee.

'No biscuits I'm afraid, just some stale flapjacks, didn't think you'd be interested in those,' he informed Andrew as he handed over the polystyrene cup. 'Any news?' he added as he carefully lowered himself into a chair.

'No, they're still in there. Poor thing being poked and prodded to make sure that nothing untoward has happened.'

'They have to check.'

'I know, but I also know that nothing has happened to her.'

'How can you be so sure?'

'It's just a feeling really.'

Father Gregory nodded but continued to study Andrew's face as if hoping to find the real answer there.

'If I knew the real answer I would tell you,' Andrew prepared to say, but The Good Vicar deftly changed the subject.

'Any idea how long the DNA tests will take on that poor girl's remains?'

Father Gregory was off and running then, explaining to Andrew's glazed-over ears about police procedure and all that good stuff. Andrew settled back and let the words wash over him, too tired even to think.

'Mr Compton,' the doctor interrupted Father Gregory. Andrew stood up quickly.

'Yes?'

'I just wanted to inform you that your…er…granddaughter appears fine. A little dehydrated but no internal or external injuries. In fact she is in very good health.'

'Thank you doctor, may I see her?'

The doctor glanced quickly at Father Gregory, then back at Andrew.

'I'm sorry, but I have been instructed by the police that only the girl's mother may see her.'

'But…' Andrew was about to embark on a tirade, explaining that it was his granddaughter for goodness sake and he was a priest, a man of the cloth, he still had his collar on to prove it. He was not a paedophile. A priest would never…

That's not the best argument is it, he thought to himself and lowered his eyes, maddened that he felt guilty without having done anything wrong.

The doctor took his leave quickly, seeing his opportunity to avoid any embarrassing confrontations.

Father Gregory guided Andrew back to his seat.

'Are you okay?'

'Fine…fine. It's all rather annoying this…' He looked up and saw the detective from the storm drain approaching them.

'Father Gregory, Father Andrew,' he nodded as he drew near. 'I just thought I'd let you know,' he addressed Father Gregory, 'that the forensic chaps believe that those remains were placed in the drain very recently, possibly even a few hours before we found them. We're busy looking into that,' he said and gave Andrew a look drenched in suspicion before taking his leave of them.

---oOo---

How dare they suspect him, he seethed quietly as he paced up and down the waiting room. They hadn't even asked for his alibi. A quick investigation of the time line, when last was Arkayic seen in London and when was he with Father Gregory or the Bridges? It was physically impossible for him to have put Arkayic or those remains there.

Slowly he calmed himself and began to regret dismissing Father Gregory.

'I'll be fine, Marge and the kids should be here soon.'

He had begun to understand that the puzzled looks he got from his colleague were not trying to decide if he was mad or not, but rather trying to comprehend what was happening to him. Perhaps he should be more open with Father Gregory.

He looked round the quiet waiting room and suddenly hated being there. It was like purgatory, not sick enough to be in bed, but not well enough to leave. He tried to think if any of his congregation were in hospital at the moment, it would give him something to do to pass the time.

The only one that came to mind was Linda McLeod and there was no way he was going to visit her, he did not wish to run into her brick-throwing husband.

Was there anybody else?

Marge's voice came back to him suddenly. *Always thinking of others, never anything left for me* and it shocked him as the truth of her accusation hit home.

But, he protested, I am not thinking of others now, I am thinking of myself. I'm bored waiting and want a distraction, I don't care if there are people here who could do with a visit.

The Good Vicar raised an eyebrow. 'Have you stopped to wonder what that would look like to those close to you like Marge? You know why you're doing it, but how would it appear to someone who can't read your inner thoughts?'

Andrew grunted out loud, then quickly glanced round the waiting room. A woman who sat with a small child looked up at him and then away, not wanting to have to deal with the loony priest who was talking to himself. The other two occupants of the room were too caught up in their own madness to take heed of a grunting priest.

'You're a fine one to talk,' he admonished the Good Vicar. 'It is usually for your sake, your reputation that I do all this caring for others stuff. It's your bloody job, you're the one who needs to be the goody goody helping everyone out. All this is done for you. I don't want to bloody do this stuff, I don't give a toss about others. I want out, but I'm stuck in this shitty body with you and trapped here. I can't leave you to make a life for me, little old Andrew Compton, not Father Andrew, not The Good Bloody Vicar. I just want out!'

The Good Vicar was shocked. He stared at Andrew and neither noticed the woman suggest to her small child that they go for a little walk while nervously glancing in their direction.

'Andrew,' The Good Vicar's voice was calm. Andrew knew the voice all too well. It had often been used to draw the sting out of hysterical parishioners trying to cope with a tragedy. He didn't want to relinquish his sting but felt that it was being slowly drawn from him, The Good Vicar was good with people remember.

'Andrew, please. This is what I am. I would love to grant you your freedom, we should all be free, although lord knows what sort of trouble you'd get into left to your own devices. I shudder to think. We need to work together, we have to make the most...'

The Good Vicar's riposte was cut short by a cry from just outside the waiting room.

'Doctor! Someone get a doctor quick!'

Andrew and the remaining occupants of the waiting room looked up as a young man staggered into the room. Attached to him and practically being dragged along, his face bloodied and bruised was, The Heathen.

---o0o---

He was caught between showing Marge and Jane to the room where Arkayic was and telling Marge that her lover was down the corridor, badly beaten. But common sense prevailed and he let The Good Vicar hug the two nearly hysterical women and lead them to his granddaughter without mentioning Brian.

He had only had time to place a quick call to Pat before Marge and Jane arrived. She didn't have any transport so Andrew promised to send Sean as soon as they arrived. *Always thinking of others.*

Jane was in tears and frantically grabbing at Arkayic as soon as she entered the room. Marge was a close second to reach the child who seemed to think the attention was hilarious. Andrew stopped Sean at the door and quickly appraised him of the situation. Sean nodded and quietly headed off.

He stood a few paces away, giving the women their relief space. Eventually Marge noticed him and came over, her eyes downcast, too embarrassed to meet his.

'Andrew.' It was almost a whisper. 'I'm...' Was there a sob there? He like to think that there was one. 'I'm so sorry. I shouldn't have doubted you. I should have listened to you, but I just thought that you were trying to get me back and I wasn't ready for that. I'm so sorry.' She fell into his arms and was sobbing loudly.

He felt remote. There were no feelings of love or compassion, just a terrible emptiness and he wanted to cry for himself. Jane glanced up at him at that moment and he saw her face soften to him.

Suddenly he wanted to laugh. All that animosity that she had towards him was being dissolved in a misunderstanding. His moist eyes were not from feelings for them and their pain, they were selfish, feeling sorry for himself moist eyes. Through all his thoughts he managed a gentle smile which Jane returned. His further lack of feeling at the returned smile caused him to sob slightly.

'It's okay daddy, she's fine.' This was getting stupid. Each little crumbling of the wall between them brought on further self-pity which was mis-read and brought on more agitation.

'Where is Sean?' Marge saved the day. She pushed herself slightly off Andrew's shoulder and he looked around in the direction she was facing, a reflex reaction.

'Oh, I sent him to fetch Pat.'

'Pat? Why?' There was no hint that Marge knew anything of his affair with her lover's wife.

'You'd better sit,' the Good Vicar stepped into his role and guided a now concerned looking Marge to a chair while he shot an *it's okay* look at his daughter.

'Brian was brought in about half an hour ago. He had been pretty badly beaten up, but will be fine.' He added the last bit quickly in response to Marge's widening eyes.

'Oh my god. What happened?'

'Don't know yet. He was barely conscious, but the doctor assured me that he would be okay. I rang Pat, but she doesn't have a car so I said I would send Sean as soon as he got here.'

Marge sat staring at him, her face a mixture of horror and guilt. He could sense that she was aching to go and see her lover and a vision of her pulling aside her blouse to offer up her breast flashed briefly through his mind.

'You should go and see him, before Pat gets here. It wouldn't be fair on her. Go quickly.' The Good Vicar stared at Andrew for a while then nodded his reluctant approval.

'Quickly. I'll stay with Jane, is that okay love?' He addressed his daughter and got the same astonished look in reply but this came with a confused nod.

Marge needed the nod from Jane before she could go and this came with slightly less confusion. Andrew watched his wife hurry out into the corridor then, turning back to his daughter cursed himself for engineering time alone with her. What the hell would they talk about?

'She's fine, not a scratch,' Jane bounced Arkayic gently on her hip. She was staring at her child, avoiding Andrew's eyes. Arkayic gurgled and reached for Jane's nose.

'That's good.' He wanted to say more, continue talking about anything but what he knew would be asked, if not now, eventually. He opened his mouth then shut it again. *I knew she would be,* was not what he wanted to say, that would be inviting the question.

'Daddy?' She looked at him now, fear and puzzlement flaring in her eyes. 'How did you know not to come down to London?'

---o0o---

Thank God for paperwork. Even The Good Vicar seemed relieved that the police chose that moment to arrive to 'get everything down.'

It was going to be harrowing for Jane this interview and he would have preferred it if Marge had been there. But this was vastly preferable to having to try and answer Jane's question. He needed to answer it for himself before he could answer it for others. Besides, Marge shouldn't be too long. Where was she? Pat would be here soon and it would not be fair on her to find The Heathen with his lover. He sat down next to Jane and patted her knee gently in a gesture of comfort. She smiled weakly then turned a concerned face to the policeman. Andrew was relieved that it was not The Sniff Detective.

'When did you notice that she was missing? Have you any idea who could have taken her? Have you contacted the police in London to let them know that you have found your daughter?'

Andrew drifted off. He felt that he was watching a TV detective show. Where was bloody Marge? He would have to go and fetch her soon. How was Pat going to feel about The Heathen now that he needed her? Would she forget him and return to her husband, dump him completely? What about Marge? Was she going to come running back to him now? He became aware that the policeman was looking at him expectantly.

'I'm sorry?'

'Sir, I was wondering if you are able to account for your whereabouts today?'

So they did suspect him. He glanced quickly at Jane who was staring at him, a look of horror spreading across her face.

Not you too.

'I was with Father Gregory, the prison pastor and then I went to visit a family nearby. I can give you the details. I travelled with Mrs Pat Squires. You can check with her if you like.' He found himself strangely relaxed about answering, they were just eliminating the suspects, standard procedure.

The officer nodded and Marge walked back into the room.

'How is he?' The Good Vicar's voice showed real concern which surprised Marge.

'He's woken up but still very groggy. The police are with him now.'

The officer raised a questioning eyebrow.

'One of my parish member's husband was brought in about an hour ago. He'd been beaten up.' Andrew answered the eyebrow.

'I see. Shouldn't you go and see him yourself Father?'

'I will in minute but my family needs me now.' It felt strangely good saying that. Not good from a he was doing the right thing point of view, but good from a he was proving Marge wrong point of view.

'I see, but your wife…'

'My wife is a good friend of the family, we discussed it and thought it best that she go see him while I stayed here with my daughter. The man's wife is due here soon and I will go and see them both as soon as we are done here.' Well something a bit like that he added to The Good Vicar.

The policeman nodded and folded up his notebook. 'I think that will be all for now. If we find any leads as to who did this, we'll let you know.'

They watched him leave then Andrew turned to Marge. This was going to be delicate. He had just made the comment about being with his family, now he wanted to tell her that he was going to see Pat. Marge beat him to it.

'You'd best go check on Pat. Sean can take us home.'

Which home, he wanted to ask, but he saw in her look that he was not going to be alone in the house that evening.

'I'll see you in a bit.'

He waited for them to disappear down the passage, then headed off to find Pat.

She was in the small ward, sitting next to the bed. The Heathen's face peeked over the bed sheets in a similar manner to the way Peggy had stared lifelessly out at the world. His eyes were puffy slits and it was difficult to tell if he was awake or not.

Pat looked up as he approached, her eyes wet with tears.

'How is he?' The Good Vicar asked.

'He's sleeping, they sedated him. He will be okay. Andrew, why would anyone have done such a thing to him? He would never harm a fly.'

He sighed inwardly at the level of concern she was showing for him, but said, 'Did he say who did this to him?'

She looked at the bruised face, then swallowed hard before saying, 'A group of youngsters came after him, calling him a paedophile. He has no idea where they came up with that, but even more worrying, he cannot recall the few hours leading up to the attack. The last thing he remembers was trying to see Marge in London, then the next thing he was being attacked just outside our house. He can't recall what happened in between.'

---oOo---

'You sure you'll be okay?' He wanted her to invite him in, but at the same time felt a guilty twinge about his family waiting at home for him. Why the guilt, he wondered. Had his own little speech about being with his family when they needed him actually made an impact on himself?

'Do you think…'

'Yes?'

'No, I shouldn't ask, you need to go home.'

Ask damn it, ask! 'What is it Pat?'

'I was going to ask if you would stay for a quick cup of tea, just to settle me down, but you should go. Jane and Marge need you now.'

After taking a second to lock The Unsuspecting Good Vicar into a room, Andrew settled into The Beaten Up Heathen's comfortable chair. It felt good to be in it.

The Good Vicar had been contemplating Brian's amnesia and had not been following the conversation. Andrew had his suspicions about this, but his thoughts were concentrated on summonsing up The Stud Muffin.

'Here we go.' Pat smiled sadly as she returned with the tray. There were biscuits, custard creams. Oh how he loved this woman.

Her hands shook as she poured the tea, but when she looked up at him she seemed to gain strength and smiled again, this time less sadly. She handed him his tea without a single rattle of the cup and quickly followed it up with a biscuit.

'Thank you for staying. I feel a bit guilty but I am pretty shaken up by this whole thing. I never knew that Brian had come back and then to get attacked a block or two away from the house, we've never had that sort of trouble here.' She shuddered. 'Andrew, I'm afraid to stay here alone tonight.'

He quickly swallowed the mouthful of biscuit, his heart racing at what he thought was a proposal for him to spend the night.

'I could...'

'No Andrew,' she was horrified, 'What would Marge think. I know she wronged you and she has a speck in her eye, but we have a log in ours that we need to get rid of first.'

The crumbs of the custard cream suddenly tasted sour in his mouth. He was the one who was supposed to do the preaching.

'Oh, I wasn't going to suggest that, I was going to say that I could call Eve and see if you could stay with her, I sure she won't mind.'

Pat dropped her gaze. 'I'm sorry Andrew. I guess that I wanted you to stay, but I'm feeling guilty about it. Please call Eve.' She sucked in a sob and remained sitting with her eyes downcast.

'You're a bastard,' he told himself before downing the last of his tea and standing up. He put his hand on her shoulder for a second then moved towards the hall. 'I'll only be a minute, do you mind if I call Marge as well?'

'No, go ahead, that's a good idea.'

No it's not a good idea, it's a bloody lousy idea. I don't want to talk to Marge. Why did I suggest it?

He dialled Eve's number and listened to the hollow ringing on the other side.

'Strange,' he muttered to himself, 'she should be at home.' He let it ring a few more times then hung up and stood in the gloomy hallway wondering if he should call Marge but feeling vaguely concerned about Eve's whereabouts. He was just about to pick up the phone again when the front doorbell rang, startling him.

He automatically reached for the door handle and only as he pulled the door open, he realised it was not his home for him to be answering the door.

'Father Andrew! I'm glad you're here,' a giggle flooded over into a wobbly laugh.

'Why? What's happened Eve?' He was alarmed. She stared at him for a second as her body dropped from choppy waves to calm lapping giggles.

'Surely you've heard about Brian. Good God, don't you know? Didn't he tell you?'

'Didn't who tell me what?'

'Brian was beaten up,' she sob chuckled.

'Yes, yes we know, come in Eve. Pat's in the living room. I was just trying to call you, I think Pat should stay with you tonight, is that okay?'

She squeezed herself next to him in the narrow passageway and he felt the warmth and giggle judders of her body.

'Of course, she's more than welcome. In fact I insist.'

She began to make her way through to the living room when Andrew suddenly asked, 'Eve, who told you about Brian?' He didn't know where the question had come from.

'That youngster, you know the one we have our suspicions about.'

---o0o---

The Rat! How had The Rat known? Had he seen it happen? Had he been part of the gang who had made it happen? Or had he orchestrated it to happen? A trip to Geoffrey Deane's memorial bench seemed to loom as Andrew made the short trip home from Pat's.

At least she would be okay. Eve would mother her to sleep this evening.

Sleep. He suddenly realised that another night on the couch was on the cards, what with the full house again. He wondered what, if anything, Marge and Jane would say, or even Sean for that matter. How had he known to stay put instead of rushing off to London? More specifically, how was he possibly going to explain to them when he hardly knew how to explain it to himself?

He turned the corner and as he neared his house his blood froze. A group of youths loitered near his front gate.

---oOo---

He staggered into the front room and collapsed into a chair. He could not stop shaking. Sean jumped up to help him.

'Dad! Dad, are you okay? What happened? Mom!'

Marge came running through from the kitchen closely followed by Jane.

'I'm fine. I'm fine.' He waved away the flapping attention.

'What happened Andrew? You're shaking.'

He wished they would stop fussing and offer him some tea for his nerves.

'I'm fine honestly. I just need a minute.'

They all stared at him expectantly. 'That's not a minute,' he screamed soundlessly at his family.

'Do you want some tea?' Ah, at least someone was thinking.

'Yes please.' Strange that it was the only other male in the house that offered. Weren't women supposed to be more attuned to people's needs, motherly instincts and all that.

Marge moved to go herself, but Sean waved her away saying, 'I know where everything is mum. You stay with dad.'

Was he trying to get them back together, Andrew wondered and then noticing the look on Marge's face added, I don't think he needs to encourage her much.

He sank further into the chair, not sure if he liked the thought of getting back with Marge.

'I'm okay,' he said, injecting as much confidence into his voice as he could muster. He would have preferred The Good Vicar to have made this statement, he was good at reassuring people. But this was not his territory and he was nowhere to be found.

He wanted Sean to return quickly so he could tell them all what had happened and get this out the way.

'Where's Arkayic?' He asked suddenly.

'She's asleep in the spare room,' Jane answered but there was doubt in her voice. 'I'll go and check on her quickly.'

'She's fine,' Andrew called after her without opening his mouth.

Great he was left alone with Marge. What would they talk about in the few seconds they had together? He turned to her, looking for his cue in her face and watched the irritation cloud her features as the chirrup of the phone slowly sank into his hearing.

Great, he was left alone now. He smiled inwardly and felt his body relax.

'Love.' Why did she use that word now, after all that had happened? Was it purely out of habit?

'There is a man on the phone, says he needs to talk to you urgently. David Bridges? Wasn't he the one...?'

He nodded quickly and pushed himself up wondering what Bridges could possibly want from him.

---oOo---

'But Andrew, you're in no state to go out and what about Arkayic? What if...?'

'She'll be fine, don't worry. Sean's here as well. You'll all be fine. Look I have to go.' *Always thinking of others*. No damn it, this involves all of us. I'm not just doing this for the Bridges.

'But Andrew, you haven't even told us what happened earlier, why were you in such a state?'

'No time now. I will tell you when I get back, I promise. I won't be too long. Maybe an hour or so, but I've got to do this Marge.'

He gently pulled himself free of her grasp and, grabbing his car keys from the hall table headed out onto the dark street.

He ignored the sniff that came from the bushes near his house and only wondered briefly why it was followed by a giggle.

---o0o---

She did look attractive without the madness in her eyes. He detected a note of jealousy from the Naked Woman who was barely visible in the dull street light.

'Thank you for coming Father.' The eyes no longer accused but rather brimmed with gratitude, puzzlement and fear. He had to read the eyes twice to make sure of the last emotion.

'Yes, thank you.' Her voice was pleasant and the smile, although coloured with sadness, was warm.

He smiled back, marvelling at the results of his prayer and ignoring the glares of the Naked Woman who seemed to be feeling left out.

'Are you sure you want to do this?' The Good Vicar was on hand.

David Bridges glanced across at his wife who nodded.

'Yes, it's been too long. I have to face up to this and move on.'

Andrew let The Good Vicar agree with a nod of the eyes.

'Shall we?' He gestured down the small path that led off the road.

'Have you got a torch?' David asked, flicking the switch on his own.

'Good point. I should have one in the back of the car, give me a minute.'

The path was uneven and difficult to negotiate in the swaying torch light, but they stumbled quite quickly along till it eventually evened out into a worn path, through a small wooded area. The torch light gave life to the shadows and an eerie funk pervaded the air.

They reached a fork in the path and David led them to the left.

'Not far now,' he called over his shoulder. His confident strides betraying what he would probably deny if asked – he came here regularly.

About a hundred yards down the path he turned off into the under-growth, his feet swishing through the leaves and plants.

'Careful now, Father,' he called back as Andrew picked his way slowly behind the couple.

After scrambling along for a few moments David slowed then stopped. He shone the beam of his torch into a small hollow at the base of a large tree.

'Here,' he whispered. 'This is where they found her.'

Andrew half expected to see a curled up body in the light, but there was nothing, just brambles and roots.

He watched as Kirsten Bridges moved slowly forward, her gaze almost trance-like as her eyes stayed glued to the spot that her daughter's body had been found, bloodied and battered.

Andrew wanted to look away, to look at the Naked Woman and see how she was reacting to this, but he found that she was clothed by the darkness so he returned his gaze to the grieving mother.

She had reached the spot where David's torch beam was pointing and slowly knelt and caressed the earth. Her arm movement slowed until it stopped and then her shoulders shuddered as the first sobs took hold.

David was next to her and holding her tight as her grief, previously denied to her by the shock induced madness, overflowed.

The wind that had been rustling in the leaves died away and a silence flowed around them as the wood gave its respect to the dead.

Slowly the sobbing died down to a final spasm of her body and then complete silence engulfed them. It seemed like an eternity that they stood motionless in their tableau.

Eventually Kirsty gave a small sniff, then smiled gently at her husband and drew his face to hers and gave him a kiss. Andrew moved to look away, but she was pushing herself to her feet.

'Father, please say a prayer for her soul.'

The Good Vicar nodded and took a few steps closer to the spot. He took Kirsty's hand gently, lowered his head and began to pray while Andrew turned his face and wept bitterly for the loss this good couple were feeling. How could God let this happen? He knew all the theological arguments he had been taught on the subject but none made sense to him at the moment.

The Good Vicar finished his prayers and looked up at the couple who, raising their faces smiled sadly.

Andrew moved the torch to start lighting the path back and shone the beam into the face of Paul McCready.

---oOo---

Bugger off, leave me alone.

'Andrew, you can't just keep us guessing. It's not fair. Twice you've walked in here tonight on the verge of collapse from fright and you've not said a word. What is going on?'

Where's Pat? I want Pat here. I want you to go back to London and leave me with Pat. She understands me.

He stopped his thoughts and sighed. No, Pat did not understand him either. Not even The Good Vicar understood him.

'Okay, I'm okay now. Can I get a cup of tea please? Then I'll tell you what happened.' He felt the tension in his body ease slightly as he said this, but also felt the onset of a headache.

Jane did the tea-run this time, and he heard her pop in to check on Arkayic while the kettle boiled. Sean stared at him strangely as Marge took his unresisting hand and stroked it gently. He should meet her eyes but he was not ready for the love he knew would be there, so he stared at her hand on his.

The silence of the room began to irk and he wanted desperately for it to end. Someone say something he screamed silently.

The clatter of cups from the kitchen made him look up and meet Sean's gaze.

'Dad,' he swallowed hard and then continued, 'dad what's going on? What's happening to you?'

'I don't know son.' He placed his free hand over Marge's without realising it.

'I don't know,' he repeated, 'I mean I can tell you what's been happening but I don't know the why…or the how for that matter.'

Jane's arrival with the tea caused them all to sit forward in their chairs and Andrew freed his hands which he suddenly became aware of as he took the offered cup. No biscuits, oh well, he sighed inwardly.

He settled back and sipped his tea, soaking in the sweetness of the hot liquid.

His third sip was a mischievous one, designed deliberately to keep his family in suspense. The first two sips had restored him sufficiently to allow himself this defiant act and he had to work hard not to smile out loud.

'Okay, I'll start by explaining my first appearance this evening. It's the simpler of the two.' It made earthly sense that one.

'I got back from dropping Pat off. She was in quite a state but fortunately Eve had heard the news and came over. She's taken Pat back to her place for the night.' Why did they need to know all that? Was he just comforting himself with that detail?

'As I returned, there was a group of youngsters hanging around outside. You didn't see them?'

He watched each member of his family shake their heads, their eyes not leaving him. Marge put a reassuring hand on his again, making it impossible for him to have more tea without pulling away so he went on.

'Well after what had happened to Brian and this whole ordeal with McCready I thought they were here to beat me up too. I parked the car and…'

'Andrew! Why didn't you go to the police, or drive off.'

He turned to face Marge, astonished at her suggestion. It made so much sense and yet it had never crossed his mind at the time. Why had he stopped and confronted those youths? He stared at her for a second then looked down at his hand clasped in hers.

'I don't know. I guess I wasn't thinking straight.' He eased his hand away from hers and took a sip of tea.

'Anyway, nothing happened. I mean they didn't beat me up did they?'

'What did they do?' Sean leaned forward.

'Evening Vicar,' the tallest one, probably the leader said while some of the group blocked his route to the house. He realised with horror that others were moving round the back of him to prevent him returning to his car. His legs felt ready to buckle under him, but he managed to summons up some strength and pull himself up to his full height.

'Good evening, gentlemen, may I help you?' He marvelled at how his voice did not betray the panic that shuddered inside him.

'You the one that's been talking to that paedo?'

'What have you heard?' He stared straight back into the youngster's unflinching eyes.

'We've heard that you got him to tell where he dumped Shirley Creswell's body.'

'I… er.'

'That there is James Creswell. Shirley was his sister.' He nodded toward a short, slightly chubby lad who looked away when Andrew followed the inclination of the leader's head.

'He just wants to thank you Vicar, he says that now they can bury Shirley proper like.'

The chubby one gave the slightest nod of the head to concur.

'Keep up the good work Vicar.' The youngster's hand shot out and Andrew jumped back almost knocking into the small group behind him. He stared down at the offered hand and realised that there was not a knife in it, but it was inviting a handshake.

'So that's why I was so shaken when I got in. I thought they were going to kill me. I hadn't fully digested what they said.' He took another sip of tea and smiled at his family.

How, he asked himself, would he explain the McCready apparition?

---oOo---

He wondered as he looked at Marge's head lying peacefully on the pillow, how many men got to feel guilty about sleeping with their wife because they felt they were cheating on their lover. His pang of guilt was blunted slightly by the perceived cooling in Pat's feelings toward him.

The Stud Muffin had sneaked into the bedroom unexpectedly when, after preparing for a night on the sofa, Marge had said, 'Don't be silly Andrew, you'll be more comfortable in our bed.'

He had tried to blank out the hint of hero worship he read in her eyes, but it had been there. All he had done was not run to her side when she needed him based on a strange feeling that he should stay where he was. Hardly the stuff of heroes.

And he had admitted to his entire family that he was hallucinating. Surely people of valour don't see ghosts. But he had been there to rescue Arkayic and that seemed to qualify him for the heroes' club.

The sex had been surprisingly good, the best he could remember with Marge, although a don't get carried away voice did whisper to him, 'surely you had better as youngsters.' Still it was the best in recent memory.

'Also the only sex in recent memory,' the little voice had taunted.

He smiled wryly at the voice and Marge's eyelids fluttered as she began to wake.

He wanted to turn away from her, he didn't want her waking image to be him looking into her eyes and smiling, but The Good Vicar prevented him from moving.

---oOo---

They know, he told himself. They must have heard.

'How's my little Arkayic?' He wanted a distraction and used his granddaughter to good effect. She bounced on her mother's knee, applauding the way Andrew had tried to diffuse the embarrassment that he felt.

Sean and Jane smiled at him, their eyes saying 'you're back together, you and mum. We heard the noises from your bedroom last night and we are a family again.'

He glanced at Marge out of the corner of his eye and she, catching his look, quickly began to examine her hands, a shy smile playing on her lips.'

'May I? he asked Jane holding out his hands to pick up Arkayic.

Who kidnapped you and brought you here? He asked her laughing eyes. Was it The Heathen?

Arkayic nodded her head and then touched his nose and giggled.

'She seems fine,' he told the room.

'Slept right through,' Jane added proudly.

Why did he do it?

Arkayic shrugged her shoulders, catching Andrew by surprise. The nodding of the head had been a coincidence, but twice?

'How did you sleep, daddy?'

She had not called him that for years, certainly not in that gentle tone. He swallowed.

'Oh, fine. Quite well actually.' Don't look at Marge, don't look at Marge. Damn!

He turned back to Arkayic. Did he say anything, The Heathen?

'That's good, I was worried that you wouldn't, given your strange vision of McCready last night.'

'Cready!' Arkayic was gleeful at having said her first word. Andrew stared at her in horror.

It had taken a while for him to finally be alone. Sean had lingered for as long as he could before leaving for work and Jane and Marge had insisted on chatting with him, trying to coax out more from him about how he had known to stay at home and not join Sean in going to London.

He had gone over the same ground in numerous way, as The Good Vicar trying to make sense of God directing his life, as Andrew just trying to make sense and once even as The Stud Muffin, making out that it was his wondrous charm and intellect that made him stay. This latter version he cut short when he noticed that Marge seemed to be falling for it.

Finally they had given up when they realised he really did not know what had made him make the decision he had. They had tidied up the breakfast dishes and only as she made her way upstairs to shower did Andrew notice how worn her pale blue dressing gown looked.

They were out now. Shopping. He sat at his desk, his hands aching to pick up the phone and call Pat. Maybe he could offer to take her to see The Heathen. But that would defeat the object of calling her. You want to see her to re-kindle your affair, not re-unite her with her husband, he told himself. He couldn't think of any other excuse to call her though.

He turned his mind to things that still puzzled him. Who had beaten Brian up, and why? Why had The Heathen, if Arkayic was to be believed, taken his granddaughter to the storm drain, and had he moved the remains of Shirley Creswell there also? Where had he got them from?

Then there was Kirsty Bridge. What had happened there? Was he really capable, through the power of prayer, to heal? Even The Good Vicar didn't dare believe that to be true, despite the evidence. He had a funny feeling that he would see the Bridges in church on Sunday. He only hoped that The Naked Woman would be tucked away under a sleeve. He would struggle to deliver his sermon with her around.

The change in attitude of his family also unsettled him. Was this true forgiveness they were giving him, not that he felt he needed to be forgiven? Or was it temporary forgiveness brought on by the current situation and the emotions surrounding it all? Would they go back to despising him once the memory of his 'heroics' the day Arkayic disappeared, faded?

He snatched up the phone suddenly, wanting to run away from his thoughts.

'Andrew, I was just about to call you. The dna matched, those were Shirley Creswell's remains. The police just confirmed it.'

'That's good.'

It didn't feel good, it felt evil. 'Have the family been informed?' The Good Vicar was at his post.

'I believe they've got someone on their way there now. We're bracing ourselves for another media circus. Can you...'

'No Gregory. Please keep my name out of it if you can. I can't handle the attention at the moment. Please. Can you do that for me?'

There was a silence on the other side for a moment, then the voice came back, 'Okay Andrew, sure no problem. You've been through a lot. I'll have a word with the guard to keep his mouth shut, although I don't think he'll be a problem.'

'Thank you, I really appreciate this. Sorry to leave you to face them on your own though.'

Father Gregory chuckled, 'Don't worry about that. I think you need to concentrate on getting the rest of the information out of McCready. Hopefully he will not mention you to anyone.'

'Oh I think he knows not to say anything.' In fact he knows a whole lot more than we do about what's happening here, orchestrating it even. He thought about his decision to confide more in Father Gregory, but his little aside was, he felt, a little too extreme. He had to ease his colleague in.

'I think we'll have a few more surprises though before we're done with this whole thing. At the moment though I'm at a bit of a loss as to how we proceed.'

As he said it, the strange question he had posed to Eve came back to him. Who had told her about Brian? In their rush to see to Pat's well-being, he had not been able to pursue that further.

'Well good luck with that, let me know if you need any help. I'll keep praying for you.'

'Thanks. Thanks Gregory.'

He hung up and started dialling Eve's number. Somehow, he knew that he would soon be heading up to Geoffrey Deane's memorial bench again.

---oOo---

Sex with Kirsty Bridges had not been the last thing on his mind as he had made his way up The Ridge to the bench. It was such an alien and un-conceivable thought that it would not even have made last place on a list of thoughts.

Yet it had happened, or at least he thought it had happened. It had felt too real to be a dream, but given his dreams of late, he could not be absolutely sure.

She had been there on the bench waiting for him and, as the haze of strangeness began to melt, he recalled with some distress his lack of surprise at seeing her there.

'Hi.'

Why not *what are you doing here?* his mind had asked.

She had smiled sweetly and nodded a greeting back.

'Please come and sit.' Like it was her lounge. He half expected to be offered tea and biscuits. He searched her eyes for any signs of the madness that had plagued her before, but there was no hint of it.

She shifted closer to him on the bench.

'I wanted to thank you for what you've done for us. We can live again.'

He nodded slowly, feeling any control he may have had over his circumstances fading fast. There was a small twinkle of realisation that Kirsty was not able to direct her own emotions either and as that small pinpoint of sanity had flicked and dimmed to nothing, their lips had met.

It had been neither perfunctory nor passionate. It was not fumbled nor forced. But there had been a kind of natural flow to it, like they were fulfilling a destiny.

And in that cloudy fog of muted emotions, one feeling had spiked and that was a sense that he was righting a wrong. He was filling the womb that had felt so empty since Chantelle Bridges had died. He could visualise clearly his seed taking root in that barren soil.

He closed his eyes as he neared his climax, a sense of relief and goodness washing over him.

Then as the warm pleasure began to shudder through his body, he opened his eyes and looked into the inky blue tattooed eyes of The Naked Woman from David's bicep. She winked at him, then flung her head back as her orgasm took hold, juddering herself back into the shape of Kirsty.

She had sorted herself out quickly and taken her leave as though nothing had happened, and, as he sat for a few moments longer on the bench, he wondered if anything had in fact happened.

The Good Vicar was at a loss for words. He was seething with anger that Andrew had taken advantage of a vulnerable woman, and yet he had been there and seen it all happen, but he had been unable to even call out one word of protest, despite being given every freedom he needed from Andrew. It was not Andrew that had stopped him crying out. There had been another force. It had felt like a good force, but he could not bring himself to believe that God would condone such an act.

'Here's your tea, Father, and a biscuit.' Eve giggled and waited to be thanked for procuring a jammy dodger despite having been convinced that there were none left.

---oOo---

'That youngster, you know.' She tapped the side of her nose and gave a little laugh.

'Where did you see him?'

'Nowhere, he came to my door.'

'He came to your door?'

'Yes, rang the doorbell. Gave me a little fright as I had just settled down to watch the telly, you know how I like my evening cuppa when I watch the soaps,' she sighed at the loss of her cup of tea, then smiled an *oops how selfish of me to be moaning about something so trivial when others have such bigger problems* smile and gave an apologetic twitter.

'What did he say?' Andrew ignored the apology.

Eve looked away, blushing slightly, her body shuddering with silent embarrassed laughter.

'Well,' she managed, 'it was very odd. He said, and these are his words, he said that the vicar's lover's husband had been beaten up.'

She looked up now, her eyes questioning him while she said, 'It took me a little while to work out what he was talking about. He kept saying the vicar's lover. Eventually I worked out that it must be Pat.'

Andrew concentrated on keeping his lower jaw in close proximity to his upper one.

'I'm…I'm…' he managed to say, and fortunately before he could add, '…so sorry you had to find out from The Rat,' Eve went on.

'Well, I guessed that since you had been spending quite a bit of time with her sorting out Peggy's funeral and all, and what with Brian having left Pat. And Marge…I'm sorry Andrew. Anyway I figured that this young lad had assumed that you and Pat were lovers. Kids can have the strangest imaginations can't they?' The question mark in her eyes had not faded, but it was joined by a look that pleaded with him to agree with her.

He chuckled, measuring out his mirth carefully to ensure it wasn't a *guilty as charged*, over-compensating laugh. 'Me and Pat lovers, ha ha, he thought that me and Pat…'

The movement at the vestry door caught his eye and he looked up at Jane and Marge, shopping bags weighing them down.

Don't look guilty, don't look guilty. Shit!

---oOo---

'Andrew.' The Bishop's voice was its usual self and he felt a strong urge to throw the telephone across the room.

'Ian, how are you?'

'I'm doing well.'

Of course you are you pious git, the papers are full of praise for the Church's involvement in getting The Paedo to talk, why wouldn't you be doing well?

He manoeuvred himself through the pleasantries.

'I presume you've seen the papers?' It was now time to get down to the crux of the call.

'Yes.' He felt that more was needed, but didn't wish to give The Bishop the satisfaction. Make him work for it.

'Well?'

'Well what?' He was being childish and knew it. He blew a raspberry at the on-looking, frowning Good Vicar for good measure.

'Come on Andrew, surely you have more to say about this, after all, you have been in contact with McCready recently.' How recently did recently mean? 'Father Gregory isn't stealing all your glory is he?' Not that recently then, or at least he only suspects.

'Nope.'

'So this whole coming clean on Shirley Creswell was Gregory's doing?' The voice dripped with suspicion.

'I don't know. It's possible that my earlier visit may have softened him up.' That's right, throw the drowning man a straw.

'Come, come Andrew. There's no need to be modest, this is me you're talking to. You did visit McCready again didn't you? I'm not going to be angry that you disobeyed me. I only want to know the facts. Did you see him again?'

There was barely a pause before he replied, 'No.'

'Really, are you sure?'

The Good Vicar meanwhile began screaming in his mind, 'You can't lie to The Bishop!' He was apoplectic.

'Oh shut up!' He'd had enough of this goody two shoes.

'What!' Ian's voice told him that his command to The Good Vicar had escaped via the vocal chords.

---oOo---

'I'm going to take Pat to see Brian, may be a couple of hours.'

'Okay love.' There wasn't even a tone in there that said *always thinking of others.* He smiled quietly as he opened the front door. The smile faded as he saw the small, hooded figure at the gate, hands thrust deep into pockets. It sniffed loudly.

'Orite Vikka?'

Andrew nodded. 'I'm fine thank you,' he walked down the path as defiantly as possible, he didn't feel defiant, but needed to make the appearance, if only for himself.

'Lot's 'appening innit?'

Andrew translated for The Good Vicar and, stopping at the gate, turned his full attention on to The Rat.

'Yes, and how much do you know about all of it?'

'Doan know nuffink Vikka.' Andrew glance at The Rat's face for a second, too scared to stare for long.

The face was neutral, it neither gave that penetrating look that he struggled to hold, nor was there any hint of the innocent, seductive look of Alex.

'Nothing? Then why did you say lots was happening?'

'Jus' wot I 'eard Vikka.'

'And what did you hear?'

'I 'eard that the 'eathen got it good like. In 'ospital 'e is.'

'Yes, I saw him yesterday.'

'Jew see 'im inna 'ospital?'

'Yes.'

'Were you seeing your grandorta?'

'You seem to have heard an awful lot,' Andrew was surprised how unsurprised he was about what The Rat was saying and this lack of emotion seemed to unnerve the youngster.

'It was 'im wot stuck your grandorta inna drain. Your lover's 'usband. It wos 'im,' The Rat waited for a response.

'Yes, I know.' Andrew said calmly staring straight at him. 'And how did you know?'

The Rat took a step back as if slapped, then grinned suddenly and said, 'I sore 'im.' He started to run off.

'Thanks Alex,' Andrew called after him, relishing the way his reaction had affected The Rat.

The youngster stopped and turned, then pushed back his hood and blinked innocently at Andrew, waiting to see if this had an effect. Andrew struggled to keep his features neutral despite a sudden sexual desire to grab Alex.

The boy stood for a few more seconds then ran off, leaving Andrew to calm his stirred loins, puzzling over why he had this reaction, but glad at his ability to have controlled it this time.

More disconcerting though was the seeping realisation that The Rat had referred to Brian as The Heathen. As far as he knew, he had never called him that out loud.

---oOo---

The bruised face looked back though swollen eyes. They looked frightened, like they knew that Andrew knew. But Pat was standing between them, guarding them both from the question that hung heavily in the air.

He wracked his brain to try and think of a way of getting Pat to leave for a little while so that he could ask it, but he knew, even without The Good Vicar prompting, that that would not be right.

For now he would just have to satisfy himself with observing the rebuilding of his lover's relationship with her husband. He was not enjoying it, feeling Pat slowly ebbing away from him. He wanted to snatch her back, pull her away from the abyss, but he could not.

She held Brian's hand tightly, looking into his bruised eyes and asked him how he was feeling. His answers were slightly slurred through swollen lips, but from what Andrew could gather from his words was that he was fine and from the tone that he was repentant. How he hated that tone.

He stood a pace behind Pat, observing over her shoulder. He wanted to put his hand on that shoulder and guide her away, back into his arms, but The Good Vicar was bugging him to leave the couple alone. If he wanted answers, he would not get them now. He sighed inwardly, resigning himself to the logic of The Good Vicar.

'I'll wait down the passage,' he told Pat when there was a break in the conversation. 'Brian I hope you feel better soon.'

He didn't wait for a reply, but skulked off quickly to the waiting room. His only hope now was that Pat would follow him quickly.

In the waiting room he dropped heavily into a chair and took in the other occupants of the room. The sick. What a pathetic bunch the sick were, but more pathetic were those waiting on the sick, wringing worried hands in time to the pulse of the smell of disease that beats in every hospital.

He picked up an old copy of *Hello!* magazine finding little solace in the glitzy celeb world that sparkled in the pages.

'Andrew.'

He looked up. 'Roger.' Thrown any bricks lately? The thought came so quickly and automatically that it frightened him.

'I'm glad you're here,' The Brick Thrower sounded sincere. 'Linda has taken a turn for the worse and I was wondering if you could say a prayer for her. I tried ringing you before I came here, but Marge told me that you had already left.'

What was this, let's get back into Father Andrew's good books week?

'I...er,' Roger faltered slightly before gaining confidence, 'I am sorry for all that has gone on. I was being pig-headed, but when I heard on the news that McCready had talked, well then I realised that sometimes you have to talk to these sorts to get answers from them, however repellent that may be. I have been foolish and I'm sorry.'

The Good Vicar nodded an acceptance of the apology that Andrew did not accept.

'I also heard from David Bridges, I did some legal work for them during their ordeal, I believe your prayers worked wonders for Kirsten.' The Brick Thrower smiled.

So that was it. I heard you managed to heal someone and I need someone close to me healed so let's forgive all that has passed, just like that.

The Good Vicar smiled. 'Of course. I'm just waiting here for Pat, you heard about Brian? Give me a minute to let her know where I am and then I'll come see Linda.

---o0o---

He had that feeling again, like he knew exactly what was going to happen. Linda would somehow miraculously be in remission by the morning and Roger would be gushing round his place, despite him wanting none of this to happen.

Not that he wished ill for Linda. She was a woman swallowed whole by her husband's shadow, unable to have a thought of her own and rationed to what she could say. He felt a bit sorry for her, but didn't go out of his way to do so.

'I'm going to give Brian another chance,' Pat told him what he already knew as they drove home. She waited for him to say something but there was nothing he could say.

Eventually he opened his mouth to reply, but had left it too late.

'Well? Aren't you going to say anything?'

The affair had lasted about a week and already it felt as if they were one of those long married bickering couples.

'I don't know what to say. I don't want it to end, I like you a lot.' He paused, waiting for a retort about his use of the word 'like' but she just nodded and waited for him to continue. That's what he loved about her, she didn't demand too much of him.

'But…' The word followed naturally on from the tone that the last sentence ended with, 'I can see that you are serious about Brian and what with Marge coming back too, she seems to want to patch things up again. It's all a bit too complicated. Besides, I've been giving it some thought,' for about the last ten seconds,' 'it can't really work with me being in the position I am in. I mean the scandal it would cause would not be good for the church.'

Out of the corner of his eye he saw her nod as he watched the car in front of him swerve slightly.

'I'm sorry Andrew I don't want it to end either but I…LOOK OUT!

---oOo---

The Rat was hunched over the steering wheel of the car that raced next to him. He could barely see over the dashboard, but he continued to race, glancing across at Andrew every so often to grin maniacally. Marge sat next to him in the passenger seat, her blouse open exposing her breasts. She too grinned evilly across at him every so often. The car they drove seemed to be shaped like Eve's plump body. The Naked Lady and Kirsty Bridges sat in the back giggling like little schoolgirls.

'Faster!' The Bishop commanded him from the back seat of the vehicle he was driving.

'Yes faster,' Pat had morphed into David Bridges in the seat next to him, urging him on.

He checked the rear-view mirror quickly. The Bishop was leering across at The Naked Lady who flirted back.

Far up ahead in the middle of the road stood a figure that, as the two cars hurtled straight at it, rapidly became McCready. Andrew tried to ease up on the accelerator, but the sticky molasses of the dream glued his foot down.

Just before they smashed into him, McCready flung his arms out in a crucifix pose.

---oOo---

He heard voices, urgent voices scrambling in the darkness that lay beyond him. He wanted to open his eyes but his head hurt too much.

He tried to concentrate to give meaning to the words that splattered around him like heavy raindrops.

He had a vague sensation of a body pushed up against him, a feminine scent wafted into his nostrils, blending with other, unpleasant smells that he could not recognise. Then the blackness closed around him again.

---oOo---

The bed was comfortable and, aside from a mild headache, he felt pretty good. He knew that he could open his eyes now, but was enjoying the calmness of his disposition so lay breathing slowly and rhythmically.

Slowly thoughts started to creep into his mind, uncomfortable thoughts and he shifted in the bed. The thoughts intensified as all the unsettling recent times that had begun at first to seep, now picked up pace until he could not handle the pain of the rushing memories and with a stifled cry opened his eyes.

The hospital room swirled into focus along with Marge's concerned featured features.

'I'm here Andrew.' He felt the squeeze of her hand in his.

'What happened?' The pace of his thoughts was slowing, but the image of the car in front of him suddenly jamming on brakes along with a stomach churning dread was crystallising with alarming pace.

'You had an accident dear.'

He looked at his wife properly this time. Her face seemed strangely beautiful despite the concern that was etched on it and the two glistening threads of tears down her cheeks.

He squeezed her hand this time, wanting to cut off the flow of tears, but this action just brought further sobs.

'Am I okay?' he suddenly asked. Other than his headache, he didn't feel too much pain elsewhere.

'The doctor said that you were lucky. A bit of a knock to the head but they can't find any major damage. They want to keep you in for a night, just to make sure.' She smiled sweetly and sucked back a sob.

He lay back again, feeling the relief flood through his body, then suddenly he tensed up again.

'Pat? What happened to Pat?'

Marge's flow of tears answered his question.

---o0o---

The bed was uncomfortable and his hip ached from lying on his side. He wanted to turn over but didn't have the energy, or the inclination to. Emptiness gnawed at his stomach, he had not eaten his dinner, but that was not what was causing his discomfort. Marge had left fairly soon after telling him that Pat had been killed in the accident. Visiting hours were over and now he faced a night being observed.

He tried to conjure up Pat's face in his mind, but it hovered just out of focus. Where was The Good Vicar now? He could do with that comforting voice and the right words to ease the pain he was feeling. But how could he visit himself in hospital? The Good Vicar was there to keep his life on the straight and narrow and to ease the pain in other people's lives. He could not be comforted by The Good Vicar.

He forced himself to turn, sighing loudly as he did so. He felt fine, why did he have to spend the night in bloody hospital?

'You awake Andrew?' A whisper.

'Brian?'

'Yes, they brought me in here while you were sleeping, I asked them to.'

'Brian, I'm so sorry about Pat I…'

'That's okay. It wasn't your fault.'

'But I was driving.' He half stumbled over a sob.

'And you did a good job from what I've been told. Apparently the car in front of you braked suddenly for a fox, you managed to stop without hitting him, but you were in an intersection and another car came screaming through the stop street and hit you side on, crushing the passenger side of your car.'

Andrew wondered if he could have talked so calmly about Marge being killed in a car crash as The Heathen was talking about Pat.

'The driver of this other vehicle, what happened to him?'

'Hit and run. The car was stolen and the police suspect that it was a youngster out for a joy ride.' Still no emotion.

There was a long pause then, with just a hint of a tear, 'She died instantly they said.'

Andrew swallowed hard. 'I'm sorry Brian. How are you holding up?' He managed to find The Good Vicar's voice for The Heathen and suddenly understood what Marge meant when she said that he was always there for others.

'I'm...I'm okay I guess. I was never the best of husbands. She deserved better. I think I realised very soon after we got married. She never said a thing though. I just got this feeling that she was disappointed with me, but I could never work out exactly what it was. I tried, believe me I tried really hard for those first few years, but nothing seemed to work. There was always this divide between us. Eventually I began to realise that it was the fact that I was not a Christian. Her faith was very important to her, but I could never bring myself to believe in all that...'

Andrew heard him shift uneasily in his bed.

'...that stuff. She tried hard to convert me. Never in a pushy way mind, she had too much class for that, but we would have long debates, all night sometimes. Eventually she just gave up, but you know what? She never stopped praying for me. Every night before she went to sleep she would pray. Not out loud, but I could tell from the way she looked at me that she was praying for my soul.'

He sucked in his breath sharply and was quiet for a moment except for his heavy breathing.

'Brian? You okay?'

'Yes,' he hissed. 'Just moved the wrong way, caused a shooting pain. It'll settle in a minute.'

Andrew itched to ask him about his injuries, what had led to them, and if he had in fact been the one who had kidnapped Arkayic, but felt that he couldn't interrupt Brian's confession. Besides, he was fairly sure that The Heathen would talk about it sooner or later.

'Father?' Brian was sufficiently recovered.

'Yes?'

'Will you pray for my soul every night now that Pat's gone?'

He had not expected that.

---oOo---

He sat up suddenly, his hands flying up to protect his face.

'Stop!' He was screaming.

'Andrew! Andrew! Nurse!'

Hands, soft feminine hands were holding him back, pulling gently at his arm.

'Mr Compton. It's alright Mr Compton.'

The nurse was a pretty one, curly blonde hair, pale blue eyes, soft red lips and rosy cheeks puffed up just slightly with puppy fat. She smiled gently as he calmed himself and allowed her to guide his hands back to the bed.

'You were having a nasty dream,' her voice was soothing against the harsh white light of the room. 'It's okay.'

He fought hard to bring his breathing under control, nodding slowly. 'I'm okay. I'm okay.'

The nurse put a cool hand onto his temple, then helped him ease his head onto the pillow. She let the back of her hand lightly caress his cheek before helping to tuck him up.

'There you go, Vicar,' she smiled. This was not flirting he realised, she was mothering.

He sighed and snuggled a little into the bed.

'I'm sorry for the trouble.'

'No trouble at all,' she cocked her head slightly, giving him a strange look suddenly, as if she had read something odd in his eyes. It was only for a fleeting moment before she straightened.

'You get some sleep now, everything's fine. Can I get you anything? Some water?' Her voice betrayed none of the curiosity that her look seemed to contain.

'No. Thanks. I'm fine now. Thank you.'

She smiled again then turned and, calling a 'goodnight' over her shoulder left the room, turning the light off on her way.

'You okay Andrew?' The Heathen sounded concerned. He now had a flavour of what they were up against and his fear showed in his voice.

Andrew took over control from The Stud Muffin who was still visualising the pretty, wriggling arse of Goldilocks leaving the room, she was an angel.

'I'm fine,' he said without conviction.

---oOo---

He watched the dawn fade into the room, feeling the tiredness of a sleepless night. He had managed to doze off after Brian had finished his confession, despite the contents of that confession being enough for him to stay up all night. The shock of the accident and Pat's untimely death had dragged his eyelids closed.

But the dream had snapped them open again and they had not closed since the cute blonde nurse had tucked him back in.

Was The Rat really responsible for Pat's death? The dream was telling him so. Those two beady eyes gleaming evilly under the hood as he sat hunched over the oncoming car's steering wheel was a frightening and haunting image.

Brian seemed just as haunted by his own dreams that he had confessed to. Dreams of digging up bones and kidnapping a baby girl.

Were they dreams or flashbacks to a reality that he had somehow blacked out?

'Good morning.' A tall, gangly nurse with a flat ugly face came in. Her smile, although genuine, looked like a sneer.

Andrew greeted her and looked across at Brian, he was still asleep.

'Um, nurse, is the nurse who was on night duty last night still here. I just want to apologise for the disturbance I caused?'

The tall woman looked puzzled. 'I was on duty last night, there was no disturbance.'

'But I had a nightmare. A young nurse, short, pretty girl, blonde curly hair, blue eyes. She came in to help me.'

The ugly nurse frowned. 'There is no one that looks like that on the staff here, you must have been dreaming,' she said.

---oOo---

You really should rest,' Marge chided gently.

'I can't Margie,' why Margie, why that affectionate name you sentimental fool? 'There's too much to do, too much going on.' She was right though, he should rest. He felt worn out again and guilt about Pat's death was being drip fed into his conscience, slowly filling the horrible emptiness that had gnawed away at him since the news had first hit home.

'It wasn't your fault.'

He hated the way she could read his thoughts.

'I know it's just...' It's just that I dragged her into this mess by having that stupid affair with her. '...maybe if I had swerved...'

The Good Vicar nodded his approval at the word 'stupid' and Andrew glared at him. It had not been stupid.

'...instead of braking...'

It had been needed and he wished it could still be going on.

'...then Pat would...'

He felt a rage building towards The Good Vicar but at the same time his words that had been clattering out of his sub-conscience were being noticed by his conscience and the tears that now spilt from his eyes made him choke suddenly.

'Oh Andy,' she was next to him, her arm around him, mothering him. 'Andy don't do this to yourself. It was not your fault.'

Andy? In the mists of his grief he still managed to question her shortening of his name. She had not called him that since they had been dating in uni. Andy and Margie. That's how they had been as students, but once he had started working, Andy had seemed too casual for the role and the more formal Andrew and Marjory had soaked through from work to home.

His sobs quietened under Marge's gentle caress and he felt the calmness ease back into his body. I should get up and do some-thing. But it was too comfortable and comforting in his wife's arms. Besides where would he go? What would he do?

'I think I'll go lie down for a bit.' He sounded like a little child and felt like one too.

Marge nodded and loosened her hold on him. He climbed shakily to his feet. As he headed up the stairs with Marge standing at the foot, checking his progress, he suddenly had a mad craving for rich tea biscuits. He stopped and turned. Marge took a step forward and instinctively opened her arms slightly to catch him should he fall.

'Do we have any biscuits?'

Marge stared at him for a second and he watched as her face seemed to suddenly realise that it was not a profound statement he had made, but was only a simple request.

Was she really expecting some deep and insightful words from him?

'I think so. Do you want some tea as well?'

'Um…yes please. Have we got any rich teas?' He heard his voice whining and wished it would stop. Why did he want rich teas so badly? He was begging.

'I'll see what I can find.' Marge's voice gave sound to the gentle smile on her lips.

The bed accepted him as it always did. No questions, no judgements. It just enfolded him in its comforting arms. It hadn't asked 'Where's Marge?' when she had deserted him. It didn't demand to know 'who's this?' when he had been making love to Pat. It was like a good friend who you could confide in.

'You're in luck, there were two left.' Marge placed the tea and plate with the biscuits on next to him.

'Thanks,' he smiled sweetly.

Marge hesitated then sat down next to him, her hand instinctively going to his brow and gently caressing it.

'If you want to talk about it, I'm here.'

He felt a lump rising in his throat. 'No, I'm fine. Maybe later, but I really need a nap now.'

He was closing the door gently in her face and she knew it. She looked away, then down at the floor for a second then stood, straightened her skirt and patted her hair into place.

'It'll be okay,' it was almost a whisper.

He smiled weakly back at her, feeling like a complete bastard. He made a mental note to try and talk to her later, try and let her in on the madness that was going on in his life.

As soon as the door closed behind her, he turned his attention to the biscuits and tea, and sat up in the bed.

And after giving thanks he broke the bread and said, 'This is my body, broken for you, do this in remembrance of me.'

Was this why he had wanted the rich tea so much? Could his tea and biscuits be used as symbols of the body and blood of Jesus? Some thing, a force of sorts seemed to be pushing him towards this conclusion. It felt like a good force, but this was the Lord's Supper, it was not something you messed around with.

He looked over at The Good Vicar for advice and saw the same confusion that he was feeling.

Suddenly he felt that this was it, this was the big test that would determine how the whole McCready affair would pan out. If he got this wrong then he would be damned, but if he got it right...

He stared at the biscuits for a long time. It seemed ludicrous, a small part of his mind was saying, that something so small, innocuous and mundane would have such significance.

Very slowly he reached out for the plate.

---oOo---

'You feeling better love?' Marge smiled nervously as he entered the lounge. She put her book down quickly and stood, reaching for him and pulling him into a hug, her lips brushing faintly against his cheek.

He tightened the hug and whispered 'Yes, I feel much better, thanks.'

After a moment of standing holding each other, she broke the embrace and guided him onto the sofa, the scene of her adultery.

'Andrew, I want you to know that it is over between me and Brian.'

He quickly covered the exposed breast that had sprung up in his mind and nodded. 'I had sort of figured that out the other night,' he grinned slightly lasciviously.

'Oh Andy,' she blushed and patted her hair, but made no attempt to stop him as he worked his way to uncovering the breast that his mind had so recently covered.

Half an hour later he watched her dress and then climbed into his clothes. He felt strangely invigorated by what had just happened.

---oOo---

In his study he eased himself into the chair, letting it welcome him back. He sat for a few minutes, luxuriating in the comfort that it offered, then fired up his computer. He needed to finish his sermon for tomorrow and it was already late afternoon. The faithful few would probably forgive him for not having a great sermon, presuming of course that Eve had let everyone know about the accident. His mood sunk as the accident and all its implications came back to him. Pat was gone but Marge was back. It all felt strange. Suddenly another impli- cation of the accident occurred to him and he opened the top drawer of his desk. The small, black dictaphone lay there innocently taunting him. What should he do with it now? Pat was not there to object anymore to what he did with the recording and Brian didn't really have a say in the matter. He stared at the machine for a good while without coming to a decision.

'Tea.' Marge interrupted the decision making process. At least she brought custard creams he thought closing the drawer, smiling at his wife and shelving the dictaphone for later.

Once she left his office, he set about tapping away at his computer and watching the sermon form on the screen. It was one of those that wrote themselves. He felt almost as if he were in automatic mode. It would not be a great sermon with deep insights into scripture. It would say what had been said from thousands of pulpits over the years, just the words and anecdotes were different, but it would do.

He sat back as the computer saved his document, then with a slightly smug look on his face, he clicked the print icon. The feeling of invincibility that had arisen in him after making love to Marge this morning had not dimmed.

The phone rang and he picked it up.

'Andrew Compton,' he said cheerfully. His invincibility went from one hundred to zero in a few short sentences.

---o0o---

'For what we are about to receive may the Lord make us truly grateful, for Christ's sake, amen.' The Good Vicar guided the family through grace. He had pretty much taken over since the phone call as Andrew had withdrawn and not felt much like facing the world.

From his little cocoon he watched as The Good Vicar went about his business, but now he had to emerge again. His family were sitting looking at him expectantly. Even Arkayic was staring intently. They could sense that it was The Good Vicar sitting there and all they wanted was their husband, their father, their granddad. Even The Good Vicar knew that and was urging him to take control, something that did not happen often.

'Come on, tuck in, he managed to smile and the atmosphere broke. Jane and Sean still seemed a little wary and Marge dug her fork into her potato in an unconvincing act of solidarity. It was only Arkayic who seemed to relax completely and she coo'ed then waved her plastic spoon in the air before thumping it on the table in front of her. Jane took the spoon and began to feed her while Andrew started to cut his meat. He knew he should say more to ease the tension.

'Hmm, this is delicious love.' It was thankfully his and not The Good Vicar's voice. 'You know I was thinking, we haven't really met Gary yet Sean, you should bring him over for dinner one night soon. Maybe you and Harry could come up from London as well Jane, what do you think?'

The family were surprised by the sudden invite of Sean's lover and Jane's partner, all except Arkayic who swallowed a mouthful of puréed mush and nodded approvingly at Andrew.

'That's a great idea,' Marge gushed a little too much, but it broke the ice and soon a relaxed conversation broke out round the table which allowed Andrew to tiptoe back into his private space for a little while.

Why had Linda McLeod died? That had not been expected.

---oOo---

The aisle divided the living and the dead. Standing in the pulpit he looked down at the church and on the left side sat Peggy, Pat and Linda. On the right sat Eve, Sean, Jane and Roger.

The doors at the back of the church opened and Arkayic came crawling up the aisle, her little face showing determination for the task. She reached the front row of pews and hoisted herself onto the right hand one, then peered round the side of her seat toward the back of the church.

A veiled figure began to walk up the aisle with a short hooded one swaggering along next to it. This oddly matched couple moved slowly forward and seemed to take forever to reach the front. There was something about the veiled figure that upset him, but he could not tell what it was.

At last they reached the front pew and the veiled figure moved onto the left and sat down while the hooded one seemed undecided on which side to sit. Eventually it sniffed and joined the veiled figure who threw back the veil and patted her hair into place.

Andrew woke up sweating.

---o0o---

Marge sat on the right hand side of the church as she always did. Sean, Jane and Arkayic were with her. Roger surprised him by being there and he sat on the left. Eve was on the right next to Audrey and David and Kirsty Bridges sat on the left behind Roger. The Naked Woman was nowhere to be seen as David wore a jacket hiding her.

A quick glance at Kirsty made him realise that she had recalled what had happened when they had met on the bench. She would not meet his eyes.

Most of the regulars who had deserted him the previous week were back and he felt a slight smugness towards the bishop who had fretted so over the loss of congregation. He was a bit surprised that his prayers for Linda had not produced the miracle that Roger had been hoping for.

He looked down at the notes for his sermon, then back up and was halfway through the first sentence when he saw Alex sitting in the back pew, his beautiful blue eyes staring at him with a longing that caused an ache in his heart. He wanted to abandon his post in the pulpit, run down the aisle, gather that beautiful cherub in his arms and bathe in the lust that suddenly bubbled up in him.

'Fight it!' screamed The Good Vicar as he stumbled over a sentence and gripped the sides of the lectern.

He tried to look elsewhere in the congregation to avoid eye contact with those baby blues but his eyes kept wandering back to those seductive eyes, his heart pounded and he felt the perspiration gather in the back of his shirt.

The Good Vicar soldiered on with the sermon, casting supportive looks across at Andrew as he wrestled with this temptation. *Why can't he pull that hood up and hide that beautiful face* Andrew cried out and he began to tremble.

In the midst of the heart thumps and sweat drips he saw Marge's concerned look. She was about to stand up to help him.

Suddenly he heard a voice that was familiar to him, but one he could not place.

'He did this to me too,' it said.

Andrew looked round the church, trying to locate the source of the voice. The Good Vicar was still stumbling over his words and would soon stop speaking.

Alex seemed to be glowing in the back pew, a beacon that drew his eyes. He felt his fingers loosen on the lectern and he knew where his feet were going to take him. Why in a church? Why here of all places was he going to commit such a horrible sin in front of so many witnesses.

'Andrew! No!' The Good Vicar's cry was hardly a whisper in his head and the beautiful smile on Alex's face glowed brighter.

He let go of the lectern.

---oOo---

'Roger, I'm so sorry about Linda,' Andrew struggled to do The Good Vicar's work. Roger nodded sadly, not really noticing who was speaking to him.

'She's at rest now,' was all he could muster. He seemed to be in somewhat of a daze.

Andrew glanced over at The Good Vicar who was still curled up in a corner of his mind shivering.

'You okay dad? You seemed to lose your way a bit there?' Sean looked concerned while Jane, Marge and Arkayic echoed that look a pace or two behind him as they filtered out of the church.

'I had a funny turn, but I'm alright now.'

'You must go see the doctor,' Marge said while Arkayic shook her head.

'I'm okay,' Andrew said again, 'I'll explain later.' He gave her a reassuring pat on the shoulder which doubled as a *move along you're holding up the queue* pat.

Marge gave him a puzzled look, but obeyed the pat.

Andrew worked his way through the remainder of the congregation, spending enough time with David and Kirsty Bridges to make them feel welcome without making Kirsty feel uncomfortable.

'Do stay for some tea or coffee,' he cajoled them. 'Eve, will you show David and Kirsty round to the hall please?' he asked as David showed a willingness to stay. Eve gave a hearty laugh, but added a strange conspiratorial look towards Andrew as she wobbled past.

He let the last member of the congregation go by, then stared into the church. There was no one there. Puzzled, he went back inside and moved slowly up the aisle, checking between the pews as he went.

He ended up in the Lady Chapel where he had hidden from Eve a few days earlier, but still did not find what he was looking for.

Where can she be? He wondered to himself. And why was Alex/The Rat so afraid of her, scurrying off like that at just the right moment? And whose voice was it that had said *he did that to me too*? He had heard that voice before.

---oOo---

Was it the weekly ritual of the Sunday roast that made it seem mundane? Every joint cooked to the same texture and lightly spiced in the same way. The potatoes, crispy on the outside, fluffy on the inside, just like last week. The Yorkshires always a little doughy and the gravy, Marge's Bisto special. The obligatory carrots and herd of peas neatly corralled into a corner of the plate completed the picture.

Today he embraced the mundane-ness of lunch. It was a touchstone that linked him to normality. He chewed diligently on a piece of beef, letting that familiar yet unidentified voice *he did that to me too* swill round in his mind. The Good Vicar knew that voice too, but could not place it either.

He checked his thoughts for a minute to add to the conversation at the table. Only Arkayic seemed to realise that he was not all there, which manifest itself in the occasional quizzical looks he got. But she was canny enough to be deflecting attention from him by squashing the peas on her plate with podgy fingers.

Where had she disappeared to? That was the other question that jostled for attention, that and why had The Rat been scared of her?

He was positive that she had not come out of the front door of the church, yet she had been there as he had followed the choir down the aisle, but there was no sign of her when he checked the pews later.

He discarded the naggingly familiar voice in favour of trying to resolve the issue of the disappearing woman. He pulled up the picture he had in his mind of her, the curly blonde hair and blue eyes, the slightly puffy cheeks. He had not dreamed up this woman in the hospital, she did exist. He wanted to ask his family if they had noticed her and if by any chance they knew her, but was too scared of the answer he would get.

'It's going to be a busy week isn't it love?'

He had let himself drift off too far. 'Huh?'

'I was just saying to Sean that next weekend would not be good to have Gary over as we're going to have a busy week…' She paused to check that he was with her this time. '…what with two funerals to arrange. Do you think that Brian…' She stopped again, staring at him and he felt his facial reaction to The Heathen's name being read. He gave the tiniest of nods, giving his blessing for her to continue and hoped that the kids hadn't picked up on this.

Arkayic gurgled and clapped her hands, a huge smile on her face as Marge continued, 'Poor man, do you think that he'll be well enough to attend?'

'I'll go and see him tomorrow and find out.'

There were other questions that he wanted answered by The Heathen. He looked across at Arkayic, wondering if he should take her with him to help prompt Brian's fuzzy memory.

---oOo--

The Sunday afternoon funk settled on the family and Andrew watched as Sean settled down on the sofa. He would probably not move for the rest of the day. Jane sat absent-mindedly playing with Arkayic while catching up on news about her cousins which Marge seemed only too happy to divulge.

He wanted to smile a contented, happy smile, a smile that mirrored the relaxed warmth of the setting, but he could not. He felt unsettled. The Ridge seemed to be calling to him. Someone, or something needed to speak to him at the bench, but he didn't want to go, too frightened of what might be there.

He couldn't face The Rat, even less if the boy turned up as the seductive Alex. He knew he would not have the strength to resist should that strange sexual desire flare up again.

But perhaps it would be Kirsty Bridges. Maybe his seed hadn't taken root properly as he had thought earlier, and now she was calling him back for another attempt. He must resist that call at all costs.

On the other hand, he still needed to try get the Bridges to forgive McCready. Maybe this was what was calling him there, maybe David and Kirsty would be there waiting to be convinced to do the impossible.

He glanced round at his family again, a slight melancholy took hold of him. Why couldn't he have a normal, happy family all the time? Why must he be satisfied with scraps of happiness when, for a few short hours his family were together at peace.

And now duty called. *Always thinking of others*. But what others this time? What others would he find on The Ridge. He didn't want to go, but the call of the bench was getting louder.

He glanced across at Arkayic. 'Do I really have to go?' he asked silently and felt his heart sink as the little child looked up from the flannel book she was recklessly turning the pages of and nodded forcefully, her small body rocking back and forth with the force of her conviction.

'I'm going to get a bit of fresh air,' he informed his family.

---oOo---

He sat down heavily on the bench, his breath coming quickly. His ribs ached slightly from the bruising they had got in the accident.

'Not bad for a man my age,' he mused as his breathing quickly returned to normal. 'It's quite a slope up to here and I can do it without too much effort.'

He looked round to see if anyone was there, but nothing stirred so he turned his attention to the town and began tracing the route from the Vicarage to Pat's house, but his mind excused itself from his eye's journey and, with a slight wince of pain, settled on the unsettling experience in the church earlier. How could that young lad have such an effect on him?

'He did that to me too.'

Andrew shuddered. The voice had not come from within his head, but from behind him.

He turned around very slowly.

---oOo---

Only Arkayic looked up when he returned and eased himself onto the sofa. The news about the cousins seemed inexhaustible as did the desire to hear it seem insatiable. It was almost as if mother and daughter had been locked into the room of their conversation to protect them, or to protect him.

Sean was dozing in his chair although his breathing seemed slightly unnatural, as if he too was being shut off and protected from whatever was happening.

Arkayic crawled over to him and he picked her up, bouncing her gently on his knee. Somehow knowing that The Rat/Alex had had this strange effect on another person comforted and unsettled him at the same time. He was not alone in his torment, but would he be alone in his resistance of the temptation?

The account, confession even, he had heard up on The Ridge had been harrowing and he was still having problems digesting it. Arkayic snuggled closer to him, her tiny thumb found her mouth and she sucked at it quietly. He put her arm around her and hugged gently.

Pat's features formed slowly in his mind, fuzzy at first then the edges faded into distinct lines. It comforted him that he could now see her like this, but as her face crystallised in his mind, other thoughts began to creep in, clouding the image in a horrible haze of unanswered questions and he shuddered slightly.

---oOo---

It felt odd being alone in the house with Marge. Sean had left after an early tea and not long after that they had put Jane and Arkayic on the train to London. It had been difficult saying goodbye to his grand-daughter, but she had grinned back at him and given him the thumbs up which, he supposed, boded well, although he was sceptical about it.

As he readied himself for bed, he planned out the day for tomorrow. He would go see the Heath...Brian straight after breakfast, then he needed to phone Father Gregory. He wanted, no not wanted, was being required to go and see McCready again. At least by resolving to do this, he would save himself the trouble of a dream telling him to do so. Then he needed to go see Roger about Linda's funeral and should also pop into the office to check on any admin there and ensure that The Lau...Eve was okay and was still keeping their little secret. He wondered if he would also have time to go see Kirsty Bridges. He wanted to try and understand exactly what had happened on The Ridge that day. Also he felt that he needed to check that she was okay with it.

The tea and biscuit plate from the previous day still sat on the bedside table and, as it caught his eye, he wondered if his decision not to try turn it into a Eucharist had been the right one. Time will tell, The Good Vicar tried to sound encouraging but he felt the doubt in the voice.

---oOo---

There was a sigh. Then a plopping sound as he fell into the stickiness of the dream. A scene like those in the old western movies lit up. A dusty main street lined with wooden facades. Outside the swing doors of the saloon stood Marge, Jane, Sean, Eve, Roger, Kirsty, David and Pat watching the street. They were all kitted out in cowboy/cowgirl gear.

The church bell rang out signalling high noon and he watched as a small figure appeared in the road, its Stetson pulled down low, almost like a hood. The Dream Master then turned his head so that he could see the blonde curly hair, soft red lips and pale blue eyes walking toward him from the other direction.

The two figures walked slowly towards each other then stopped about forty paces apart. The Dream Master zoomed in on The Rat's eyes, evil, snarling eyes that shot venomous looks at him to the point where it became unbearable for him to look at them.

The Dream Master turned his gaze to zoom in on the eyes of The Angel. Her eyes were soft, kind, exuding a balm to soothe the pain inflicted by The Rat's look.

His view then zoomed back to take in the whole street again and as he did, the small crowd outside the saloon rendered a chorale version of the theme to *The Good, The Bad And The Ugly*. He stifled a laugh, frightened of the retribution The Dream Master may serve up.

The Rat and The Angel took up the gunfighter pose, hands twitching over holstered weapons, neither taking unblinking eyes off the other.

Then into this scene Arkayic came crawling. She appeared from under the porch of a building and in a few quick wriggles was midway between the gunfighters. Neither of them flinched and Arkayic pushed herself unsteadily to her feet.

He cried out then, trying to alert his granddaughter to the danger, but his cry was stifled by The Dream Master and Arkayic wobbled slightly then as her confidence in being able to stand grew, she beamed a broad grin and two shots rang out.

---o0o---

He stared at the tea. A small wisp of steam rose from it and dissolved in the cool air of his study. His right hand rested lightly on his Bible, but his mind didn't know this.

What had happened to Arkayic? The shots had woken him before he could see who had survived the shootout. The theme to *The Good, The Bad And The Ugly* played continuously in his mind. *Deedle deedle dee. Dee Dee Dee.*

Stop that, he shouted soundlessly. I can't think with that racket. The sound faded slowly and his attention returned to the room. He lifted his hand from the Bible and picked up the rich tea biscuit that sat on the saucer of his teacup. Why had he taken the rich tea? There had been custard creams in the cupboard and they were his favourites, so why take the rich tea?

This was not helping. What did it matter which biscuit he took, he should go back to bed, it was just a silly dream. He started to push himself up out of his chair when he heard the light tapping on the window. His head swung round instinctively while his mind braced itself against what he might see.

But all he saw was his reflection in the darkened window. The tapping came again, this time accompanied by a muffled voice.

'Dad! Dad!'

'Sean?' He moved quickly to the window and opened it, his eyes slowly adjusted to the dark while his ears heard his son sob.

'Dad,' he said again as Sean's pale naked body began to come into focus, 'Dad, I've done a terrible thing.'

---o0o---

He found Sean's clothes where his son had said he had left them, then, looking round to ensure no one was about, he hurried back towards the car. What was he to do? His mind raced as he tried to figure out how to keep his son safe. He did feel a little resentment towards The Good

Vicar who had not uttered a word of help since Sean had explained his sin.

He wondered if he had been abandoned by The Good Vicar, but he could still sense his presence despite the lack of communication, it was however only a faint presence.

He stumbled slightly on the dark pathway and cursed Sean's stupidity at choosing this spot for his escapade, but as he steadied himself he forgave his son. This was something that Sean was equipped to deal with.

A sound up ahead made him stop. He snapped off his torch and moved quietly off the path. The darkness closed in around him and the silence hissed in his ears. He waited, then he heard it again. It sounded like a cross between a giggle and a sob. It was closer now and was accompanied by a breathless huffing.

'No! Not Eve too,' he muttered to himself and, snapping on the torch, hurried down the path towards the oncoming Laugh.

---o0o---

The kettle began to whistle its old fashioned *I'm ready* alarm and he switched it off, then poured the water into the two mugs. He was anxious to get back to Sean who needed him, but he had to see that Eve was okay first. *Always looking after others.*

'But what else can you do?'

'Oh, so you are still there,' the sarcasm coated response to the reawakening of The Good Vicar felt satisfying, but there was no time to argue with him, he had more important things to do.

He put the two tea cups onto a tray and, rifled through the cupboards for some biscuits. Jammy bloody dodgers. He cursed, but took a few of the stigmata biscuits out of the packet and put them onto a plate. Sugar is always good for someone in shock.

Eve sat on her sofa in her yellow dressing gown, her large bulk shuddering from a mixture of shivering fear, sobs and giggles. Andrew put the tray down gently on the table. He really should phone home.

'There you go, drink this.' The Good Vicar handed her a cup of tea and set about doing what he did best. He soothed the rattled nerves, calmed her sobbing frame and slowly brought her to a point where he could start extracting the story from his secretary.

But he needed to be gentler still. How do you ask a woman why they were wondering around The Ridge naked at that time of night? She was probably beginning to burn with shame at the thought that her vicar had seen her in such a state and, if she had suffered the same fate as Sean, incredibly embarrassed by what she had done.

The enormity of what Sean had done was only beginning to sink in and his brain was working overtime to try and figure out what he could do to prevent his son from getting into trouble. Now he had two people he needed to care for. He wondered how many others there might be. *He did that to me too.* Even the Good Vicar shuddered as that voice came back to him.

'I couldn't help myself Andrew.' The giggle that followed seemed out of place, almost as if she had enjoyed it. 'It was like he had some sort of power of me. I really didn't know what I was doing.'

'Who had power over you? What were you doing?' The Good Vicar kept the voice calm and gentle. He was not accusing her. Even though he knew the answers, he could not be angry with her. She needed to tell her story, get it out of her system.

'That lad, you know the one. You said he looked like a rat.' She stopped to allow a small laugh to judder through her body.

'Have some tea Eve. Take your time.'

She smiled sadly at him, nodded and obeyed his command, like a small child obeying its father. He watched her over the rim of his teacup and, catching his glance, she looked away, embarrassed by what she was about to confess. Sean had given him that same look.

'Okay?' The Good Vicar smiled and Eve gave a nervous laugh and nodded.

'Eve, I want you to tell me everything that happened. This is very important. I realise that you may be embarrassed by what has occurred, but it's really important that I know what's happened. We'll treat it like a confession. I won't mention it to anyone. Okay?'

Eve gave another sob and nodded again, then she blew her nose nosily on a tissue.

'I had my Horlicks after I finished watching TV like I normally do, it helps me sleep I find. Then I went to bed and read for a bit, Agatha Christie, I do like her books and the one I'm reading at the moment is really good one, an Inspector Poirot one.'

Just the highlights, Andrew screamed noiselessly at her while The Good Vicar adjusted the facial expression to convey the same message in a more polite form.

'Anyway I eventually switched off the light and went to sleep,' she could read faces, 'It was just after midnight that I heard the noise. It woke me. Stones being thrown against the window.

'Well I got up and put on my dressing gown and peeped through the curtains and he was there, the rat boy. Well at first I thought that he was in some kind of trouble, but he just motioned for me to come out to him. You know with his hood down he looks like a...a...' She searched for the word, then almost blurted it out, '...a cherub.'

She looked at Andrew expectantly, waiting for him to confirm that she had used the right word.

The Good Vicar rearranged the *yes, I'm listening to you* look into an *I understand, please go on* look.

'That was when I felt like I had lost control. It was like I was caught inside a trance, I knew everything that was happening but could do nothing to stop it. Well I got dressed and hurried out to him. He had moved onto the road and I followed him. I had to, I couldn't stop myself. He kept walking so I kept following him.'

'Where did you go?' Andrew was pretty sure that he knew the answer. He bit down hard on a jammy dodger, taking his growing anger at The Rat out on the defenceless biscuit.

'Up to The Ridge, to Geoff Deane's memorial bench.

'And what happened then?'

Eve turned away from him as the tears began to flow.

'When I was young, I kept telling myself that I would find the right man one day, so I saved myself for then. I wasn't the most attractive girl, but I did have boys wanting to...you know.' Her voice sounded detached, faraway. 'But up there, I couldn't help myself. I had no control over what was happening.' She turned suddenly towards him again and wailed, 'Oh Andrew, I didn't want to lose my virginity like this.'

---oOo---

'Dad! It's statutory rape. I have no defence. It felt like I was the one who was being raped, but the law would never see it that way. What can I do?' Sean paced round the lounge, his raised voice worried Andrew. It would wake Marge.

'Sean, Sean, sit down, please.'

Why didn't The Good Vicar take charge here? He fumed internally.

'You'll wake mum.'

That had the desired effect and Sean slowly lowed himself into the chair. He buried his head in his hands.

'What can I do dad? I am not a paedophile, honestly. Before tonight I had never seen a child as a sexual object. You believe me don't you?' Sean raised a questioning faced and Andrew gave a gentle nod.

'I do believe you son,' he desperately wanted to put his arm around Sean and comfort him, but couldn't bring himself to do so.

Sean studied his face, looking for any hint of a lie.

'You do?' The disbelief hurt, but he could understand where it came from.

'He did that to me too.'

'What!'

'That young lad. The Rat I call him,' he chuckled humourlessly, 'he has had that effect on me too, that powerful attraction.'

'Dad! You didn't...did you?' Sean seemed shocked and intrigued.

'I've been lucky, I've managed to resist, but I think I have had the help from a guardian angel of sorts.' It sounded corny as he said it, but that woman, the curly blonde haired nurse, she had to be an angel sent to protect him.

Sean stared at him for a long time, then shook his head slowly before looking down at the floor again.

'That doesn't really help me though,' he looked up again, the realisation that what he had just said would sound ungrateful was etched on his face. 'I'm sorry dad I...'

Andrew's eyes made a pre-emptive forgiveness strike on the apology, stopping it in its tracks.

'What are we going to do dad?' It was resigned and was accompanied by a sigh.

'Not much we can do tonight, let's try and get some sleep and we'll attack this problem tomorrow.' He turned to The Good Vicar as if to say, *How was that, did I sound caring enough?*

The Good Vicar rolled his eyes, but Sean fell for it.

'Okay,' he stared at the floor for a while longer, then, lifting his eyes, he said, 'Dad I've got to shower first, I feel grubby.'

Andrew nodded again, he knew what Sean was talking about.

'What about mum? I might wake her.'

'You go shower, I'll sort your mum out, don't worry.'

Sean searched Andrew's face again then shook his head as if trying to shake off the nightmare that was enveloping him.

'Thanks dad,' he said and climbed wearily to his feet.

Andrew stood and moved towards the stairs behind his son. Sean suddenly stopped, turned and embraced him, catching both him and The Good Vicar by surprise.

'I love you dad, no matter what, I love you.'

The embrace was gone before Andrew had a chance to raise his arms to reciprocate.

You too son. The phrase caught in his throat and he watched Sean trudge quietly up the stairs. His legs began to follow automatically, while his mind still lingered on the hug and how good it had felt.

He heard Sean moving round the bathroom and quietly pushed open the door to the bedroom. His eyes adjusted to the gloom and his heart stopped. Marge's side of the bed was empty, the bedclothes slightly ruffled where she had been sleeping.

---oOo---

'Come on son, hurry up.' He could understand Sean's reluctance to go back up The Ridge, but where else could she be?

The light from his torch picked its way along the path, but it shook unsteadily in his hand. Dawn was not too far away, but still distant enough for it to be dark.

He had not noticed the chill earlier when he had come looking for Sean's clothes, but now it bit into him. Perhaps it is cold dread that I'm feeling, his mind tried desperately not to imagine the worst.

But what was the worst. Had Marge been lured out like Sean and Eve to some sort of debauched sexual feast over which they had no control?

He could live with that, Marge would be blameless in this infidelity. An exposed breast jumped up in his mind and he reached for it, wanting to take motherly comfort from it, wanting to stave off the image of Marge going to the left side of the church in the dream, the dead side of the congregation.

In loving memory of Geoffrey Deane. They reached the bench, slightly breathless. He wanted to shout out his wife's name, but it stuck in his throat. The beam from the torch flicked over the bench and then into the darkness beyond.

Sean stood close to him, his breathing slightly laboured from the climb and, Andrew presumed, from fear.

'Dad, where is she? This was where he brought me, do you think this was where he brought mum?'

'I don't know son.' He was amazed at how calm he sounded. This was where he brought Eve too. Why was he not here with Marge, or had he already had his way with her and she was now wondering around The Ridge naked and dazed. He moved the torch to shine first on the spot where Sean had left his clothes, then where Eve had left hers. Nothing.

Neither of them could tell him what had happened after their encounter with The Rat. They could remember the act with vivid detail, perhaps too much in Eve's case, but after that it was a blur until they found themselves at the bottom of the hill without a stitch to cover the shame that welled up in them.

Surely that was where Marge was, but why had they not passed her on the way up? Maybe she had hidden when she had heard them coming. There were plenty of rocks and bushes to hide behind.

He flicked the torch around the area again in a half-hearted double check that they had not missed anything, then said, 'Let's head back, she may be down the hill already, or home even. She's going to need us.'

Sean nodded in the dim light of the torch. He had been there and his logic was on the same track as his father's. Andrew spared a second to feel a warm glow at this bond, then the cold reality hit home again and he guided the torch beam to the path down.

Another torch shone light back at him.

'David? David is that you?' Kirsty Bridges voice sounded terrified.

---oOo---

'We must go to the police, dad.'

'And tell them what? That you were having sex with an underage boy at midnight on The Ridge?'

'No! Dad!' His son turned his back on Andrew. 'But mum's missing. We have to tell them. Mum and David Bridges are missing.'

Andrew sighed and shot a glance over at Kirsty. She looked pretty sitting at the kitchen table, her small hands wrapped around the steaming tea cup, sucking the warmth and comfort from it while her eyes teetered on glazing over with the madness that had been there when he had first met her.

'No.' It was gentle now. 'Son, look I'm sorry that was a low blow, but if we go to the police there will be questions about what you were up to, questions which will be difficult to answer. The police are already suspicious of me over Arkayic's strange displacement from London. We can't involve them, not just yet anyway. Please trust me on this one.' He looked at Kirsty again as he said the last sentence and she nodded an almost trance-like nod.

A picture of The Sniff Detective flashed in his mind and he knew that his decision not to involve the police was the right one.

'Trust me son,' he said again in an almost whisper.

Sean's shoulders sagged, then he turned slowly and nodded his resignation. He moved to sit at the table, then seeing Kirsty there, he changed his mind and went and leant against the counter on the opposite side of the room.

Andrew took a sip of tea and then bit into his custard cream, enjoying the sweetness of the filling. He wanted to sit down, but, for different reasons to Sean's, he could not bring himself to sit at the same table as Kirsty. Their sexual encounter at the bench had taken on a sinister flavour given what had happened with Sean and Eve and possibly Marge and David. He took another bite of the biscuit, hoping to dispel the taste of that thought.

'Okay dad,' Sean looked down at his feet and shuffled them awkwardly, then shot a quick glance at Kirsty.

You can trust her too son, Andrew thought. She won't say anything. How he knew that he could not say.

He was worried about Eve too. She had been frightened to be left alone, but what else could he do? Bringing her over to the vicarage would have raised questions that would have been difficult to answer, but that was back then, before Marge had gone missing. It was different now. But how could he bring her here without raising suspicion. He could not tell Sean or Kirsty what had happened to Eve, The Good Vicar would not allow him to break his word that her confession would be held in the strictest confidence, unless...

He turned to Kirsty.

---o0o---

The ice cold blackness outside the window had slowly melted to a lukewarm grey. The tinny ringing of the phone in his ear disheartened him, but it was what he had expected.

'Still no reply?' Kirsty's voice was quiet but the tone told him that she shared his expectations.

'No.' It was the third time he had tried the Bridges' home. There was still no word from David.

A clatter of dishes from the kitchen told them that Eve, or less likely Sean, was busy tidying away the teacups and possibly preparing a breakfast of sorts.

'He got to her too didn't he?' Kirsty's face told him that she knew the answer already.

'How do you know?' He wasn't too sure if it was him or The Good Vicar who asked.

'You can see it in her face; that fear and shame. That's why you brought her here, not to comfort me, but to comfort her.' It wasn't an accusation, just a statement of fact.

He nodded and she smiled gently. He had been quite surprised at how easily he and Sean had divulged the full, well almost the full truth, to Kirsty. He had excluded Eve from the story of his trip up to The Ridge. He had also been surprised at how calmly Kirsty had reacted to the news.

They were alone in his study, the first time they had been alone together since that encounter on the bench.

'He would have come for me too you know,' she looked away now.

'Who?'

'That devil child.'

'The Rat?'

She gave a slight snorting laugh. 'Yes, The Rat. That's a good name for him. He would have come for me too.'

'What makes you say that?' He was intrigued, this was not madness talking.

'I don't know. It's just something I feel.'

'So why didn't he?' Andrew pressed her when she didn't offer any further explanation.

She gave an embarrassed laugh and looked away, then looked back, her expression saying, *you really don't know do you?*

'Because of you, us, we, what we did the other day.' She looked away again.' I guess this sounds crazy but when we...you know, well I felt something happen, I felt that I was being made pregnant. At the time I thought we were making a replacement for Chantelle, but now, I think it was for my protection that this happened. Me being made pregnant has somehow repelled that devil child from me.'

Andrew nodded slowly. It made sense in a strange way, despite The Good Vicar not wanting to accept it.

'But why me? If being made pregnant repelled him, why me, why not use David?' He winced inwardly at the use of the word 'use' but it was out there before he could think. Kirsty did not seem to notice.

'David is no good.' She then winced outwardly. 'That came out wrong. What I meant to say was that after Chantelle was born, David had the snip. We only wanted one child. It made sense back then, but after Chantelle was gone well...'

She didn't want to continue down that route so he changed tack. 'Why Sean?'

'He couldn't get to you so your son was the next best thing, a surrogate if you like.'

'How do you know he couldn't get to me? He did try you know.'

'Yes. I felt it in the church yesterday. It's frightening, but since I have become pregnant, I have sensed things that I don't think I would have been able to before.'

'Why Eve?' Andrew asked after digesting the reply.

'She was easy prey I guess. What does she know about him? Does she know something that he wouldn't want other people to know?'

'No, oh hang on yes, she knows that...' He stopped, remembering the fire and brimstone threat to Eve if she ever divulged that they knew that The Rat had eternal youth.

'There is something, but if I tell you, won't that endanger you?'

'I don't think so, I think that somehow my pregnancy protects me, but probably best not tempt fate.'

Andrew nodded. What Kirsty was saying made sense, it was strange. Just over a week ago, this woman would hardly talk, driven mad by the brutal loss of her only child, and now suddenly she was here, talking lucidly, making real sense of a nonsensical situation, and surprisingly calm about the fact that her husband was missing.

What had changed her so?

---oOo---

'Andrew, it's Gregory, can you come over as soon as possible.'

'What's happened?'

'McCready had some sort of a fit last night. Started around two in the morning. He's been in a coma since. Apparently he kept shouting "That'll teach The Good Vicar to ignore me".'

---oOo---

Sean was still asleep on the sofa, his even breathing at odds with the pained expression on his face. Eve, when he had popped his head round the spare room door was in a similar state.

'Tell Sean to let Jane know about their mother when he wakes up. Are you sure you'll be okay?'

Kirsty nodded. 'You go. We'll be fine. I'll take care of them.'

He felt bad about not telling her where he had to go, how do you tell a woman's whose husband had just gone missing that you were off to help the man who had murdered your child?

But Kirsty was calm and un-inquisitive. She seemed to instinctively know that what he had to do had something to do with resolving all this mess. She had changed since they had...

---oOo---

'Don't worry, the Governor has threatened to fire everyone on duty if any of this leaks to the press.'

The prison warden accompanying them pretended that he had not heard Father Gregory's quiet reassurance. Andrew could not help wondering if this was the one who had supplied his details to the press on his first visit and, deciding that he was guilty, glowered at the back of the guard's head.

His probably misguided anger didn't last long, he had bigger things to contemplate. Not only did he have to face McCready again, but he would have to do so with a reduced Good Vicar capacity. During the drive over to the prison he had looked around for his conscience companion, but had received only muted responses to his calls.

They reached a door where the prison warder stopped and indicated by a toss of the head that they should enter. Andrew glanced round quickly for The Good Vicar, but didn't find him and so followed Father Gregory into the room.

McCready lay in the single bed that the room contained. The bed clothes were pulled up almost to his chin. They rose and fell gently in time to his light breathing, but as with Sean and Eve, the regular breathing was offset by the grimace that was splashed across his face.

'He's been like that pretty much since his fit last night,' Father Gregory said without taking his eyes off the paedophile.

'What do the doctors say?'

'Same as with that blindness episode, they can't find anything wrong with him physically.'

Andrew nodded slowly and stared at the face on the pillow. With the steely-greys hidden behind their eyelid shutters, there was a lot less menace about the man.

'Is there anything you can do?' Gregory looked across at him now, a strange look on his face, like a parent appealing to the doctor to save their dying child.

Andrew scrambled around in his mind. What could he do? What would The Good Vicar do?

'I could pray for him,' he blurted out the grabbed-at solution.

His colleague nodded and both men bowed their heads. Andrew searched his mind for some words to use as a prayer, but all he got was a flash of curly blonde hair, pale blue eyes and soft red lips. The picture was in his mind for a second then gone.

'He didn't do it you know.'

'What?' Questioning.

'Chantelle Bridges, Shirley Creswell. None of them. He didn't touch any of them.'

'What!' Incredulous.

'Those murders, McCready didn't commit them.'

Father Gregory stared at Andrew, his mouth open. Had Andrew been a separate being in the room with himself he would have adopted the same disbelieving pose. It was true, he knew it was true, but had no idea how he knew it to be so.

The two men stared at each other, trying to come to grips with what had been said. A slight movement on the bed made Andrew turn.

'Thank you Father,' The Steely-Greys were active again.

---oOo---

The tea tasted bitter and horrible. How do you drink this stuff he wanted to ask the prison vicar, but refrained from doing so. He wanted to go home, back to Sean and Eve and Kirsty. They needed to continue their search for Marge and David.

He would go as soon as he could finish this discussion with Gregory. Didn't he get it? At the moment, there would be no way of proving that McCready was innocent unless they could prove who actually did commit those crimes.

He suspected that The Rat was the guilty one, but how could he even begin to prove that. *Yes Inspector, I believe that a youngster, about ten or eleven years old did it and not McCready. Yes Inspector, he looks like a rat, has supernatural powers and a distinctive sniff. I see, you believe me about everything except the sniff.*

He closed the door on that voice letting it become a muffled mumbling in his mind. Would McCready have said more if Gregory had not been there? He had had the feeling that The Paedo, or was he, had wanted to say more, but was holding back. He had to arrange time alone with McCready. Paul.

Father Gregory was looking at him expectantly. He had missed something.

'Sorry Gregory. I was, miles away, so much to think about.'

His colleague nodded his understanding. 'I was just asking if you knew where this youngster hung out, I mean does he have a home, a lair if you like?'

Andrew shook his head. 'No idea. As I said he just seems to appear and disappear as he pleases.'

A lair. He liked the word, it was a word coated in slyness and stealth with a hint of evil. He pictured a cave full of bones, a rancid smell of rotting flesh flaring up in his nostrils.

'Well if we could find where he stays, maybe the forensic boys could do something to prove McCready's innocence.'

And possibly where Marge and David are, Andrew added without saying anything.

---oOo---

He was still a bit shaken by the time he got home. It had been a narrow escape, climbing the pavement like that when he nearly nodded off. Fortunately the road had been quiet and the shock had woken him enough for the rest of the journey home to have been safer, but as he put the key into the front door, he felt the tiredness fall around his shoulders like a heavy blanket. He drew a deep breath, preparing himself for the leadership he would have to show once he got inside.

The sniff caused him to turn sharply and his eyes darted round the small front garden, desperately searching for the hooded figure that owned the sniff. The garden was empty, so he ran to the gate and wrenched it open.

'Goodness, Father Andrew, you startled me.' Audrey stumbled backwards, teeter for a heart-stopping moment, then righted herself and the glasses on her nose.

'Did you see a young lad in a hood out here just a second ago?' His voice was rough, demanding. Where was The Good Vicar?

Audrey was taken aback by the lack of Good Vicar in his voice and wobbled slightly on her heels.

'Sorry Audrey,' he calmed himself as best he could. 'I just thought I heard this lad and I need to speak to him urgently,' the voice, although not The Good Vicar's was having a positive effect on his elderly parishioner. 'You didn't perhaps see him did you?'

'Oh no, I haven't seen anyone along the street today other than you.' She screwed her face up as she studied his.

He nodded, but still glanced up and down the street himself to double check.

'You don't know where Eve is by the way?' Audrey ignored, or didn't seem to notice the mistrust of her answer.

'No.'

'Well I just popped into the church office to see if she was available for tea this afternoon and she wasn't there. The office was all locked up. That's unusual.'

'Oh silly me,' he slapped his forehead, hoping that the action didn't seem overacted. 'I forgot, I asked her to run an errand for me this morning. I'm sure she'll be in the office a bit later.' Lord forgive me. How had that lie slid so effortlessly from him?

'Oh good, I'll try on my way back then.'

The vicar would never lie to you would he? Andrew smirked to himself.

'I hope you find your young lad.' She smiled the smile that old ladies reserve for their vicar, a smile that says *that collar you wear attracts me because of the power it has over me, but it also says that you are off limits.*

He shuddered inwardly, but returned the smile with his *you flatter me, but yes I am off limits* smile, then pulled his *nice to see you but I must be off* face.

Inside, Sean was pacing the floor in the lounge while Eve fretted on the sofa. He could hear Kirsty playing a tea making tune on the cups in the kitchen.

'Dad.' Sean stopped his pacing and looked expectantly at Andrew while Eve gave a little shrieked laugh and tried to push her large frame out of the chair.

'Any news on your mother?' It was an odd way to answer the question that their eyes asked.

Sean looked crestfallen while Eve giggled nervously and shook a disappointed head, leaving Andrew feeling slightly guilty at not having any news.

He shrugged resignedly and eased himself into a chair. He wanted to be alone to think, but that was impossible.

'Did you get hold of Jane?' He changed the subject.

Sean nodded, 'Yes, she's getting the first train up. Should be here about twelve.'

'Is she bringing Arkayic, do you know?' He suddenly realised that his granddaughter was an important piece of this puzzle and felt that it was vital that she was here.

'I presume so, I didn't ask.' Sean's face changed suddenly. 'Should she have left her with Harry?'

'No, I don't think that that would have been wise.'

Sean nodded, accepting his father's opinion as gospel.

Kirsty arrived with the tea.

'I heard your voice Father and guessed that you wanted a cup.' She placed the cup down next to him and with it a plate containing two custard creams. He loved this woman. No, not in that way, he hastily explained to the absent Good Vicar, then looked up at Kirsty as he realised that he had made that excuse out of habit, The Good Vicar had deserted him.

Kirsty returned his look, then nodded slightly as if she had read his thought. To Andrew it felt as if it was The Good Vicar who had acknowledged him.

---oOo---

Arkayic wanted to go to him as soon as she and Jane got off the train. Jane was busy fretting about her mother and greeting Sean, so passed her daughter to Andrew without seeming to notice.

It soothed him having his granddaughter back, more so when she gave him a big hug and gurgled happily in his ear. He held her close, a sense that everything was going to be alright now flooded through his body, but he could not show too much of it outwardly, Jane would not tolerate him relaxing while Marge was still missing. He answered her questions as best he could, struggling to convince her that no, they should not go to the police and he would explain why later.

In the rear-view mirror, he caught a glimpse of Arkayic in her car seat. She seemed to be following the conversation intently, her small brow furrowed in concentration. When they arrived home he carried Arkayic while Sean took Jane's suitcase. Kirsty and Eve were in the lounge and they stood when the family walked in.

As Andrew opened his mouth to do the introductions Arkayic reached out to be taken by Kirsty, smiling happily.

'You're privileged,' Jane said staring in disbelief, 'she never goes to strangers.'

---oOo---

Andrew put the phone down and stared at it for a long time. Pat was dead, the funeral parlour had just reminded him of this and he felt quite flat. Marge was missing and he had hardly raised a panic within himself.

Always thinking of others. How could that be if he could not muster the requisite feelings he should be having about his wife and his lover?

Pat was dead, feel something damn it!

He tried to bring up the image of her in bed with him, tried to recapture the tenderness and love he vaguely recalled having then, but the image came up blurred, distorted by those wavy dissolve-lines they use on television.

Pat was dead. He tried to give himself another mental pinch to wake himself from his mental slumber and as if in response to this his ribs, bruised from the accident, began to ache dully.

He was in the car talking to Pat. Look out! She cried and he swerved violently to avoid the car that had braked suddenly in front of them. Then he saw it, that other car hurtling toward the passenger side of his vehicle, two rat-like eyes gleaming evilly over the steering wheel. He could hear the sniff combined with a boyish cackling laugh and then he began to feel...

---o0o---

Jane was still having a go at her brother.

'I still don't understand. That's no excuse Sean. Surely you could stop yourself, you're a gown man. You know the difference between right and wrong. What you did is disgusting, perverted!'

Eve gave a little sob, but Jane didn't notice. 'How old did you say he was? Ten? Eleven? You're a bloody paedophile, you're not my brother,' her voice was screeching now. 'My own brother. You know I have no problem with you being gay, I supported you when dad shut you out, but if I had known you were a bloody paedo I would have physically kicked you out of the house myself, you disgusting pervert you...'

'Enough!' Andrew moved into the longue. He had been caught in the doorway, unable to get past the blast of anger coming from his daughter, but now his own anger had built and he barked his command against the force of Jane's tirade.

'Enough!' Arkayic who was on her mother's hip raised her tiny arms and gave a joyful cry that sounded like a 'Yay!'

'You have no idea what's happened to Sean, no idea what we're up against here. There are forces at work, evil forces that are trying really hard to do damage to me, to my family and my friends.' He glanced at Eve as he said this. He had never regarded Eve as a friend before, but now in the face of adversity it was either friend or foe, and Eve was surely friend.

'I don't know why, or how he is doing this, but we are under attack by an evil, powerful enemy.' His voice was gentler now and he had calmed himself enough to register on the shocked look on his daughter's face. He turned to Sean who, until now had been staring at the floor, his head bowed by the weight of the guilt his sister had been laying on him. He too looked shocked and Andrew suddenly realised that he had never raised his voice to his children like that.

In the silence that followed his outburst, Jane tried to reconnect her lower jaw with her upper one, Sean resumed his study of his feet and Eve tried desperately to restrain a frightened laugh.

'Your father is right.' It was Kirsty who broke the silence, her voice strong yet comforting. 'We are at war. What this devil child has done to Sean and Eve is part of a string of despicable things and these will continue unless we do something to stop him.

Jane looked first at Eve, the shock that she was also involved clearly etched on her face.

'So what do we do now?' Sean had completed his PhD in shoegazing.

All eyes in the room turned towards Andrew.

---o0o---

In loving memory of Geoffrey Deane. The late afternoon air was slightly chilly, but was kept just on the right side of comfortable by a weak, misty sun.

Andrew surveyed his 'troops' and the laugh that bubbled up in his mind threatened to spill into the tangible world. Talk of this being a war had given a strange slant to his thinking.

Troops. A plump, elderly woman who can't stop laughing, a young gay man who had never been quite sure of himself, a young angry hippy girl, a bereaved mother who had gone from clinical insanity to clinicalness in record time and an intuitive baby.

Squad! A-ten-shun! He barked the order out in his mind, the mirth that built up again was cut short as Arkayic stiffened in her mother's arms and brought her hand to her forehead in a salute.

'Okay, this is where I first made contact with The Rat, and I've seen him here a few times. Also, we know that this was where Sean and Eve were led to. I suspect that his base is somewhere near here. It's possible that your mum,' he looked at his son and daughter, 'and your husband,' a glance at Kirsty,' are being held hostage near here. We need to find this place and hopefully we can rescue our loved ones.

'I suggest we work in pairs. Sean, you and Eve head further up The Ridge, Kirsty, you go with Jane and walk back down. I'll take Arkayic and search the area round the bench.'

Jane looked sceptically at her father and pulled her daughter closer as if to say, *No, you're not going to take my daughter, not in this dangerous climate.* But Arkayic wiggled and reached out for Andrew, then as Jane started to pull her back, she began to cry. Jane stared at her daughter and slowly, as though in a trance, she handed Arkayic over.

'Look after her,' she whispered and Andrew knew now that his daughter was beginning to understand.

---oOo---

The temperature had dropped a few degrees as he sat down on the bench. Arkayic had got progressively heavier as the afternoon wore on and she was now asleep on his shoulder. He wondered if any of the others had had any success, but doubted it. His legs welcomed the break from carrying his weight and the throbbing in his temples subsided somewhat as he relaxed his mind.

The others should be back soon. He checked his watch again, presuming that they were all still okay. That last thought didn't worry him too much, he *felt* that they were okay and took comfort from that.

His own search had been fruitless and, if truth be told half-hearted. Soon after the others had left, he had turned to his granddaughter and playfully asked, 'So Arkayic, are we going to find your Nan this afternoon?'

She had shook her head, slightly sadly he thought.

'She is okay, isn't she?' A panic arose in him.

Arkayic bounced in his arms as she nodded and gurgled.

He smiled gently at her and had begun his unenthusiastic search.

Now he watched the lazy, late afternoon traffic crawl silently round the town. Geoffrey Deane had been right.

'I did love this view.'

Andrew turned to face the voice. Geoff looked slightly transparent, but his voice was solid. Would he say more this time? Andrew wondered, would he explain what he had meant by *he did that to me too*?

'Mind if I sit?' The Vision asked, moving round to the front of the bench. Arkayic stirred in his arms and lifted her sleepy head. Instinctively Andrew tried to push her face back onto his shoulder to protect her from The Vision, while at the same time nodding his head towards Geoff to let him know that it was fine for him to sit.

Arkayic's head wiggled under his hand and he heard, or could swear he heard her say, It's Geoff,' her undeveloped tongue blurring the words.

He removed his protecting hand. Arkayic gurgled happily and reached out toward The Vision.

'Hello Arkayic,' Geoff held out a finger which she took and gripped strongly.

'What did who do to you?' Andrew almost blurted out the question. 'Last time all you said was "He did that to me too". Who did what?'

Geoff turned his gaze from Arkayic towards the town.

'You know who.'

'The Rat?'

The Vision nodded slowly, a pained expression on his face.' 'That was a long time ago,' he shook his head.

'What did he do to you?' Andrew's tone was slightly callous, he needed information and at the moment, he didn't really care how he got it.

Geoff sighed. 'I suppose it was me that started all this off, you see back then I was...well I had...' He struggled for the words. 'I had a few boys. I couldn't help myself, I am deeply ashamed at what I did.'

He turned to face the view that he loved so much, then went on in a dreamy voice, almost unaware of Andrew and Arkayic. 'Most of them turned out okay. I'm not saying that as a justification by the way, rather I'm just pleased they did. God knows it could have been a lot worse. One of them likes to fiddle with his nephew and another is pretty close to being arrested for looking at child porn on the internet, but those are the most affected of my victims.

'The others, thankfully were stronger. Oh they have hang ups but they keep them to themselves. On the whole they're pretty balanced people. One of the even married my daughter.'

Andrew nearly dropped Arkayic.

'What? Brian? You messed with Brian?' No wonder he turned out a heathen. He swallowed the last bit.

Geoff nodded without taking his eyes off the town.

'Do you know how that killed me, walking up the aisle with Pat on my arm, having to not flinch as I handed her over to him? Most fathers go on about how their son-in-laws are not good enough for their daughters. This was the reverse, the father-in-law was not good enough for his daughter's choice.

'And you know, he never mentioned it. Not to me, not to Pat. It was like he had shut that episode out of his mind completely. But I lived in fear. Every time Pat rang up, or whenever they came round I expected him to have told her and she to accuse me, but she never did. He's a good lad Brian.'

An exposed breast jumped up in Andrew's mind along with Brian's hungry lips near it. A good lad? Did this vision know what 'The Good Lad' had been up to with his wife? Andrew suddenly blushed as he wondered if Geoff knew what 'The Good Vicar' had done with his daughter.

'It's easily done,' The Vision continued. 'When you're that way inclined you have to be on your guard all the time. It's a constant struggle, every day, every time a beautiful young boy walks past you, you have to summons up all your strength to fight the urge.

'But once you let your guard down, then you're done for. You do the despicable deed and, if you get away with it, you get a little bolder. I was not struck down by lightning, I didn't have the long arm of the law bashing down my door. All it took was a few threats to the kids and you were safe, or so I thought.

'I was fine until I tried it out on The Rat. He was just like any of the others I had messed with, but once the deed was done, he changed. He seemed to gain strength from the experience and that frightened me. Here was one that was going to fight back and I knew I was in trouble.

'But he never went to the cops or to his folks, he just haunted me, appearing at odd times and places, looking at me, tempting me, seducing me. And I couldn't stop myself. It was like I had fallen in love with him, but at the same time hated him.

'Every time I went with him, I would be bubbling over with lust beforehand and then wallow in self-loathing afterwards. Each time I promised myself that this would be the last, but then he would appear again, looking like an angel and I would just give in.'

Andrew nodded, he understood about the angelic appearance.

'The Alex persona,' he said half to himself.

Geoff looked across at him now. 'Alex?'

'That's his name isn't it? To me with his hood up he's evil and he's The Rat, but with the hood down, he's the beautiful Alex.'

'But his name's not Alex. It's Paul. Paul McCready.

---oOo---

Andrew surveyed his troops and wished they weren't there. He needed to retire to his tent and strategise, but, he supposed, all the strategies in the world would be of no use if the troops were demoralised. He would have to work deep into the night formulating battle plans.

Kirsty was the one still functioning, the others were shell-shocked although Sean was showing signs of emerging from his stupor, but was not being helped by Jane who was getting progressively hysterical. He needed to nip that in the bud soon as it was contagious. Eve was a giggling wreck and Arkayic was asleep on Jane's lap.

Kirsty had managed to prepare a very good shepherd's pie, one which Andrew secretly admitted was better than Marge had ever managed. He found himself trying to recall his sexual encounter with Kirsty, eagerly anticipating the arousal that this would bring, but nothing came, just shards of a memory that seemed to have been deliberately shattered in an attempt to destroy the evidence. Where was that damned Good Vicar? This was his fault, couldn't he have at least let him have a memory to cling on to. He was about to let out a large sigh of contempt at what he now believed was the departed Good Vicar when Jane's hysterics broke through his thoughts.

'I'm calling the police, we can't hang around hoping that we stumble across this Rat's cave or house or whatever. How do we even know that's where mum is? She could be anywhere, she may have been involved in an accident. We must do something. I'm calling the cops.' She moved towards the door.

'Your mother is being held hostage by The Rat. The police will be of no use, we have to solve this one ourselves.' Even Kirsty looked surprised at the conviction of her own words.

---o0o---

Some of Marge's sleeping pills had eventually got Eve to sleep. She had got progressively worse during the evening. It wasn't the worried-about-mum hysteria that Jane had shown, it was more a slow draining away of sanity and it scared Andrew. He could handle Jane, and Kirsty's words had had a profound effect in bringing her back from the brink, but Eve…

'She's going over to the other side.' Kirsty placed a cup of coffee in front of him in the kitchen.

'What?'

'He's coming for Eve tonight, he's going to take her away and she won't come back.'

Andrew raised alarmed eyes.

'Oh, she'll be back physically, but she'll never be the same Eve. She's changed, I've noticed and I'm afraid that the change is irreversible.'

'What can we do?'

'We can try standing guard, prevent her leaving the house, but I don't think that'll be enough.'

---o0o---

The coffee tasted bitter, but then it would with two heaped spoons of granules. Andrew winced as he swallowed another mouthful. He had nearly dozed off and hoped that the caffeine kick would not only prevent him falling asleep, but also rid him of the growing nausea of tiredness.

He checked the clock. Still another hour before he could go and wake Kirsty for her watch. He opened a cupboard and sighed. They were out of biscuits. After another mouthful of the vile coffee he felt a little more awake and drained the rest of the cup in a few quick gulps. He shuddered against the taste then dumped the cup in the sink. He should check on Eve.

The hall was dark and he steadied himself against the wall, feeling his way along gingerly. As he reached the bottom of the stairs, his eyes were pulled towards the front door and he felt sure he saw movement through the small frosted glass window.

He paused, his heart pounding loudly in his chest. Had The Rat come for Eve as Kirsty had predicted? Very slowly he let go of the banister that he had rested his hand on and took a tentative step towards the door.

---o0o---

'Eve's gone.' Kirsty was awake immediately. Her eyes had opened as he entered the room and they showed little sign of her having been asleep, but he felt that she had been.

Her words were a statement rather than a question.

He nodded slowly, then shook his head, trying to dismiss the sadness that had accumulated there.

Kirsty sat up, swinging her legs off the couch. She looked exceedingly pretty and for just a second Andrew longed to be with her, but in a more intimate way, a more memorable way than the clinical encounter on The Ridge.

The urge passed quickly, but left a vague warm glow in its wake.

Kirsty rubbed her eyes then looked at him.

'Get some sleep, there's no point staying up now, we can't do anything. We'll start again in the morning.'

The words were soothing and he nodded before turning and leaving. He paused again once in the hall. Where was he going to sleep? Jane and Sean were sharing his bed and he didn't have the stomach to go to the now vacant spare bed. He could go back into the lounge and use the other couch, the adultery couch, but was worried that it may become the scene of new adultery should he venture back there at the moment.

That left his study. He could get a bit of shut eye in his chair, after all he had managed to doze off there numerous times when the dullness of the sermon he was preparing overwhelmed him. Funnily those usually ended up being re-written into some of his best material.

He would need a turnaround like that tomorrow he thought as he lowered himself into the welcoming chair. He felt his tension ease itself out of his body.

'How on earth did The Rat get her through that small window?' He asked the room quietly, then sat bolt upright, pulling all the dissipating tension back into his body. The Angel at the front door, had she been a diversion? Had she lured him out of the house so that The Rat could steal Eve away?

---o0o---

He felt soft lips brush against his cheek and a cool hand flit across his brow. His nostrils filled with a delicate scent of goodness. He didn't want to open his eyes, scared that The Dream Master was toying with him – was it The Rat hiding behind his eyelids?

The Dream Master allowed lips to be gently pressed onto his forehead and the volume was turned up on the gentle fragrance. He had to open his eyes.

Full red lips, curly golden hair and beautiful blue eyes pulled themselves out of the hazy image that greeted him. He opened his mouth to speak, but a soft finger on his lips prevented him doing so.

'She had to leave.' The words dripped like pearls from the full lips. 'She belongs to him now. There is nothing we can do. She could not stay as she would contaminate the house with the evil that has now taken hold of her. I am sorry Andrew. It had to be done.'

The fingers reached out and gently closed his eyes in the dream, then he opened them on the dull morning light of his study.

---o0o---

'…sometime during the night. We're not sure exactly when. We tried staying awake to stand guard, but he still managed to take her.' He could hear Kirsty's voice in the kitchen as he padded quietly down the passage.

'Daddy!' Jane greeted him with a large hug, obviously glad that he too had not been snatched away during the night. Arkayic cooed gently on Kirsty's lap.

'Eve's gone,' Jane sobbed into his chest.

'I know,' he told the top of her head.

'What's going on daddy? Is mum going to be alright?' She disengaged herself from his chest and looked up into his eyes.

He managed to hold her look as he scrambled around for The Good Vicar and then watched the panic grow in his daughter's eyes as she seemed to read the puzzlement in his own. Where was The Good

Vicar? He couldn't take the look Jane was giving him and in despair he looked across at Arkayic and Kirsty. They both nodded at him.

'Yes, your mum is going to be fine,' he said it with a conviction that surprised himself.

He looked at Jane who stared at him for a second, then across at Kirsty, then back at him. The panic subsided in her eyes and was replaced with a confused look.

'Go see if Sean's up, we need to plan what we're going to do today.' He couldn't take the look from Jane anymore.

She nodded slowly, then a panic took hold of her eyes that mirrored itself in Andrew's emotions. Was Sean okay? He held his nerve while Jane let go of hers and dashed out of the kitchen to check on her brother.

'Sean is fine,' Kirsty said calmly as soon as Jane's footsteps hit the stairs. 'I checked in on him a few minutes ago. He may have been having a nightmare, but otherwise he was okay.'

Andrew nodded slowly then moved across the room to put the kettle on. All he felt like for breakfast was a packet of custard creams, but he couldn't do that in front of everyone, besides which did they even have any? He couldn't recall.

He fumbled in the cupboard for the tea bags while throwing an offering of 'Tea?' over his shoulder.

'Thanks,' Kirsty replied gently.

He could hear Jane's footsteps returning down the stairs and he turned to greet her. As he did so Arkayic began to bounce excitedly on Kirsty's lap.

'Gamma! Gamma!' she gurgled.

'No love, that's your mother,' he said gently, moving towards her, holding out expectant hands to pick her up.

'Andrew.' Kirsty's voice froze him. 'Andrew, the front door!'

He nearly knocked Jane over as he hurried out the kitchen. He wasn't sure, but he thought he heard her say, *Sean's fine*, but the words brushed his eardrums like the caress of a butterfly's wings.

Her dishevelled greying hair had not been patted into place for a while, but at least she was clothed. Having comforted himself with that fact, he could now register the shock that her glazed over eyes gave him.

'Marge!'

'Mummy!' There was that butterfly again.

She stood for a second, arms relaxed at her sides, then slowly raised them at an angle, opening her fists to show her palms.

The angry red wounds revealed themselves, one on each of the offered hands and as he stared at them, they dissolved into jammy dodgers.

'Mummy!' Jane was trying to push past him, but he held his ground in the doorway.

Marge's fingers closed around the biscuits and crushed them, letting the crumbs pour out onto the pathway. As they fell, so too did the glazed look from her eyes and she blinked.

'Andrew.' The word left her with consciousness and he caught her as she began to collapse.

---o0o---

'Dad, Jane's right, we must call a doctor.' Sean paced the front room in his boxer shorts, his eyes constantly flicking from his father to his mother. The latter lay on the adultery sofa, a pillow propping up her head. Her breathing was relaxed and her face appeared serene.

'We can't Sean. She'll be fine.' He wished he believed that, but the conviction he had had earlier about how events would unfold had all but drained away.

'She'll be fine.' He tried to convince himself. 'Where's Kirsty?'

Jane looked annoyed. Why ask for Kirsty when you need to take care of your wife, my mother, her face said, but her mouth only said, 'In the kitchen with Arkayic.'

Arkayic. As he thought it, he heard his granddaughter's voice coming closer up the passage. 'Gamma! Gamma!'

Kirsty arrived at the door a second behind Arkayic who was scrambling frantically on all fours. 'Gamma!' She reached the sofa and tugged at Marge's blouse, pulling it askew and slightly revealing the sensible bra. Andrew shuddered as the act of adultery sprung up in his mind, but then relaxed as that quickly faded, brushed away by Marge's eyelashes as she opened her eyes slowly.

'Mum!' Jane and Sean were united in their cry, but neither moved.

'Andrew?' Marge blinked and looked around. He was beside her, helping her sit up. 'What happened Andrew? I have had the most awful nightmare.'

---o0o---

Her left thumb gently massaged her right palm. A small wisp of steam curled up from the untouched cup of tea in front of her. Her eyes flittered nervously across the faces that watched her, eager faces that craved details, details that her face said she would rather forget.

The silence hurt. Andrew wanted to say something to break it, but he knew that Marge had to be the first one to talk. They were all waiting for her to be ready.

'Gamma?' Arkayic's voice was gentle. Her small delicate face showed intense concentration. Andrew could have kissed her.

Marge stirred and looked across at her granddaughter. A far away smile came closer then retreated again. She reached out for Arkayic and Jane handed her over. Arkayic clambered into the expectant arms and snuggled up to the adulterous breast.

'It was horrible.' Her voice was hanging out with the smile. 'Every single one of them. I could feel their names burning inside me as we moved them. Linda Parker, Kylie McLear, Fiona Droight, Shannon Leary, Constance Fish, Kerry-Ann Stokes, Lisa Plummer, Cheryl Staines, Diane Gates...'

The names dropped heavily in the room as Marge listed all those who had disappeared, presumed to have been taken by McCready.

She finished the list and fell silent. The others in the room stared at her then suddenly Kirsty asked, 'Was there a man with you in your dream?'

Marge looked up startled, her eyes quickly asking the question. Who is this woman? In the scramble that had followed her arrival back home, there had been no introductions.

'This is Kirsty, Kirsty Bridges. Chantelle Bridges mother.' Andrew answered her eyes and watched the realisation start dawning.

Kirsty smiled a brief pleased to meet you, then her features returned to their previous worried state.

'Was there a man with you in this dream, about five foot six, dark hair, a tattoo down his left arm?' She leaned closer as she asked.

'David.' The involuntary word shocked the whisperer of it. She stared at Kirsty for a second, then Andrew watched as panic began to fill her face. She turned to him.

'Andy? It was a dream, please tell me it was a dream.'

---oOo---

The urge to swing by the storm drain was great, but he knew that he couldn't. His presence there would be highly suspicious, besides which, Father Gregory could handle things on that front.

He had been rather startled by Andrew's revelations, but had agreed to make it look like McCready had been confessing again. The problem was that the police already knew that the first set of remains that they had found there had been recently moved, and that they were the only remains in the drain. Even if they believed that McCready had confessed, there would be the question of who moved the bones. He did not relish another visit from The Sniff Detective.

Kirsty sat quietly in the passenger seat. She had listened to what Marge had said with growing agitation. At first Andrew thought it was as a result of her recalling Chantelle's death, but as Marge's panicked whispers continued, he realised it was David that Kirsty was concerned about.

'He's not as strong as your Marge.' Kirsty was reading his thoughts.

'He'll be okay, I'm sure.' Andrew responded and dropped further behind the car in front of him. They were nearing the scene of the accident that had killed Pat and, apart from the obvious nervousness, a small part of Andrew's mind was telling him that they could ill afford to lose Marge's car as well, not at this time.

Once safely through the intersection that still had some scattered glass lying in it, Andrew relaxed slightly and began thinking of his family. There had been no protest from Sean and Jane at his leaving them to look after their mother. It was like they had just accepted that he would be *thinking of others* as he announced that he would take the agitated Kirsty home. What he hadn't said was that he would possibly go on to visit Brian afterward. There were questions that needed to be answered, but first he had to deal with whatever they would find at the Bridges' house.

---oOo---

He stood on the pavement outside their house. From the way he carried himself Andrew could tell that he was dazed. Even though they were over half a block away, he could see this. Kirsty caught her breath and stifled a cry. Instinctively he patted her thigh in a comforting gesture.

He pulled up in a parking about four cars down from where David stood and they jumped out.

'David!' Kirsty cried and began to run to him, then stopped as the figure on the pavement turned slowly to face them. As he did so, he exposed The Naked Woman and in that instant Andrew thought he saw shame in her eyes, shame for her crass nudity and moreover shame and shock at what she had seen. She wanted to look away, but her inky permanence held her eyes fixed on Andrew, even when he lifted his to the vacant ones of her owner.

Kirsty waited a step or two away from David, too scared to reach out and touch him. They stood for a second, locked in a strange triangle like the gunfighters of his dream, each waiting for the other to blink.

Then in agonisingly slow movements, David brought his hands out from behind his back. In his left hand he held a small beige disc which, as his movements began to speed up slightly, Andrew recognised as a rich tea biscuit.

Suddenly the biscuit was held aloft as Andrew had so often held the host above his head at the Eucharist. David's eyes closed and his lips parted slightly as he prepared to say the words of the prayer that Andrew knew so well. His whole being screamed out that he should stop David, not let him continue with this irreligious act, but he stood rooted to the spot, unable to move.

It was Kirsty that reacted, springing forward and jumping to knock the biscuit from her husband's hands. It flew into the road and exploded into crumbs.

Life flooded into David's eyes followed quickly by horror. He blinked rapidly as he took in his surroundings, then slowly sank to his knees.

'Kirsty! What have I done!?' He howled into his hands as he covered his face.

---oOo---

The house no longer screamed out its emptiness, but it still did not feel comfortable. David was far from comfortable, he paced restlessly around the lounge as Kirsty updated him on all that had happened.

He shuddered as she relayed Marge's story, even whispering under his breath her name, *Margie,* a tender whisper, but it was not an adulterous one, more a brotherly one.

'They're probably at the storm drain already,' Andrew took over from Kirsty when they reached this point in the story. 'I'd advise you not to go there, you will only cast suspicion on yourself.'

'Suspicion? On me? Why? I was a victim in this remember. My daughter,' he paused and glanced at Kirsty to check that the mention of Chantelle had not upset her before going on, 'was murdered by that bastard. Why would they suspect me? I am trying to find answers as to why he did this.'

It was a fair point, but Andrew still felt uncomfortable with David returning to the scene. He may implicate Marge if the cops decided that his presence was suspicious and began to interrogate him. *He's not as strong as your Marge.* Kirsty's words came back to him. An implicated Marge would undoubtedly lead back to him despite his being completely innocent in all this.

'At least wait until it's on the news, then they will be less likely to question your being there.'

David hesitated while Andrew watched the logic sink in. The Naked Woman, feeling at home again in familiar surroundings gave Andrew a flirtatious look. If only she could talk, he thought.

'You're right,' David sighed, then moved across to the radio which he turned on. 'Ten minutes to news time,' he added, glancing at the clock on the wall.

'Do you know where the bodies came from,' Andrew asked suddenly. 'I mean where did you carry them from?'

'Andrew!' Kirsty admonished him,' he's been through a lot, he doesn't want to remember what's happened.' The tone was sensible, like The Good Vicar's used to be.

'It's important,' he retorted ignoring the tone. 'We have to find The Rat and stop him.'

'Stop him doing what? What is he going to do next?' Kirsty looked frightened.

I don't know, but I have a horrible feeling that he was clearing out those children's remains so that he can start collecting some fresh ones. David, you have to remember where the bodies were stored before you moved them?'

---o0o---

There was one more place to try. Someone else had been employed to move the bones. Besides he needed to discuss Pat's funeral.

Brian was looking much better.

'I should be out of here tomorrow. Have to take it easy, but the doc says I'm going to be fine.'

He was almost too upbeat. Where was his remorse at losing his wife?

'Have you got someone to look after you?' The question had its desired effect, reminding The Heathen that he no longer had a wife to look after him, and his eyes saddened.

'My sister is coming down first thing in the morning.' He sank back on the pillow and was quiet for a moment. Andrew let him re-digest his loss. He had seen it often in the bereaved, those times where the mundaneness of normal life conspires to let you forget your grief and believe that all is well. The denial stage. And then along comes a man in a collar to bring you back down to earth with a bump. God, he was tired of playing the role of emotional gravity.

Without The Good Vicar he plunged in, hoping that Andrew Compton would cope. The voice that came out of his mouth had sufficient elements of the right tone and his words, judging by Brian's reaction to them, seemed to be the right ones.

Pat's funeral was set for the following Monday and the arrangements followed a similar line to those that Peggy's had, with the exception of the question of recording it.

Once they had finished this discussion, Andrew moved uneasily in his chair and tried to mould the questions in his mind into acceptable words. He had two things that he wanted answered. Firstly, he had to see if Brian could recall where he had moved the remains of Shirley Creswell from. That must surely be where The Rat's lair was. If he could find that, he could get to The Rat and stop him.

The second question was more a want to know than a need-to-know one. He wanted to know how Brian, given what Geoff had done to him, could possibly marry his abuser's daughter and consign himself to either keeping their horrible little secret, or risk alienating himself from his wife by bringing the accusation to light. He knew that this question would go unasked.

'Brian, I'm sorry to bring this up, but I need to ask you about what happened just before you were beaten up.' He watched the man in the bed wince. 'It's important. I need to know everything that you can remember. I think that we can safely assume from what you have told me so far that it was you who moved Shirley Creswell's remains, even if you were under an influence of sorts.' He kept his voice low, almost at a whisper.

'Before you deny it, let me explain that both Marge and David Bridges, the father of Chantelle Bridges who was the one that Mc-Cready got done for, both of them have had similar experiences to what you had. As we speak, the police are busy recovering the remains of every one of McCready's victims from the same storm drain where you deposited Shirley's body.

'Someone, and I think I know who it is, took control of them and directed them the way you were used. I need you to tell me everything, anything you can remember. I have to stop this person before they start killing again.'

Brian stared at him, a mixture of fear and horror on his face.

'Brian,' his voice was gentle, almost Good Vicar quality. 'Please, this is very important. I need to know what you can remember, anything at all, even the smallest detail could help.'

Andrew watched him closely as he moved uncomfortably in the bed then, lying back and closing his eyes, he uttered a half sob and said, 'I really don't know Andrew. I've been going over it again and again in my mind and it's still fuzzy. I can remember heading off to see Marge in London,' he didn't flinch at this confession, 'then the next thing I remember clearly was that group of young thugs shouting at me and calling me a paedo just before they beat me up.'

'And nothing in-between?'

No. Nothing. Just dreams…nightmares. I was carrying this little girl. She was dying, her head had been bashed in. There was blood everywhere. It was so horrible.'

'Where were you in the dream? Can you remember any landmarks? Anything?'

Brian shook his head. 'No, nothing at all, it was dark, no buildings or landmarks of any sorts, just darkness. I'm sorry Andrew I really can't recall anything.'

'That's okay.' No it's not okay damn it! Can't you remember what you've done, any bloody fool can remember what they've done you imbecile. There was no Good Vicar to reprimand him for his thoughts so he did it himself. It was just the frustration talking.

'It's okay,' he said again. 'If you do remember anything, please let me know. As I said anything, even the smallest detail may help.' He stood to leave. 'I'll be in touch about the funeral.' He was almost at the door, his disappointment weighing heavily on his mind.

'Andrew wait.' He turned and Brian looked furtively around the room, double checking that they were alone.

'The kid, the one who made me do this, he looks a bit like a rat.'

Andrew nodded with his eyes and returned to his seat. 'Go on.'

'Well, I wanted to say something earlier but I was embarrassed.'

'Embarrassed?'

'Well, this kid…'

'Call him The Rat. That's my name for him.'

Brian raised a surprised eyebrow then smiled slightly. 'Oh, like you call me The Heathen?'

It was Andrew's eyebrow's turn to express themselves. 'I…I…how did you know?'

Brian's laugh was warm. 'He told. The Rat. You certainly sum up people well with your names. The Rat, that's just a perfect description and, I suppose, The Heathen sums me up quite well, although after this whole ordeal, my beliefs have been shaken up, you may have to start calling me The Doubting Heathen,' he chuckled and Andrew's laugh was relief-drenched.

'What did you call Pat?'

Love. 'I didn't really have a nickname for her, but I do call Eve The Laugh.'

Brian's mirth was cut short by a pain in his ribs. He drew in a sharp breath, then after a few seconds smiled again.

'That's a good one.' He lay back on the pillow again, letting the pain subside and the smile fade.

'That boy, The Rat, when I was supposedly doing his bidding, there is one thing I do remember.' Andrew leaned forward slightly. 'I remember it because it hit a nerve with me, something that I had tried to forget, he dragged it up again.'

'Go on.' Andrew did his best Good Vicar impersonation.

'Well, he said that we had something in common.' Brian stopped for a second, trying to force the unpleasantness out of what he was about to say. 'He said that, like me, he had been abused by Geoff Deane, my father-in-law. Now there's no way he could have been abused by Geoff, he wouldn't have been born by the time Geoff died, but how the hell could he know that I had been abused by Geoff. There I said it. I was abused by Geoffrey Deane.' He looked around as though expecting some sort of shift to occur in the universe now that he had admitted it out loud, but there was nothing.

'You seemed unmoved by that,' he said at last. Andrew cursed the missing Good Vicar. He would have known to act surprised.

Instead he heard the words, 'I knew that already,' escape from his lips and again he cursed silently.

'You knew! How could you have known, I never told a soul.'

But a soul told me.

Fortunately he had grasped enough control of himself again to not blurt out that thought. Instead he said, 'The Rat ratted on you.' It looked like he would get an answer to the unasked question after all.

---o0o---

He was at a loss as to what to do next. He had exhausted all avenues in trying to establish the location of The Rat's headquarters. The power the little rodent exerted over his victims had completely blocked out all pertinent details in their minds and he had no more victims that he knew of to talk to. The storm drain was still out of the question so home seemed the only option.

Marge was looking much better. She had washed and her hair was now neatly brushed, although that did not stop her patting it nervously as she sipped her tea.

Andrew disguised the emptiness he was feeling about the whole affair and the dread that The Rat was winning this battle. He spoke in his best Good Vicar impersonation voice as he updated the family on his lack of success. He tried to hint at passageways that connected the looming cul-de-sac with the next road but wasn't convincing himself and, judging by the looks he got, he was not convincing his audience either, not even Arkayic responded to his words.

He was tempted to put on the radio to hear the BBC voice tell him what he already knew about the storm drain, but refrained from doing so. He knew the details already and he had an irrational thought that by listening to the story he would be confirming his role (some would say guilt) in the whole sordid affair.

The inactivity began to gnaw at him. He felt a desperate need to be doing something, trying to stop The Rat before the killing began again. His family seemed to be settling into a post ordeal state of relaxation, even Arkayic lay peacefully on Sean's lap. Something would happen eventually he thought and let himself be lulled by those around him into foregoing his agitation.

His thoughts drifted back to his conversation with Brian and the f-word jumped into his mind. Forgiveness. Brian had not used the word, but all he had described about his relationship with Geoff certainly had the attributes of forgiveness.

It shocked him now as he thought about it that a heathen could be capable of forgiveness and this in turn shocked him that he could have thought that. Where in any of his theological books did it reserve that virtue for the sole use of Christians?

He could not even begin to imagine how he would have felt in Brian's shoes and, to his credit, did not even try. He did feel a slight sense of awe at what Brian seemed to have achieved.

His thoughts were interrupted by the front doorbell which injected tension back into his body. He quickly tried to disguise it, not wanting to contaminate his family, but they were a step ahead of him already.

'Audrey,' the relief was only momentary as the worried expression of his elderly congregation member followed the recognition of who it was.

'Father Andrew, you must come quickly. It's Eve. I don't know what's wrong with her.'

---oOo---

She was sitting at her desk, her clothes looked dirty and dishevelled. The blouse was slightly ripped and her ample bosom threatened to bust out of its confines. She was laughing. No, that was not the right word, laughing was what she used to do. Now she was cackling.

Her eyes had caught whatever disease her laugh had as they stared evilly out of what was once a pleasant face. She did not show any signs of recognising Andrew or Audrey.

'This is how I found her,' Audrey whispered. 'What's happened? Do you think that she's been,' she paused, the word was almost as embarrassing to say as the act would be for her to admit, 'raped?' It was practically inaudible.

Yes, both physically and spiritually.

'I don't know. Eve! Eve!' He clicked his fingers in front of her but this only seemed to make her cackle louder and her eyes sink further into their madness. He dared not touch her.

'We'd better call the police.' Audrey's presence gave him no alternative, he could not hide this one under the carpet. She was not wrapped up in this affair, she was an outsider and he knew his influence over her would be limited. Damn you Eve, you're making things bloody difficult.

He reached for the phone which rang under his hand and he withdrew it quickly as if burned. Then calming himself he picked it up.

'Andrew? It's Roger, I'm glad I caught you. Your daughter said you would be at the office. I was wondering if I could come and see you to discuss the arrangements for Linda's funeral.'

'Not now Roger, we've got an emergency here.' He slammed the phone down and picked it up again.

Maybe if it had not been Roger the Bloody Brick Thrower, Roger the I Can Walk Out of Your Service Deserter, then maybe he would have made an effort to summons up some sort of an imitation of The God Vicar, but he could not be asked, not for Roger.

He dialled the police station's number, cursing both Roger and Eve in his mind and blocking out Audrey's terrified stare. Eve was a diversion, a trap even. The Rat was getting worried, but Andrew was more worried that he was falling into this trap and he could see no alternative. Damn The Rat! Damn him to hell! He cursed.

---o0o---

She had done remarkably well given the incredibly short notice. The stumbling over her words and panic in her voice were just perfect. The calming down at the behest of the voice on the other end of the phone was spot on. There should be no suspicion as long as Audrey played along.

He had felt a bit devious telling her that the ambulance would respond quicker to a call from a distressed female rather than a male voice. That may actually be true, but the deviousness was his unvoiced reason for handing responsibility over to her.

The deception deepened when, after Audrey had made the call, he had said he needed to go see Roger to apologise. Audrey was caught between looking after her friend and making sure that the bereaved were taken care of, but she followed the view that the Vicar must be right and let him go with minimal fuss.

He was halfway home when he decided that he should really go and see Roger. He would just be a distraction otherwise.

'I'm sorry Roger, Eve was ill and we needed to call the paramedics. I was panicking.' He tried to measure the grovelling in his voice to be enough to appease, but not enough to degrade himself. Roger didn't seem to notice. It was hard to believe that someone who seemed to treat his wife as a servant could be so devastated by her passing. Maybe he's thinking you just can't get the staff these days. Andrew tried not to smile at that thought. He really did need to forgive Roger, but he didn't have the energy now.

They went through the funeral arrangements in autopilot mode, neither showing any particular passion for the task, a task made more difficult by the lack of biscuits with the awful tea. At least Linda could make a good cuppa even if they never had biscuits.

'I think that about does it,' Andrew said moving to stand. He wanted to get out of there.

'Andrew, there is something I need to tell you.' Roger was suddenly more alive but also nervous.

Andrew eased back in his chair despite thinking 'What now?'

'I don't suppose you're going to believe me, but this is the God's honest truth.' He stopped and tried to read Andrew's expression which was desperately scrambling around for the right one to settle on.

Roger hesitated until Andrew managed to find his *go on, I'm listening with an open mind* look.

'Well that night, the one when I threw that brick. Andrew, you've known me a good many years, you know that it's not in my nature to do such things.' He paused waiting for the agreeing nod which Andrew provided. 'I wasn't myself that night. I was,' he groped around for the correct words, 'I was under some sort of undue influence.'

'The Rat.' The words left Andrew along with all the bitter feelings he held had towards Roger.

'What?' Roger's voice held more surprise than question in it. 'You know.'

'I didn't know, but I should have. How foolish of me. Roger I'm very sorry, I have been blaming you for your actions, but it has not been your fault. The Rat, you seem to know who I'm referring to, has been causing havoc in the town of late. You are not alone in falling under his influence.' He watched the relief drain into Roger's face and felt a small warm glow ignite in himself. He had done a Good Vicarly deed and brought relief to a parishioner's woes without the help of The Good Vicar.

At the front door they shook hands warmly.

'I'll see you at the funeral then,' Roger gave a sad smile.

Andrew nodded and returned the smile despite the thought 'that's if I'm still around then,' passing through his mind.

---oOo---

Jane greeted him at the door. 'They've taken Eve to hospital. Audrey just dropped by. They think she's had a nervous breakdown of sorts.'

He nodded at the news.

'Is she going to be okay daddy?' Her eyes looked sad, like she already knew the answer.

'I...I don't think so.' He swallowed hard and looked back to the street to prevent his daughter seeing the welling up in his eyes. He would miss The Laugh he suddenly realised. With all the horrible and sad things that happened in this world, people who could be happy and laugh should be treasured. They were special people, people sent to remind us about the bright side of life. But The Laugh was gone. She was now The Cackle. How he wished he had not seen her in that state. It would be an image that would always be there, hiding The Laugh away from his memory.

That bloody Rat! His blood boiled suddenly and he turned, dry-eyed to face his daughter who stepped back, fearful of the vengeful look in his eyes.

'We have to find The Rat,' he muttered to himself and pushed past Jane as politely as he could.

The Rat had made his life a misery these last few weeks and he now burned for revenge against that little brat. But where the hell was he, where was that little shit's base?

'Er...Roger got hold of you I guess.' Jane's voice followed him into the lounge.

'Yes.' The response was unfairly gruff.

He sank into the adultery sofa wondering what to do next. He was at a dead end, but he could not just sit around and wait for The Rat to appear, he had to do something.

Arkayic! The thought suddenly occurred to him. She must have seen where Brian had picked up Shirley Creswell's remains from. He turned his eyes to the small figure that sat on the floor, her back to him, gently thumping a cuddly sheep on the carpet.

Maybe if he took her out for a walk and asked her to point in the direction that Brian had gone he could find The Rat's lair.

It was risky. If he did find The Rat, it was highly likely that there would be a confrontation of sorts and then having Arkayic would be a huge disadvantage. How could he protect his granddaughter while having to use all his mental powers to overcome The Rat?

He toyed with the idea, torn between his love of Arkayic and his duty to the greater good. He was nearing a decision when the phone rang.

---o0o---

I suppose it makes sense, he told himself. But how did he know about Harry? As far as he knew only he and Marge really knew about Harry. All they had told people was that Jane was living with 'a nice young man' up in London. Neither he nor Marge had wanted to admit to people here that Harry was a lazy layabout with questionable hygiene.

But the fact remained, they had contacted Harry to play messenger.

'Um…Andrew?' It had been a great start to the call and had taken him a few seconds to realise who was calling.

'Yes? Is that you Harry?'

'Um…yeah.'

'Is everything okay? Do you want Jane?' You good for nothing excuse for a human being, I was in the middle of trying to think.

'Yes…er…no.'

'What?'

'Um…yes, everything is okay and, er, no, I don't want Jane, no, actually I don't not want to talk to Jane, but it's like…'

Get to the bloody point you moron! Andrew screamed mental vibes down the phone.

'…I've got a message for you.'

'What?' His voice kept his mind's outburst a secret.

'A message...for you.'

'Yes?' He waited then when no response came he forced himself to calmly ask, 'Who's the message from, Harry?'

'Well, um, it's actually someone who was giving a message from someone else, um, this is like third hand.' Tell me the bloody message! 'Well, um, this priest dude, Gregory he said his name was, he, er, he like said that he couldn't call you directly, you would know why, but, um, anyway he said to tell you that his, um, his charge, yeah that was the word he used, his charge. Anyways, he said that this other dude had said *the things have happened*. He, um, said that you would like know what he meant.'

Andrew gripped the receiver tightly as his eyes moved to the drawer that contained the dictaphone. He drew his breath in sharply. Mc-Cready! *Things have happened.* He would now be told the link between McCready and Peggy...and Geoff.

'Go on.' His voice was unsteady now, betraying the shaking of his hands.

'Um, that was about it. Things have happened. Oh and this Gregory dude said you must meet him for coffee now. You'd know where. Er, he said it was like urgent.'

'Thanks Harry.' For a Neanderthal you have done well to remember all that.

'No worries. Um, er, is Jane like coming back soon, it's just that I need some shirts ironed.'

Despite himself, Andrew smiled at the idea that Jane would go running back to London just to iron some of Harry's shirts.

'I think she'll be home soon Harry,' he said in a voice that The Good Vicar would have been proud of.

---oOo---

It was a different waitress this time. This one had none of the nervousness that the last one had had, but also lacked any sort of initiative to serve them that the nervous girl had had.

She was pretty though, green grey eyes; blonde hair, artificially curled and rosy pink cheeks. She also, Andrew noted while berating himself for noting, had much larger breasts than the flat chested girl of earlier. In fact she looked vaguely like his angel.

He waited patiently for her to finish chatting to a young man whom she clearly had a thing for but he seemed too busy trying to get her to like him to notice that she did. Andrew smiled quietly at the scene, it was a brief distraction to the agitation he felt that Gregory was not there already. He could do with a coffee though. And a flapjack, no make that a blueberry muffin.

His indecisiveness irritated his agitation. He should have ordered something rather than saying he was waiting for someone. At least the afternoon tea crowd was beginning to thin out, but surely they would be wanting to close up soon.

'Andrew, so sorry I'm late.' Gregory glanced nervously round the shop before sitting. 'Had to make sure I wasn't followed. The press are having a field day as you can imagine. Can I get you a coffee? We need to be quick though.'

The young man tried, unsuccessfully, to hide his disappointment when Father Gregory summonsed the waitress. She seemed nonplussed as well, but brightened a little as Gregory said, 'Could we have two coffees, just filter is fine.'

Their drinks did not keep the young lovers apart long.

'McCready wants to see you, but we must work quickly. The press are still at the storm drain so I have arranged to move McCready to a secret secure location. He'll be under guard but you'll have time with him alone. Drink up, we must move.'

As the two vicars hurried out the shop Andrew, noticing that the waitress was at the till on the other side of the shop dealing with their bill and rather generous tip, leaned closer to the young man as he walked passed and whispered, 'She likes you, go for it.'

He smiled at his good deed and in response to quizzical, half amused look the young man gave him. He suddenly felt good. A large piece of his puzzle was about to fall into place.

---oOo---

It was strange seeing The Steel-Greys in a more relaxed setting. A safe house Father Gregory had called it.

The number of armed guards around the place did not make Andrew feel safe, it was more his growing conviction that McCready, or should that be McCready senior, was innocent of the crimes of which he had been convicted, that gave him that feeling.

He met McCready's eyes which seemed softer and more grey. He nodded a greeting and moved into the chair opposite the sofa on which The Paedo was sitting. No, not The Paedo, he was innocent remember Andrew reminded himself,

Father Gregory enquired if they wanted anything. 'Tea? Coffee?'

'No thanks.' This was not a time for tea. Tea was too trivial for this meeting.

As he had explained on the way over, McCready would only talk if he was given a private audience with Andrew, so having made the drinks offer, Gregory left the room, closing the door quietly behind him. Andrew wondered if the place was bugged. Probably, but he wasn't going to mention that to McCready. It was unlikely that he would talk if he thought others were listening.

'This place is most likely bugged,' McCready began, his voice soft, almost gentle but loud enough for any hidden microphone to pick up.

Andrew stifled his grin and gave an unconvincing shrug. 'They said nothing to me about having bugged the place.'

'And you a Vicar, Father. You would not lie to me would you?' He didn't expect an answer and Andrew nodded to confirm that he was not going to supply one.

'Not that it matters, Father, I have nothing to hide.' He wrote on an imaginary pad of paper with an invisible pen, then asked the question with his eyes.

Andrew reached in his pocket and took out his notebook that he always carried with him. To jot down sermon ideas, you never know when you could be inspired. He opened it on the first page and felt a pang of sadness that it was blank.

'I promised to tell you, Father what the connection is between me and Peggy Deane once certain things had happened. In return you promised to let me listen to the recording of her funeral. Do we still have a deal on that, Father?'

Andrew nodded and patted his breast pocket to indicate that the dictaphone was there, then handed over the notebook and a pen while he addressed the hidden microphones.

'I have the recording with me, but if I recall our deal is not only that you have to reveal your connection to Peggy Deane, but also that the connection would warrant you listening to the recording.

The Steel-Greys looked up sharply from the frantic writing that McCready's hand was engaged in. They relaxed quickly as they read Andrew's expression which told him that he would hear the recording no matter what.

'Peggy Deane was a very good woman. One of the kindest I knew. She would have gone to the police, but I persuaded her not to. I think that if she had known about the others then, she would stopped her old man, Father.' The hand was writing furiously again while he spoke.

'Hang on. Gone to the police? What for?' Andrew knew the answer, but thought that those listening in on the conversation needed some enlightenment.

McCready looked up and half grinned. He could see where Andrew was coming from.

'Sorry, Father, got ahead of myself there. Peggy Deane's old man Geoffrey was a paedophile. Big time. There were very few kids in the village who were not affected by him. He even buggered old Brian, who married his daughter. He was the worst Geoff. The things he made us do. I won't go into details, but some of the things he did scarred us for life.' He resumed his writing and was already onto the fourth page of the notebook. Andrew was amazed at how he could maintain the thread of his conversation while writing a whole other story in the book.

'When Peggy caught him at it with me, it was one of his 'lighter' days. If he hadn't been less abusive then than another time, maybe I wouldn't have been able to stop her going to the police. I don't know if what I did was right but I could see that she was hugely torn. She loved Geoff dearly but was also appalled at catching him in such a compromising position. It was tearing her apart, trying to decide if she should report him and lose her husband, or do nothing and let him continue with his sordid ways.'

He stopped writing and stared at a corner of the room for a moment. Andrew followed his gaze, then realised that McCready was looking at a scene sometime in the past in some other room.

'It was strange. I wasn't begging her to leave the police out of it because I was scared of reprisals from Geoff, it was because she radiated this sense of such goodness at that moment that I felt that I would do anything, even endure all the perversions and humiliations that Geoff could deal out, just to prevent this wonderful woman from being hurt.

'So there I was, Father, pleading for my persecutor as he fumbled to make himself decent again. It took a lot of effort on my part and, Father, to this day I still don't know why I did it, but I'm glad I did.' He finished writing and closed the notebook, staring at the cover for a few seconds.

'I don't know how she did it, or what she did, but Geoffrey Deane never touched another kid again. People say that you can never cure a paedophile, that they will always have those urges, and I don't know if Geoff ever had those urges again, but one thing for sure he never acted on them again if he did.'

He handed the notebook and pen to Andrew.

'Not only that,' he put his hand on Andrew's to stop him opening the book, 'but when she found out about the others, she counselled every one of us that had been abused.' He gestured to Andrew that he should put the book into his pocket and mouthed the word 'later' before going on. 'That's how Brian was able to marry Pat. Peggy's counselling brought him to a point of fully forgiving Geoff for his transgressions.'

Andrew reluctantly obeyed the gesture and put the book into his pocket and brought out the dictaphone in the same movement. McCready's eyes followed his hand as it brought the machine to rest on the table between them. He watched the man reach out to pick the machine up, then change his mind and gently stroked it for a second before looking up and nodding thanks.

'A lot of people would look at Geoff's behaviour towards me to explain the murders that led to me being locked up, but believe me it would have been a lot worse had it not been for Peggy taking me under her wing. I owe a lot to her even though I've let her down. That is the reason I wanted to hear her funeral service, I wanted to hear that she was at peace because I could see that she carried the guilt that Geoff should have carried. She took all that guilt onto her shoulders and she did it for us, for everyone that Geoff abused. She was a saint.'

The Steel-Greys met Andrew's eyes now, then indicated the dictaphone and asked the question.

'One more thing before I can let you have the recording,' Andrew suddenly became aware of the ears that were probably hanging on to their every word. 'I know it was not part of the agreement, but I need to know who you got to move the remains of those children.' Please don't say Marge or David, please say you don't know.

'Your secretary Eve.' He didn't miss a beat. 'She was my partner in all my crimes.'

---oOo---

The outer room was abuzz as Andrew moved into it. He was dazed. Why had McCready fingered Eve? Not only named her as the mover of the bodies, but also as his accomplice in the crimes. There had never been any talk of a second person involved in the murders. Why name Eve? There was no way she was involved in this. Or was there? Had Marge and Brian's 'visions' of moving the bodies been just dreams?

'Are you okay Andrew? Here, sit down.' Gregory guided him into a chair. 'Let me get you some tea.'

He nodded as he sunk into the chair. Tea, the answer to all life's problems. There was a lot of activity around him, men, policemen most likely, were talking into phones while others were grabbing jackets and moving to the door, but this was angry static buzzing around outside the cocoon of his confusion.

A tea cup rattled in front of him and a kind arm was laid gently on his shoulder.

'Andrew.' Gregory's voice coaxed him back into the noise of the room and he blinked, shook his head and then nodded.

'I'm okay, just a little shocked that's all. I mean Eve. I would never have thought.'

'You should go home, there is nothing you can do now. Are you okay to drive or should I get someone to take you?'

Andrew took a sip of tea and blinked again to try and rid himself of the horrible accusation he had just heard. The tea did more to help than the blinking.

'I'll be okay. Give me a few minutes. This tea is good.' He smiled at his colleague who studied his face for a second before smiling back.

'You've done well Andrew, amazingly well, but it's over now, you can relax. You've been through one hang of an ordeal, you deserve some rest.'

But it's not over yet, his mind screamed from behind his tired, accepting expression. The Rat is still out there.

He managed to nod his head, despite his thoughts.

'I'm fine. I'll be okay. Just let me finish my tea. You don't have any biscuits by any chance?'

'I'll see if I can rustle some up,' Gregory gave him an encouraging pat on the back as he stood to go in search of the biscuits.

The tea was helping and Andrew now looked round the room. Most of the police had vacated it and in the descending calm, he imagined he could hear his own voice coming from the tinny speaker of the dictaphone in the next room and a picture of McCready sitting listening intently, rose in his mind.

'You must go home now, you need to read the note McCready wrote to you.'

He looked up into the beautiful face of The Angel. How did she get in here?

'You must go now.' Her voice was soft and soothing, but with a hint of urgency.

He nodded and stood to go find Gregory. He had taken a few steps when he suddenly turned to ask The Angel how she had got into the house, but she was nowhere to be seen.

---oOo---

Despite all that had happened, despite the moments of closeness he had felt to his family over the last couple of weeks, he now realised just how much of a chasm lay between him and his wife and children. The only one whom he seemed to connect with was Arkayic and she was asleep.

Marge and Jane sat in front of the telly, absorbed in a bland soap opera. Again he got the feeling that they were being cocooned for their own protection.

They hardly looked up when he walked in, although Jane did mumble that Sean had gone home. Hopefully it meant one less person to worry about. Hopefully he had made it home this time without any interference from The Rat.

He made tea, took some through to Marge and Jane, then returned to the kitchen for his cup. He paused by the biscuit cupboard then giving into temptation opened it and sighed. Jammy Dodgers. That was odd, Marge never bought stigmata biscuits. Maybe it had been Jane or Sean. Bottom line was that was all there was to be had.

In his study he carefully placed his tea on the coaster, then put the plate of biscuits next to his Bible. He eased himself into his chair, feeling the weary aches being drawn out of his body into the comfortable cushioning foam.

The notebook in his pocket felt light in comparison to the heaviness of the dictaphone that he had now relinquished. He thought for a minute of Pat, of their short-lived affair and wondered what would have become if them had she survived.

'You're delaying.'

He looked round the room, expecting to see The Angel, but there was nothing there, just the lingering vibrations of her voice.

He sighed and reached for the notebook which he placed on the desk in front of him, then he reached for his tea to steel himself. The biscuits distracted him and he took one up instead of the tea. He stared at the raw red wound centre and suddenly felt as though he was being pulled into that angry void. Colours, bright and harsh, flashed in his head and hurt his eyes.

With some effort he averted his gaze from the biscuit and putting it down quickly on the plate he grabbed his tea and took a large, scalding gulp. He breathed out the pain of the boiling drink in a rasping gasp and steadied his hands on his desk. I must read the note from Mc-Cready, he thought, but the biscuits were attracting his attention again.

He picked one up, avoiding eye contact with it. He weighed it in his hand and felt it tingle somewhat. Without thinking he laid it flat on his palm, red eye up. Then he took the other and laid it on the opposing palm, as he had done before, as Marge had done when she arrived back from her ordeal. The tingling intensified, then at a rapid pace grew to a delicious pain. The deliciousness faded quickly, leaving only an intense pain that reached unbearable and went beyond that before he could move to drop the biscuits. They burned in his hand.

He wanted to cry out, but the pain had spread across his chest in a tight band that trapped his breath inside him. His mind screamed at him to drop the biscuits, to throw them across the room, but he could not move. His eyes bulged in their sockets and through the thick fog of pain, he thought he saw his palms bleeding from the ugly gashes on them.

Then just as he felt he could endure it no longer, he felt a force of such intense goodness that the pain paled into insignificance against the shame he now felt. Every sin he had ever committed, the large one of his adultery, the impatient, at times nasty thoughts that often raced through his mind, even the little white lies, every sin throbbed through his racing mind and stood naked before the goodness. He wanted to scream out at the shame he felt, but no sound came.

With an extreme effort he curled his fingers round the biscuits and felt them begin to crumble in his hands. The goodness, shame and pain crumbled with them and at last, gasping for breath, he felt calm enough to open his eyes.

The Angel sat in the chair opposite, her beautiful face exuded an air of serenity, her blue eyes looked straight at him, through him, into his soul.

'You are ready now,' her voice melted into his mind. 'You have faced pure goodness and survived, now you must face pure evil and do the same.'

He stared at her for a moment, then down at the biscuit crumbs on his desk. They held no clue as to what was going on so he looked back up at the empty chair opposite him.

'I should have gone out and got custard creams,' he muttered to himself. 'This would not have happened with custard creams.'

---oOo---

Dear Father Andrew. By the time you read this, you will know whether the room we are in was bugged. I want to start by apologising for bringing Eve into this, but as I think you are already aware, she is long past redemption and this may be the only way to keep her safe from the one you call The Rat.

You should know that she is now carrying his child. We can only hope that the child does not inherit the evil that The Rat has.

I am writing this note to try and explain to you what has happened. Those who may be listening to our conversation will not understand this, but, I believe that you now have sufficient knowledge of The Rat to perhaps grasp this. Getting this knowledge is the 'certain things' of which I spoke.

I did not kill any of those children, it was The Rat that is guilty of those crimes. You will probably be asking yourself how then was my DNA found on the murder weapon in the Chantelle Bridges' case. It was my DNA, but it was also The Rat's DNA. We share our DNA as we are the same person, we just inhabit two separate bodies. I know this is an outrageous claim, but I will try and explain what happened.

The first time that Geoffrey Deane abused me, I had a very strange, intense dream that night. In it I was standing at a fork in the road. The one direction was good, the other evil. I knew I had to choose then whether I would allow the abuse to take me down the path of evil where I would grow up to abuse others, or to be strong and overcome it, grow up to be good.

I was a good kid, but the anger that Geoffrey Deane's act had awoken in me was very powerful and frightening. In my dream I stood at that junction all night, trying to decide, but I could not bring myself to choose either path. The dream obviously decided for me and split me into two people, one good, one evil. The Rat was in bed next to me when I awoke. He was the mirror image of me, but I could sense that he was evil.

I managed to physically kick him out the house, hoping that he would go away, but he hung around town. He seemed to have this aura about him so that no one recognised him as being the spitting image of me, only I could see that.

I began to grow older but he stayed the same age, as though he were destined to be stuck in that day when 'we' were abused, when the anger and shame were so acute. This all happened when I was twelve.

When I was fifteen, my family moved away and I hoped that I could be rid of The Rat, but strange dreams of him haunted me and I could feel the evil deeds that he wished to commit. I also realised that I had some level of control over his actions.

I learned to focus that control and prevent him from doing the things he most wanted to do. However, that control was not to last. As the age gap between us grew, I found I was less able to hold him back. When he began his killing spree a few years back, I was then only having intermittent control over him. I soon realised what he was doing and came back to try and stop him, thinking that being closer would increase my power over him. But that didn't happen. He engineered things so that I was arrested and with my/his DNA being on the cricket bat, I ended up in prison.

At least here I was closer to him and, not having the distraction of work, I could strengthen my control over him. That is probably why the killings stopped when I was arrested, but I think it was also him retreating slightly as he had got away with his crimes and thought it best to lie low for a while to let things cool off.

He has grown stronger though, my control over him has dwindled again and I can only direct him occasionally and for limited periods. He is going to embark on another killing spree very soon, I feel that. You are my only hope to stop him.

I will be making a concerted effort in the next few days to deliver him to you. I cannot predict when or how this will happen, or even if I can do it, but remain vigilant and be prepared to face him at any moment. You must deal with him then, we may not get another chance. He must be stopped.

God bless you Father Andrew.

---oOo---

'How's David doing?'

'He's fine, exhausted. He's sleeping now. I didn't want to leave him, but I had to come over. How's Marge?'

'Also sleeping. She was very tired too. Jane's asleep as well.

Kirsty nodded slowly. 'What's going on Andrew?' He loved the way she called him by his Christian name, no Father Andrew. It was friendly yet held no hint of the strange intimacy they had shared.

'I'm not sure myself, but I'll try and explain. You want some tea first?' It was a bit late to be offering tea, but he needed some to calm his nerves from the fright he had got when Kirsty had tapped on the front door.

'No thanks, but make yourself one, you look like you need it,' she gave a motherly smile.

'They've got Eve in custody, but I think she'll end up in an institution,' he explained as he assembled his tea. 'Poor thing, they're probably going to say that her state was brought on by the violence of the crimes she helped him commit. It's unfair that she has to suffer in all this.'

Kirsty nodded her agreement while he automatically opened the biscuit cupboard then, feeling a slight tingle in his palms, shut it again. Must get some harmless custard creams, he told himself.

'Come, let's go into the front room where we can talk.'

He sat in the adultery sofa and Kirsty sat in the other one, a respectable distance apart he thought.

'Now, tell me what's happening and don't deny that there is something on the go, I can feel that something major is about to take place.' Her voice was strong, commanding.

He didn't leave out anything, even going to fetch the note from McCready for Kirsty to read. She took it all in, her face serious, at times grim.

'That poor man,' she said when she had finished reading the note. 'I never thought I would ever feel anything but hatred for him, but now...' She turned the last page of McCready's writing absent-mindedly and stared at the fresh blank page for a moment.

'I don't suppose they will let me visit him?'

Andrew shook his head. 'Not at the moment. I don't think so.'

'I'd like to apologise for hating him so much. I guess that sounds silly.'

Andrew shook his head again and then fell silent for a minute.

'I want to help you with this Rat business. I want to be here when McCready,' the name slid easily off her tongue, there was no flinching like previous times, 'when he delivers The Rat to you.'

I'm not sure that he'll be delivering The Rat, I think it'll be more like just giving a small window of opportunity to get at him. Andrew nodded and kept his thought private. He would need all the help he could get so no point discouraging an ally.

He was just grasping at loose ends of conversation starters when he heard the sound. A sort of slide and then a bump, slide and bump.

Startled eyes threw alarmed looks while hearts pumped furious tattoos.

Slide and bump, slide and bump. The noise got closer. We're not ready yet, Andrew wanted to yell out. Come back later. But he knew he must get control of himself and fast. This was his chance, possibly the only chance he would have.

Slide and bump, slide and bump. It was nearly there. Then a short pause before the lounge door began to yield to the slight pressure behind it.

Deliver us from evil. Deliver us from evil. He grabbed at the snippet of a well-worn prayer and made it an instant mantra.

The door continued to open slowly.

---oOo---

It was no good shaking like this. He needed to keep his nerve. If only The Good Vicar was still around. He could have talked him down from the mental table he had jumped onto.

'Look Andrew, there is no Rat here, not even a mouse.' The voice was not clear like it used to be, it was muffled and slightly distant, but it was The Good Vicar. He glanced round the room quickly, almost expecting to see a physical manifestation of his departed conscience, but his eyes settled on his granddaughter who was tugging herself onto her feet using the pleat of his trouser leg.

'Gumpa,' she gurgled and looked quizzically at him, her face asking why he was so surprised to see her and why had he not picked her up yet.

'How did you get out of your bedroom,' he asked as he heaved her onto his lap.

She giggled and rocked backwards and forward on his lap.

'You gave us a huge fright,' he admonished her in a friendly voice and she stopped her giggling and leaned into his stomach, spreading her little arms in an incomplete hug.

He glanced across at Kirsty, expecting to see her smiling, but her face was white with fear.

'What...'

'Shhh! Did you hear that?'

He felt Arkayic tense up in his lap.

'Yat?' she whispered.

He should have put Arkayic back in her room, but she had clung to him so tightly. Besides, he reasoned with himself, I did not have the time. The Rat would have been out of sight before I could have got back downstairs.

He prayed quickly and furiously that God would protect his grand-daughter through this ordeal. And me, he added suddenly remembering that he too was in great danger. Oh, and Kirsty as well. He was reminded of her petite presence as she puffed slightly, trying to keep up.

He could just make out the small figure of The Rat up ahead in the gloom. A fingernail moon clung to the sky and cast a slight glow on the path. He could not work out if The Rat was aware that he was being followed or not.

He had an image in his mind of an evil grin on that little rat face as he lured his prey into the trap of his lair. His stomach knotted at that picture and he held Arkayic closer to him.

The Rat had announced his presence by walking confidently down the street, rattling a stick against the garden gates and whistling a cheerful tune. In the light of the street lamp, Andrew had got a good look at his face despite the hood and, although he could not swear to it, had thought that the boy that walked down the street was oblivious of what he was doing, there seemed to be a vacancy to his eyes.

'McCready's got control of him,' he had muttered under his breath.

'Yat,' Arkayic had repeated and looked at him.

How long would McCready maintain control? He watched the shadowy figure scurry further up The Ridge, expecting it to stop, turn and charge back down at them swinging a cricket bat. Instinctively his hand covered Arkayic's exposed head.

They were nearing Geoffrey Deane's bench and Andrew grew more nervous. How would he confront The Rat? What powers would The Rat use against him? How much control would McCready be able to have over the kid? And what, if he could overpower The Rat, what would he do? Take him in for questioning? Give him a stern talking to? Exorcise him? He'd never exorcised anyone let alone witnessed an exorcism except for seeing that horrible movie.

He had not really had a chance to think through what to do. 'Deal with him,' McCready's note had said.

Deal with him? How? He wanted to turn to Kirsty and ask her advice, but was afraid to turn round in case he lost sight of The Rat.

'Andrew.' The whisper came in answer to his thoughts. 'Give me Arkayic, you can't take her into battle with you.'

It made sense, but he didn't want to let go of his granddaughter.

'Andrew, you have to, you don't have a choice.' It was like The Good Vicar speaking and he reluctantly slowed his pace till Kirsty was next to him.

'Take care of her,' he pleaded then, after kissing Arkayic on the head, handed her over. She went willingly which was a slight relief.

'If anything happens to me...'

Kirsty nodded, then flicked her head in the direction of The Rat. 'Go get him,' she whispered.

---o0o---

He could just make out the bench in the gloom up ahead, but was unsure if there was a figure sitting on it or if that was merely a distortion of the dark. He heard his breath, fast and hard as it echoed in his ears, his exhale blowing clouds of steam into the cold night air.

His mind still raced with the question of what he was going to do when he confronted The Rat and as he neared the bench it rang out the alarm that he was completely unarmed.

He looked around desperately for something to protect or perhaps attack with. He picked up and discarded a large stick which crumbled in his hand. He stopped. Had he heard a noise? A stifled laugh or was it a scream? His hand pawed the ground and closed around a sizable rock without informing his mind of its actions.

He hurried forward, heart thrashing, eyes glued to the bench. *In loving memory.* Would his family erect a memorial to him if he was to perish tonight on The Ridge? Would there be an 'In loving memory of Andrew Compton' plaque erected somewhere, or would it say *Here lies a neglecting father and adulterous husband, best forgotten*?

The bench faded into clarity as he approached. To his growing horror, he realised that there was no-one there. He had lost The Rat. A curse fell silently from his lips and splashed on the pathway.

There was that sound again, a muffled giggle. His head swung wildly round trying to trace the sound as it pinballed around the darkness. The blackness closed in around him as a cloud passed across the moon and he groped for and sat on the bench to steady his nerve.

The cloud drifted lazily on, ignoring the tension on The Ridge. It had nowhere particular to be and all night to get there. The slither of a moon smiled its silvery grin down on the bench, at odds with the grimness of the person sitting there.

As the pale glow returned he heard the noise a third time and saw a figure half stumbling up the slope towards him.

'Kirst...' The rest of her name was swallowed as a small figure stuck its head out from behind his companion.

'Evenin' vikka.' The voice slithered across the small divide between them. 'Look wot I found.' He nodded his hooded head at Kirsty.

Andrew's eyes flicked quickly between The Rat's evil ones, Kirsty's frightened ones and Arkayic's questioning ones.

'Andrew, he's got a knife,' Kirsty blurted out the news, terror quivered in her voice.

'Shut it, bitch.' The Rat made a move behind Kirsty's back and she straightened, trying to get away from the sharp point of the knife. Andrew flinched as though the blade had poked his own back.

'Doan worry vikka, the knife snot for ya,' he moved slightly further out from behind Kirsty, but maintained his grip on her free arm and kept his knife hand behind her back. 'Ya see I'm no longa intristid in ya, maybe we can 'ave a bit o' fun layta, like wot me 'n' Sean 'ad, but thass diffrint.'

Andrew stared at the lips that moved beneath the hood, evil, sneering lips. What were they saying?

'I no longa wanna kill ya, ya no longa my enemy so I can 'ave my fun with ya differently. But I do now wanna kill your lady friend here.'

'Why?' His voice seemed to come from a different body, a different planet.

'The evil lips twisted into a grin. 'You bloody fik or wot vikka? You wos never my enemy. The Bloody Good Vikka, thass 'oo I want dead and 'e's no longa in you so I doan need to kill ya. Bloody cleva that vikka running away 'n' 'iding inside this bitch.' He pricked Kirsty's back again and she let out a muffled groan. 'Shut it!' The Rat commanded.

The Good Vicar inside Kirsty. That didn't make sense. How could that have happened? His mind flew back to the strange platonic sex he had had with Kirsty on the very bench on which he now sat. The Good Vicar was in an unborn child that was clinging to the side of Kirsty's womb.

'Andrew, do something,' Kirsty's voice was the mingled plea of a desperate, scared woman and the sensible, but very edgy voice of The Good Vicar.

'One more sound from you bitch and you'll ge' it, unnerstan.' The Rat twisted her arm slightly and applied more pressure with the knife. He seemed surprisingly strong for such a small boy. Kirsty sucked in her breath and grimaced at the pain.

'Leave her alone,' hardly a commanding tone.

The Rat responded with a harsh laugh. 'Sorry vikka. Nuffink you can do, I'm gonna kill off The Good Vikka, then 'ave my fun wiff you 'n' maybe 'ave yor grandorta for afters. 'S a pity I 'ave to kill this bitch, she's quite pretty, like 'er dorta wos.'

Kirsty gave a moan at the mention of Chantelle.

'Enuff now,' The Rat's tone changed. ''S gettin' cold out 'ere an' I'm sick of this bitch's moanin'.'

In a quick movement he stepped out from behind Kirsty, raised his arm, the blade glinting briefly in the moonlight, then brought it down with great force towards Kirsty's belly.

Andrew watched in horror. As the knife hurtled towards its target, he saw Arkayic wriggle free from Kirsty's grip and drop in front of her stomach, creating a tiny human shield from the oncoming attack.

The knife plunged into the tiny body.

---o0o---

He knelt over the bloodied body, a huge sob shuddered through his frame. The pale moon gave a serene glow to the innocent young face that stared lifelessly back at him.

He drew in a rasping breath and buried his face in his hands. His body was ahead of his mind in expressing emotion. His mind was empty, grasping frantically around for explanations, but his body knew how to react.

'Andrew.' A gentle hand was on his shoulder, drawing his eyes away from the body. He blinked, trying to focus his tear-filled eyes on the owner of the voice. His mind knew the voice, but he needed the proof that only his eyes could give.

'Is...?' The voice couldn't finish the question.

'Dead? I think so.' He cleared his throat and blinked away the tears. He turned his eyes back to the body and blinked again as it seemed to fade in front of his eyes. He jumped back in fright, issuing a muted cry. The body was disappearing, rapidly blending in with its surroundings, until he could no longer see it.

A small voice echoed in his brain as he pushed himself unsteadily to his feet.

'Gumpa?'

---o0o---

The dawn began to slowly brush away the gloom of the night, colouring in the details on the silhouettes in his office.

Andrew sat motionless in his chair, his eyes focussing on a point between himself and the wall. He was still not sure what had happened up on The Ridge and Kirsty could not fill in the details either. He called his mind back from its mid-air spot and cajoled it to go over the sequence of events again and, despite it painting the same picture each time, he threatened that if it didn't tell the truth this time he would place it in the care of the nearest mental health institution.

His mind sighed and said, 'I've shown you the truth, hundreds of times. This is what really happened.'

'Once more,' he begged, 'humour me. If you tell the same story again this time I promise I'll believe you.'

His mind gave him a sceptical look, but rewound to the moment The Rat raised his arm to strike.

Andrew watched as the film played through again in his head. The Rat's arm began its sweeping descent, the knife cutting through the air. He saw Arkayic's eyes widen and a determined look settle on her face. She wiggled furiously, escaping from Kirsty's fumbling grasp and began falling, timing her descent perfectly to be right between the oncoming knife and Kirsty's belly a fraction of a second before the knife would have torn into Kirsty's flesh.

There! Stop there, back up then play back frame by frame, he commanded his mind as he sat up in his chair.

Why? What have you seen? His mind asked

Just back it up and can you zoom in a bit?

His mind made the necessary adjustments and they watched as the knife edged closer to Arkayic's body. Then it touched the little green jumper that she had on and then he saw the blade pierce the clothing.

Stop! There! See! He wanted to jump up and point, but his mind could see it as well. As the blade moved into Arkayic's body, it was no longer Arkayic's face on those small shoulders, it was the face of an angel, his Angel.

The blade was in and out in a fraction of a second in real time, but in a frame by frame analysis it took ages as it sank to its hilt and then made a slow withdrawal.

As the tip became visible again the face changed back to Arkayic's. He had examined the jumper before they had headed back down The Ridge again and it was intact. Where Arkayic had been for that fraction of a second was anybody's guess and he was too tired to be anybody. All he knew was that she was in a safe place while The Angel took the knife stab that would have been fatal for Arkayic. He wondered if angels died like mortals did, then said a quick prayer of thanks and an additional one for the soul, if they have souls, of The Angel.

Do you want to see the rest again? His mind asked.

No, I know what happens after that. He could not face his own rage that followed, the lashing out at The Rat with the stone he still held, the blood that flowed from his forehead as he staggered back, the force of the blow surprising him.

He had seen too many times for his liking the replay of his hands gripping the throat of the startled boy, felt too many times the uncontrollable rage that overrode the desperate pleading in those pretty blue eyes that stared back at him as the hood was thrown off the head.

He certainly did not want to experience that moment when he saw the life leaving the little body and he felt his fingers slowly relaxing.

Had he really taken a human's life? He did not want to answer that. The Rat was not human, he told himself. He shuddered and then looked round his study. The light outside was now bright and he could hear movement in the kitchen.

He rubbed his eyes and pushed himself wearily to his feet.

---o0o---

The Pale Blue Dressing Gown was at the fridge. It would take out three eggs this time, the usual two and one extra for Jane.

'Morning love,' he gave her a peck on the cheek and wondered how long it would be before she ran off with The Heathen again. He was, after all, available now.

He flicked on the radio as he moved to sit down.

'...in his prison cell.' The BBC voice said. 'McCready who was serving a life sentence for the murder of Chantelle Bridges was pronounced dead by the prison doctor in the early hours of this morning.'

'McCready? Wasn't he the one you had that dream...'

'Shhh!' He silenced The Pale Blue Dressing Gown with a flap of his hand.

'Sources at Dartmoor Prison have said that it appeared that Mc-Cready had been strangled, although prison officials have refused to comment until a full autopsy has been performed...'

He sank back into his chair and stared at his glass of orange juice.

'It's over,' he whispered to the orange juice. The juice didn't answer.

---o0o---

The large nurse crossed herself as she left the small padded room. There was something about the new admission that made her feel uneasy. The cackling laugh, the wild staring eyes that seemed to look into your soul. No, things were not right with this patient. She shut the door and turned the key. In the room the cackle subsided as the patient felt a movement in her belly. The movement felt evil and to the patient that felt good.

---o0o---

www.ingramcontent.com/pod-product-compliance
Lightning Source LLC
Chambersburg PA
CBHW070217030726
47505CB00006B/1715